UPSTATE EXPECTATIONS

ERIN MARIE BASSETT

For You, Dear Reader. Please enjoy.

PROLOGUE

Just Another Manic Monday

Nora

"Ugh, what am I looking at here?"

"A cat's butthole." I announce from a few feet away. "Sir Harold knocked my phone over while I went to grab a drink."

I come back to the table, shoo my life partner slash pet, Sir Harold of Manhattenshire, off to the side, and prop up my phone again so my best friend, Liz Collins, can stare back at me.

It's Monday night and we're eating dinner together on FaceTime like we have every week for the last four years.

"I had a feeling that's what that was. I'm not sure I'm hungry anymore." Liz says as she takes a huge bite of a panini.

"You better be hungry," I hear her fiancé Kyle mutter behind her, "you requested two sandwiches."

"Hi Kyle." I call to the phone.

"Hi Nora."

"Hey, back off, this is my girl date, get your own friends."

"I have my own friends, I'm headed to meet them in twenty minutes."

"Anyway," I sing song, "How was your weekend Liz?"

"Good! I got to shoot an engagement session. They were so cute and in love."

"Are you going to get your own engagement photos taken?" I ask. A few months ago Kyle brought Liz to the city for a long weekend before the camp he runs started for the summer. He proposed in Central Park, in a spot where he literally ran into her four years ago.

He had me hide nearby to get pictures so there are some but I'm not the professional photographer in the room so they're not great.

"I dunno, depends on if Kyle wants them or not. We don't really need them for an official announcement or anything. Everyone in Lakeville knows we're engaged and has invited themselves to the wedding."

"Ew."

"Stop."

"Fine, but I do not find small town life appealing at all." I take a bite of my meal-prepped chicken fajita bowl.

"Ooo that looks good," Liz picks up the phone and spins it around, "Kyle look at what Nora made. I want that."

"It's a fajita bowl." I lift it up to show Kyle.

"Did you really spend your whole day cooking yesterday?" Liz asks as she returns the phone to rest in front of her.

"You know it. Meal Prep or Die."

"I don't understand you."

"Yeah well I can't live off of granola bars from the office like you used to. You're lucky Kyle cooks for you."

"Don't I know it!" Liz says as she takes a big bite of her panini. "So," she starts as she chews, "what does your week look like?"

"Same old, same old. Staff meeting tomorrow morning, prospect meetings on Wednesday and Friday. Maybe one on Thursday, I'm waiting for their assistant to confirm." I take a bite and continue talking while I'm chewing. Liz and I ignore the rules of polite society on these calls. "Actually, the one on Friday should be good. Darlene Smithe who graduated from Cornell and then married another alumni. He went on to do some major research projects for Cornell and MIT but she raked in the cash as the first woman to run a private equity firm back in the 80s."

"She sounds like a badass." Liz says. "Are the meetings all in town this week or are you traveling?"

"All in town. I actually don't travel until after Labor Day. Schools are back in session now so people are busy on campus."

"Makes sense. Any word on the promotion?" Liz asks.

"Not really, Trisha keeps alluding to it so I know it's on their radar. Hopefully before the end of the year I'll know more."

"You'll kill it." She takes a bite of her panini. "OH! Did you try the under-eye patches Imogen Skye recommended? I just ordered some."

"Yes! I meant to tell you. They are amazing."

"Maybe we should add a face mask element into our Monday night calls?" Liz ponders.

"Maybe, but you know I've got my skincare routine locked down. I don't do anything different except for a Thursday night mask if I don't have a dinner."

"To get your face ready for the weekend?" Liz asks as she wiggles her eyebrows.

"You know it." I smile as I chew a bite of dinner.

"Although, you haven't really shared any crazy stories lately."

I try to keep my facial features relaxed and hope that my friend doesn't start to do the actual math. It's been three months since I've hooked up with a guy which can officially be described as a dry spell. And is out of character for me.

Truth? I haven't wanted to go out as much as I used to.

The whole thing was getting boring. The dressing up, visiting the same bars, chatting up the same types of guys. I've been slowing down my routine for awhile now.

"Well you know how the city gets in the summer, it's all tourists. No thanks." I try to sound nonchalant.

"True," Liz concedes. "Hey, let me guess the rest of your schedule this week!"

I laugh nervously, "sure, knock yourself out."

"Tomorrow after work you'll get your nails done. But not a pedicure because you got one last week. And you'll pick up your dry cleaning."

"So far you're not wrong." I tell her.

"Wednesday night is carry out night and if you're having fajitas for dinner all week you'll get Thai."

"Thai Nine is the best."

"Ugh, I miss that place." Liz takes another bite of her sandwich. "Okay, Thursday you'll wash your sheets."

I don't respond because, one, she's right, but two, I see Kyle walk behind her and drop another half sandwich on her plate before kissing her on the head.

"Good bye Kyle." I call out.

"Bye Nora!" He calls back before he whispers "see you later babe, love you."

I watch my friend's face bloom with affection. Her eyes and smile soften and she sighs with contentment before turning back to the screen.

"Sorry," she mutters.

"Don't be, you're cute." I smile.

"Yeah but I don't want to be the girl who like flaunts her relationship in front of her single friends."

"Since when do I care about being single? I'm single by choice. This isn't news to you."

"No, you're right. Nora Judithany Heely," she starts.

"Not my middle name." I mutter under my breath.

"Will never have a boyfriend."

1

When It Rains, It Pours

JIMMY

There were several reasons why I didn't want to attend the Home Builders Convention in New York City this week. One, my truck barely fits in any city parking places. Two, people in the city are grumpy. And three, I don't really care about networking. My sister and I rebuild homes in our hometown, Lakeville, NY, nowhere else. And that's all I want to do.

After a week of me giving friendly smiles to strangers and getting nothing in return, what feels like hours of small talk, and countless introductions to people I barely remember, driving home in this rain storm is the cherry on top of my I-don't-want-to-be-here sundae. My wipers are moving back and forth violently across my windshield. The squeaking sound is drowning out the latest Hayes Farrow hit playing on the country station. Lightning cracks across the sky and the wind is pushing against my truck like it wants to start a fight. I take my foot of the gas for a second to relax my hold on the steering wheel and that's when I first see the flashing lights ahead.

Hazards are on about 100 yards in front of me. The storm clouds have darkened the sky and it feels much later than it is. Unfortunately I don't have my jump kit or tool box with me, but maybe I can offer this driver a ride to town. My tires crunch on the gravel as I pull my truck off behind the little black sports car, put on my own hazards, and step out to see what's going on.

I can see one person in the driver's seat. The rain reflects in my headlights which makes it difficult to see anything else clearly. As I reach the driver's side window, a swish of long hair is flicked over a shoulder revealing the slender curve of a woman's neck, her slim shoulder rolling forward as she reaches towards the center console. I scan my eyes further and stop at the hem of her skirt that cuts a straight line across her trim thighs.

This might just be my lucky day.

I clear my throat, ready to muster my best "How can I help you ma'am" charm. As I raise a knuckle to rap on the window, she turns and lets out a blood curdling scream.

"NO! I'm poor! I'm skinny! Definitely not a good snack!" She yells at the window. Even through the glass and the downpour I heard her clearly.

"Ma'am, open up, I am not going to murder you. And I have snacks in my truck so I'm good."

She cracks an inch of the window down. I see her holding a pen in her hand like a slasher knife. Her face is still in the shadows but I see a chin that comes to a soft point under full and pouty lips.

"You have snacks?" The lips ask.

I laugh. "Yeah, snacks, a blanket, and a cell phone

charger."

"And you're not going to murder me?"

"No ma'am."

She rolls up her window. I stand up straight and slick my wet hair back with one of my hands. I close my eyes to wipe some of the rain from my brow when the door flies open and slams into my legs.

"Fuck!" I yell out as I bend over to grab my shin.

"Oh shit, I'm sorry! I thought you moved. Took the old car door right to the junk huh?"

"Not to the junk, to the shin." I correct her even though I'm wincing in pain.

"Ah, good then, shins can be fixed." She climbs out of the car and closes the door. Her spicy perfume blends with the earthy smell of rain and I raise my head to watch her as she hurries past me. My eyes settle on her shiny black high heels as she pulls a wheely suitcase with leopard spots out of the trunk. She pops the handle and starts walking to my truck with one arm over her head to shield her from the downpour.

What kind of woman gets caught on the side of the road in upstate New York in a pencil skirt and heels? Pharmaceutical Rep? Political Analyst? Either way, my money is that she's from the city. City girls and me don't mix. Best to get her somewhere safe and head home like I'd planned.

She hits the button on her key fob and her car beeps as it locks which jolts me into action. My boots slosh in the puddles on the side of the road as I jog up to her. When I reach her we're almost to my truck and I grab the suitcase out of her hand. She mutters a tentative thanks and follows me to the passenger side.

I open the door for her and she just stands there. The light from the cab of the truck illuminates her features and I quickly catalog the auburn red hair, gold hoop earrings, silky white top, and gold chain of her purse on her shoulder.

"Up you go." I say in a teasing tone.

"Ugh, actually."

"What's the matter?"

She pauses and looks down at the running board. Then without warning, she hikes her pencil skirt up her thighs so she can lift her leg enough to climb up into the seat. My jaw hits the floor as she gives me a view of her thighs. There is barely an inch of fabric until the point where her legs meet her hips. City girl or not, I'm imagining some fancy panties on her.

I swallow hard, shut her door, and then put her suitcase into the backseat. I make my way around to the driver's side door and climb in.

"I don't know what kind of small town weirdo you are but I will tell you this; be sure to fuck me before you murder me because I am great in bed." She says as she buckles herself in.

"Ma'am, I'm not gonna murder you. I'm just going to get you out of this storm."

Better not make any promises about fucking just yet.

Lightning cracks just ahead of us and the thunder rumbles immediately. She lets out a little yelp next to me. I know better than to be a sitting duck in a lightning storm. I put the truck in drive and pull out from the side of the road.

Once we're past her car I run a hand through my wet hair and pull a little at the collar of my wet t-shirt. The AC is blasting which makes my nipples stand up straight. I chance a glimpse over at the girl in the front seat and notice that her nipples are hard and pressing against her silky top.

I clear my throat. "So, where ya headed?"

"Umm, I'll have to wait for my phone to charge a bit to get the address."

"What town is it at least?"

"Lakeville, we're not far."

"Yeah I know Lakeville." Interesting. My hometown is the type where everybody knows your business as well as you do. I don't have much to hide so it's endearing, but there are rarely secrets. I don't tune in to the gossip but I think I would have heard if a cute redhead was moving to town.

I drive slowly because the 10 miles to Lakeville will go by quickly and if her phone is totally dead we might need some time for it to recharge. She's sitting straight as a rod, her hair damp against her head with little droplets falling off the ends. She's cradling her phone in her lap looking down at it and her knee is bouncing up and down. I look back up at her face and she's biting her plush bottom lip.

"So I should tell you that even though I don't know where I'm going, my friends Liz and Kyle are expecting me and they're probably worried sick. Like they'll be calling the sheriff or whatever you townies use for law enforcement."

"Yeah, we townies respect Joseph, he's been the sheriff goin' on twenty years now. Good fella. Always volunteering his time. And his wife makes a delicious apple pie."

Honestly I have no idea if Susan makes apple pie but this girl seems to think I'm a country bumpkin so I'm leaning into it a little bit. My little sister, Angie, was in school with Liz, I've known her all my life. Kyle is Liz's fiancé who moved here when the foundation his aunt runs started operating the camp just outside of town. He's a good guy, we've gone out fishing a few times and have hung out at bonfires.

And I know exactly where they live because I redid their screened in porch after they bought their house. But I don't feel like sharing that information with the city slicker sitting in my front seat just yet.

"Your friends will be able to bring you back to your car in the morning. You're about 10 miles outside of town."

"Oh, good. Okay. And I guess they'll have gas, or there's a tow truck in town? When my phone died I figured I was close enough but then the gas tank just kept getting lower and lower and the storm kept getting stronger so I pulled over. The whole time I was just envisioning the headlines." She lifts her hand to scroll the message across the front page. "City Girl Gets Abducted On The Side of the Road. Friends Say She Was One of a Kind."

She's one of a kind all right.

"And I should not have been listening to that true crime podcast while driving upstate by myself but the story is just so interesting! It's part of why my phone died so not only did I lose my GPS, I didn't get to hear where they found the girl. I'll have to catch up with it tomorrow even though Liz hates that shit. She's such a goody too shoes sometimes. I mean, don't get me wrong, the girl can party, but once she called me after Kyle got extra handsy while he was behind her and she was shocked that it would feel good. I mean c'mon girl! Everyone knows that's the second best orgasm a girl can have. The first obviously being when— OH! My phone is back on. Okay. First things first, GPS."

Wait.

Go back.

What is the best kind of orgasm a girl can have?

"Now I'm dying to listen to the podcast again, oh, ha, get it, dying? But since you haven't heard any of it yet I'll wait. You really have to let the tension build before getting to the climax."

Does she know she's turning me on with the way she talks?

"Oh, GPS says we're a minute away. How'd you do that?"

"I know where Liz and Kyle live. I live in Lakeville too."

"Oh, well you could have just said so." She scoffs.

I pull up in front of the house, put the truck in park, and turn off my lights. Liz and Kyle live in a cul du sac and their neighbors don't need my headlights shining in their living room.

Lightning cracks again and she visibly startles. She takes a deep breath and turns towards me in her seat. It's dark in the truck and even though I can't make out the details very well I can tell she's a beautiful woman.

And her nipples are still pressing against her shirt.

She extends her hand to shake. I grasp it in mine and, shit you not, lightning flashes outside.

Suddenly she launches herself towards me and I barely catch her by the waist before she's straddling my legs. Her skirt is bunched around her waist and she pauses before sinking both hands into my hair and leaning in for a kiss. I respond by grabbing her ass, finding the edge of the lacy underwear I expected was there, and pulling her down onto the erection that started to build when she mentioned orgasms a few minutes ago.

She lets out a little whimper as she rolls her hips over me. She's clutching my jaw in her hands and keeping her mouth pressed up to mine, her deep inhales through her nose spurring me on. I test her by pushing my tongue past her lips and am rewarded for my bravery when she opens her mouth to me. Our tongues meet and dance against each other, pushing and pulling with each swipe.

I have no idea who this woman is but she tastes like rain and vanilla and adventure. Every place our bodies meet turns to fire and my muscles tense with the effort of keeping her pressed against me.

I drag my hands up her back. Her shirt is damp from the rain and clings to my fingertips. I reach her ribcage and spread my hands wide across her sides. My thumb just an inch from the bottom of her breasts. Expecting this to end at any moment, and not wanting to push my luck, I stay right there, slowly caressing the skin under her tits with my thumbs.

She moans and arches her back which pushes her tits forward and right up against my chest.

"Please." She whispers.

I growl as I cup her. I can feel her nipples through the thin layer of lace.

My cock is painfully pressing against the inside of my jeans. I'm still gripping her breasts when she starts to rock against me. Her hips roll back and forth in a salacious rhythm as I roll her taught nipples between my thumb and forefinger.

I haven't dry humped a girl since high school but that's exactly what's happening in my truck right now. It's hot. Made hotter because this girl is a complete stranger. This feels dangerous and fleeting.

She breaks the kiss and presses her hands into my shoulders and uses the leverage to grind herself down. She flips her head back and her wet hair slaps against the steering wheel. She grinds harder and I feel my balls tighten.

Fuck, I'm going to come in my jeans.

She leans forward and presses our foreheads together, still riding my lap. I move my hands back to her ass and hold on tight. Her breathing gets more shallow and little whispers of "yes" escape her lips.

She inhales a succession of short breaths before letting out a squeak as her legs stiffen and squeeze around mine.

I slide myself down a few inches in my seat which gives her direct access to the bulging fly of my jeans. She scoots forward and lets herself go.

It's dark in the cab but I can see the tension in her face melt away as she comes. Her eyebrows ease and the flex in jaw loosens. She slows her hips but stays pressed against me. Seeking out the last bit of friction for herself.

It's on the smallest roll of her hips that my stomach bottoms out. I dig my fingers into her hips and slowly roll her over my dick again.

Once.

Twice.

Third time's the charm.

My cock swells and I grunt as my orgasm rips through me leaving my legs numb.

She takes a deep breath.

I do the same.

I look up at her and see a fire in her eyes that I'm sure is matched in mine.

With one last kiss she leans over and grabs her phone and purse from the passenger seat. Then she pops open my door, slides off my lap, and adjusts her skirt as she hits the ground. She closes the door and walks quickly around the front of my truck, the headlights reflecting off her rain wet clothing. Her red hair like a flame as she pushes it off her shoulder. My head is on a swivel locked into her movements.

Who is she?

What the fuck just happened?

How can I make it happen again?

She opens the back passenger side door and grabs her bag. The in the sultriest voice I have ever heard she says, "Thanks for the ride," before closing the door and walking up to the house.

I watch her walk up to the door. When she's inside I pull my hands down my face and blink a few times before driving home to my apartment.

2

Dry Cereal and Coffee With Heat

Nora

"Ohmigod, I feel like a Jane Austen character."

"It's not that bad."

I give my adorable but clearly suffering from heat stroke best friend a look over my sunglasses. We're siting in her screened in porch in the blistering upstate heat and humidity after a storm knocked out the power last night.

The same storm that got me stranded on the side of the road. Which I reacted to by dry humping a hottie in a truck.

I've been told I use sex as a deflection or validation tool. But my therapist doesn't know shit. I learned more about my mental health from my cat than I ever did from that quack. Obviously, I jumped on that guy as way to thank him for stopping and taking me to Liz's.

That's all.

Definitely wasn't chasing an orgasm to make me forget about my problems.

Nope. Not this girl.

Liz picks up her hand fan and starts flapping it violently near her face. Now, if we were one of JA's characters that fan would probably be delicate lace with a little ribbon for keeping it safely around our gloved wrists. But we're not. The best we could do was to make a folded palm fan out of a cereal box.

Cereal that we had to eat without milk because Liz didn't want to open the fridge again and let the cold air out.

Dry cereal people.

That was my breakfast.

Heat, humidity, dry cereal, and thinking about my ride here last night has me feeling hot and bothered. Literally and figuratively. I don't see any way it can get fixed without air conditioning.

How Liz can just sit here and act all chill like her thighs aren't fusing with the patio furniture I'll never know.

"It is that bad. All we have are room temperature drinks, books, and board games. No music on in the background just the disturbing hum of cicadas." I shudder. "So creepy. Seriously, they are creatures of the underworld."

"Wow," Liz says while shifting in her chair to square her shoulders at me. "Nora, I know you aren't a morning person but you've become a bonafide city snob! Remember you are the one who called me at 5pm yesterday and asked if you could come stay for the week. It was your choice to be here and now you're complaining and moping instead of just enjoying this beautiful day."

I stare back at her silently and I can tell she think she won. That I'm sitting here contrite and contemplative.

Wrong.

I'm stewing.

Emotionally and physically.

"You're right," I slyly concede, I catch her smile, "I am a city snob. But you know what? I'm proud of it. And you would have been too if you didn't just up and leave four years ago!" I grumble.

"That's not fair. You know that's not how it happened." She's right, I do know, and I feel a little bad for saying otherwise. "Plus, I couldn't be happier here. I like my life. Don't take your discomfort out on me. I won't be dragged down by it."

With that, Liz stands up and walks back into the fires of hell. I mean the house. Maybe I was a little harsh there. Alright, fine, probably a lot harsh. It wasn't her fault that the firm I work for, Fosters, Henderson & Associates, totally dicked her over with a job offer four years ago. Liz is a creative type, a little clumsy, and completely lovable. She, Kyle, and I met four years ago as interns. I got a bestie. She got bestie and a fiancé and now they're happily shacked up in this volcano adjacent mid century ranch.

I haven't found another good girlfriend in the city. I didn't look too hard at first, hoping Liz would get a job and move back. Then when Kyle told me he was moving up here I knew she was going to stay. At that point, instead of friend hunting I focused on work and picking up men if I needed company.

And up until yesterday, I was killing it. I was working at a stable, well-paying job helping major universities raise money from wealthy-as-fuck donors. I went to college on scholarship so when I get someone to pay it forward, I'm helping another Nora Heely from blue collar New Jersey attend an Ivy League school.

Then things changed in the blink of an eye. Or rather, a lack of blinking. I woke up on Friday and quickly discovered that my grey American standard rescue cat, Sir Harold of Manhattenshire, had died. He's been in my life for three full years. The longest relationship I've ever had. Honestly, the only relationship I've ever had. And he just up and kicked it with no warning. I woke up on Friday and he didn't.

I had a meeting with a prospect for a major donation to Cornell at 10am. So I wrapped Sir Harold up in a kitchen towel and made room for him in my freezer. I cried while I showered, cried while I tried to put on make up, and cried in the cab on my way to the meeting.

When I got there, my client, Dave, took in my appearance and his eyes about doubled in size. We were ushered to our table where our prospect was already seated.

She was wearing a Chanel coat, pearls, red lipstick. The classic uptight New York wealthy widow uniform. I sat down next to her, introduced myself as a consultant who works closely with Cornell and when she held out her hand to shake mine I noticed a cat charm on her bracelet and I broke down.

Wailed.

She was very kind and asked me what was wrong. Without thinking, I told her the entire story of Sir Harold and I. How I made eye contact with his pale green eyes through the window of the shelter. How he immediately snarled at me. How I knew in that moment that we had to spend the rest of our lives together. How I shopped for cat toys before the adoption was even approved.

Dave sat patiently through all of this. After I got the story out, Darlene, the prospect, patted my hand and said, "Ah dearie, we all have pets we love more than we expect to. Mine was Princess Allegra, a long haired Persian mix, she was a rescue as well. Got her right after my Horace died."

We smiled at each other and Dave took this break in the action to get the conversation directed towards her donation to the school. Things were going well but when Dave asked if we could draw up the paperwork and send it to her attorney she hesitated.

She looked at me.

I froze.

"On second thought, I think my money could be better used by an animal shelter like the one you got your Harold at. What was the name of it again?"

Not wanting to be rude I told her.

Just a few hours later, I was put on a leave of absence for a "Conflict of Interest" breach of contract. Allegedly, I used a prospect of one of Fosters' clients for my own personal gain.

Not what happened.

Well, not what I intended to have happen. I was just a grief stricken cat lady who tried to power through and went to work instead of taking a day off.

I took a cab home in a daze. Bouncing in the backseat with some of the personal effects from my desk in a box on my lap; a cat mug, an extra pair of heels, and my spare makeup. I opened my apartment door, set down the box, and sank to the floor and cried. Once the tears stopped, I stood up, wiped my eyes, and formulated a plan. I called Liz, shared about Sir Harold, and told her I was going to take some time off. I asked if I could come up to Lakeville. She said, well yelled, "of course!", and then I packed all my summer weekend casual clothes into my suitcase and hit the road.

I'd take this weekend in Lakeville to regroup. And on Monday, I'll start calling my boss, Trisha, to see what I can do to get un-furloughed.

Liz steps back out on to the porch. "Okay, let's go."

I look up at her and she's wearing a vintage band t-shirt, jean shorts, and a pair of sandals that look like they're made for competitive hiking. She has a crocheted bag slung over her shoulder and I barely withhold my distaste at the sight of it.

"Where are we going? Mr. Darcy's house?"

"Nora, you know that isn't walking distance from here." She deadpans. "Mr. Bingley's could be if we go now."

"Ugh, fine but as much as I feel like Eliza Bennet right now I am not fond of walking." I say in my best Kiera Knightly impression.

"Noted. You're more of a Lydia anyway," she mutters. "Let's go."

I slip on my platform slides because they're the only non-heeled sandal I brought. My current wardrobe doesn't really scream comfortable-for-small-town-excursions.

Liz gives me a walking tour as we make our way towards downtown Lakeville. She points out the road that goes towards her parent's house. She points out Sunfish Park, which is tough to miss. It's a sprawling green space right along the lake. A gazebo holds court at one end and pathways with benches zig zag through the park. There's a small beach and a dock with a few boats and jet skis tied to it. We continue walking and we pass the municipal building, a boutique, and a hardware store before arriving at Scoops & Sips Café.

A little bell chimes as we step in and even though there

isn't air conditioning, the atmosphere is refreshing.

Liz greets the owners, Sandy and Mitchell Wright, who are scooping ice into cups. The sight brings tears to my eyes. I'm tempted to ask for a cup of just plain ice to hold against my heated skin but I refrain. I order my iced coffee and step to the side where the creamers are. I add a splash of almond milk and stir while Liz chats and waits for the pastries she ordered.

I take a small sip of my coffee through the straw, trying to pace myself, and a satisfied moan escapes my lips.

"Was that good for you?" a husky voice behind me asks.

I spin and find myself eye to chest, broad chest, of a man. Slowly I pull my gaze up to his face and whoa mama.

A square jaw covered in thick, well trimmed, scruff. His full lips are curved into a small smirk in the middle of the dark brown beard. Further up his brown eyes sparkle with hints of gold flecked throughout. Short curls of thick brown hair peek out under a tan baseball cap.

He's the type of guy that I would definitely approach at a bar in the city if he didn't approach me first. Although his hair is longer than the financial district men I typically see, he's clean cut and manly. In the city he'd be in a suit, no tie, the first few buttons of his dress shirt undone to show off his man cleavage. Instead the lumberjack in front of me has a washed out green henley shirt on, the sleeves fitting tight around his biceps. And he's wearing jeans even though it is easily a triple digit heat index today.

I take a small step back because he's definitely in my personal space and that's when I realize who it is. This is *the* guy. The one who gave me a ride last night. Who got me off through my clothes, which was a whole new level of hot.

Since I'm only here a week and we've already hooked up in a sense, I decide to be the flirtatious main character of my story. I smile knowingly up at him and say, "It's good but I can think of better ways to start my day."

Good line right?

Satisfied, I start to walk away, leave 'em wanting more as they say, when he chimes back in.

"Me too, but usually that requires you being in bed with me."

I'm sorry, what now?

Who says stuff like that out loud?

To strangers?

Okay, not quite strangers but still.

I thought city boys moved fast, all performance, no preamble, but they've got nothing on this guy. Unlike my usual guy, the playful glint in his eyes is more charming than daring. But I'm not going to let one comment throw me off my game.

Think, Nora, think.

Oh, I got it.

"Usually? I would think that's the only way."

"Well no," he leans in closer to whisper in my ear. His hot breath on my outer ear sends shivers down my spine and his fresh scent already carries a hit of musky sweat. My eyes are focused on a curl of his hair sticking out under his hat against the nape of his neck. "There's always the shower, the wall, the counter," he pauses, "my truck. Plenty of places to have a good time."

My iced coffee, with a splash of almond milk, has combined with the dry cereal and turned into cement in my stomach. My body stalls out while my mind envisions sex in all those places. With him. Chills are racing down my back from his breath near my ear and while, yes, it is hotter than hades here, the chills are making me flush instead of shiver. I know it is my turn to speak but I can't manage to get a full breath.

He pulls back, stands up straight, smiles, and tips his baseball hat before running his hand through his thick hair and replacing it. I pivot slowly to watch him as he steps around me and walks away.

Ladies, his backside is just as nice as his front side.

Noticing that isn't helping the chills plus flush cheeks plus wet cement sensation I'm working through.

"I see you met Jimmy," Liz says as she walks over and hands me a pastry box. She adds some half and half to her iced coffee.

"Ha, um yeah, I guess I did." I blink a few times.

"You okay?" Liz looks at me like I might actually have heat stroke. And who knows, maybe I do. Aren't the symptoms shortness of breath (check), racing heart (check), flushed cheeks (check), throbbing between your legs (check).

Okay maybe Dr. Google doesn't list that last one but they should. It's debilitating.

Liz steps towards the door and I slowly follow. She holds open the door and reaches out to take the box of pastries from me.

"Nah, I've got it." I tell her as I step out onto the sidewalk.

I'm still looking at Jimmy's retreating figure as he crosses the street. He does this little skip jog thing and the word "SEXY" flashes like a neon sign in my mind. He unlocks his truck and reaches in.

In my truck, gulp.

Condensation from my iced coffee falls and hits my foot which brings me back to the present. I turn to and see Liz is watching me with an amused look on her face.

"What?" I challenge.

"Ooh, nothing." She says through a grin.

3

Asking Questions

JIMMY

I noticed her as soon as she stepped into the coffee shop. How could I not? All my thoughts in the last twelve hours have been of her. She was breathtaking last night but in the light of day, man. She was stunning.

She was dressed to the nines in short jean shorts that hugged her ass and a cream colored strapless top. My gaze wandered down her body to her shoes which were a mile high.

I couldn't stop myself, I had to get close to her again. When I smelled her spicy perfume it triggered an uncomfortable reaction in my chest. Then she turned and seared me with her sapphire blue eyes.

I panicked. The blue was like a fragment of sky in the middle of her face. The feeling of sunshine and a breeze frozen in time. All I could do was get closer, my hands twitched to touch her.

Chimes ring overhead as I press my back into the door of my family's hardware store, Lewis Hardware. My sister Angie is sitting at the register.

"Hey. Any idea how long Liz's friend is staying in town?" I ask.

"Nope." She pops the P.

I continue walking towards the office in the back and I think I've ended the conversation but I should have known better. Angie is a little sister. The kind with relentless questions and endless energy for testing patience. And an uncanny ability to zero in on the hot button issue that is most sensitive to her pressing.

"Why?" She asks as she pushes off the stool and walks behind me towards the office.

Why? Why did I ask? Because while getting coffee, like I always do on Saturday mornings before coming in to balance the books, I managed to talk dirty to the girl who I picked up on the side of the highway last night in a storm. The same girl I then dry humped in my truck before dropping her off.

"Oh no reason, just met her at the coffee shop."

"Yeah?" Angie wiggles her eyebrows as she comes into the office and flops onto the sofa.

"Yeah." I try to shrug it off and pivot towards the filing cabinet but I haven't set my coffee down yet so my hands are full and I have to pivot back.

Nothing gets past Angie.

"You think she's cute."

It wasn't a question.

"Seriously, are you twelve?" I try to deflect.

"Twice that actually. I turned a full two dozen last May. You were there, at the party," she suddenly turns mock serious. "Oh no, Jimmy, are you losing your memory in your old age?"

I laugh because Angie can diffuse any situation with humor.

I got the charm, the handyman skills. She got the artistic genes and the sense of humor. Together we make a good team.

It's why owning a business together works so well. We work together remodeling homes in Lakeville and the surrounding towns. She does the design, I do the construction, and we share the responsibility of managing Lewis Hardware which my grandfather started back in 1954. My grandpa, James Arthur Lewis, better known around town as Pops, ran it for sixty years before officially passing it down to my dad.

I set my coffee on my desk and reach to switch on the lamp, turn the knob, and nothing.

Oh yeah, the power is out.

"Are you able to take cash today?" I ask Angie.

"Yeah, or I'll just open up a tab like the good ole days."

"What good ole days?"

"You know, like back in Pops' day. You had a tab at your local shops and would pay them like once a week or something." She shrugs. "I dunno. I wasn't there. But you were old man, what was it like?"

"That's your second age dig in as many minutes. What's with you today?"

"Nothing." She says an octave higher than necessary.

And before she was even finished saying the word she hops off the sofa and shuffles out of the office. Moments later I hear the stool at the front counter scratch across the ancient tile floor.

I'm guessing it's about a boy.

Now it's my turn to tease her and I take a breath fuel my efforts, when I remember that I barely dodged the questions about Miss Magnetic Blue Eyes. Not wanting to tempt fate I decide to let it slide.

From the door of the office I can see her toeing the ground in front of her. Arms crossed over her chest. Head down.

"Hey, what's up?" I ask as I walk towards the front of the store. Time to put my big brother pants on and help her out, minus the teasing.

"Ugh, it's nothing. I mean, not exactly nothing but it's not important."

She looks up at me and I give her a knowing look and lower my chin. Silently saying go on.

"Fine. So I hung out with a guy last night, and before you start asking a ton of questions, yes you know him, and yes you like him, or at least you did before he started to date your sister, but I'm getting ahead of myself because it wasn't even a date. It was accidentally seeing each other at the market and talking for awhile, and me walking back to his place with him, but not going up because it started to rain so I just drove home. And all this is irrelevant anyways. I'll never go on a date with anyone in this town because you know every guy, and are friends with them or their family, and I'm always your little sister. It's not fair."

I look at Angie while she catches her breath. Her posture has changed. Now she's standing square on both feet, legs hip width apart with her hands propped on her hips. I wait to say anything until she looks up at me.

"Feel good to get that off your chest?"

"Actually, yeah, huh, who knew I was hanging on to that?" She shrugs and sits back down on the stool. "Well, as I was saying, I went on a non-date date last night. And when I got home I didn't charge my phone so now it's dead and the power is out. I don't know if he's texted me. I think it went well and I want to go hang out again, but I don't know if I can be the one to ask him out, and now he can't reach me because my phone is dead. OH! I could email him."

She turns to the computer at the front desk and I'm going to give her three, two, one.

"Oh yeah, computers need power." Her shoulders slump forward as her hands fall to her lap.

"So does Wi-Fi."

"Not helpful." She deadpans.

I try not to laugh.

"You're just going to have to wait it out I guess." I say with a shrug.

"Yeah, I guess." She sits back down on the stool with a sigh. I nudge her shoulder with a friendly punch and she gives me a half smile. I return it and then walk back to the office. I take a sip of coffee before I sit at the desk and sort through a stack of mail.

It's pretty slow for a Saturday since the power is out. Angie and I mop the floors and tidy the shelves while we talk about next steps at the Fallons' house, our current remodeling project. It was a total gut job and we're both glad the drywall and floors are finally in.

I head back to the office and write a note to myself to bring the laser level to the job tomorrow. I peel the paper off the notepad and fold it before sliding it into my pocket. I stand up and the door chimes.

"Jimmy! It's Kyle!" Angie yells from the front.

"Be right there!" I call back.

I walk out of the office and flip the light switch at the door and nothing happens. I laugh at myself for being such a creature of habit and walk up to the front of the store shaking my head.

"Hey man! How's it going." Kyle and I exchange a man hug with a good slap to the back from each of us.

"I'm good. I wanted to invite you both to a bonfire at our place tonight. We're gonna go full camping style, food over the fire, s'mores, whiskey, beers. After I take Nora to get her car I'm going to drive over to Avon to get ice so BYOB even if it's warm."

Her name is Nora.

"Sounds fun," I look to Angie who is smiling and nodding. "We'll be there."

"Awesome, I'm making the rounds but everyone is welcome so invite whoever."

"Will do. See you later."

4

Far Cry From My Usual Saturday Night

Nora

Forget Georgian Society, I'm living in the Stone Age.

How did Betty Rubble pull off such a cute look? She didn't have electricity or hot water. And she probably used a fossil as a hairbrush. Certainly my handmade Italian brush with an ergonomic design is better than that.

Even with the latest in hair brush technology at my disposal my hair is frizzy. The sun set an hour ago but it did little to cool the air. It's like the bayou out here. I'm sticky with sweat. And Liz insisted both of us walk through a cloud of bug spray, which does not blend well with my perfume.

She and Kyle are sitting on the other side of the bonfire with their friends laughing and chatting. I'm sitting on a log holding a stick with a hot dog skewered on it. I've been instructed to rotate it evenly.

After the coffee shop visit, where Jimmy talked dirty in my ear, sent shivers down my spine, and kicked off the sexiest of mental montages, Liz and I walked around town.

We didn't go into any stores but we window shopped and

Liz introduced me to everyone we passed. I snuck a peek in the window of Lewis Hardware and saw a cute girl sitting at the counter. Liz told me Jimmy's family has owned the store forever. He and his sister run it now and they have a side business remodeling homes. She showed me their social media accounts and the projects are really good. I've never wanted a white picket fence sort of thing but I'll admit I would add it to a faves list on the real estate app I sometimes browse.

I tried not to be too nosey about Jimmy's life because Liz would see right through me. On the way back to her house she continued the walking tour of Lakeville. We walked past the Chow Down diner which she told me only serves pancakes during the week. We peeked in the windows of a cute clothing boutique called Gina's. And we laughed a little standing outside The Christmas Year Round shop, because what small town doesn't have one of those.

When we arrived at the house Kyle was there with a greasy looking man holding a red gas canister in his hands. Eugene Tarf, auto body shop owner and gas station proprietor of Lakeville, drove Kyle and me out to my car in his tow truck and helped us refill the gas tank.

Kyle decided to lean into this no-power situation and organized a bonfire party. There are coolers of beer, hot dogs, and s'mores fixings. This is a far cry from my usual Saturday night where I'd be at a bar with my legs crossed, shoulders rolled back, and elbow perched on the back of the stool. Open, but not desperate. Welcoming but not friendly.

I twirl my hot dog a bit and look around. It doesn't take much imagination to see a bonfire becoming some sort of trendy dining experience in the city. People would flock to cook for themselves over an open fire.

And, actually focusing on cooking my hot dog has kept my mind off Sir Harold and my job, or lack thereof. Without my phone, that hadn't recharged much before I left Jimmy's truck, I didn't have access to my podcast. No TV, movies, or even a freaking radio, all day today leaving my thoughts as my main source of entertainment. They kept running away and going down worst case scenario paths. What if I don't get my job back? What if I can't make rent?

What if?

What if?

What if?

And each time I came to the same answer.

I don't know.

And I am not comfortable with that conclusion.

My mind is buzzing. No wait, that's coming from next to my ear. Instinctively I wind up and swat at the mosquito. I pull my hand away to see a squished beast that must be genetically engineered for massive size. The satisfaction of killing the bug is short lived. In one swift movement, I managed to slap myself in the face and drop my hotdog into the fire.

"Everything alright?" a voice asks from behind me. I turn to see Jimmy smirking. His whole face participates in the smile with lines crinkling his eyes drawing me to their chocolate depths. I take in his appearance, a pair of shorts that were tailor made for him, showing off the perfect amount of man thigh, which is two inches above the knee. He's sporting a green t-shirt that deliciously hangs off the kind of pecks a girl dreams about. I know because I dreamt about them last night. That tan baseball hat is in place, and it looks like it has been molded to his head over his longer-than-a-city-boy's hair, which is curling out over the sides. His dark brown eyes sparkle as they catch the firelight and shadows fill the crinkles at the corner of his eyes, inviting me for a closer look.

He's still smirking knowingly and I remember that he asked if everything is alright and no, in fact, everything is not alright.

Not even close.

I'm stinky.

I'm sweaty.

I'm hungry.

I'm sad.

I'm scared.

I'm crying.

Dang it, I am crying. I feel a big tear hit my cheek.

Jimmy must see it too because his eyes soften from teasing to tender.

"Hardly, but I'll manage." I get out with a smile but I can tell he doesn't buy it.

"I'll get you another." He picks up the stick I dropped, and hands it to me. He pulls the charred hot dog off and takes it with him. He steps over to the cooler and I quickly try to smooth my hair down while his back is turned. I'm pushing my luck but I lean forward and jiggle my tits up in my shirt and I slyly manage this move as if I'm checking my legs for mosquito bites.

I have four, for the record.

"Here you go." Jimmy hands me a beer and takes the stick out of my hand before threading two hot dogs onto it. He moves the stick into the hand that is holding his beer and switches his cap around backwards.

I swallow my tongue a little bit.

Who knew backwards baseball hats were such a turn on?

He sits down on one of the log benches surrounding the fire. He nods towards the spot next to him and so I sit down too. Usually I don't like decisions being made for me but I'm willing to do what he says, no questions asked.

"First bonfire?" He asks after a sip of beer.

"Is it that obvious?"

He chuckles. "Nah, only to us seasoned pros." I watch his hand rotate the stick over the fire. His hands look strong, veiny, and my skin warms remembering how they felt on me last night.

He leans a little closer to me and says, "I'm Jimmy by the way."

"Oh! Yes, Hi, Nora." I say while pointing to myself. By the grace of Princess Kate I don't blurt out "Liz told me your life story."

"Nora," the way he says it sends a shiver down my spine, he's testing the word on his tongue. "Nice to meet you. How do you know Liz and Kyle?"

"We all worked the same internship in the city together four years ago and became fast friends. We've stayed in touch with weekly FaceTimes."

"Wow, weekly?"

"Yep. Every Monday at 7:30. I came up to Lakeville for one day the summer after Liz moved back but I haven't had a chance to visit since then."

Truth? I hadn't wanted to visit. Liz went through such a rough time when she first left the city I was afraid of how I'd find her. That and I was focused on my job and not much else.

Then once Kyle moved here I didn't want to disturb their domestic bliss.

"How long you staying?" Jimmy asks breaking me from my thoughts.

"Oh, umm, just the week I think."

He perks up. "You've picked a good week. First a power outage to welcome you to town,"

"Well, I think technically my welcome was getting rescued outside of town and then, well, you know." And by the way he narrows his eyes I can tell that he does.

"Right." He coughs out. "That, and then Float Fest is on Saturday."

"That's the annual boat parade?"

"The very one."

I remember Liz telling us all about it during our internship and mentioning it in our calls. Every family with a boat decorates it, invites their friends out, and then everyone cruises all afternoon around the lake. There's a big carnival at night.

Jimmy leans forward and I follow his gaze. I don't see anything besides his hands holding the stick roasting the hotdogs. He stands and I watch him check the hotdogs, then walk over to a card table and plates them for us.

"Mustard?" He calls over.

"Yes please."

He comes back, hands me a plate with a hotdog, pasta salad, and a small pile of fruit. He sits down again, pivots, and holds his hotdog up to me.

"Cheers Nora." He says while making full eye contact. Leaving me burning up from the inside out with such an intense gaze on me.

"Cheers Jimmy." I reply and feel my face flush.

He keeps his gaze locked on mine, smirks, and takes a huge bite of his hotdog. I watch him chew which oddly doesn't gross me out like it should. The mechanics of chewing is now intriguing.

"Jimmy! There you are!" Across the fire I see a girl in a cute floral minidress, her hair in french braided pig tails. She's got little white sneakers on. I look down at my kitten heel flip flops and add a cute pair of tennis shoes to my mental shopping list.

She rounds the fire and Jimmy gives her a wave. He's still chewing and I have yet to take a bite so I stick out my hand, "Hi, I'm Nora!"

"Nora! Hello! I'm Angie, Jimmy's sister. It's so nice to meet you." She says with a wide smile.

"Hi! It's so good to meet you. Liz showed me the social accounts for your houses and I loved them."

Angie's smile falters for a split second as she quickly flicks her eyes to Jimmy.

"You should come by the Fallons' house tomorrow and check out the current job then."

"Sure, I'd love to."

She smiles and walks away to get a drink and I take a bite of my hotdog. It honestly tastes incredible for being a hotdog. Either it's the open flame or the fact that a hot guy made it for me. I can't be sure.

"So," I feel Jimmy's gaze turn towards me. "If you saw Angie's socials then you knew who I was."

"Guilty." I say with a mouthful. I swallow. "Liz showed me earlier today. But I had no idea before then, pinky swear." I hold up my finger to him.

"Ha, no need to pinky swear, that shit's serious." He lowers my hand. His lingers on top of mine for a second longer than necessary before he slowly pulls it back to his lap. "You really liked the houses? You weren't just saying that?"

"No! Not at all. They're amazing. Some of the before and afters were amazing. Every once in a while I get obsessed with looking up homes online. Or watching the Homecraft Network for hours. But then I take a look around my humble one bedroom apartment and realize that I'd be totally overwhelmed by anything bigger."

"I get that. The first place I redid was the apartment over the store. Angie is still living at home but I know she's dying for me to move to a house so she can have the apartment. I just don't see the need."

"That sweet girl is still living at home? That's all the reason you need! What is she 23?"

"24."

"Oh yeah, definitely. She's gotta get her own space. If only to have a place to let her vibrators air dry."

Jimmy coughs on the pasta salad he had just taken a forkful of. "What?!" he chokes out. His voice is strained like Italian dressing is stuck in his vocal cords.

"Sorry. I just meant she needs a space to call her own. Every woman does in their early twenties."

He takes a sip of his beer and turns to look at me. I try not to fold under his scrutiny.

"I suppose you're right."

"Oh, okay, yeah." I mutter in response as I try to read his expression. Was it bad form to suggest his sister has not just one vibrator, but enough to necessitate a weekly group cleaning and air drying routine? I watch as he drains his beer, turns back to the fire, and rests his forearms on his knees. He looks like he's deep in thought.

"I'll grab you another beer." I say as I stand up abruptly. I grab his plate, empty beer, and walk over towards the cooler.

When I return I stop next to him. He's still staring at the fire so I stare at it too. I lower the beer down to him without looking. I feel him take it and then I feel the back of his hand graze down my calf.

There's no way to hide the goosebumps that erupt across my skin. A wobbly sensation knocks my knees about and I need to move.

I take a step back but I don't get far. The heel of my sandal is stuck in the grass. I yank up my leg to free my shoe but it doesn't budge. I yank again, harder, and lift my arms to help my efforts.

Turns out, I overcorrected. Seconds later my world is tilted on it's axis. I am careening forward, windmill arms and all. The beer I was holding tumbles to the ground and I feel it splash on my feet as my hands connect with something firm and warm.

"You okay?" Jimmy asks looking at me.

"Think so." I mumble as I stare at my hands planted on his chest. He nods and helps me stand up straight. Then he holds my hand while I, successfully, step around him and sit down.

Jimmy's hand releases mine and then stiffly moves back and joins his other around his beer. He leans forward again on his elbows and looks at the fire. I admire his profile and watch as the amber shadows cast by the firelight dance across his features. His shoulders are rolled forward, his forearm muscles flex as he spins his beer bottle around in his hands.

Our bodies are inches apart and the air between us is alive with possibility. My body hums with anticipation as I drag my gaze down to the space that separates our legs.

And like it's operating under a magnetic pull, my knee slides to the side and rests along his.

I stare and wait for him to pull back. To adjust his leg. He doesn't. Instead his eyes travel from the point where our knees are touching up my leg, to my waist, my chest, and finally his molten chocolate eyes meet mine.

5

In A Hurry To Go Slow

JIMMY

Nora stares at me and I take another swig of beer. It is bitter and sour. I know enough to know answers aren't found at the bottom of a bottle. Courage doesn't live there either. I've lost my taste for alcohol tonight. Instead I want to taste the strawberry blonde with eyes as deep as the ocean. The one who makes me think shit like that and surprises me from one moment to the next.

And each time she mentions something like a vibrator, or our time together last night, or is simply close enough for me to touch my restraint tightens, ready to snap. Our knees are touching and it's as if that spot is the epicenter of an earthquake.

Her outfit doesn't help steady my body or mind either. She's in a tank top that looks like a corset. With short frayed denim shorts that expose a sliver of her round ass. Her hair is up and sleeked back in a ponytail. Her lipstick has faded slightly leaving a red stain on her lips. Her eyelids and cheeks are shimmering in the firelight.

When she was standing in front of me I couldn't keep my

hand off of her. I was staring into the fire and remembering the weight of her body over mine last night and just the feeling of her calf drove me wild. Nora does something to me.

"What?" She asks, pulling me from my thoughts.

"Nothing, just thinking," I scratch my beard and look down at her feet, "those shoes aren't really made for bonfire nights."

She looks down at them too and shrugs "No, I suppose not. I guess I'm more prepared for pavement."

"Here." I offer and then I reach down and hold her ankle as I slide off one sandal. I hear her suck in a deep inhale. I need oxygen too, my head is spinning. I dangle the first sandal on my finger. She grabs it and pulls it into her chest like it is a child's treasured stuffed animal.

I smirk and slide off her other shoe. When I hand her the second one she takes it and burns me with her stare.

Listen, I know I'm an attractive man. One, I can see myself in the mirror. And two, I often get, umm, a positive response from women. When I leave Lakeville for a night out, I don't have trouble catching an attractive girl's eye. When I was in the city last week for the Home Builder's Conference, I heard girls muttering 'he's hot' or 'look at him' as they walked past. I caught a few others pointing.

I imagine it's what girls feel when men stand still at a job site and catcall at them while they're walking by. Part of it was embarrassing and awkward but another part of it kinda felt good. Not that I would ever make a move on some random girl walking by.

Well, unless she jumped on me in my truck.

The moment I think about it I flick my gaze up to Nora's. I watch as the tip of her tongue glides over her bottom lip before she pulls her lip between her teeth.

I'm gone.

Lust travels through my body faster than a freight train. Something primal takes over. I stand quickly and look around for a place to take her. I'm like a caveman. Every moment I wait to get her somewhere private feels like an eternity.

"What are you looking for?" She knowingly asks.

"Somewhere private. I need to kiss you again but I don't want an audience."

"Oh. Umm, we could go up to the house. No one is up there."

"C'mon." And I grab her hand and drag her up with me.

"Ew, my feet are getting dirty."

I look down at her and see that she's standing on her tip toes looking down at her feet. She slowly picks up one foot and takes a tiny step forward. I don't have time for this but the way she's bending over a little makes her breasts look like they could spill from her top so I admire the view for a moment.

Okay, moment over. Caveman Jimmy growls and swoops down to scoop her up in my arms. I'm carrying her like a bride up to the house and there is no way everyone here hasn't seen it. Her squeal of laughter doesn't help us fly under the radar.

Nora's long legs hang over my arm and my palm burns against her smooth skin. She tosses her arms around my neck, her sandals clapping against my back as I walk quickly towards the house. Her spicy scent draws me closer and I pull her into my chest. She tightens her grip around my neck.

At the screen door I set Nora down and open it. She saunters in with her strappy sandals hanging over her shoulder. She then goes to the back door of the house and opens it while facing me.

I cross the three steps to her and crash my mouth into hers as she steps backwards into the house. Her hands travel up my chest as her sandals fall to the ground. We spin into the room while our mouths are still connected and I push the door closed. When I hear it shut I reach down and hoist her legs up around my waist.

She locks her ankles around my back and I carry her to the arm of the sofa where I set her down and lean her back slightly. I run my hand down from her collarbone to the center of her chest. She reaches for the hem of my shirt.

I stand up to help get my shirt off and while my head is still inside the fabric the room is flooded with light. The TV starts blaring. The microwave beeps.

I finish taking off my shirt and Nora is looking up at me wide eyed.

"Glad the lights came on so I could see this." She says while pushing her hands up my abs, through my trimmed chest hair to my shoulders.

I hear a whistle from outside. Nora smiles slyly at me. She might not be embarrassed but I do not want a spotlight on this. On us.

"C'mon." I grunt as I slip my shirt back on over my head. I bend down and grab her shoes.

"Where are we going now?"

"My place."

I don't give her a chance to argue, or put her shoes on, before I pick her up again and take her to my truck. I set her into the front seat and stare at the piece of her sandy red hair that has fallen from her ponytail, framing her face. She's holding her chin high with her hands folded around her shoes in her lap.

We drive in silence for the few minutes from Liz and Kyle's to my apartment. I park in the back and walk around the truck to help her out.

"A girl could get used to this." She quips as I pick her up and begin carrying her to the door leading to the apartment.

"I could get used to it too." I say as I turn my head and nibble at her jaw. She laughs and tightens her grip around my neck.

When we get upstairs I set her down and turn on the lights.

"So you redid this place?" She asks as she looks around. I watch her walk into the main living area. If I hadn't been the one to lay these floors myself I'd swear the foundation of the place wasn't level. It feels like someone has stuck a pile of cinderblocks under one side. My world is titled towards her.

"Yes." I say as I take a step forward.

"Wow, impressive." She says while she looks back over her shoulder at me. I see a twinkle in her eye and return her smile with one of my own.

"I didn't drag you back here to talk though."

"Oh, no?" She teases.

"No."

"Well, why did you drag me back here then?" She cocks a hip out to the side. She's still in her bare feet and holding her sandals in her hand.

"You know why Nora."

Her eyes darken and she drops her shoes before taking two steps to me and reaching for the button of my shorts. Without another word I take my shirt off and let her unzip my fly. She trails the lightest of touches along my bulging boxer briefs as she slides my shorts down my hips.

I reach up for her top and pause, realizing I don't know how to take it off of her. She puts her hands on the center seam and undoes one little hook at the top.

Nope. I don't have that kind of patience. I grip her top between my fingers and tug, hard. The sound of her shirt ripping apart fills the room and we both freeze for a moment before I toss what is left of her shirt to the side. Nora's breath is heavy and our eyes lock. My calloused hands grate against her milky skin as I tease my fingertips down her chest, across her pebbled nipples, and down her stomach to the button of her shorts. Nora's eyes simmer as I slowly unzip her fly. Now all I hear is the crunch of the zipper's teeth echoing off the walls.

She shifts her hips side to side and the shorts slide down her legs revealing a black lacy thong. I reach down, grip her ass, and pull her to me. All that separates us is the thin lace of her panties and the cotton of my briefs. I sling my hand around her waist, lift her, and walk towards the bed.

"Nora," I whisper as I set her down on the bed with one knee resting between her legs. "I can't seem to stop myself around you."

"Then don't." She whispers back before our mouths crash together again.

6

The Thing About Rules

Nora

Just another minute.

Then I'll get up.

One more minute of being curled up in Jimmy's arms.

Spooning is not a place I've been before. In fact I've avoided it like skinny jeans since they were dubbed uncool.

I peek over my shoulder and see Jimmy snoring softly next to me. I watch as his chest rises and falls and his eyes flutter under their lids. Meanwhile over here I'm dealing with shallow breaths and fluttering heartbeats. The weight of his arm over my waist feels, well it feels. I'm not sure what to make of it.

With my eyes wide open I softly trace a path up his arm from his wrist to his elbow. The hair on his arm catches in my nails as I travel but he doesn't stir.

I roll back over and look out his bedroom window from where I'm snuggled in under his arm. This is the first time tonight that I've stopped to think. Up until this moment I was all sensations. The pressure of Jimmy's hands on my body. The rough texture of his beard everywhere he kissed me. My body softened in his embrace and I let impulses lead the way.

Well, shame on me because those impulses have driven me to a place I've never been before.

I was ready to let him screw me six ways to Sunday on the sofa, in Liz's house, with the lights on, with a party raging outside. But going back to his place made everything better.

And a little bit worse.

Jimmy's bed is comfortable, worn in. His sheets smell like him with an extra dash of musk. When he carried me in here and all but tossed me on the bed I told myself it wasn't really breaking my one-and-done hook up rule because, technically, we didn't sleep together in his truck.

And thank the goddess of orgasms for that loophole.

Now, three intense orgasms later, I'm tucked in Jimmy's bed with his arm wrapped around me. It's not just the cuddling that's new, being in a man's bed at all.

I like a home field advantage. Or a neutral ground. Give me my bed or somewhere random. I never go home with the guy. No, he comes to mine. Because then I never have to worry about this moment right here.

The one where sex is over and I have to leave.

But I'm in more than just that pickle.

You remember when he tore my shirt off? Unbelievably hot I know, and I experienced a tiny orgasm at that moment too. However, now the issue is that I don't have a shirt to wear home.

Second issue is that he drove here and I doubt the cab situation is the same in Lakeville as it is in the city.

So I'm shirtless and stranded.

Jimmy is snoring softly behind me. I catch a smile growing

across my face because I am thoroughly enjoying this. My mother would roll over in her grave, if she were dead.

"Men have used women for centuries, now we get to use them." Is her somewhat feminist mantra. The problem is she never got to the using them part. She would get caught up with some guy, think that she had the upper hand, and then when she felt like he was almost done with her she'd go find the next guy.

She always had a backup man.

An out.

And that's pretty much the only advice I've taken from my mother. Always have an out. Which is why it's unusual for me to follow sensations instead of a strategy.

In the city, I control the night. If a man is interested I make it seem like the idea of bringing him home with me just popped into my pretty little head but no, I've been plotting it for hours. At this point I don't even have to actively plot. It's just how I operate.

Jimmy stirs behind me and pulls me closer to him. Sparks fly throughout my body as his chest presses into my back. The weight of his thigh against mine has images of sturdy tree trunks running through my mind.

Okay, enough. Who thinks that sort of thing? Did I get zapped by lightning last night and not realize it? Have I done some sort of freaky Friday switch or something?

Because the Nora Heely of two days ago would never consider snuggling up to a guy and spending the night. Would never envision herself safely nestled in a forest with him.

That's something a love sick, naïve, romantic girl would do. Not me. Okay, time's up. On an inhale I slowly lift his arm and slide out of bed. Jimmy shifts a little but doesn't wake up.

Phew.

First things first, a shirt. I don't think the citizens of Lakeville would be thrilled with me walking home topless. Even if my tits are, well, the tits.

I tiptoe over to his closet and pull down the first button down shirt I see. It's plain white and starched stiff. This isn't the time to be picky so I slip it over my shoulders, fasten the middle two buttons, and head for the living room where my shorts are.

I have no clue where my thong ended up so we'll just leave that one as a souvenir.

Ah, there they are. I bend over to pick my shorts up.

"What are you doing?"

I let out a little yelp as I spin and clutch my shorts to my chest. My heart is racing, from being snuck up on no other reason. Definitely has nothing to do with Jimmy standing shirtless in his bedroom doorway in low slung athletic shorts. My eyes scan the clipped chest hair covering his pecs, abs, and zero in on the thicket of hair, disappearing in the waistband of his shorts, which does nothing to slow my pulse.

"I was gonna call Liz for a ride home."

"You don't have to do that," he says.

"Well, you drove me here and I don't exactly know my way back, so…"

"No, I mean, you don't have to leave."

"Oh, well, I don't usually, umm, yeah, I don't usually spend the night with guys."

"Nora, there's no way in hell you haven't done any of that," he throws his thumb over his shoulder at his bedroom, "before.

The way you," he swallows, "well, yeah, it doesn't seem like you are a novice."

I chuckle "Oh, yeah, I've done, umm, that, before. A lot. Not like, a lot a lot but like a healthy amount."

"No judgement here," he holds up his hands, "I'm hoping you and I can do it a lot a lot."

I smile. He's charming.

Dangerous.

"We'll see what happens." I fish for my phone in the pocket of shorts that I'm still holding to my chest instead of putting on. "I'll just text Liz."

"Don't."

I look up at him and he is staring at me with such intensity that my knees quiver.

"Stay."

Let the record show that I don't appreciate his one word commands on an equality level. But whoa mama, they are speaking to my lady parts. Still, lady parts got me here and I'm not sure I can trust them to get me out of here. He catches my hesitation and walks over to me. He brings the backs of his knuckles to my cheek and brushes lightly up to my hair.

His fingers thread into the strands as he rakes the hair away from my face and settles his hands at the back of my neck. I watch as he lowers his mouth to kiss me. My pulse picks up and a pressure builds between my legs.

He brings one hand down from my shoulder and gently tugs at my shorts so I release them. They drop to the floor with a thud which reminds me that my phone is still in the pocket. His hand returns to my waist and he grips my side and leans me back slightly.

Again my mind empties and I follow what feels good. I respond to the places his hands travel. Both of us murmur into each other's mouths. He taste like him, it's unique and unlike anything I've experienced before. Satisfaction simmers under my skin. We deepen our kiss and he slides his hand to the front of my hip and down. I pivot my leg open slightly for him and he runs the hand that was in my hair down to my waist. My arms float up around his neck and I pull myself even closer to him. He removes his hand from between my legs and I whimper.

"You're wet for me already," he whispers against my ear as he pulls my thigh up to rest on his hip.

"Yeah" I exhale. Like I had some say in how my body responds to him. He continues to work his fingers along my folds until my thighs begin to shake.

"Yes, Jimmy, yes." I whisper.

A falling sensation courses through my body. I tighten my arms around his neck and my hand finds the back of his head. My fingers weave through his thick hair and I grasp the strands as an anchor in this storm.

"I've got you Nora." Jimmy grunts as his arm around my waist flexes which pulls me closer to him.

His beard scrapes my neck as he nips and kisses along my collarbone. I whimper as every inch of me lights up. His thumb taps against my my most sensitive parts and my body bows involuntarily in his arms. A sharp cry erupts from my chest as every muscle in me tenses. He grunts and increases the speed and intensity as his fingers continue their dance. My body snaps, and my eyes fly open as the combination of his words, his sounds, and his touch overwhelms me. I watch as he watches me surrender all my control.

My insides flutter and I roll my hips to counter the friction Jimmy is applying with his fingers. Tidal waves of electricity rush through my veins. Liquid warmth follows in their wake.

His hand at my back splays wide as my body relaxes. Our heavy breaths are in sync as he pushes my leg down and my feet find solid ground again.

When he stands up straight my arms trail down his and he flexes his biceps under my touch. I grip back, digging my nails in. Jimmy leans down and places a kiss on my neck, right behind my ear. I tilt my head to make more room. The need to be surrounded by him is overwhelming my decision making ability.

"Get back in my bed." He grumbles before putting both hands on my waist and turning me towards his bedroom.

I nod, biting my lip, as he pushes me towards his bed.

Expecting him to want to continue what he started in the living room I begin to unbutton his shirt. He stops me as he lays his hand over mine on the buttons

"We're going to sleep. That's all. You can wear this if you want or sleep without it but I don't expect anything from you."

"Oh. Okay."

I look down to where his gym shorts are tented and then watch as he steps back and rounds the bed to the other side. He climbs in and pulls the covers back for me.

He just wants to sleep?

My brain cannot compute.

No one who is as good at sex as we seem to be just sleeps.

Or maybe I was right all along and he really is some small town murderer. He attracts unsuspecting women and gets them to stay with him by delivering multiple orgasms in a short period of time. Half of me is disturbed by how quickly my mind goes to "murderer". I blame my true crime podcasts for that, but I can't ignore the facts.

Liz told me earlier he hasn't dated anyone in Lakeville in a while. When he rescued me on Friday was he coming back from a date? Is she tied up in some shed outside of town?

These thoughts run through my head as I watch him plug in his phone and set it on the bedside table. He seems so normal.

Too normal?

Hesitantly I slide myself into bed because I don't want to do something to piss him off. I lay down with my back towards him and I tuck my arm under the pillow.

He slides up behind me and spoons me. Again my nervous system is flooded with dueling sensations of comfort and fear.

"Good night Nora."

"Umm, yeah, good night Jimmy."

"You okay?"

"Mhmm," I hum but it doesn't sound convincing.

He shifts up to his elbow and rests his head on his hand. With his other hand he gently pulls on my shoulder so I roll onto my back and look up at him. "What's wrong?" He asks.

"Nothing. I'm fine."

"Which is girl for 'something, I'm the opposite of fine'." He informs me.

Touché.

"Like I said earlier, I don't do the whole sleep over thing."

"Well, there's a first time for everything." He says matter of factly.

"I guess so."

"Do you want to text Liz and tell her where you are?"

Okay, a murderer probably wouldn't say something like that. Unless he's trying to throw me off the scent and make me feel safe.

I stifle a yawn. "Yeah, I'll grab my phone." And I slide out of bed to get my shorts. I send Liz a quick text and return to bed.

If I wake up tied to the headboard, well, shame on me.

...

The sun is shining in through the windows when I open my eyes. I guess it's too much to ask to close the curtains. But also, bravo Jimmy for having curtains.

Jimmy.

Quick check. I'm still in his shirt, I'm still in his bed, I'm not tied up.

Which, honestly, is a little disappointing. I bet being tied up by him would be an out of this world experience.

A clunk in the kitchen draws my attention. I toss off the covers and walk to the door of his bedroom.

A girl could get used to this.

Standing at the stove is a shirtless Jimmy, gym shorts slung low on his hips, delicious back dimples on display. By the looks of it he's scrambling eggs. There's a plate of fruit already on the counter and a loaf of bread sitting next to the toaster.

I've never had a guy make me breakfast before.

Before my no sleepovers policy was instated I had a few guys buy me breakfast. But that was like four years ago so it's been a while.

Well, there's a first time for everything.

I walk out to the counter and take a seat on one of the stools.

"Whatcha got going on there?" I ask.

Jimmy spins around with a ginormous smile on his face. It's infectious and my body decides to return the smile. The way his whole face crinkles into the smile makes my stomach feel like it's jumping on a trampoline.

"Good morning! I'm making eggs." His eyes turn serious. "I hope scrambled is okay. I know from Runaway Bride that how you take your eggs is a big deal but this is the only way I know how to cook eggs." He points to the side. "Can you pop some bread in the toaster?"

My smile freezes in place as I process. First, a reference to a classic rom-com movie. Second, admitting he has limitations. Third, asking me to help like I belong here.

It would be a cold day in hell before a power suit admitted to not knowing something. Even the ones who are willing to take direction in bed. Not everyone can be a stallion with you right off the bat.

Well, I guess Jimmy has been.

I slide two pieces of bread into the slots and turn around to face him with my hands behind me on the counter. He turns and smiles at me and I am glad to be holding on to something because it is another megawatt smile. Charm oozes out of him and I feel my defenses turn slack.

"Alright, eggs are almost ready." He says while he claps his hands together and walks over to a cabinet for plates. As he brings them over to the stove there's a knock on his door.

We both look questioningly at each other.

"Are you expecting someone?" I ask.

"No. Are you?"

I chuckle. "No, Liz knows I'm here but I doubt she'd come and fetch me. She's got a photoshoot today."

Jimmy crosses over to the door and opens it. His is sister Angie starts talking the instant the door is opened.

"Okay, so don't kill me, but, oh you should put on a shirt, or don't but, okay, yeah, umm, you know how—" she stops when she sees me.

"Oh whoops! Sorry, okay, didn't know you were umm, entertaining."

I give her a little wave "Hi Angie."

"Angie, what are you doing here?" Jimmy asks, crossing his arms and widening his stance.

"Right." She gives her chin a little nod and squares her shoulders. "Remember how you met with that producer at the Home Builders Convention last week and she said 'see you soon' and you didn't really know what she was talking about?"

Jimmy unhooks one hand and rolls his palm for her to continue.

"Well, she's here. Like, downstairs. They're going to start shooting some footage for the pilot today."

"Angie! What the fuck?"

"I know, I know, sorry! I didn't think she would like make it happen so quickly. And then the power went out and I missed her email saying that she was coming today."

"I'll just, yeah." I say as I grab my shorts and walk to the bedroom.

"Nora, wait." Jimmy says as he does his little jog step after me. It was the same one he did across the street yesterday. His shoulders flex up to his ears with the first few steps.

"Nora. Don't go," his shoulders relax and he turns to point at the kitchen. "You haven't had breakfast."

"No, it's fine. Don't worry about it." I look down at his sleep rumpled button down. "Can I umm, borrow this?"

"Of course, keep it."

"Oh no, that's not necessary. I'll get it back to you in a few days. I assume Lakeville doesn't have same day dry cleaning."

"No we don't but don't worry about it. I don't have a clue what Angie has up her sleeve so I don't know when I'll be free again. Or," he pauses, "come along with us today. Yeah, that could be fun."

"Jimmy," I put my hands on his biceps, yum. Focus, Nora. "Don't worry about it. I'm going to head back to Liz and Kyle's. Last night, well the last two nights, have been super fun but I'm not from here and I don't do small town boyfriends."

He bristles, and I didn't really mean to insult him but everything I said was the truth. The affection I've developed for him in the last day and a half is trouble with a capital T.

He reaches up and runs his knuckles along my cheek like he did last night. I am one degree away from melting. As Jimmy's head lowers to mine my eyes flutter closed and his warmth envelopes me. He presses a featherweight kiss to my cheek and then whispers, "Nora, there's nothing small…town about me."

7

Funny Meeting You Here

JIMMY

I watch as the blue in her eyes turns stormy. She holds my gaze for a breath before blinking deliberately and stepping back. Without a word Nora slips into her shorts and fastens them. The she ties the front of my shirt into a little knot. When she looks up at me again the heat in her eyes is gone.

Iceberg straight ahead.

I reach my hand out to catch her at the waist but she drops her shoulder and moves past me. She toes her shoes on and walks to the door.

"Guys, I'm so sorry." Angie offers. "I mean you're my brother so gross but Nora, sisters before misters and all that. It won't happen again."

"Don't worry about it." Nora says brightly as she turns the door knob to leave. "Have fun today. I'll see you around."

And with that she walks through the door and pulls it closed behind her. As soon as the door shuts I turn towards Angie who is grimacing.

"Jimmy, don't look at me like that! I said I'm sorry. And actually, if you would be the one to man the business email account we probably wouldn't be in this situation."

"Don't turn this on me." I pause, pinch the top of my nose, and take a deep breath. "Now, start from the top. What's going on?"

"Marla Johnson, the producer from the Homecraft Network, is downstairs and she wants to talk to us."

"Just talk?"

"Well, no, she wants to talk and then shoot some preliminary footage as like a test sort of thing. To see if we can hack it as TV stars."

I roll my eyes. When Angie got a message from the Homecraft Network a few months ago about a show I told her to ignore it. She said she was just going to follow up to be polite but then last week this Marla lady cornered me at the convention and introduced herself.

She kept saying things like 'we're so excited' and 'we'll get going soon'. I forgot to talk to Angie about it because in the last 48 hours Nora rocked my world off it's axis.

Last night was no exception. I feel a phantom of Nora on my fingers as I turn towards my room to get dressed. I'm no more than two steps away when there is a knock at the front door. I look at Angie who springs into action to answer it.

"Hi Marla! Oh, my." Angie gasps as a camera man strolls in, obviously recording.

"Hey! What are you doing?" I demand.

"Oh, we just wanted to get some footage of the apartment. This is the first space you redid right?" Marla answers.

"Yeah, but I'm not ready for you to film it." As I say that the camera man pans around and gets a few seconds of me standing there shirtless before I turn my back and march through my bedroom door.

"Not a morning person huh?" I hear Marla ask Angie as I close the door.

I actually am a morning person. But I'm not a person who likes when the best morning he's had in a while gets interrupted by his younger sister and a camera crew.

I quickly get dressed and run a little styling cream through my hair, regrettably undoing the way Nora's fingers had played with it last night.

I heard her when she said she didn't do relationships. And it's not like I've been sitting around here trying to find a girlfriend either. But I know in my bones we're not done with each other yet. There is no denying the connection we already have. I can't shake the feeling that she was trying to convince herself she didn't do boyfriends more than she was trying to convince me.

I need to get my head in the game and figure out what Angie has gotten us into. But before I do, I press both hands into the counter and hang my head as I take one more moment to let the feeling of Nora wash over me.

Stepping back into the main room again I see that Angie has served up the breakfast I never got to eat. I step over and dig in because if I know anything, it's that getting hangry today is not in anyone's best interest.

"We could definitely do that." Angie says to Marla.

"Do what?"

"Marla wants us to take her and Dax," she gestures to the camera man, "around on a tour of Lakeville. Talk about some of the properties we've already finished. I figured that was a good place to start."

"Alright, seems reasonable. Will this footage be used in the show?" I ask Marla.

"Probably not, but it'll give us a sense for how comfortable you are on camera and if it goes well we can reshoot it later for the pilot." She says as she types something on her phone.

"Okay, let's get this over with." I say.

"That's the spirit." Angie says flatly as she gives me a look that says "screw this up and I'll kill you."

Moments later, Angie is in the front seat of my truck giving Marla and Dax the story on every storefront we pass.

"That is T.H.E. Library. I actually helped with some of the concepts for their recent remodel."

"When was the library project completed?" Marla asks as she types something in her phone.

"No, T.H.E. Library. It's named after Tessa Harper Edwards who was the woman to spearheaded the world-record campaign back in the 1950s." Angie clarifies.

"I'm sorry, what?" Marla asks looking up from her phone.

"Tessa Harper Edwards helped to organize the longest continuous domino chain reaction with hardcover books back in 1952. Lakeville still holds the record. Anyway, story goes that everyone just dropped their books off at the library afterwards and she helped get it all organized. When the certificate was awarded they surprised Tessa by renaming the library after her. So it's T.H.E. Library of Lakeville."

I glance up and watch Marla and Dax's faces take in the quirks of our hometown. Dax simply smiles to himself. Marla's eyes grow wide for a second before she mouths "wow" to herself and goes back to her phone.

I make the turn out of downtown onto Cherry Street and

head towards the lake. The other direction leads to the Inn and the camp grounds. I doubt Marla cares about seeing that today. Most of the homes in Lakeville are here on the east side of the lake and the views are beautiful, especially on a sunny morning like today.

The first place I ever redid was the apartment over the store. After my high school girlfriend, Bethany, left town, going back to the house we rented together was painful. Kyle was renting the apartment above the store at the time but he and Liz had just bought a house which meant he was moving out. Pops was the one who suggested I convert the old storage area and make the whole floor an apartment. He helped me with the initial plans but I did all the work.

I focused all my energy on the project, finishing it in four months. The day I moved my stuff in, Angie moved back from college. I helped her unpack at home and we went out to dinner with Dad. The next day, Angie helped me out at the hardware store while she applied for interior design jobs.

That afternoon, Sandy Wright stuck her head into the office and asked me to see the apartment. I took her up and she gushed over the space and what a good job I did.

Then she started to tell me about updates she and Mitchell wanted to make to their mid-century modern home. I pulled Angie into the conversation and together we came up with a plan. Sandy and Mitch didn't need much convincing so we got to work. Word travels fast in a small town and soon we had three more requests.

Angie dove head first into getting this business set up for us. She created the website and the social media accounts. She posts often, sharing tips and inspiration and I hardly know what else because I just focus on the work.

"The first house we did together is just up ahead." Angie shares.

"Do you think they'd let us look inside?" Marla asks.

"Let's just drive past today, we can ask everyone about being on camera later." I say, not wanting to interrupt Mitchell's Sunday morning.

When we turn onto their street my shoulders stiffen. Angie notices the truck just after I do and our gazes lock. Her's seems to say 'it'll be fine, just keep driving' and mine says 'if he gives me shit I'm not responsible for what I say back'.

Because that's the truth. If Dad tries to stop and talk to me, I'm going to shut down. What little the camera crew was hoping to get out of me will be gone.

He has a way of zapping all the energy from the room.

"That's the first home over there." I say while pointing out the window and barely slowing down.

"Oh! It looks like they're home and outside, let's stop." Marla says.

Angie and I exchange another look and I pull to a stop on the opposite side of the street.

"Well, well, well, what do we have here?" Dad's voice carries from the side yard towards us. It looks like he's helping to clear some branches that fell during the storm.

"Hey Dad." Angie says as she walks over to him and gives him a kiss on the cheek. "What are you up to?"

"Well Mitchell told me yesterday morning that these branches had fallen. After I cleaned up our own damn yard by myself, I came by and saw that they were still layin' here. So I stopped and got to work. Someone has to keep this town clean."

He's making a point to say he's the one to keep the town clean. Not me. I try not to take it personally. He knows damn well that I was the one who kept the family store running and did handyman work for everyone around town after Mom got sick. After she died I finished high school, then I got Angie through high school and off to college too.

A tightness closes in on my chest just thinking about that time. How our family went from a pillar of this town to the one everyone pities. How Dad could barely manage to get out of bed after she died. How I had to step up and be the man of the house while I was still figuring out how to drive.

It's been 15 years.

Angie knows the dynamic between Dad and me is bad so she steps in to talk to him before I get the chance to reply with some snarky comment. Marla and Dax are recording behind my shoulder. The last thing I want is for this to become a family drama so I turn to them and just start talking about the project.

"Mitchell and Sandy own Scoops & Sips Café, the coffee shop in town, and they saw all the work I was doing on the apartment above the store. Mitch stopped by one day while I was painting and was impressed with how I reconfigured the old storage space."

As I retell the story my chest fills with pride because Mitchell was one of the men who stepped up as a father figure when Dad couldn't. Pops was there too but Mitchell would bring me a coffee at the store and talk with me about weather, baseball, town events. He made it feel normal to be 18 years old and at the helm of a third generation family business.

"Then Sandy stopped by and she started talking about making updates to their place. Angie had just gotten home from school and was working in the store so I told her about it. She immediately started working on a design plan and a color scheme and she came with me to see their house.

"When we walked in I could see the way the plan could unfold. How we could not just update the space but transform it for them. They're both great people and have strong community connections. I couldn't wait to give them a space they deserve."

Marla had stopped what she was doing on her phone during my speech and when I finish she says "and cut" and a huge smile spreads across her face. Dax sets the camera down and holds out a hand for me to shake.

"That was awesome man. I wish we could have been here to film this house! This show is going to be so 'feel good'. I can't wait."

The front screen door opens with a whine and closes with a slap. I turn around and see Sandy walking towards us.

"Good morning." She says in a friendly but suspicious way. "I'm Sandy, owner of this here home, can I help you?"

Marla steps forward and extends a hand to shake.

"Marla Johnson, producer for the Homecraft Network. This is Dax Lowry, one of our talented camera men."

Dax holds out his had and smiles.

"Oh! I had no idea!" She pats at her hair and straightens her clothes. "I thought you might be here with the news or something. I hadn't heard any scuttlebutt but with the power outage we've all been a little behind. I think the biggest news in town is the arrival of that firecracker redhead who is staying with Lizzy for the week."

One of Marla's eyebrow raises and she eyes me. Hopefully not putting together that the firecracker redhead is the one who left my apartment in my shirt just fifteen minutes ago.

"Marla was asking Angie and me to show her some of the properties we've worked on. Naturally I started here first." I say to Sandy to move the conversation along.

"And a fine job they did too! C'mon in, I used the power outage yesterday for old fashioned cleaning time, elbow grease comes at a high premium these days. Then this morning I was able to run the vacuum over everything. It's the spiffiest it'll be until Mitchell comes back inside from the yard."

I gesture for Sandy to lead the way as Dax lifts the camera in front of him again. Marla gives me the go ahead arm and I remember that she's not supposed to be on camera at all so I follow Sandy up the walkway.

"Mitchell and I moved in, gosh, back in the 80s, 1983 I suppose. Fresh newlyweds and even though the home was 25 years old, we could barely afford it. We pinched pennies and made it work," she chuckles to herself. "I remember Mitchy telling me to reuse coffee beans for a second day and I laughed in his face! It was just a few years later that we opened Scoops & Sips. That was after the diner closed of course.

"We painted and did small projects over the years, but nothing major, We just kept putting it off. Then Jimmy did such a fine job on his own apartment after all that sad business with Bethany and that on the heels of his Ma, we knew he'd be the one to help us update our home. Then Angie came back from school with all her fancy software and I was sold. We didn't even talk to another contractor or designer, just went with these two Lewis kids because we trusted em.”

I see Dax pivot in my direction so I just smile and shrug. I'm not going to address firecracker redheads, Bethany, or Mom, so it's time to start talking about the space.

“This all used to be open.” I say as I point towards the glass doors to the office. “Sandy wanted a spot for coffee shop business to live at home. She also wanted a spot to host the Tome Raider monthly book club meeting so we created this seating area off the kitchen.” I walk backwards bringing Dax with me around the wall.

Angie designed a reading nook with a small curved sofa and a chaise lounge. The dining chairs she picked out are plush and comfortable so the Tome Raiders could pull them over and gather up in the winter to discuss their latest selection. Or, honestly, they probably discuss town gossip more than the book.

“The majority of our budget was spent on an updated kitchen. The original layout was a large square room but we shifted things to create an L-shape and added an island. Then this wall became a pantry.”

“Yes, it has made cooking and hosting so much easier! Mitchy and I never got to have our own kids but when our families come for Thanksgiving the kitchen is full of kids trying to grab at desserts.” She smiles fondly at the memory. “We used to be stepping on them and tripping over toys in the old kitchen, now they know to stick to the pantry side or risk losing dessert privileges all together.” She says gravely.

“You wouldn't.” I chuckle.

“Jimmy, be glad you haven't tried to sneak a bite of my sister Sheila's cranberry crumble blondies before dinner.”

Sandy lowers her voice, "She makes you live to regret it." And then she comically shudders.

I laugh and see Marla smile. Maybe this is going well. I look past Dax and see Angie standing in the front yard. Dad isn't with her but she's waving to someone.

Marla says "and cut" again before pulling out her phone and typing away. She starts walking out the front door, Dax follows. I turn and give Sandy a quick hug.

"Thanks for letting them in and giving us a tour. I didn't know they were coming today otherwise I would have given you a heads up."

"Don't worry about it Jimmy, I'm glad to see you gettin' some attention for these skills of yours." She says as she starts to walk towards the front door.

I mutter thanks again and then step outside. The sun is bright and I can't quite make out who Angie is talking to until I take another step off the porch and realize it's Nora.

Dax has lifted his camera up in front of him to film them and the hairs on the back of my neck stand on end.

Nora sees me. She offers a quick little wave and a smile. Behind me the door opens again and Sandy comes out to the front step next to me.

"Oh! It's that friend of Liz's." She says to no-one in particular but loud enough for everyone to hear. "Hello deary! I'm Sandy, I'm so glad to meet you. How long are you staying in Lakeville?"

"Hello Sandy," Nora says, "I plan to be here just through this week." She flicks her gaze up to me and a heat builds in my stomach.

"Well then you'll be here for Float Fest! What fun!" Sandy

claps her hands together. "And I just love when we have you city girls come up to visit us. This fashion sense of yours is adorable! Where did you get such a perfectly cut boyfriend style shirt? I'll have to tell Gina to order some for the boutique."

"Oh, uhh," Nora says and she pulls on the tie she made in the front of the shirt. She doesn't look at me but Angie does and that's all it takes for Sandy to put two and two together.

"It's Jimmy's?!" She hollers.

"Nora had to borrow a shirt after the bonfire last night." I say to Sandy while hoping, praying, that's enough information for us to go with right now.

"She had it on when we got to his place this morning." Marla whispers to Sandy.

"My oh my." Sandy says as she looks between us. "Only staying the week huh darlin'? We'll see about that."

8

News Travels Fast Around Here

Nora

"Okay, time to go!" Angie says.

I look at Jimmy wondering what is going on and what he wants me to do. He glances to his right and that's when I see a man who looks exactly like Jimmy, just a generation older, leaning against the hood of a truck, shaking his head.

"Angie, you take Marla and Dax back to the store in Dad's truck." Jimmy calls out as he starts walking in my direction. Then he turns his gaze on me. "You, come with me."

Before I can say that I'm fine to walk back to Liz's by myself Jimmy grabs my hand and starts marching me back towards his truck. He walks me all the way around to the passenger side where he opens the door for me and holds my hand as I climb up into the cab. He doesn't close the door right away but instead leans his head down close to mine, his hands resting on the top of the door.

"What are you doing out here?"

"I'm walking home." I say brightly. "Liz drew me a map for how to get to her place." I flash him the neon pink sticky note with a crude map drawn on it.

"I'll take you."

He closes the door and rounds the front of the truck. I see his sister get behind the wheel of his dad's truck and she shoots me a sympathetic look. I definitely did not expect to run into them when I was walking back nor did I expect that Sandy lady to air all the dirty laundry.

"Sorry about that." He says as he closes his door and starts the truck.

"Sorry about what?"

"Sandy, my dad, the camera. This morning. I dunno, everything." He says with a shrug.

"Oh, it's fine. It'll make a good story one day. I'm sure it's already the most popular post on the Lakeville gossip pages."

He laughs. "Yeah, Sandy is definitely going tell everyone that the firecracker redhead was seen walking around in Jimmy Lewis's only dress shirt."

"This is your only dress shirt?" I ask while holding it out in front of me by the buttons. What kind of guy only has one dress shirt? The men I hook up with in the city only have dress shirts.

"Ha yeah, keep it around for weddings and funerals. And apparently for girls who wear shirts I have to rip off."

I flush reliving the moment he tore off my top last night. I'm sure when my bodice ripped, revealed my heaving breasts, somewhere a romance writer got her wings.

We pull up to a stop sign and Jimmy turns in his seat. I turn to look at him too.

"I'd like to take you out for dinner Nora."

"No." My stern response startles both of us. He looks like I just kicked his puppy. "Sorry, it isn't personal. I don't do relationships."

"So you've said." He mutters as he turns back towards the road and drives through the intersection. The atmosphere inside his truck has changed.

It's the truth. Saying no isn't personal to Jimmy. He has surprised me at every turn. When Sandy asked me how long I was staying, saying just a week felt wrong. It felt like a week wouldn't be enough.

But I don't belong here. My life is in the city. Or what's left of my life. Tomorrow is Monday and I can't hide from my problems anymore. I need to make a plan and get back on track.

My shoulders slump forward and I pivot towards the window. I don't know how to explain to Jimmy that I am not the girl for him. I'm not the girl for anyone. That I do things on my own. We've hooked up twice and, on top of that, I spent the night at his place. I feel like I'm in a midlife crisis.

Well, quarter life crisis, fingers crossed.

He pulls up in front of Liz's house and puts the truck in park. I don't know what to say to him or how to explain it.

So I don't.

I reach for the handle and start to mutter another sorry under my breath when his hand reaches out and grabs hold of my arm. I look to his hand first, then up to his face.

"Nora, I haven't felt this strongly about a gir—" he starts.

"Nope. Jimmy, I'm gonna stop you right there." He's still holding my arm and his touch is soothing. Hot. Distracting. I shake the feelings out of my head and continue. "I didn't come up here to become the main character in a city-girl-falls-for-hometown-hero story. I came up here because my life fell apart on Friday and I had no where else to go. Maybe I'm admitting too much to you but I've already broken all my rules when it comes to men in the last few days so here we are. Please don't fall in love with me. I'm not worth it, and I'm not staying."

With that I grab the door handle, pop the door, and hop down before he can say anything else. I reach for the spot where his hand was on my arm, cover it with my palm, and squeeze myself in a hug.

His vulnerability and openness throws me off balance. I can handle the guys who are in it for the hook up and ready to go after that. I cannot handle guys having feelings.

I cannot handle having my own feelings.

And it's time for me to bury these feelings I seem to have developed. After all, I am my mother's daughter and a long term relationship is not in the cards. I won't end up pregnant in a small town only for the guy to leave for bigger things. The only person I can count on is myself.

Once inside Liz's house I head straight for the guest room. I yank off Jimmy's shirt and toss it on the floor. Instantly I am flooded with guilt and pick it back up. I shake it straight and start to fold it. His scent wafts in my direction and I bring the shirt to my nose and inhale.

The shirt smells like him even though he claims he never wears it. The fresh, woodsy, salty scent triggers a flood of warmth throughout my body. My knees tremble for a moment.

No. I toss the intoxicating garment onto the bed like it burned me. I quickly wrap my breasts in my arms and spin out of the room to head for the shower.

9

Drop this? No way in hell my friend.

Nora

There is nothing hot water and high quality products can't fix. Even lingering thoughts about a certain small town contractor.

Although, full disclosure, I did think about him while I maneuvered the shower head where I needed it most.

I followed that self care with some solid towel time. A full ten minutes of scrolling videos on my phone while sitting on the end of the bed in my towel. Eventually I changed into my matching linen short and tank set before I returned to the bathroom. I ran through my skincare routine, returning each bottle to it's rightful place in the line up, and then I applied some minimal makeup. Finished up with working my sea salt volume spray in my hair and voila! Nora is back in action.

I pick up the the neon sticky note map Liz drew for me and decide to walk into town. I pack up my purse, slip in to my strappy block heel sandals, and head out.

While I'm walking I realize it's Sunday afternoon and that's normally when I FaceTime with my mom. She might not understand what I do for a living, and she will definitely question why I'm not in the city, but I need to check in.

My face appears on the screen as the call connects and I brush my hair forward over my shoulders before trying to fluff it up on top.

"Hi Nora," Mom's face appears on the screen. She looks tired. More tired than usual. Her eyeliner has smudged enough to tell me she didn't wash it off last night.

"Hey Mom. How are you?"

"Eh, fine. Fucking Brandon didn't show up for our date last night so I had Eddy drive me over to his place. That skank Melody's car was in his driveway. Eddy helped me egg Brandon's truck and then we went out drinkin."

"Wow, what a night." I shouldn't have been worried about her asking me questions. She's barely registered that I'm walking outside and not sitting in my apartment.

"Yeah, then Brandon started callin' me this morning all like 'I'm sorry' but I ain't got time for that shit. He and I was supposed to run a job for Terrence this week but I had a feeling he was strayin' so I told Terrance I was gonna do it with Eddy. Now Brandon, the shithead, will be out a paycheck. Serves him fuckin right."

"What's the job Mom?"

"If I tell you, I'll have to kill you." She cackles before her laugh turns into a hack of a cough, telling me that she's started smoking again.

"Fair enough. Well I'm just walking to meet a friend and thought I'd check in."

"You're walking? Are the cabbies on strike?"

"No, I'm, umm, actually upstate visiting my friend Liz."

"The photographer one?"

"Yeah."

"How long you gonna be up there? Just the weekend?"

"Might stay this week. Work isn't busy right now." For me at least.

"Hmm, well, enjoy yourself I guess. I gotta go, Eddy is here."

"Okay, bye Mom."

"Bye."

I hang up and am glad to have gotten through that conversation without having to tell her many details. She at least knows where I am. Sort of. It doesn't matter anyhow, she's got enough going on in her own world right now.

I check my sticky note and slow down my pace a bit. I take in my surroundings as I approach the town.

The lake is off to my left and the sun is glistening on the water as it ripples in the light breeze. It's not painfully humid today but it still warm. A few families are playing together in the park and several people are walking dogs along the lake.

I turn back towards town and just ahead is a boutique with several cute outfits in the front window. I stop to peek in through the front of the shop and stand up suddenly when I realize someone in the store is waving at me.

Angie steps out of the boutique with the dress she's trying on gaping open in the front.

"Nora! Get in here. I need help." She reaches for my hand and drags me inside as she continues.

"I have a sense for design and putting things together if we're talking paint colors and upholstery swatches but when it comes to clothes, I'm totally lost. And people in Lakeville don't really get dressed up so I don't get much inspiration. But I'm seeing a guy tomorrow night and I need to impress him."

"Well I think if you showed up like that he'd be all yours." I nod towards her unbuttoned dress.

"Oh, whoops." She mumbles as she starts to button it up. Once it's done she starts to spin halfway in each direction looking at herself in the mirror.

"It's cute right?"

"Very." I tell her, because it is, but a floral skater style dress is what Liz would wear on a date.

"But you hate it."

"No! I don't hate it. It is really cute. It just isn't my style."

"Well it is my style I guess but that hasn't really worked for me in the dating department so maybe I need to try something different."

"The most important thing is to be comfortable." I turn around and pull a black tank top off the rack and hold it up in front of me. "For me, my clothes are my armor. When I get dressed to go out at night I want something that will force me to sit up straight and display my boobs."

"And that works?"

"Every time."

"Okay then. Dress me. Tell me what to wear. I can't get this guy to see me as a woman, he just sees a little girl."

"Oh yeah, an outfit from my wardrobe definitely says woman." I start to walk along the racks of clothing. I pick up a pair of white shorts, a mini skirt, and a slip dress.

I reach through the curtain of the dressing room to hand the items to Angie but she grabs my wrist and pulls me in with her.

"Ohmigod Nora, he texted. Like out of the blue texted. That's a good sign right?"

"Totally." Although honestly, I have no clue, I don't text guys. Considering all the hookups I've partaken in I have very few numbers in my phone.

"What should I text him back?"

"I have no idea, what did he say?"

Angie clears her throat. "Better bring it to trivia tomorrow exclamation point."

"That's it?"

"No good?" She asks as her arms slap down at her sides. "Ugh, I thought it was good. He used an exclamation point."

"No! I'm sure it's great. I just, ugh, don't really text with guys."

"What do you mean you don't text with guys?"

"I pick them up at bars, bring them home, and then kick them out before morning."

"Why? Don't you want to get to know them?"

I laugh. "No, not really. I usually make my choice based on looks alone. It's almost better not knowing if there is more under the surface. Although, most of the guys are like financial district bros, they're heartless anyways."

"That's so sad." She pauses. Maybe it's sad to her but, I'm happy enough with my system.

"It works." I say and then I hand her the slip dress. "Put this on and then wear the mini skirt over it."

"Ooo cute! Okay!" Angie says and I step out of the room to let her change. "I'm just going to write back a cute little 'you too' so he knows I read the text."

"You do that."

"So you're done with Jimmy?"

"What?"

"Well, you said you don't really get to know the guys you hook up with and I don't know what happened last night but I haven't seen Jimmy drag a girl out of a party ever. He seemed pretty intent on…well he's my brother so I'm not going to say it but you get the idea."

I laugh, "Yeah, I do. I get it. And I dunno. He and I have actually hooked up twice and I spent the night at his place so I've already broken the rules with him."

"Twice! When was the other time?"

"Friday night, he picked me up on the side of the road. I actually told him to have sex with me before he murdered me because I was a good lay."

"Ha! That's a good line. I bet it rattled him. But he's not a murder. He's more like a puppy."

"I've figured that out." I pause as she steps out of the dressing room. "Now, that outfit is hot."

"It is, isn't it?" Angie confirms with a wide smile.

"Yes. And with a little smoky eye makeup and soft curls he won't be able to keep his hands off you."

"That's the goal."

"So, your brother started saying something earlier and didn't get to finish because I cut him off. He said he hasn't felt this way about a girl since…"

"Bethany."

"Maybe? Who was she?"

"His ex. They started dating in high school, right when Mom got sick. I left for college and Jimmy stayed but I always got the sense he was kind of waiting for me to come back before he left to do something else. But when I graduated and came back he wanted to stay in Lakeville."

Angie walks back in to the dressing room.

"Now try the black tank top and white shorts. I'll go find you a belt." I say, because hearing more of Jimmy's story isn't going to help me be done with him.

"Alright, so anyways," she raises her voice so it carries through the store. "Jimmy got the store and within a few months Bethany left. She said she couldn't stay in this small town forever and she was done waiting for him."

"Oh man, that's rough." And exactly what I'm going to do to him. I'm going back to the city. That's where my whole life is. Dead cat in the freezer and all.

"He's okay now but it was bad at first. Dad was really low then too. I had one semester left at school so I wasn't around to help either of them. Luckily Pops let Jimmy remodel the apartment. He poured himself into that project and it distracted him long enough to kind of move on."

"When was this?"

"Umm, like two years ago." Angie says as she steps out of the dressing room with the black and white outfit on.

"This is a good look too but the dress and skirt are super hot."

"Well hopefully he'll be asking me out again so I'll get both."

"I like your thinking." I say as I hand her a skinny black belt. As she threads it through the loops of the white shorts, she looks over her shoulder at the shop keeper.

"Don't worry, she has her ear buds in and hasn't heard me telling you Jimmy's sad love story. Gina is a terrible gossip so everyone would know you were asking about Jimmy and that I told you everything by the time we left the store."

"You sure the ear buds aren't decoys?"

"What do you mean?"

"Like she just has them in but nothing is playing."

"Oh shit, I never thought of that." She pauses and then she snaps her fingers while leering at the woman.

No reaction.

Either this gal is looking for her Oscar or she really can't hear us.

"I think we're good." I say as Angie starts doing a weird yelp sort of sound.

"Okay because I would feel really rotten if Jimmy found out I told you all that."

"I understand. Secret's safe with me."

"I know. I trust you. You're good people Nora, I can tell."

Thankfully I don't have to respond to that because she's walking back into the dressing room to change. When she brings her items up to the counter I'm looking through the jewelry display on a little table near the front. Gina finishes ringing her up and then as the two of us reach the door she calls after us.

"And, I guess I should warn you, I already texted the Tome Raider group chat that you were sniffing around about Jimmy."

Angie and I exchange a look of panic before she bursts out in laughter. I surprise myself when I follow suit and the two of us walk out onto the sidewalk in a fit of giggles.

"What's so funny?" Liz asks from across the street. She looks both ways before crossing over to us.

"Gina got our goose. Bad." Angie says with big eyes.

"Oh no, you shared secrets in front of her? You know better Angie! The Tome Raiders will be all over this. What was the secret?"

"That Nora likes Jimmy." Angie says while inspecting her manicure.

"No. That is not what the secret was. I just asked about his past." I clarify looking at Liz.

Liz knows better than anyone that I don't date. I hook up and don't get emotionally involved.

"Hmm, maybe she only asked about him but the question is," Liz turns to Angie holding her chin, "why did she ask about him?"

Angie picks up the thread and pulls. "That, my friend, is an excellent question. Could it be because she's, interested?"

"Shut up you two. Liz, you know better, and Angie we don't know each other but let me tell you I don't get interested in guys. Period."

"It sounds like you're trying to convince yourself pretty hard my friend." Liz prods.

"No it doesn't." I protest.

"It does."

"It doesn't."

"I think it does."

"I say it doesn't."

"I'm confused." Angie admits which ends the volley between Liz and me.

"Let me set the record straight," I say to them both. "Yes, I've hooked up with him twice and—"

"Twice?!" Liz shouts.

"Shhhh! Keep your voice down." I scold. "And yes, twice.

First was on Friday night when he picked me up after my car ran out of gas. Then again last night."

"When's the last time you've tapped the same ass twice?"

"Ohmigod can you not say it like that?"

"Fine," Liz concedes. "When was the last time you saw the same man more than once."

"Internship summer, with Jeff."

"Oh.My.God." Liz mouths but doesn't make a sound.

"When was that?"Angie asks, engrossed.

"Four years ago." Liz answers.

"Holy crap." Angie whispers.

"Alright. Enough. It is not a big deal." I try to wrap up this conversation.

"And you stayed at his place last night? Sandy said you were wearing his shirt this morning when she saw you." Liz says as she crosses her arms over her middle.

"Geez news travels fast around here. Yes, okay, fine. I admit I stayed at his place last night. And then I had to wear his shirt home because mine, got, umm, ripped."

"He freaking ripped your bodice." Liz says like it's this great injustice to her.

"He's my brother so it's gross but if it were anyone else that'd be so hot."

"It was." I admit.

"And then this afternoon, several hours later, you're pestering his sister for information about his past?" Liz says like she's a prosecutor about to land her final argument.

Well, guilty as charged.

"Not exactly but sure, since I can tell you're not going to drop this."

"Drop this? No way in hell my friend. We talk every week and I can't keep track of all the different bros you've told me about. In the last four years there has not been one repeat and the most information I got on the guys was whether he was too tall or not tall enough."

"That is a very important factor." I protest.

"I agree, but that's not my point."

"What's the right height?" Angie asks.

"Five to eight inches taller than you. Up to ten if you wear heels all the time." I answer. Yes, I've done the math.

"Back to my point," Liz interjects. "My point is that in all these years you've never ever been curious about a guy's backstory. Until now."

"Maybe your boring small town is causing me to hemorrhage brain cells or something." Nothing like being called out on your crush to bring out the petulant child in you.

"Not cool." Liz says and she starts walking away.

"Liz, wait, I didn't mean it." I start to walk after her and then turn to Angie. "It was fun shopping, thanks for chatting, and I'll see you around."

I pivot and catch up to Liz.

"It's okay to tell me that you like him." She says quietly.

"I know, but I'd have to admit it to myself first."

10

Slow Day for Memory Lane

JIMMY

A ring of the bell alerts me to the front door of the store opening. I call "Hi, be there in a minute," from the office where I'm reviewing the slips we collected over the weekend when the power was out.

"Don't bother, I know where things are."

Dad.

I wonder what brings him in today. And what state he's in. Angie said yesterday that he seemed okay when she was talking to him. And for Jim, okay is about as good as it gets.

I should give him more credit. My mom was the love of his life. The way my mom used to talk about their younger days made me believe in true love. She said it was a real life country song. A romance for the ages.

Because of her I believed in true, life-long love. I still do. Bethany took that belief away from me for a while. Although, it didn't take long for me to realize that I wasn't heartbroken over her. We didn't share true, can't live without you, *won't* live without you, love. We were companions at best. Roommates at worst.

After my head cleared, and the remodeling business with Angie started growing, I decided I could be patient. That I didn't have to get married young like my parents. I focused on myself, my family, my friends. And if the right girl came along I'd know it.

Immediately my mind flashes with the image of Nora this morning in my shirt. I was ready to tell Marla and Dax to fuck off. If I hadn't been ambushed, and if she hadn't been so eager to leave, I would have.

Told them to fuck off that is.

The sound of items being set on the counter brings me back to the present. Steeling myself for an early morning conversation with Dad I roll my shoulders back and walk towards the front of the store. He's gathered a few plumbing fittings which tells me the half bath is acting up again.

"What's the project Dad?" I ask in as casual a voice as I can. We don't do small talk, we yell or he dishes out comments that lay blame on me for everything.

"Half bath." He mutters.

And that's all I'm going to get out of him. I put the pack of plumbers putty and new locknut in a small brown bag for him. He reaches for his wallet but I hold out my hand to stop him.

"C'mon Dad, you don't have to pay for these."

"I'm not gonna take any special treatment."

"Fine." I ring him up and he hands over cash. I hand him the change and he looks up at me. Our eyes connect and there is something different in them. His eyes seem brighter.

"So Angie told me about your little show. What is it, you aren't gettin' enough attention around town so you had to go national?"

Now, if anyone else said that I'd laugh and take it as a joke. But it's coming from Dad and I'm offended.

"Exactly. Hoping it goes global, you know with the internet and all." I reply full of sarcasm.

"Don't get smart with me. I was just tryin' to have a conversation." He turns towards the door, "I'll be back when the goddamned washers need to be replaced too." He says as he steps out the door.

I stand at the counter, mouth fixed in a tight line, as I watch him round the front of his truck and get in.

Was he serious? He really did just want to talk? He and I haven't had just a talk in a long time. Years.

Mom had been sick for a few years and when the cancer spread there was no stopping it. She died when I was 16, Angie was 9. She was strong and patient and incredibly caring until her very last breath.

The town banded around us. Pops did more at the store again while Dad grieved. Dad didn't want us to comfort him nor could he comfort us. I started to do more at the store after school and on the weekends.

The first month was awful, Dad never left their bedroom. Pops and Gran all but moved in with us. Neighbors brought over food. Bethany helped Angie with girl stuff when I didn't know where to begin.

The second month was worse. Dad was out of bed but he was drinking. Morning and night. He tried to go back to work at the store but he'd pass out drunk in the office or knock displays over. Pops had to keep working.

Two years later, I graduated high school and stayed in town. Angie needed someone at home. Pops needed someone at the store. And Gran's memory wasn't what it had been. She forgot to pick up Angie a few times after soccer practice and would mix up names and faces.

That summer was the worst of it. Angie was about to start middle school and for some reason the girls in her class ignored her all summer long. Gran became a different person. Pops and I were spread thin keeping the store going, caring for Gran and Angie, and keeping Dad out of trouble.

Well as much as we could.

He got pulled over for a DUI that summer. He spent the night in the drunk tank. He called me from the station to pick him up but I was with Bethany. She had been complaining that I wasn't spending time with her.

So I chose a girl over my Dad and when I picked him up in the morning, after dropping Bethany off at her house, he laid into me about loyalty and family first and that some skirt is never the priority.

It stung. Logically I knew he was lashing out because he was in pain. He was angry at the world for taking away the love of his life. But I hated him for giving in to his pain. I resented him for leaving me to fend for myself, and everyone else.

Before school started for Angie that fall I moved us in with Pops and Gran. She didn't need to see Dad the way he was and I hoped that doing so would force him to snap out of it.

It didn't.

His drinking got worse.

That next spring Gran was moved to a home in Avon for Alzheimer's care and a few nights later Pops sat down with me on his porch and handed me a beer.

"Jimmy, I've made some decisions."

"What kind?"

"Well, first of all I need to be closer to Dolly. Your Gran is the best woman on the planet and even though she's not the same as she was, I need to be near her. My…" he chokes up and taps on his heart, "my heart is breaking and I can't just leave her."

I twirl the bottle in my hand. If he leaves, where does that leave me? Angie? Dad?

"This house is paid for, you're gonna keep it and keep Angie here with you. You're also going to take over the store."

"But Dad is suppos—"

"Well grandson, your Dad can't."

We both look out over the street together in silence. Deep down I knew my Dad couldn't take over the store. I had plans to leave Lakeville. I was going to go to engineering school. I was going to move up and out.

But if I go, then there's no one here to take care of everything. Angie would have no one to look out for her. The store would have to be sold or at least operated by someone else and in it's entire history only a Lewis man has been at the helm. First Pops, then Dad, then Pops again, and now me.

A few weeks later Pops moved out, Bethany was finishing her first year of classes at the community college in Rochester and Angie was finishing her first year of middle school.

I was waking up in the morning, dropping Angie off at school, and then spending the day at the store where I had to manage it all. Dad would stop in a few times a week and try to help but I would end up re-doing whatever he had attempted.

This was life for the next five years. Bethany got her

nursing degree and started working at the regional hospital. Angie was making her way through middle, and then high school, and I was running the store.

Gran passed away the spring of Angie's senior year.

Pops moved back into the house after that. Bethany was renting a duplex in town and I would spend most nights there.

When Angie left for college it left Pops in the house all alone. I was worried about him, I didn't want him to deteriorate like Dad. Over the next three years I would have dinner or share a drink with him after I closed the store for the day. I had just gotten back from his place one night when Bethany laid out her ultimatum.

"Now that Angie is almost done with school, are you going to go?"

That had always been the plan. Get Angie through school and then I'd go. But it was January and I hadn't applied anywhere.

"I dunno, I haven't really thought about it." I replied, which was a half truth. I didn't know how to tell her that I had lost my interest in going. I was 29. Friends of ours had gone to school and graduated already. Some had gotten advanced degrees. I'd be the oldest freshman if I went now and on top of all that, I liked working at the store.

I liked helping our neighbors with their projects. I liked solving problems with them. I liked being able to walk down the street and know everyone.

Plus I had a girl and was planning to ask her to marry me. I had the ring on hold with the jeweler. Just needed a couple more paychecks to make it mine.

I was comfortable. Happy.

"Well, I thought Angie was coming back and then you and I would go. We'd start our lives."

"Our lives have started Beth, we have a life here in Lakeville."

"Yeah, but I don't want to be in Lakeville forever."

"What do you mean?"

"I mean we used to talk about getting out. Moving away. Trying new things. Adventures. And now," she sighs, "now I feel like you're happy to just stay here."

"Bethany, I am happy to stay here." I say with some question to my voice. But I hadn't said a truer statement.

"Well, I'm not."

And that weekend she moved away.

I was devastated. I moved back in with Pops and after a few days of wallowing he gave me the idea to remodel the apartment above the store.

I managed to take this trip down memory lane without another customer coming in. That's a Monday for you. I flip the sign on the door to closed and lock up.

Upstairs in my apartment I crack open the windows. The summer breeze is breaking through the humidity today and the fresh air feels good. I can hear kids playing in the park, the crack of a baseball bat ringing through the air. Dogs barking. Boats churning. Occasionally a car drives by. I settle in on my sofa and listen to the soundtrack of summer.

Monday night is trivia night at The Whale. It's most popular during the summer when kids are back from college and they all pile in. My buddies and I used to be regulars. Holden Monaghan, Jack Richmond, Cole Dunham, and I called ourselves the Smarty Pants. When we were a few buckets in, we'd joke about being the Smarty Panty Melters. Though none of us had the balls to make that the official team name.

I laugh thinking about the time we erased the specials board to map out all the states that touch Route 66 and how Rick, who owns The Whale, hollered at us for twenty minutes.

It was worth it though, we won.

I crack open a beer and smile at the memory. It's been a while since I've visited The Whale on a Monday night and it might just be time to revisit the old stomping grounds.

11

Good Heads Think Alike

Nora

"So what do you townies do for fun on Monday nights?"

Liz looks over her shoulder at me from the kitchen. She's chopping vegetables while Kyle gets chicken ready to grill. They figured out long ago that she's the sous chef in the relationship.

"Normally I keep my butt home and FaceTime with you."

"True, but now you have me IRL so let's go do something fun."

"You could come to The Whale." Kyle says as he pushes backwards through the screen door.

"That dive bar in town?" I barely hide the ick from my voice.

"The only bar in town." Liz corrects as she drags the vegetables off the chopping board into a bowl.

"Well if that's the case then why the hell not. I am bored out of my mind. I listened to the second to last episode of my podcast about the girl that was stashed away in a basement for eight years and I wanted to savor the end of the story so I'm saving the last episode for tomorrow. Then I tried to read one of your romances but ugh the characters were so sappy! And predictable. I mean *of course* they're going to fall for each other."

"Hey, don't hate on my HEAs."

"Your what?"

"Happily Ever Afters." Liz says with emphasis as she plops down on the sofa next to me.

"Ohmigod, there are acronyms?"

"Girl, you have no idea. The world of romance novels is a place of acronyms, tropes, and," she leans in and whispers, "some really hot smut."

I laugh. "Smut?! Like you're reading porn?"

"I prefer to call it Cliterature, but yes, it's porn. Kyle has even started to figure out that when I'm halfway through a book he's in for a treat."

"Ew."

"Don't even. I know you. I had to start using headphones for our Monday night chats because I don't need Kyle knowing all the things that are possible for blow jobs."

"Point. I do know what I'm doing in that department. But it's interesting to think that I could freshen up my material. Although, getting to be with a different guy each time keeps it fresh."

Liz levels a look at me over the rim of her wineglass.

"What?" But I think I already know.

"Let's pretend it's Monday Night FaceTime." She turns towards me and crosses her legs on the sofa. She holds up her hand like she has her phone in it. She rolls her shoulders and clears her throat. The final part of her prep is to plaster a fake smile on her face. "Tell me about the guy you hooked up with this weekend."

"You already know."

She lowers her hand and levels me with a disappointed look.

"I do, but I want to watch you squirm because I have never seen you blush about a boy before."

I reach up and feel my heated cheeks and then move my hands to cover my mouth because it is involuntarily breaking into a smile.

"Shit Liz, I don't know what's going on." I'm still covering my mouth while I talk and she reaches up to pull my hands down. "In the last four days everything in my life has changed. First, Sir Harold, then the furlough, then developing a crush on Jimmy. What is happening to me?"

"Furlough? What do you mean? I thought you were just taking a vacation?"

Shit, I forgot. I hadn't told her yet.

"Ahh, not exactly. I was really upset on Friday morning after finding Sir Harold dead and accidentally tanked a prospect meeting. Well fast forward, and Patricia, you remember her?" Liz confirms by shivering. "She called me into her office that afternoon to say I was on furlough until further notice. They're paying me 50% of my salary while I just sit and wait around for their decision."

"Really?"

"Yeah, it's torture. I can't access my email or anything so I'm just sitting around waiting for a call. They said I personally solicited a client, which is not what happened but you know as well as I do that the code of conduct is king and there's no wiggle room."

"I do." Liz says as she looks down at the glass in her lap.

"I was fucking thriving too. I was running all of the east coast schools and Trisha said by the end of the year I'd be promoted to Partner. My book was solid. Clients and prospects respected my opinion." I pause, considering. "Actually, that's probably why Darlene decided to donate to an animal shelter instead of Cornell."

"Wait, back up, that's what happened?"

"I was crying into my frittata about Sir Harold who was wrapped up in a towel in my freezer, well he still is, anyway, we bonded because she had a rescue cat too. I was able to get the convo around to the school but at the end she said she was going to look into giving to a shelter."

"Couldn't she designate her gift to Cornell's vet school?"

"Oh fuck. That would have been perfect. I was so far off my game that morning. I didn't make that connection."

"I'm sure it's not too late. Can you call her?"

"No, I don't have access to her info since it's all in the Fosters system. I'll have to wait and hope they give me my job back."

"They will, they'd be stupid to let you go. You've been such an asset for them these last few years."

"I agree."

"Dinner's ready!" Kyle shouts from the back yard.

Liz and I stand up and grab the salad and plates and head outside for dinner.

"Nora and I are gonna head to The Whale tonight," Liz says as we sit down.

"Hell yeah! It's trivia night. The Nine Inch Males are gonna kick some butt."

"Say ass like everyone else, Kyle." I tease.

"Too much time spent around kids. My mouth is officially PG."

I flash my eyes over to Liz who blushes immediately. I know for a fact that his mouth does plenty of X-rated things. I smile because this feels like the summer they first got together and I would tease her at work about how much she liked him. Kyle being the gentleman he is would get in on the teasing just enough to be endearing, never off putting.

We finish our dinner, Kyle tells us about the campers who arrived today for the last week of summer camp. Liz shares about the families that she's booked for photoshoots for their holiday cards. She also renewed her contract with a lifestyle blog for exclusive stock photos. Then there was something about a pet food campaign.

I don't have much to add to the conversation. I don't have any news about work, or funny cat stories, and while I did talk to my mom yesterday it was same old same old there. I'm enjoying my meal, settling in to the slower pace a little bit, and mentally planning my outfit for the night.

...

Kyle holds open the door for me and Liz and we walk into The Whale. Immediately my nostrils sting with the stench of stale beer while my eyes adjust to the low light. After two steps I notice that my shoes are sticking to the floor.

Liz leads me towards a high top while Kyle goes to the bar for a bucket of beer. The walls of the large room are wood paneled and the decor is somewhere between nautical fishing town and a grandparent's basement. Large ropes swing from one spot to another on the wall and there's a pool table in one corner with two mismatched sofas around it. Low booths line the wall opposite the bar and high top tables fill in the space between. Behind the booths there are collage picture frames on the wall and a collection of beer signs. Glass jar candles are on each table and little table top tents inform us that it is trivia night. The crowd is energetic and almost every table is full.

I spin a little in my stool and take in the citizens of Lakeville who are here for trivia night. The guys are mostly wearing t-shirts. Some have chino shorts on but most have gym shorts. They're all in sneakers or sandals. The women aren't any fancier.

When I told Liz I was going to change for going out she looked at me funny but didn't protest. I came out of the guest room a few minutes later in my cream bodysuit and cut off denim shorts. I paired this look with gold hoops, my gold ankle strap sandals, and my black quilted purse with a gold chain strap. Liz clapped and stood up from the sofa saying "okay, let's go!" And I was surprised that she wanted to wear her bike shorts and oversized band t-shirt out tonight. With her professional grade hiking sandals. Now that I see the outfits on the other patrons I'm less surprised.

Most of the girls our age are in leggings or bike shorts with baggy t-shirts or tank tops. One has a tennis skirt on. Their hair is up in messy buns or ponytails and they're all wearing sneakers or sandals.

I recognize Sandy and Gina sitting at a table with two other women. Sandy waves and I lift my hand back in response. At least they're wearing linen pants and striped t-shirts.

I turn back towards our table as Kyle drops off a bucket with six beer bottles on ice. He pulls one out and takes a sip before kissing Liz on the temple and walking over to a booth where three other guys are sitting.

"He comes for trivia most Mondays. That's Levi, Holden, and Cole. Levi is a high school teacher, Holden is a veterinarian, and Cole just took over his family's farm outside of town. Holden and Cole are from Lakeville. Levi moved up here a few years ago."

"He's cute." I tell Liz as my eyes connect with the clean shaven blond one in a buttoned up short sleeve chambray shirt. The only guy in a button up in the bar. He holds his beer up in a salute across the bar. I smile.

"Don't start." Liz warns.

"Why? He is cute. I am single. And I haven't been to a bar and not picked up a guy in like four years."

"Old habits die hard huh?"

"Exactly Liz, exactly." I say as I tip the beer to my mouth. The door behind us swings open and light from the early evening spills in. Liz can see the door from her seat and her eyes go wide. I turn to see what she's looking at.

It's Angie. In her slip dress and leather skirt date night outfit. And heels. And her hair is curled in soft waves. Her makeup looks fabulous.

But, she looks like she belongs in a cocktail lounge in Hell's Kitchen, not The Whale in Lakeville, on a Monday.

Whoops.

She smiles when she sees us and walks over to our table.

"Ohmigod, thank heavens you're here." She says as she sits

down at our table with us and grabs a beer.

"Hey Angie," Liz says. "You look great."

"Thank you! Nora helped me pick it out yesterday." She says proudly as she sits up straighter. Liz looks at me and I give a tiny shrug.

I might have picked a different outfit for her if I knew her trivia date was here, and that people dress like they're about to do yard work, but whatever, too late now. She's owning her outfit. And confidence can get you twice as far as competence.

"I'm so nervous." Angie whispers. She takes a drag from the beer bottle and hisses her displeasure before knocking back another. "I nipped into Dad's gin while I was getting ready." She looks around the bar anxiously. "When he suggested we meet at The Whale tonight I figured trivia would be a fun bonding thing but I forgot that the whole town shows up to play too."

"But a group date is a good idea. It helps keep conversation going. There's less pressure." Liz offers.

"I guess so. I just want him to see me as a grownup."

"I'm sure he will." Liz placates as she stands to get a few glasses of water for us.

Angie turns to me and puts her hand on my harm. "Nora," she starts seriously. "Thank you." She leans closer and I can smell the gin on her breath. "I feel so freaking sexy tonight."

"You're welcome Angie. My pleasure." Liz comes back and sets down the waters. I take a sip from mine, hoping Angie takes the hint, but she just takes another swig of beer.

"Tell us about this guy you're meeting." Liz says.

"Well, I've known him forever and," she sighs, "I'm in love. I mean, obviously I'm not going to tell him that, but I am. He's perfect. He's cute, smart, funny. Loves animals. The only problem is that he's been Jimmy's best friend forever and he only sees me as Jimmy's kid sister."

"Wait, Holden Monaghan is your date?" Liz asks surprised.

"Yeah, why? Oh god, you think he's out of my league. I knew it. I knew—"

"No! That's not what I meant at all. He's a great guy. And, actually you two would be perfect together." Liz continues.

I just sit there quietly because I know he's the friend I made eyes at earlier when we sat down. And I know that he's here for trivia night with his buddies. Liz gives me a look that asks 'how are we going to coach our girl through this?'

"We didn't set up a time but like he knows when trivia starts right? Should I text him?" Angie reaches down for her phone.

I need to act quickly. Honesty is the best policy right?

"Angie, hon, he's already here." I tell her slowly.

"What?!" She spins in her stool and her hair slaps my face as she whips her head around. The moment she sees him in the booth with Kyle she freezes.

He looks up and they make eye contact. His eyes flick between Angie and me and I can feel her deflating next to me like a balloon.

Holden asks Kyle to move so he can get out of the booth and we all watch as he walks over to our table.

"Hey Angie, wow, you look great." He says as he places his hand in the middle of her back and leans in to give her a kiss on the cheek. He turns and does the same to Liz and then stands up and looks me in the eye.

He extends a hand and introduces himself. "Hi, I'm

Holden."

"Charmed I'm sure." I reply. "Liz, can you come with me to order some drinks at the bar?"

"Yep!" And she hops off the bar stool. We saddle up and lean against the bar, every so often turning around to check in. Angie is doing a pretty good job with her body language. Her legs are crossed in his direction, her arms are open with one resting on the table, the other on her lap. My only critique is that she's swiveling her seat a little too much.

They're chatting but he never makes a move to sit down at the table. Liz and I order G&Ts and start to slowly sip them while we try not to be obvious as we watch their conversation.

In all my years of picking up guys I've never thought about what it might look like from the outside. But watching Angie flirt, she just did the touch-the-bicep move, and watching Holden respond is fascinating.

It could almost be narrated for a nature documentary.

"Watch as the young female slowly arches her back to put her breasts on more prominent display."

"See how the male responds by..." wait, shit, that's a high five.

I watch as Holden returns to his table and Angie slowly spins back towards us. Liz and I exchange a quick look and hustle back. As we do, the door opens, and even as I squint against the light, I can tell it's Jimmy.

And I do not feel comfortable with the swarm of butterflies that suddenly take flight as I take in his tall, broad frame. As he comes into the bar I notice the way his jeans hug his muscular thighs and my eyes zero in on his fly and the butterflies fan out and race through my bloodstream.

I bite my lip thinking about how he slid down just an inch in the seat to give me more friction against those jeans.

"Hey gals." He says as he steps up to our table. He gives Angie a quick hug and smiles at Liz before turning towards me. He hesitates for a millisecond before leaning in and kissing me next to my ear.

He lingers and I enjoy the mixture of his fresh soap smell and his cologne. My arms twitch with the temptation to reach up and circle them around his neck but I notch my shoulders down into their sockets and stay put.

I've been there, done that, so I'm finished.

Right?

I catch Liz's eye and her eyebrows raise to the ceiling. Is it possible she can read my mind? Not wanting to give anything else away I turn towards Angie who is reaching for her second beer and has a defeated look on her face.

Jimmy stands, takes the last beer in our bucket and props one hand on the back of my stool and one foot on it's bottom rung.

"You're all dressed up Ange." He says after a sip of beer. I admit I watched him bring the bottle to his lips.

"Yeah, for no reason." She slumps.

"What do you mean? What happened?" Liz asks.

"He was excited that I came to Trivia Night and he was glad that I already had a team because theirs was full."

"Ouch. Brutal." Liz says and I reach out and put a hand on her shoulder.

"Well then, we'll just have to show off how fun you are." I say. I turn towards Jimmy, "Jimbo."

"Don't call me that." He mumbles.

"You're on our team." I finish, ignoring him. I turn to Liz and Angie. "What's our team name gonna be?"

"Trebek Fan Club?" Liz offers.

"The Wise Crackers?" Angie says.

"Oh that's a good one. But I think we need something spicy." I tap my chin as I think. "Got it. Good Heads."

Liz blushes and nods quickly.

Angie doesn't seem to get it.

A deep voice chimes in. "No."

"C'mon!" I slap his shoulder with the back of my hand. "It goes both ways! This table has," I pause, "or more accurately gives, and gets, Good Head."

"No." He says again, and takes a sip of his beer.

"OHMIGOD I get it. Yes. Love it. Okay, I'll go sign us up." And Angie slips off her stool and saunters up to the corner of the bar where the signup sheet is. She comes back with a cocktail and our dry erase board.

12

If That's What She Wants, That's What She'll Get

JIMMY

Never in all my years has The Whale hosted a raunchy trivia night. But that's tonight's theme. I have a feeling the Tome Raiders had a say in it.

So far I've had to consider and try to answer the following questions.

Q: Axillism is the use of what body part during sex?
A: Arm pit.

Q: What common bathroom item was originally sold as a cure for gonorrhea?
A: Listerine.

Q: How many different types of kisses are detailed in the Kama Sutra?
A: 10.

I hate to admit that I've learned a thing or two.
But I will willingly admit that I have enjoyed answering the

questions with Nora.

"Okay Marys," oh yeah, Nora has been calling the three of us Marys all night. Apparently our lack of sexual knowledge compared to hers is virginal. "I have carried this team all night. We're neck and neck with The Nine Inch Males, and I refuse to let the Blow Jobs lose."

"Good Heads," I correct her.

"Right." She takes a look at her drink. "Anyways, Good Heads" she claps her hands together, "we got tits."

"This." I correct.

"No, I meant tits." She smiles up at me and her sassy attitude has me hooked.

"The question is…" Rick announces over the microphone. "What rude-sounding name is both a word for male genitalia and male lobsters?"

Immediately Nora and Liz throw out ideas, rapid fire.

"Dicks."

"Wangs."

"Members?"

"No. Oh, Tool!"

"O'Toole?"

"No. Just Tool."

"Oh."

"Cock."

"Joystick?"

"Weenie?"

"Pickle."

"Dong."

"Knob."

I sit back in amazement. There really are a lot of words for dick out there.

Angie hasn't said anything. In fact she's been quiet for a few questions now. I look in front of her and there are two empty cocktail glasses. And I know our table has been cleared a few times tonight so I wonder how much she's had.

I got the impression she was here for a date and I'm guessing he never showed. I also want to ask if she borrowed this outfit from Nora because it does not look like anything I've seen Angie wear before.

"Peen?"

"Oh, could be."

"Pecker."

"Dang, that's good too." Liz says.

"Ten seconds." Rick announces.

"Shit we gotta pick one." Liz says.

"I'm going to go with 'Peen' it seems scientific-ish." Nora says and she writes Peen on the dry erase board.

"Okay teams, hold up your answers." Rick announces. "And I see that two teams got it correct. The answer was 'Cocks'."

"Fuck." Nora says, frustrated.

"Peen is better." Liz says as she pats Nora's hand from across the table and slurps her gin and tonic loudly through the straw.

Angie goes to stand up but slides off her stool. I'm standing on the other side of Nora and as I jump around to catch her, Nora grabs her by the arm and holds her up.

"I got her," Nora says to me. "Why don't you close up and I'll take her to the bathroom."

"I don't have to go to the bafroom." Ange slurs.

"I know, but a little water on your neck will help." Nora says as she loops her arm behind Angie's and guides her to the bathroom.

Liz looks at me and kind of shrugs. I go to the bar to close our tab and Liz heads over to Kyle's table.

A minute later, Nora comes out of the bathroom with Angie and she's standing up a little straighter but that's where the improvement ends. I meet them at the door and go to take Angie off Nora's hands so she can go back in with Liz.

"Nah." Nora says to me quietly, "She'll save face if I walk out with her." And right after that she lets out a loud joyful laugh and kind of slaps Angie's arm. "Oh. My. God. *Angie!* You're bad!"

Before Angie or I can say anything Nora has ushered her out of the bar. As I stand holding the door open I see Holden turn over his shoulder to watch us leave. I lift my hand in a wave and follow the girls out.

Angie shakes free of Nora's grasp.

"Who wouldn't want to get with this?" She says as she gestures up and down her body. She is walking backwards down the middle of the street towards the store.

"Well love, as hot as you are I'm not into chicks and that there is your brother so, no." Nora says with a lit of teasing her her voice.

"Fine. But like generally speaking. C'mon. I'm a catch."

"That I can agree with," I say as I guide her around to my apartment entrance. There's no way I'm taking her home to Dad's like this.

"I'll just, umm, head back then." Nora turns the statement into a question by lifting her pitch at the end.

"No! Come with us!" Angie says as she starts to climb the stairs. She's using the railing like it's a rock climbing rope and putting one hand over the other as she ascends.

Nora looks up at me and I step a little closer. The temptation to touch her, caress her, kiss her, has been strong all night. She's wearing a pair of denim cut offs and her cream colored top is skin tight. Her gold sandals have a small heel to them. Her strawberry lemonade hair is down, falling in soft waves around her face.

She's fucking gorgeous.

"You heard the lady," I say as I hold open the door for her.

She smiles and walks past me. I wait a few steps before I start so I have an eye level view of her ass as we go upstairs.

"Get a good look?" She whispers as we reach the top.

"As good as you got when I first came into the bar tonight."

"You saw that?"

Yeah I saw it.

"Yep. Busted."

I unlock the door to the apartment and Angie rushes in. Nora stands on the landing with me for an extra beat before stepping past me inside.

"Jimmy, where are your snacks?" Angie whines from the kitchen. I head in and open a cabinet to pull out a bag of pretzels and a box of cereal. She squeals with delight and takes both over to my sofa.

"Is that generic brand cereal?" Nora asks.

"Yeah."

"Interesting." Nora comments.

"Why?"

"I've just never met a person who buys generic brand

cereal and actually eats it instead of donating it to a homeless shelter right away."

"Good point Nora." Angie chimes in from the sofa as she chews. "This is gross Jimmy, get better cereal."

I roll my eyes at Angie and then turn to find Nora looking at me. She's got her hands stuffed into her back pockets. I linger for a moment longer, focused on the way her chest is pushing forward. When I return to look at her face she smirking. I nod towards the sofa and she steps around and takes a seat next to Angie.

Angie turns on the TV to the Homecraft Network and beckons me over. I sit at the other end of the sofa from where Nora just sat down. The show comes back on and Angie starts mumbling and telling us that she would have done something or other different. She's popping pretzels in her mouth and talking while she chews so we really aren't getting much detail.

"Jimmy? Can you get me some water?" Angie asks. The pretzels and concentrating on the TV seem to be helping her, she's slowly coming back from oblivion.

"Sure thing." I stand and get a glass of water for her, and one for Nora. Before I walk back to the sofa I look at the two of them. Angie is chatting with Nora and Nora is smiling back and looks totally relaxed.

Bethany and Angie never really got along. Bethany wasn't thrilled about being her mother figure. So while she did help me when Angie needed someone to teach her how to use a tampon, they weren't really friends.

Already this feels different. Like Angie and Nora are friends.

"I'm sorry tonight didn't work out the way you wanted." Nora consoles Angie as I walk over with their waters. "Thanks." Nora says when I hand it to her and there is true appreciation in her eyes.

"What did you want tonight?" I ask as I sit down.

Angie sighs. "Just to be seen as an adult I guess," she says as she stares forward at the show.

I look at Nora over Angie's head for more information. She offers a tiny shoulder shrug and turns back to the TV.

The show is more interesting than I expected. They had some structural issues to figure out and I learned a few things. The credits are rolling as the next show starts and I look over to see Angie passed out against Nora's shoulder.

Nora senses me looking her way. She turns and smiles.

I stand and get a blanket to cover Angie up. I also grab a pillow from my bed and slowly we maneuver Angie off Nora's shoulder and down onto the pillow. Nora takes off Angie's shoes and sets them on the floor by the sofa. She stands and brushes her hands down her shorts.

"Alright, I'll just, ugh, go I guess." She kind of looks around as she says it.

"You can stay." I offer.

"No, I don't want to impose. I just, ugh does Lakeville have Uber drivers?"

"Drivers, multiple? No. Driver, singular. Yes."

"Figures. And, just have to ask, are you the Uber driver?"

"Nope." I smile.

"Why are you smiling?"

"Because the Uber driver just passed out on your shoulder."

Nora looks down at Angie who is sleeping with her mouth

open and looks back to me. Putting two and two together she pivots towards my bedroom. I grin and follow behind her, but at the door I crash into a pillow.

"What are you doing?" I ask Nora who is clutching a pillow to her chest.

"I'm going to sleep on the couch."

"Nora, don't be ridiculous. You're going to sleep in my bed. I've kept my hands off of you all night but I can't hold out any longer."

"Well you'll have to. I didn't come here to hook up. I told you Jimmy. I don't do dating."

"Fine, but you can't sleep on the sofa, there isn't room."

She looks past my shoulder to the one square of cushion available and then looks back up at me.

"Fine."

She pivots back into my room. She throws the pillow down, sits on the end of the bed, and slides off her shoes. I watch as she places both hands on the bed next to her and her shoulders creep up towards her ears.

"Umm, mind if I use the bathroom?" She asks.

"Please, go ahead. There's an extra toothbrush in the drawer if you want to use it."

"Oh, okay, thank you."

I watch as she walks into the bathroom and closes the door. I sit on my bed and stare at the closed bathroom door. I remember my mom telling me about how important ending your day with your partner can be. About sharing that moment as part of your routine. I also remember when Bethany and I moved in together. I was stressed out with the store, and Angie, and Dad, and Pops, which meant that by the end of the day I had little energy left for her.

I rub both sides of my beard in my hands to dislodge the fantasy of brushing my teeth next to Nora. It's a more uncomfortable fantasy than the images that ran through my mind during raunchy trivia.

Then I chuckle to myself as I imagine how hard she'd freak out if I went in there and picked up my toothbrush. Everything she's said has had "NO COMMITMENT" stamped on it.

And underlined.

She is not interested in settling down.

The door opens and she walks out. "All yours."

I head in, remove my contacts, piss, brush my teeth, and head back into the bedroom. Nora is sitting on the side of my bed fully clothed.

"What's up? Why aren't you in bed?"

"Oh, um, I was hoping I could borrow a t-shirt. This thong body suit is not going to be comfortable to sleep in."

I have to swallow the drool that has pooled in my mouth as the image of her ass in a thong comes to mind. "Here you go." I toss her a t-shirt and strip down to my briefs.

"Ugh, not fair Jimmy!" She says.

I turn around. "What's not fair?"

"I was all set on not hooking up with you again. Convinced myself that it would be a terrible idea. But then," she crosses over to me, "you whip out these!" She reaches around my back and presses her fingers into the muscle divots right above my ass. "Frickin' back divots. My kryptonite."

I laugh. "Seriously? That's your kryptonite?"

"Yes, ugh." She marches back to her side of the bed where she drops her shorts, reaches between her legs and swiftly unsnaps her body suit. I watch as she pulls it up over her head revealing her perfect, naked body. She grumbles something while pulling her arms through the sleeves of my t-shirt and then popping it over her head.

She seems frustrated when she reaches up around her neck to pull her hair out of the collar. Nora whips back the covers, slides into bed, huffs, and then rolls on her side facing away from where I'll be getting in on my side.

I pull back the covers and sit down with my back towards her. I smile as I slowly reach to plug in my phone because I can feel the mattress shift as she turns to look at my back.

If it's my back muscles she wants, it's my back muscles she'll get.

I reach up overhead and grasp one wrist and stretch from side to side. Then I switch. All the while knowing my muscles are firing off with each movement.

"Ugh!" I hear and then the bed bounces as she rolls back.

I tuck my legs into the sheets and lay on my side so I'm looking at her back. Her red hair is fanned out over my pillow and her small shoulder is drowned in my t-shirt. I'm tempted to do a little chef's kiss gesture because this woman right here is perfection. But I do not want Nora to catch me doing that so I just think it instead.

"Nora?"

"What?"

"You sound mad." I tease.

"I'm not mad, I'm frustrated."

"Sexually frustrated?" I whisper.

"Yes." She whispers back.

"I can help you with that you know."

"Trust me, I know." She says as she slowly starts to roll back towards me. It's just an inch but it feels like a mile.

"Can I ask you something?" I reach up and run some of her sunrise colored hair over my finger.

"Sure."

"Why are back divots your kryptonite?"

She rolls all the way to her back and looks up at me. She takes a deep breath before answering.

"Because in my mind it means you have strong forward and back movement." She says.

"Do you mean, thrusting?" I smile.

"Yes. Yes I do mean thrusting. And while I can't see a guy's back while he's pistoning in and out pf me, I can feel those divots working with my hands and I can imagine the strength being poured into the movement."

"Sounds like you really like that."

She licks her lips. "Yeah, I do."

I let the air sit heavy between us. My cock is half hard just having this quick conversation about what she likes but I don't want her to think I'm some fuck buddy.

No, this is more for me.

I'm newly determined to make her want me. To miss me. To make her crave me. Nora is already so much more than a hookup to me.

I lift my hand and brush my knuckles from her temple down to her jaw. My fingers curl around the back of her neck while my thumb holds her jaw up towards me. As I lean down her eyes close, and when I'm an inch from her lips I say "that's good to know," before giving her a featherlight kiss.

I pull back and her eyes flutter open in surprise.

"Good night Nora, see you in the morning." And I roll over and face away from her so she can get a full view of my back.

I hear her let out a puff of air and then her arms slam into the mattress before she rolls onto her side. I close my eyes and relive the evening. I remember how she cared for Angie tonight. How she bantered with Liz at trivia. How she's open about her attraction to me. That will be my starting point in my mission to make her fall for me.

13

Great Question Katherine

Nora

I woke up to Jimmy stretching his back in front of me.

Again.

The boy knows how to show off.

If I thought for one second he was serious and not messing with me I'd be kissing, nibbling, sucking, my way up and down his spine.

He stands up and crosses over to the bathroom. As soon as the door closes I run two fingers down my abdomen. I am already so on edge that when they reach my clit a zing of lust shoots through my veins and settles in my toes. Within thirty seconds I've defused the situation.

Sort of.

My vagina and I both know that quick little jill off won't be enough to keep me calm today. No, she knows what she wants, and ever since Jimmy walked into the bar yesterday she's wanted him.

He steps out of the bathroom and as I stand up to head in he drops his briefs right in front of me so I get a full view of his naked back side. Ugh, the ass only adds to the impression that he was a model for some sexy marble statues. He's freaking delicious.

I let out a whiney huff of air as I pass him and go into the bathroom. I close the door while looking back at him and he catches me.

He smiles.

He winks.

He flexes his ass muscles.

Jerk.

I pee, brush my teeth, splash some water on my face, use my fingers to clean up my eye makeup, and finger comb my hair. When I step out of the bathroom Jimmy isn't there so I slip back into my body suit and shorts.

I head out to the main room. Jimmy is standing over the back of the sofa talking to Angie. I can't hear what they're saying. He's just in a pair of gym shorts so, again, his back is on full display.

The urge to walk over and run my hands from those dimples up over his shoulders is overwhelming.

I've got it bad.

Angie sits up and she sees me. "Nora! You stayed over again?!"

"Only because my Uber driver was passed out on the sofa."

"Oh whoops, I forgot that people might want rides home last night. I hope everyone's okay."

"I'm sure they are." Jimmy offers.

"Welp, I better get back to Dad's and change and I'll meet you at the store Jimmy. Remember Marla and Dax are coming back this afternoon."

"Thanks for the heads up." He mutters.

"Hey, I gave you almost six whole hours this time! Not my fault I was focused on myself yesterday."

Angie is at the door and she slings her bag over her shoulder.

"Thanks for letting me crash, Jimmy and thank you," she looks at me, "for being my wing woman last night."

"Not sure how good I am if I didn't get you laid."

"True, but for me, a night out where I felt grown up and pretty is a win, even if I didn't end up with a guy."

She shrugs and then opens the door and heads out. I turn towards Jimmy who is watching me but I can't discern what's going through his mind.

Normally my mind reading with men only includes two messages; "wants to fuck," or "does not want to fuck," and that has gotten me pretty far in life.

But with Jimmy, I get the "wants to fuck" vibe and then there is also this "wants to talk" vibe. Which is new.

"I'm glad I get a do-over." He says as he turns towards the stove. I walk over to the kitchen island and lean against it. I place my forearms and palms down on the cool stainless steel surface.

"What do you mean?" I ask.

"Well, the last chance I had to feed you breakfast was rudely interrupted."

"True. But who am I to interfere with stardom."

"Ha, hardly. I'm not sure why they picked Angie and me." He says as he crosses over to the fridge and pulls out the eggs. He sets them on the counter and pulls a mixing bowl off the shelf beneath the island. "When she applied she said all she had to do was write up a little bit about what we do and share our social media handles."

"And then they just showed up with a camera?" I ask.

"Well, no, they contacted her via e-mail and asked if we would have a call to discuss. So we had that call, I dunno like three months ago. And this time Angie and I both got to talk about what we do and how we feel when we do it.

"The call ended with like 'we'll be in touch' and next thing I know Marla is introducing herself at the Home Builders Convention last week and a few days later she's here in Lakeville with a camera man."

"Do you want to do the show?"

"Yes and no. It would bring more money to our business which would help us do better jobs and work for more people. I just don't want it to be a distraction."

"You really love what you do, don't you?"

"I do. I love working with my hands. Creating something from a pile of supplies. I want to learn more about repurposing and refinishing furniture. But the best part, no contest, is seeing the people's faces when they walk into their updated space."

"That's so cool." I say.

Jimmy has finished whisking the eggs and he turns towards the stove. "What's your job like Nora?"

"High pressure. Old school. I help universities approach donor prospects for major financial contributions."

"Oh wow."

"Yeah, so when a university builds a new science building and it's named after someone I helped make that happen."

"That's cool. Why'd you get into that?"

"I wanted to help spread the wealth. Help people and schools put their resources to good use."

"Makes sense." His back is still towards me and he's stirring the eggs in the pan. There are little muscles firing off across his shoulders. They're hypnotizing.

"Did you always want to be a, uh," what is his job? Contractor? Builder? Store owner? All three? Something else? "Contractor?"

He laughs, thank goodness. He turns the stove off and pulls the pan to the side. "Yes and no. I helped in the store all the time growing up, helped my Dad with projects around the house when I wasn't playing baseball, and when I was in high school I was looking at engineering schools."

"Oh yeah? Where'd you go?"

"Well, I didn't." He says as he pulls a baking sheet out of the oven.

"Oh."

He turns around and I am hit with his mega watt smile. "Nah, it's fine. My mom passed away from cancer when I was in high school. Angie was finishing 4th grade. My Dad, well, he didn't handle his grief so I stayed here. Pops gave me the store when Gran got sick, I helped Angie start, and finish, high school and then go off to college."

He walks over to the island and hands me a plate. There are scrambled eggs, bacon, a slice of toast, and strawberries. His plate has eggs, bacon, strawberries and a small little salad.

"I had always helped Pops and Dad with projects on their own homes. And when folks came into the store with questions I had to figure out how to solve them. Sometimes I'd help them actually fix the issue at home." He takes a bite and looks at me. "I didn't know I could do a whole home project until I built this place." He circles his fork around to indicate the apartment.

"It's very impressive." I say with a smile while taking a bite of eggs.

"What can I say, I'm impressive." He winks at me as he shovels a forkful of salad into his mouth.

Feeling spicy I pick up a strawberry and while making full eye contact with him I place it in my mouth and make a show of taking a bite.

His chewing slows down as he watches my lips.

I'm impressive too.

The intensity in his eyes ignites a fire in my belly which chases away the discomfort that was building as we talked about my job.

Jimmy clears his throat. "What, uh, are your plans for today?"

"Well, I need to get back to Liz's and I have one episode of my podcast left so I might take a walk and listen to that. When does shooting start for you?"

"At one. I'll head over to the Fallons' house this morning and get started. We're focused on the bathrooms in the house today. Cabinets, fixtures, tile, as much as we can get done."

"Who works at the store while you're on a job?"

"Angie usually. She will swing by to check the tile and faucets this morning to make sure the right ones got delivered but then she'll head back to the store. We do the projects together but we don't always work together."

"How are they going to do that for the show?"

"They'll film her visits and make it seem like she comes to

the site all the time. And I'll be there when the homeowners see their place for the first time. After she's decorated it."

"I guess that's how most of those shows work."

"Yeah, Marla actually calls it a Brains and Brawn format. I don't know if that's like an industry thing or just her own term. But she said it has worked for shows in the past."

"Interesting." I finish my breakfast and stand to take my plate to the sink. I feel, more than I hear, Jimmy follow me, it's like I'm tuned into his frequency.

I set my plate in the sink and he reaches around me and sets his down while pressing his chest into my back. I turn so his chest is pressing up against mine and lift my chin so I'm looking at his face.

"Did you enjoy your breakfast?" He asks.

"Mmhmm." I hum.

"Maybe we can do it again sometime."

"Maybe." I reply. That's the best I can give him.

He nods and steps back so I can walk back to the bedroom. I put on my shoes, pick up my phone, and check it. Nothing. I put it in my back pocket, grab my purse, and walk back out to the main space.

"I'll drive you back." He says as he walks past me into his bedroom.

"Oh, okay sure."

Jimmy comes back out of his room with a navy Lewis Hardware t-shirt on that does almost as much for me as seeing him with his shirt off. The way the sleeve pulls against the curve of his bicep has me clenching around nothing. His baseball cap is settled over his shaggy chocolate colored hair and my fingers itch to play with the curls that run along the edge.

The thrill of hooking up with someone new is the whole unexpected element of it. The novelty. I can get a pretty good read early on if they're good enough to let them lead the way. Or if they need some coaching, I'll gladly get in the drivers seat.

With Jimmy it has been both. The first night I was in charge but he knew how to take it further. The second night he initiated things but he knew when to let me lead.

It is a give and take.

I always thought sex with the same guy over and over again would be boring. And yet, being with Jimmy more than once has not only satisfied me, but has me wanting more.

"Ready?" He asks.

"Hands." I reply. Still half living my day dream about the things his hands could do with me.

"Huh?" He questions.

"Ah, nothing. Sorry."

He looks at me sideways with a small smirk on his lips. Those lips. I wanted to crash myself into him last night but I didn't. I wouldn't let myself. Now that he's walking towards me my mind is racing.

Is he going to kiss me?

I lick my lips.

Does he want this too?

I lift my chin.

Are we both experiencing this heat?

I hold my breath.

He stops in front of me and slowly reaches his arm out. I freeze, waiting to feel his strong arm lock around me. I would have a hard time not letting my knees buckle.

I'm at the edge again, from just being near him.

He smiles and I feel the smile on my own face spreading.

I hear a click and my lust filled haze vanishes as I realize he only moved toward me to reach the door knob. He pulls the door open and I blink rapidly up at his stupid, attractive face.

"After you." He says.

I try not to huff like a 2nd grader who didn't get her way but I'm finding it increasingly difficult to keep my chill. I stomp towards the stairs and with each step down I tell myself to cool it.

Get it together Nora.

You don't need a man Nora.

You don't want a man Nora.

One and done Nora.

It's worked up until now.

It'll work again.

Why mess with a good thing?

Just move on Nora.

Get back to Liz's and chill out.

Take a shower.

Don't think about Jimmy in the shower.

Don't!

Bad brain.

And we reach the door that leads out to the parking spot behind the store. I push the door open hard and it flies back against the wall.

"Whoa girl, easy." Jimmy says with a laugh.

I round to the passenger side and whip the door open when he unlocks it. I climb up and forcibly sit in the seat.

"Nora, everything okay?" He pivots towards me once he sits down in his seat. His arm draped over the steering wheel. And that casual move alone has my lady parts buzzing.

"Fine."

He gives me a 'get real' look.

I cross my arms with a pitiful humph.

"Hmm. Seems like you're frustrated again."

The inner 2nd grader comes out. I pivot towards him, "Maybe I am."

"Anything I can do about it."

"No." I say with a head shake.

"Okay." He sounds too chipper as he turns to put the key in the ignition. "If you think of something, all you have to do is ask."

"That won't be necessary." I reply as flatly as I can.

He turns the key, the engine starts, and just the small vibration of the truck sends shivers up my spine and I feel the urge to purr. I lick my lips and try to swallow but it does nothing to help my dry mouth.

He puts the truck in reverse and swings his arm over the headrest of my seat. Again his arms and broad chest are on display. I stare as his pecs tighten with his movements under the well worn cotton of his t-shirt. His eyes flick to mine and I am caught red handed.

I blink and turn my gaze out the front window and his hand brushes my shoulder as he brings his arm back to the center console.

The five minute drive to Liz and Kyle's is silent. We pass a few other cars on the way and Jimmy gives them a wave. I focus on keeping my eyes forward but watch out of the corner of my eye as his fingers drum on the arm rest in beat with the song.

We pull up in front of their house and there's a car I don't recognize in the driveway. Jimmy puts the truck in park and turns towards me.

"Have a good day Nora. See you around." He says with a confident smile.

"Yeah, you too." I mumble as I open the door and slide out of the seat in a daze.

I'm halfway up the driveway when Liz's mom, Katherine Collins, comes bounding out the front door.

"Nora! Hello!" She shouts. Then she turns and starts waving her arm wildly towards Jimmy. "And Jimmy! What fun to see you here too!"

Jimmy leans down so he can see better out the passenger side window. "Hello Mrs. Collins." He says. "Have fun with the set up." And with that he drives forward, loops around the cul du sac, and as he drives past us on the way out he holds up his big manly hand in a wave.

"Nora, I'm glad you're here. I need some of your fashion sense for the decor."

"What decor?"

"For the boat silly! Float Fest is Saturday and this year I *will* have a better float than Gina Papadakis." Liz's mom mutters as she loops her arm in mine and pulls me with her into the house.

When I step in the front door my eyes are assaulted. It's like an attic and a party supply store had twins and the afterbirth is in front of me. Everywhere I look there are rolls of fabric, fake greenery, paper lanterns, streamers, and as I pan my view further to the right, celebrity cut outs?

Katherine claps her hands together. "Okay, so I want a swanky French Riviera vibe." That helps to explain the James Bond cut out, and maybe the Michelle Obama one too. Where did she even get that?

"I already told Charles that we were going to put the celebrities on the roof of the pontoon. Like it's a night club or something. Then I want to put beaded curtains around the whole thing. Or velvet. What's that old TV show quote, I'd drape myself in velvet if it was socially acceptable?"

"I'm not sure."

"No matter, I already got a bunch of plastic champagne flutes so even though Charles insists on the pony keg he will drink the beer out of a flute. This pontoon will be sophisticated." She finishes with determination. Hands on her hips she turns towards me. "So, what do you think?"

"Well I love it. I'm worried about velvet and water, and it being like 90 degrees, but besides that, very doable."

"Oh, I didn't think of that. Okay, scratch the velvet. But the beaded curtain thing, that's cute right?"

"Very."

"Now," she steps into the living room and starts lifting up bags and bolts of fabric, looking for something. "I had those wooden beads somewhere. Nora, be a dear and check over by Jason."

"Jason?"

She points towards the celebrity cut outs and sure as shit, behind Bond, Michelle, and Elle Woods, is a Jason Voorhees cut out. Ski mask, machete, and all.

The true crime podcaster in me loves it.

The girl who has been recruited to make this pontoon boat swanky is having trouble picturing Jason Voorhees on board.

But down by his feet is a bag full of wooden beads. "Got 'em Mrs. Collins."

"It's Katherine."

"Alright, where do you want the beads?"

"We're going to paint them, what do you think," she lifts a handled top container that is almost two feet tall. "Maroon? Teal? Oh, hold on. I'll just search images of the French Riviera again."

I carry the beads over towards her and look over her shoulder as she unlocks her phone. The first thing that pops up is her TikTok account and before she quickly swipes it away I swear I saw a video of Jimmy with his shirt off. I'd know that back anywhere.

"Hmm, what do you think?" Katherine says as she tilts her phone in my direction. "Orange would be too Italian right?"

"Right." I answer. "I think teal would work. And that'll look good against the water too."

She lets her phone drop down to her leg. "Yes! Oh goodness why didn't I think of that. Okay, teal it is." And she takes a big step over two bags filled with plastic flamingo parts before going out to the porch. "We'll paint out here."

I follow her to the screened in porch. She opens up the paint container and pulls out two small brushes, a paper plate, and a sponge before closing that section of the plastic storage tote and opening the next. Once she finds the paint bottle she wants, she starts shaking it. Her bracelets making it a melodic affair.

"So Nora, tell me what's new."

"Umm, nothing really."

She levels me with a stare over her reading glasses. "Not what I hear."

I laugh. "What do you hear?"

"That you're going hot and heavy with our own Jimmy Lewis."

"Who said that?"

"Well, Gina dropped it in the Tome Raiders book club chat yesterday. Sandy confirmed it. And I got to see him drop, you, off, this morning." She emphasizes each word, "that's triple confirmation territory when the Lakeville gossip standard only requires, well, none."

"It's not what it looks like."

"Then what is it?"

Great question, Katherine.

What is going on with Jimmy and me? We're not dating. I don't do that. We obviously have physical chemistry but last night we didn't hook up and I still want to hang out with him. I want to talk to him more.

I'm sure there's a name for this and that other people have experienced it before but this is all new to me.

"I'm not sure what it is. We did hook up, not gonna lie about that, but last night I just stayed over because it was late after we got Angie tucked in."

"Yes, Gina said that Angie drank a lot last night. That's not like her."

"It was a weird night for her."

"Gina said she was all dressed up." Katherine leans back in her chair to view my outfit. "And that you had helped her pick out an outfit for a date in the store on Sunday."

"Yeah, I bumped into her there and gave her some ideas."

"And that you asked about Jimmy's past."

"I was curious okay!" I know I sound like a defensive teenager but that's what a mom's questions will do to a girl.

"Well, curiosity aside, Jimmy is the best kind of people. He cares so deeply for the ones he loves. We were all just shocked when that Bethany left. I mean, I had a hunch she wasn't the right match for him but to leave after everything they'd been through?" Katherine shakes her head. "It was just a shame."

I don't have anything to say to that so I focus on painting my bead. Images of a younger Jimmy stepping up when his family needed him playing in my mind.

"How's your mom?" Katherine asks after a few minutes.

"I talked to her yesterday, she's fine."

"Yeah? That's good." And I'm glad she doesn't push for more. Fine is going to have to be enough. Liz has told her parents a little bit about my relationship with my mom but mostly about my past, not the present.

I told Liz it was fine if she shared. That I'm not ashamed of my past but that I didn't really want to waste anyone's time going through the current details.

"How are Maggie and Charlie Jr?" I ask.

"Charlie Jr is doing great! He's now the Director in the emergency department. The hours are a little more manageable than they were when he was a resident and attending. I'm hoping he finds a girl soon."

"Is he looking for a girl?"

"He doesn't say he is, but that doesn't mean anything."

"What do you mean?"

"All I care about is whether his heart is open. You might

not be looking for love but that's usually when it finds you."

Huh, interesting.

"And Maggie?"

"She's a lost cause."

"What?" I laugh.

"She is looking so hard for love that she'll never find it. The girl goes on a hundred dates a month but none of the men are ever good enough." Katherine shakes her head and picks up the next bead. "One had nose hair, I told her he could trim it but she was already done with him."

I laugh, because, yeah, nose hair is a hard pass.

"Another one had a, and I quote, weird voice, so she didn't go on a second date with him."

"Well, a voice is kind of a tough one to look past."

"I suppose you're right."

"Those two are such opposites. Charlie Jr rarely goes on dates. Maggie goes on them constantly. I'm not sure which is better."

"Not sure it matters."

"I suppose you're right. They have to figure it out in their own way. Lizzy helped Charles see that with her whole photography business. I'll have to learn to accept it when it comes to their love lives."

"I guess you will."

We sit back and continue painting beads for an hour while Katherine fills me in on all the Lakeville gossip.

How Mrs. Cartwrite filed a complaint over her neighbors flower garden. Apparently Mrs. Wallner's crawling rose shrub had spread into Mrs. Cartwrite's property. The town's garden council, which both women are members of, had an official review, town hall debate, and ruling. The bush could stay but it would need to be trimmed regularly.

"Well, we did it." Katherine says as she sets her paint brush down. I look around and the table is covered in teal beads. Hundreds of them.

"Tomorrow I'll be back to string them." And she stands up and carries the paper plate with paint on it to the trash. She washes off her brushes and leaves them on a paper towel on the counter. She surveys the piles of items scattered through the living and dining room.

"I suppose I should tidy this a bit huh?"

"I'll help." I say with a smile. "I'm just going to wash up."

In the bathroom I wash my hands and scrub off the teal paint left on my fingers. My phone starts to buzz in my back pocket. I quickly dry my hands and reach for it.

Fosters.

I clear my throat and answer.

"Hello, this is Nora Heely."

"Hi Nora. It's Trisha." My boss.

"Hi Trisha. How's it going?"

"Fine. You?"

"Fine." This is painfully awkward.

"Okay, I'm just going to cut to the chase." I take a deep breath and sit down on the edge of the tub. "Mr. Foster is mad. He had this whole 'I can't believe we trusted her' rant on Friday. Yesterday he seemed a little more level headed but he insisted on a full review of every prospect meeting you've ever handled."

"Seriously?" I ask.

"Yeah, so until that review is completed he won't make a

decision on your employment status."

"Okay. Is there anything I can do?"

"No, just hang tight."

"Okay. Thanks."

"Yeah, bye Nora.."

"Bye Trisha."

I hang up the phone and let my arms hang lifeless between my legs. I'm perched on the edge of this tub and it mirrors the edge my life is on.

One wrong move and I plunge backwards into a hole. No job. No paycheck. Starting over.

Or I wait it out, balance, breathe, and everything goes back to the way it was.

I lean forward and backwards a little bit to test the feeling each way. Forward feels more stable but heavy somehow. Gravity pulling me into myself until my lungs are crushed up against my ribs. Backwards is scary but exhilarating. I feel the strength in my core as I test the limit, the quickening of my heart rate as I push myself a degree further.

I wonder which way things will go?

14

At The End of the Day

JIMMY

When I got to the Fallons' house this morning the drywall in the bathroom was ready to go. I opened up the boxes of tile and texted pictures to Angie. She gave me a thumbs up but then immediately called to clarify that I was not to start installing anything until she got here in person to take a look.

While I waited for Angie to stop by I installed the shower and bath surrounds and started on the vanities.

A little after noon Marla and Dax showed up. They asked me to come out to the front lawn and do a 'talking head' where I just tell the camera what I've been working on. Marla would let me talk for a minute and then ask a question for me to answer. It was easy but I was itching to get back to work.

I was in the middle of telling them about the Amish cabinetry guy we used for the custom vanity in the primary bathroom when Angie pulled up. Dax filmed her getting out of the car and walking up to me. Marla made Angie put on a microphone and then get back in her car and do it again.

So Angie reversed a block, pulled back up, got out, and we went through the whole song and dance again. It was awkward.

Marla is typing away in her phone and she barely lifts her head and says "Alright, walk to the house and show her the tile samples."

So we head inside, Dax on our heels.

"I organized it by space. So this is the floor tile, back splash and shower tile for the primary bathroom." I say as I point to a group of boxes on the floor. "And then here are the ones for the second bath."

"Oh, don't you just love this green?" Angie says as she pulls out a sheet of the backsplash tile. It's a glass tile in a deep emerald green. It'll be beautiful anytime of day because of the way the light shines through the window in the bathroom.

"It's going to look so good in there." I say.

"Okay, and then the floor tiles are in the checkerboard pattern alternating between the grey and white marble."

"Yep."

Angie moves over to the kids' bath tiles and looks up at me.

"What if we did a fun little message in the penny tiles?"

"What do you have in mind?"

"I'm not sure yet, I'll have to think about it. But you can go ahead and do the other tiles first, I'll come up with something by the end of the day."

"Alright, I'm starting in the primary anyways. I want to get that room done so the guys can get in and finish with painting the bedroom this week."

"Good. And I got an update on the hanging chair that is going in the boys' room. It should be delivered Friday so you'll have the hardware you need."

"That works. Did you pick a paint for Olivia's room?"

"I've narrowed it down to the final two. I'll put the order in at the store when I decide."

I smile at her. We really do work well together. I don't know if working on other people's homes would be as much fun if Angie wasn't doing it with me.

"Anything else?" I ask.

"Nope." She pops the P.

"And cut." Marla says and Dax lowers the camera. I forgot they were there. "That was perfect you two!" She turns to Dax. "Lets make sure we tell Anna that we need to capture them on the first go." They start walking back out the front door. "Because you saw that re-do of Angie's arrival right? Brutal."

Angie turns to me with her hands in her back pockets and grimaces. I laugh and raise my hand to her for a high five and she jumps as our palms connect.

"That was fun! I actually forgot they were there." She says.

"Me too. Glad they liked what they saw." I reach into my back pocket and pull out the mic pack and unclip the mic from my shirt. Angie does the same and then starts wrapping the cord around the pack.

I hand her mine and she walks towards the front door.

"Alright, I'm headed back to the store. See you at dinner tonight." I roll my eyes. "You promised." She scolds.

"I know. Alright, let me get to work."

Angie walks out, leaving me with boxes of tile that need to be carried upstairs and racing thoughts about dinner with Dad and Pops tonight.

...

One thing I hate about a job site is the lack of air

conditioning. I handle heat well enough but the combination of today's humidity and being in a small, mostly interior, room like the bathroom, means I am dripping with sweat.

I stand up and stretch. My shirt is sticking to my back. I reach back to the neck and pull it off. I could probably use a break but I'mm in a groove so I make a pencil mark halfway across the wall from where I am now. That'll be my stopping point.

I pop my headphones back in and find myself singing along to the songs as I work. My mind wanders to Nora as different song lyrics filter through my brain.

The sunshine in her hair. The cherry red lipstick. The cutoff shorts. Hell even the power ballads about getting revenge on a cheating boyfriend have me thinking of her because I can easily imagine the aftermath of Nora scorned.

My balls shrivel up a little bit thinking about it.

I've got one more row of subway tiles to go before my break line so I turn up the volume a little higher and get to work. One song later and I'm done. Well for now.

I stand up from where I was crouching, stretch my back by placing my hands on my lower back and pushing forward, and then I turn around to find Dax recording me.

"Oh hey man. I didn't know you were there." I say as I pull my headphones out.

"Just grabbing a bit of footage." He says. "It looks great in here."

I put my headphones in their case and slide it into my pocket. "Yeah, it's coming together."

I step out into the hallway and Dax follows behind me down the stairs. I'm not sure if he's still recording. I get outside and all the way to my truck before remembering that I left my shirt on the vanity. I turn around to go get it when I hear a catcall whistle from across the street.

I turn around as I hear "Yeah baby, give the ladies what they want!"

"Hi Gina." I say unenthusiastically and offer her a quick wave. Gina Papadakis is the town divorcée. She's been through three husbands now, and while I appreciate the sentiment it's a little weird that she's offering up catcalls to a man who is young enough to be her son.

I jog back into the house, up the stairs, and grab my shirt. I slip it back on and the fabric is still damp from my sweat earlier. It's early afternoon, hottest part of the day. I decide to head home, shower, and then come back to finish up later.

...

I stand up and brush my hands off. The wall tile in the primary bathroom is done. I came back after my shower and got to work. I reach into my pocket to stop my music and as I lift my phone I see the time.

8:04 pm

And I see the three missed calls and seven texts from Angie.

Dinner.

Shit.

I forgot.

I was supposed to meet her at Pops' at 6. Two hours ago. Dinner will be done with by now.

"Shit, shit, shit." I mutter as I grab my stuff and take the stairs down two at a time. I lock the front door and jump in my truck as I dial.

"Where the fuck are you?" Angie whisper yells.

"Sorry, sorry. Ange, I'm so sorry."

"Fine. You're sorry. But what happened?"

"I lost track of time. My phone was on do not disturb."

"Sure."

"I did! I went back to the site to finish the tile and just kept going, I didn't check the time until I was done. I had no idea it got so late."

"The tile is finished?" This is a peace offering if I've ever heard one.

"Yes. The primary bath tile is finished. Tomorrow I'll get started on the kids' bathroom."

"Well, good job I guess, that puts us a little bit ahead of schedule doesn't it."

"It does."

There's a pause. My unasked question hangs between us.

"How was it?"

"Fine."

"Fine, fine or *fine*?"

"The latter."

"Shit. Sorry. What happened."

"Well it started out normal enough. There was some bickering about baseball, Pops asked Dad what he's been working on, Dad told him to mind his own business. You know, normal dysfunctional grown men stuff."

"Sorry Ange."

"Actually, it's fine. It would have been worse if you were there I think. Pops said he would stop by the store soon to catch up."

"Okay, so what am I going to have to do to make this up to you?"

"I haven't decided on your sentencing yet."

"Fair."

"Yeah." She says as she trails off.

"Alright, well, have a good night Angie, again, I'm so sorry, I'll see you tomorrow."

"Night Jimmy."

I hang up and turn on to Cherry Blossom Drive towards town. As I drive past Sunfish Park I turn and look quickly across the open green space. There's a gazebo in the center where concerts are held in the summer. Local cover bands come and play for a few hours and Lakeville residents set up blankets and picnic. Sometimes there are family movie nights and at Halloween they do a screening of a classic slasher film.

As I bring my eyes back to the road, a swish of red hair catches my eye. I come to a complete stop at the corner and look to my left.

Nora is sitting on a bench, elbows resting on her knees, and her shoulders are shaking like she's sobbing.

My heart rate picks up as the fight response courses through my veins. The thought of her hurting has me throwing the truck in park, turning off the ignition, and barreling towards her. I'm just reaching the grass when she looks up. She throws her arms in the air and lets them flop back down on her legs.

"Nora? What's wrong?"

"Nothing." She sniffles and uses the back of her hands to wipe away tears.

"Are you hurt?" I say as I crouch down in front of her, my hands finding her thighs without a second thought.

She looks at my hands and then flashes her eyes up to mine.

"No, I'm not hurt." She says, her voice thick with tears.

"Did something happen? Why are you out here alone?"

"No, nothing happened actually. That's the problem. No this is just your standard walk after dinner with a stop for a quick public sob."

I chuckle. "Don't all your murder podcasts tell you not to walk around alone at night."

She perks up. "First, the correct term is 'True Crime'. Second, yes in fact they do, and they tell me to be especially wary of handsome strangers."

"Handsome huh?" I grin.

"You know you are." She says before straightening up and sitting tall. "And, uh," she looks down at her feet, "my shoe strap broke so I'm not sure how I'm going to walk home."

I look down at her feet and see that a strap is ripped right out of the sole and that the only other thing keeping this shoe on her foot is a tiny band across her toes. I put my hand on her ankle and slowly slide the shoe off her foot. I unbuckle the other one and do the same. Leaving her barefoot.

She's wearing the cutoff shorts from last night, and actually the top looks the same.

"Have you changed since last night?" I ask as I stand up and move to sit on the bench next to her. I sling my arm along the backrest.

She looks down at herself. "Ugh, no. I guess I haven't. I got distracted."

"Yeah? What distracted you?"

"Katherine, Liz's mom. She has all these plans for Float Fest. So I spent my morning painting beads with Michelle Obama and Jason from Friday the 13th."

I laugh, "What?"

"Yes, oh and James Bond. From like the 80s. I'm not sure if the theme is top secret but she's got big plans to blow this competition out of the water."

"She'll have a tough time beating Gina."

"That's what she said too! She said it was her mission this year to one-up her. What does Gina do to win such pontoon boat decorating respect?"

"Well, last year she, went with a crab fishing boat theme. She had the cage things on the front and everything. She served up crab appetizers and hired male models to be the fishermen."

"Sorry I missed that." She laughs.

"Yeah, it was something to see. The year before that? She did a Rose Bowl Parade thing where she covered her boat in carnations. The bees were a little annoying but the boat looked amazing."

"Wow, any idea what she's doing this year?"

"No, this is the only thing around here that stays a secret."

"Hmm, well I'll have to double down on my efforts to bring home a win for Katherine."

"They're lucky to have you on their team." I say as I reach forward and pull a strand of her hair through my thumb and forefinger.

Nora turns towards me, looks down at the hands folded in her lap, and then looks back up. She takes a deep breath, "I sort of lost my job."

"When? Today?"

"No, Friday." Friday? I remember Friday. Hell yeah I do. I keep my eyes trained on her and she continues. "There was a miscommunication between a prospect, me, and my client. A few hours later I was put on leave. My boss called this afternoon to tell me they're doing a full investigation. I don't know when it will be done. I don't know if I have a job to go back to. I don't know what's next."

"Shit, That sucks." Because it does. Uncertainty is one of the worst feelings. It's this poisonous cocktail of anxiety, worry and, worst of all, hope.

"Yeah. I guess I'm realizing I don't do too well when things are out of my control."

"Not many people do." I say. I think of my dad and how he responded to Mom's cancer. And then on the other hand I think of Pops and how he took action when Gran started to get sick.

They both lost the women they love but their reactions to it were completely opposite. I lost a woman, who I loved at the time, and I split the difference between them.

"What's your plan?"

"I don't know." She whispers. She looks up at me.

"That's okay."

"Is it?" She asks. She crosses her legs and turns towards me on the bench. "I've always had a plan. Always. As a kid, my plans involved chores and doing people's laundry for money. As a teen I planned everything for school and college applications while working two jobs. As a college student I planned my course work to get me the most bang for my buck. I planned my internships. I planned my applications. I planned my career.

"And I stuck to those plans. It got me far. The first unplanned thing I did was to adopt Sir Harold. Then the stupid old cat went and died and I ended up destroying my career."

She slumps forward with her face in her hands and she starts crying again. I freeze momentarily as I work through everything she just said. I'm sad for her, a little confused, and sorry, not sorry, aroused by the smell of her perfume wafting my way.

I reach my hand that was resting on the back of the bench down and place it on her shoulder. She slumps forward. Her head lands in my lap and she curls up into the fetal position and continues to cry.

Helping teenage Angie through some of her most dramatic times has prepared me for this moment. Nora is spiraling. She feels out of control. She needs to release this anxiety before she can move on or see things differently.

I rest my hand on her bicep and let her cry. Some of her hair falls across her face and I gently push it back over her shoulder and watch her face as her crying slows and her breathing regulates.

She turns a little bit and looks up at me.

Our eyes connect, her blue eyes clouded with tears and dim in the light of the streetlamp overhead.

"Thank you Jimmy." She whispers.

"For what?" I ask.

"For not leaving."

"You're welcome."

She smiles.

15

Undermined by Purple Slippers

Nora

I roll my head back down so my cheek rests against Jimmy's leg. I have never had my head in a man's lap while his clothes were on. It feels more intimate this way.

This afternoon was exhausting. After the call with Trisha, Katherine had me help her clean up the house before she left to make dinner. Liz got home, then Kyle, they cooked, and we ate. Liz kept asking me questions and I kept dodging them as best I could.

The thought I've been stuck on all day is, without my job, who am I?

I texted Trisha knowing it was against the rules. I told her I had an idea for fixing the cat lady thing.

No response.

I started to think about who I could pass a message through but this summer's interns are already gone and I never worked with the one who got an offer. The competitive nature of landing deals means I didn't make too many friendships within the walls of Fosters, Henderson & Associates.

Liz's idea about donating to the veterinary program was pure genius. Goes to show how off my game I am that I didn't think of it. And, unfortunately unless Trisha answers my calls no one will ever hear the idea.

After helping Liz and Kyle with the dishes they settled in to watch reruns of Suits, and I told them I wanted to take a walk. I slipped on my sandals and started to head towards town.

When I was across the street from the park I got a text from my Mom.

Mom

Do you still have that savings account at the credit union?

The one she had me set up in high school and then drained two weeks before I graduated? That one?

No, I closed it.

Then nothing. I rolled my eyes and continued towards the park when my sandal strap ripped. I sat down on the bench to look at it more closely but couldn't get a good look because the tears were welling up in my eyes.

I gave in and sobbed. My shoulders shook as my stomach clenched and my lungs worked to keep up. Hot tears pooled in my palms as I held my face in my hands.

And then Jimmy showed up.

I was raw, I was full of emotion about my job, my mom, Sir Harold, friendships, him, everything. And for him to simply listen, not try to solve it, was exactly what I needed. To let me cry and release the tension that was building inside me.

I didn't know that's what I needed.

But he did.

My head is still resting on his lap and I feel him looking down at me. I blot at my face with the back of my hand to dry any remaining tear stains. My breathing evens out as I stare off into the dark around the lake.

Jimmy shifts and pulls his phone out of his pocket. With one hand he taps out a message. I hear it send then he slides his phone away, and his other hand begins to play with my hair.

I turn and shift onto my back so I'm looking up at him and he tilts his head down at me, "How was your day?" I ask in a playful tone.

He smiles. "My day is great."

"Is?"

"It's not over yet."

I push myself up to sitting and turn towards him. "It's not?"

"No, I was driving home after spending the whole day tiling a bathroom when I spotted a pretty girl and came over to talk to her."

I blush. "Yeah? Then what?"

"She was having a bad day but she shared her burden with me." I look down at my hands clasped in my lap. He reaches out and tilts my chin up to him so I'm forced to look at him and his stupid attractive face. "And I was happy to be there for her."

"Yeah?"

"Yeah." He says. His gaze shifts behind my shoulder and I hear a car pulling up. I turn around and see Angie stepping out of her car and walking towards us. She's got a pair of purple fluffy slippers in her hand.

"Here you go." She says as she hands the slippers to me.

"Uhh, thanks." I say and I look at Jimmy.

"Thank you Angie." He says.

"I'm still pissed at you." She says as she points at him. "And deciding your punishment."

Amused, I look at him. "What did you do?"

"I'll explain as I walk you home." He turns to Angie, "Good night Angie."

"Good night James." She whines before sticking her tongue out at him.

I chuckle as I slide my feet into the slippers and Jimmy holds out his hand to help me stand up. He links my arm in his and my fingers instinctively curl into his bicep. He looks down at me and flexes quickly. I laugh.

"There it is." He says.

"What?"

"Your smile. It's like freshly baked chocolate chip cookies on a cold day."

"Haven't heard that one before." I tease.

"I was trying to be original."

"Three and a half stars."

"Ouch." He says as he presses a palm to his chest. "But the bar has been set I guess."

"So why is Angie pissed at you?"

"Ehh, I missed dinner with her, Dad, and Pops."

"That sounds bad."

"It is and it isn't. I left her alone to play referee between those two which is why she's pissed but I also saved her from having to referee between Dad and me too. She didn't see that as a fair trade."

"I see. What will the punishment be?"

"Not sure. Last time, when I forgot to come over and dig out the driveway after a snow storm, I had to stand barefoot in the snow for fifteen minutes which was how long it took her to dig a path for her car that morning."

"Seems fair."

"She's always fair."

"How did the tiling go?" I ask as he turns me down Liz and Kyle's street.

"Really well. The primary bathroom is done. Angie came up with an idea to put a word in the penny tile for the kids bath. She said she'd decide what it is tonight. Something fun, silly."

"That's cute."

"You're cute."

I stop dead in my tracks which pulls Jimmy to a stop too.

"No." I say quickly. Like I'm scolding a puppy.

"What do you mean 'no'?" He asks.

"Stop flirting with me."

"Why?"

"Because you don't want anything to do with me."

"How do you know that?" He challenges.

"Jimmy, there are so many reasons. I'm not from here, I live in the city. I might not have a job to go back to and I might still have a dead cat in my freezer, but I am not staying. I am not flirt-with material."

"I disagree." He leans in and our noses almost touch. "Also, we're going to talk about the dead cat in the freezer thing at a later date."

He grins.

"I'm serious. I don't want you getting attached or getting hurt. I'm trying to manage expectations here."

"I'm a big boy."

"Jimmy." I level with him.

"Nora." He levels back.

I cross my arms and steady my stance. The fuzzy purple slippers take a little bit of credibility out from under me but I will not let this crush go any further.

"Have dinner with me." It isn't an ask this time.

"No." I say out loud even though a voice in my head just giggled 'yes'.

"Have dinner with me." He repeats.

"No." And I have a tough time not smirking.

"Nora," he warns, "I'm not going to say this again. Dinner, Thursday, 7pm. Meet me at The Whale and we'll go from there."

With that he steps up, places a kiss to my temple, and walks away.

I watch him retreat down the sidewalk and then cross the street back towards town. Once he's out of sight I turn around and scuff my way up Liz's driveway and let myself in.

Liz mutters a hello over her shoulder from the sofa and I mumble one back as I walk back to my room. Once I close the door behind me I bite back the smile that spreads across my face.

...

My alarm sounds and I reach over to turn it off. My temple thuds with a headache as soon as I open my eyes so I quickly squeeze them shut. I roll back onto my back and take a deep breath. My limbs feel heavy and sluggish as I roll up.

I didn't drink last night so this must be my first ever emotional hangover. I slowly blink open my eyes and see Angie's slippers on the floor. I stand, slip into them, and shuffle to the kitchen for water.

I turn the corner of the hallway and am greeted by the scene of Katherine struggling to get through the front door carrying three giant shopping bags stuffed to the gills.

"Here, let me help." I say as I reach for one of the bags she has balanced on top of her arms.

"Ah, thank you Nora." She says as she makes her way through the door and sets everything down with a clunk.

"What's all this?" I ask peeking into one of the bags.

"I raided the party store again."

"You what?"

"I went and bought up as many different decorations as I could. If Gina doesn't have anything to work with then my chances of winning are even higher." She says as she steps into the living room and takes a seat.

She turns the TV on to one of the national breakfast shows and kicks her feet up on the coffee table like she didn't just spend five hundred dollars to sabotage her nemesis.

I walk back over to the kitchen for water and find myself drawn into a segment about a baby chimpanzee at a North Carolina zoo who befriended an owl that was nesting just outside his enclosure.

The segment ends and the hosts return to the screen. They're talking about the segment coming up next and how excited they are about it. Something about a new show that the Homecraft Network just announced.

I wonder if that's the same channel making Jimmy's show.

I head back down the hallway to wash up and get dressed. Maybe have some ibuprofen for this headache. I hear jingles for medications and toilet paper as I put on my olive green knit slip dress. The show's theme plays. I can't hear what the hosts are saying but suddenly Katherine sucks in a big gasp of air.

Worried that she's choking or collapsing with a heart attack I come running down the hall. "What? What is it?"

I turn the corner to find Katherine just staring at the TV. I look over her shoulder and see a TikTok video of a guy dismantling a kitchen. I look closer and recognize the very muscular back on the screen.

Jimmy.

Then he turns to the camera and smiles and the clip ends.

The hosts reappear on the screen and under them the banner reads "Showbiz Scoop".

One host is fanning herself with her note cards. The other turns towards the camera.

"He can come to my house for *repairs* any day."

"Clean out the pipes right?" The other one jokes.

"In all seriousness, this series of salacious videos caught the eye of Homecraft Network producer Marla Johnson and she fast tracked a pilot featuring Jimmy Lewis and his interior designer sister. They upgrade homes in upstate New York."

"Yes ladies, the girl talking in the videos is his sister and as far as we know he's single!"

"I have a feeling this will be a popular show when it hits the air."

"I would have to agree." And then the host shifts and begins talking about Imogen Star and her baseball player boyfriend.

Katherine and I look at each other in shock. Her eyes wide in amazement she reaches for her phone and begins typing on it at a pace I hadn't seen from anyone over sixty in my life.

"What are you doing?" I ask her.

"Texting the Tome Raiders." She tells me before she hits send. She looks up at me, "I wonder if Sandy saw this?"

16

Or Are You Just Happy To See Me?

JIMMY

Weird.

Mitchell winked at me when I went in for my coffee this morning.

He's a friendly man but not that friendly.

Maybe he had something in his eye.

I get to the door of the hardware store as Steve steps up too. I unlock the door and pull it open for him but he says "Oh no, after you hot stuff." With a laugh.

Also weird.

I turn on the lights as Steve heads for the paint section and I'm wondering if his wife has finally picked a color for the walls of the nursery. Angie gave her a few choices after their gender reveal party and that feels like a while ago.

I drop my wallet on the desk in the back and my phone buzzes with a text.

Kyle S: Girl are you a construction worker?

What the hell? I swipe open the message.

KYLE

Because you're erecting my pole.

Gross.

What the duck was that?

I'm coming up with pick-up lines for you.
You're gonna need em.

Why would I need pick-up lines?

Did Nora say something to Liz and Kyle last night? That's gotta be good right?

🔗 The Morning Show Showbiz Buzz

I click on the link and two ladies with way too much makeup on are talking about a Homecraft Network show. Then, it cuts to a TikTok video and I appear, working at the Fallons' house. I'm demoing the kitchen with my shirt off. Suddenly the video moves to slow motion as I turn around and smile at the camera.

It's from a TikTok account I've never heard of. I don't have the app so I quickly download it, make an account, and then search the handle.

There, right before my eyes, are dozens of videos of me, with my shirt off, working on various projects. Most of them are in slow motion. I click on one and the comments all say something about thirst, or traps, or being my good girl.

The door chimes with someone entering and I turn around to see Angie standing near the checkout looking contrite.

"Ah, hey Jimbo."

"Don't call me that."

"Ooo-kay. Well, umm, how are you today?"

Little siblings shouldn't get away with everything they try to pull. I decide to temper my anger and play dumb.

"Good actually, Mitchell was very nice and winked at me when I got my coffee. Steve, who is in the back looking at paint, you might want to help him later, called me hot stuff, and Kyle sent me some pick-up lines that I can use."

"Oh, that's nice."

"Yeah, and after I accept the deliveries this morning I'm going back to the Fallons' to start in the kids' bathroom. It's going to be a hot one so maybe I'll WORK. WITH. MY. SHIRT. OFF."

"So you know."

"I'm starting to know."

"Okay, listen. I uploaded the first one on accident. I was showing off some behind the scenes footage of the detail work you were doing, sanding down a shelf so it had a beveled edge. I zoomed out and you were working without a shirt. I didn't even think about it because you never wear a shirt when you're working, so I posted it. I woke up the next morning to thousands of notifications, shares, likes, comments. So I kind of started a behind-the-scenes account for our business that features you working shirtless."

"So you made soft porn of your brother and shared it online?" I deadpan.

"Ew! No. Gross. Well," she thinks about it and then shakes her head to dislodge the thoughts. "No. Not what happened."

"When did Marla contact you?"

"After Imogen Skye shared one of your videos and it went viral." And she has the smarts to be sheepish about this.

"Angie! Seriously?" I yell. I can't keep my anger down anymore.

"I know, I know, I'm sorry okay?"

"We're even." I point at her.

She looks at me like she doesn't understand.

"For me missing dinner last night. We're even. I would argue that I owe you a sentence but I'm too pissed to care right now." I pause and look down at my phone where another video is playing. "No more. Got it?"

"Loud and clear." She says. She pivots away from me and hollers "Steve! I'll come help you make a decision." And she scurries away down the aisle.

I turn towards the office and feel my phone buzz with new notifications. Not wanting to deal with any of it I turn my phone off and sit down at my desk.

The front door chimes and I have a feeling I won't be left alone today.

"Just a minute!" I call with frustration. I take a deep breath, slip off my cap, run my hands through my hair, and stand up. When I look towards the door of my office, Nora is walking in. She stops when our eyes connect.

My blood pressure eases as I take her in. My heart is pounding for a different reason. The green dress she's wearing hugs her body, showing every curve. The green makes her red hair shine and her blue eyes sparkle. She looks gorgeous, like a spring morning.

I round my desk and she takes another step into my office. "Hey Gorgeous." I say. "Nice shoes."

She looks down at the purple slippers Angie dropped off for her yesterday. She looks back up at me and shrugs. "They're insanely comfortable. I'm not giving them back."

I lean back and sit on the edge of the desk. She's just out of arms' reach. We look at each other and both of us are frozen to the spot.

"I didn't expect to see you today." I say.

"I thought maybe you'd need a friend." She says as she takes a half step closer to me.

She blinks and I think my chance to hold her is gone until she takes two quick steps forward and presses her body against mine.

Her arms fling around my neck and she squeezes. I wrap my arms around her and nuzzle my head into the side of her neck. Her floral and spice perfume sends a signal straight south and my arousal thuds against my fly.

I kiss her neck, softly, testing. She leans her head a little further away making more of her neck available to me and I continue to kiss along her pulse up to her jaw.

She pulls herself back a bit. Her eyes are closed and her fingers thread through the hair at the back of my head. I run one hand up to the base of her neck and bring her mouth to mine as the other hand slides down her back to her hip where I pull her closer to me.

Nora steps between my legs and tilts her head so she can deepen the kiss. I settle back and put her in control of our connection. As our kiss continues, Nora consumes me. My body and soul working together to tattoo her on my heart.

Someone clears their throat and it isn't Nora or me.

I break the kiss and allow Nora to slide her head to my shoulder. I look over hers and see Angie standing with her hand clasped over her eyes.

"What?" I growl.

"Ah, the lumber delivery is here." She squeaks out and she quickly turns away.

I slide my hands to Nora's waist and pull her back so she's standing in front of me. She rolls her shoulders back and stands up straight.

"Remember, don't." She whispers.

"Don't what?"

"Go falling in love with me." And with that she brings her hand to my face, her thumb runs over my kiss-wet lips. Then she pulls her hand back and curls it into her chest.

She turns around and walks out. I hear her talking with Angie but I can't hear what they're saying. Instead I take a few breaths, let my body settle down, and head towards the loading dock in the back.

...

Luckily Mike, the lumber delivery driver, didn't know about my social media fame. But that's where my luck ran out.

On the drive over to the Fallons' I got honked at, catcalled, and whistled at. I have a feeling I'm never going to live this down. I pull my truck into the driveway and see that Marla and Dax are already there.

"Good morning super star!" Marla announces when I get

out of the truck. The camera is already pointed at me and I scowl.

"We need to talk." I mutter as I get closer to her.

"About what?"

"About the fact that you decided to do this show based on just barely safe for work videos."

"What's there to talk about?" And she has the audacity to look confused at my anger.

"Marla, I did not agree to do this show to become some celebrity or a sex symbol." I shudder at the thought. "I am a small town, family business owner who helps people improve their homes."

"And you look really good while doing it." Marla adds.

I roll my eyes. "Let me just ask this, if it hadn't been for the videos would you have contacted us about the show?"

"Probably not. No."

At least I have my answer. I don't feel any better about the situation. I feel used, exposed. When Angie first got me on board with doing the show she sold me on the fact that it would bring money into Lakeville and we'd be able to do more for the town with more resources.

That's still true.

And while it was annoying to get the attention from people in town, do I really care if strangers watch videos of me? Especially since I didn't make them trying to get attention. My well-intentioned but misguided sibling did it.

Marla gets a phone call and walks across to the other side of the drive way to take it. Dax is kind of avoiding eye contact with me and while that's annoying I'm going to let it slide while I think about my situation.

Do I want to worry about videos of me on TikTok?

Do I want to care that the videos are the reason we got this opportunity?

Can I go back to a time when I didn't even know they existed and continue to operate as usual?

Maybe I'll just keep my shirt on when the camera is around.

But then I consider that it's only 10 in the morning and the day is already uncomfortable. August in upstate New York is hot and muggy. If this morning hadn't happened, I would already have taken my shirt off to work. But today I'm going to suffer through and keep this worn cotton on my shoulders. I'm not sure I'm ready to exploit myself for this opportunity.

It's the principle of the matter.

Okay, it's settled.

Work as usual, head down, but with a shirt on.

Angie texted me late last night with some pictures of the word 'fresh' inlaid in penny tile. We went back and forth and decided on a script style. She's headed up to Rochester tomorrow to pick up the few sheets of tiles we need for the wording and I'll mark the space out in the tiles today.

I head up the stairs and get started. Marla and Dax follow.

"Can you put your mic on?" Dax asks.

"Oh, yeah sure."

I string the mic cord up through my shirt and it gets caught a little so my abs are showing. I look up and see that Dax is recording.

Is this whole thing a practical joke? Maybe it is. I mean, bravo to Angie for all this planning and coordination and I'll give her credit, the production value is high. And she's got the whole town fooled.

I could be embarrassed. Humiliated. But I'm starting to believe that Angie is going to jump out of the closet later and yell, "Punked!"

Or maybe this is serious and the primarily female demographic of the Homecraft Network is demanding content like this.

Want the truth about what is really bothering me? Here it is. I only want one woman to see me without my clothes on. Nora. She agreed, in her way, to go out to dinner with me. I couldn't fall asleep last night because I was trying to plan something special. And then this morning when she walked into my office and offered me comfort I wanted to drag her upstairs with me and shut out the world.

There has to be a future for us.

And I can tell that frightens her.

It frightens me too, but instead of walking away from the unknown, I'm drawn to it. To her. She's smart, she's confident, she's hot as hell.

And I know she finds me attractive, it is written all over her face. Yesterday morning it was amusing to see her flustered. Knowing she was battling herself to keep away from me.

I lean back on my heels and smirk. She wants me. I'm sure she does. But something is holding her back.

An idea pops into my head. A way to catch her affection.

I turn around and look at Dax. He's leaning against the door frame and holding the camera up.

"Hey man, cut for a second."

"Sure. What's up?" He sets the camera down on the counter.

"Where's Marla?"

"She's outside on a call with LA. They are figuring out how to capitalize on the segment this morning."

I manage to refrain from an eye roll and remember that this could be an opportunity for the town.

"You've been in this business for a while right?"

"A few years." He chuckles. He's in his late forties at least.

"Okay so tell me. Do you think it's a good idea to play up my, ah, appeal?"

He smiles. "You have to consider the options. One is that you don't play into it and your show is just about a brother and a sister who renovate homes in their hometown. Or on the other hand," he holds out his hand palm facing up and lifts it a bit, "you could stand out and make your show unique."

"Wouldn't I become a joke?"

"Yeah, but we could figure out how to make it seem like you're in on the joke. You could turn to me and say 'you ready for this?' and then you take your shirt off. If the audience knows you're in on the joke then they're laughing with you, not at you."

I think about it, that's an interesting point. I could make it cheesy but also give the people what they want.

"Would Marla be mad if we make it a joke?"

"Marla wants to make money." He looks over his shoulder and then back at me. "Honestly? I think people would be weirded out if they tuned in to see you renovate a home and ended up with a striptease. I think joke is the way to go."

"I do too." I stand up straight. "Is the lighting good?"

"It's perfect."

I turn towards him, clear my throat, and nod at the camera.

He picks it up and gets it situated. He gives me a quick nod and flashes his gaze up to me before I see him go back to the view finder.

"You ready for this?" I ask.

Pause.

Then I reach behind my head and pull my shirt off by the collar. Once it's off I run my hand down my chest to wipe some of the sweat away.

Dax silently chuckles and then turns the camera off.

"Perfect man." He says and he reaches out to shake my hand.

"I hate to admit it, and you can never tell Angie because I'm going to hold this over her head forever, but that was kind of fun."

I hand him my phone.

"Okay, help me with another."

17

Nips, Pool Noodles, and Balloons, Oh My.

Nora

"My fingers are cramping." I complain. For the last hour and a half I have been stringing beads to create curtains for a pontoon boat. Each strand is five feet long.

And we need fifty of them.

We still don't know what Gina's plans are so it is all hands on deck to make this pontoon boat the swankiest in history.

The Tome Raiders chat has been blowing up as the news of Jimmy's morning show fame started spreading. Even Liz texted to say she got asked by some old college friend if she knew him.

I stand up and crack my knuckles while Katherine finishes typing something on her phone.

"Okay then, let's take a bead break. We need to make outfits for our guests."

I look at her for any sign that she's joking.

There is none.

She's serious. She wants to dress up the celebrity cut outs like they are paper dolls.

She stands and walks into the living room and starts to unroll the black velvet fabric. I watch from the kitchen as I pour myself a glass of water.

"Michelle could wear a gown from this. And," she points to a navy blue fabric, "Timothy Dalton can get a suit out of that."

"Who's Timothy Dalton?"

She looks at me like I just asked if the Pope was Catholic.

"Who is Timothy Dalton?" She repeats. "He's James Bond."

"Oh! Okay, yes a suit for James Bond."

"Now, our friend Jason will be a little bit of a challenge."

"Yeah, vintage goalie mask doesn't exactly scream sexy sophisticated."

"True," Katherine says while tapping her chin. "Actually, what if…"

She trails off lost in thought and doesn't finish her sentence. She starts digging around in the giant bags of items and then brandishes a black marker like a sword.

"Let's make him a thief! We can color his mask so it looks like a ski mask and turn the machete into one of those black bank bags with a dollar sign on the front."

"That's actually a really cute idea Mrs. Collins."

"Call me Katherine silly."

"Right, I forgot."

"So Nora, where did you run off to this morning?"

"Oh, I ah," might as well be honest, there's no way someone didn't see me, "I went to check on Jimmy."

"You've taken a shine to him, haven't you?"

"Sort of."

She looks at me over her reading glasses. Passes her gaze

up and down my face and then turns back to the velvet fabric.

"What?" I challenge.

"Nothing." She says.

Now it's my turn to look her up and down.

"Jimmy is a special boy, that's all. Well, he's hardly a boy anymore. He's a man. But he's been through a lot and this town cares about him."

I'm about to say that *I care about him* but I pull my lips together tight to prevent me from speaking up. A battle of wills is taking place between one part of me that doesn't feel ready to admit that I am developing feelings and an increasingly larger part of me that does.

"Let's get back to those beads." Katherine says. And she turns to walk back to the kitchen counter.

Earlier, when the news segment finished I bolted out the door, heading straight to the hardware store. When I saw Jimmy by his desk he looked worried. My body reacted before my mind did and I threw my arms around him. Then his kiss to my neck sent a heat wave through me.

It felt like he relaxed in my arms. Like some of the worry left his shoulders. I couldn't look at him though. I knew I would see lust, or worse, love in his eyes. Instead I leaned in and kissed him. Hopefully conveying that I was there for him without having to say it.

As I start to string beads again I can feel the way his hands held me while we kissed. The blend of strength and tenderness. He all but admitted yesterday that he cares about me and his touch today confirmed it.

"What's that smile for?" Katherine asks breaking me from my thoughts.

I take a deep breath and look at her. "How did you and Charles fall in love?"

"Oh my! I haven't told you the story?" I shake my head. "Well, get comfortable because it is a doozy."

"A doozy?"

"I don't know, it's the first word that came to mind." I chuckle. "Let's see now, we first met in middle school."

"Really?"

"Yes, and even though middle school is much worse now with all the social media it was still brutal back then. We were all on the verge of puberty and some days it felt like the world revolved around boys and other days they were infested with cooties and you wouldn't touch them with a 10 foot pole for fear of being infected."

"I feel that way now."

"Bet you wouldn't mind catching cooties from Jimmy though would ya?" She teases and I blush. "Anyways, he was the shortest kid on the basketball team and I was the most uncoordinated cheerleader so we spent some time together at the end of the bench. He was nice, but he was new in town and that gave him a mysterious appeal."

"Can 10-year-olds be mysterious?"

"Nora, you have no idea."

I bark out a laugh, "really?"

"Yes, but he wouldn't go steady with any of the girls so we all decided he was gay. Turns out he had a crush on a girl from his old school and wasn't ready to let her go.

"But the gay thing stuck, for better or worse, and he started high school with that on his shoulders. By then he was one of the taller guys on the basketball team and I had traded in my poms for textbooks.

"I had a few other boyfriends in high school, Eugene the mechanic being one of them," she winks at me, yay for her but also, ew, he's greasy. "And then we all went our separate ways for college."

"I thought you got together in college?"

"Listen to the story dear, it's more fun that way."

"Fine."

"Where was I? Oh yes, we all went our separate ways for college. My mother was determined for me to graduate with something besides my M.R.S. degree so I picked nursing. The summer after my freshman year I came home and tutored kids to make money.

"Charles had come home that summer too and he would show up places I was. Now this was before all that GPS and Track My Phone nonsense mind you. He had to do it the old fashioned way," she pauses, "stalking."

I sputter a laugh into my water glass. "Seriously? He stalked you?"

"But in a sweet way, not a scary way. After seeing him at the diner or in the park or at the library when I was tutoring I stopped him and asked him what was going on. He was so startled that I was talking to him that he blurted out that he wanted to take me out to dinner.

"I smiled and said no."

"Why did you say no?"

"Because I was 19 and had a life planned. I wasn't about to date someone from my hometown and settle down."

"But you did end up doing that?"

"Yes. We ended up seeing each other at the Float Fest

carnival and he asked again if we could have dinner together. Before I had a chance to answer he got us hot dogs, handed me one, and took a big bite out of his. He smiled at me while he chewed and it made his eyes crinkle at the sides and I'd never seen anyone cuter in my life."

"That is so sweet, Katherine."

"So we spent that night, ah, what is it you kids say? Chilling? And then we stayed in touch as we went back to school. It wasn't easy but we wrote letters and made calls once a week. Meet up in Lakeville when we could."

"When did he ask you to marry him?"

"He knew I wanted a career and a family. The easiest way to do that was to have the career first. I moved to Albany to start my nursing program and he moved to Boston to start his Masters. We made a plan together. We would work towards our advanced degrees, get married, then he'd finish his PhD and I'd keep working as a nurse.

"Once his PhD was done we moved back to Lakeville so I could be near my parents. I was pregnant with Charlie Jr and then Maggie followed pretty quickly. Once they were both in school, I went back to work. My mother helped with childcare and Charles' schedule meant he could take them to school in the morning.

"By the time Lizzy came along we were a well-oiled machine."

"Sounds like it."

"We were open with each other early on, and we kept talking. It allowed us to support one another and be there if one of us needed the extra coverage."

"You might have the model marriage." I joke.

"Not sure about that but I do know how good I have it. I saw plenty of my friends and coworkers struggle with it all. Don't ask me how I got so lucky, but I am grateful I did."

There really isn't anything to say in response to that. Charles and Katherine's marriage really is the ideal. And the home Liz grew up in is pretty much the opposite of mine.

I know Liz said she felt ignored growing up, and after listening to Katherine talk about her job I could understand how Liz might feel that way, but she was never neglected.

Katherine and I delve into a silence as we string beads. I'm not sure what is on her mind but mine is racing with questions.

Would I want a relationship if it was like theirs?

Have I been saying I don't because I didn't have an example to follow?

Is it possible to have that kind of relationship?

Have I wasted too much time?

If I don't have a job can I bring my whole self to a relationship?

Am I considering Jimmy because I don't have anything else in my life right now and he just popped up out of nowhere?

Is he a crutch?

Or, is it possible he'd be the person who could support me while I figure out what's next?

I'm startled out of my spiraling thought process, thank goodness, when the screen door of the porch opens and slams shut.

"Mom! Get this. I have an idea of what Gina's theme is going to be." Liz whispers as she joins us in the kitchen.

"Why are you whispering?" I whisper.

"Because, Gina could have bugged the place." Liz says as

her eyes scan the corners of the room and her mom nods her head.

"Right." I say with an eye roll. One quick glance at the clock tells me that 2:07 in the afternoon is a good a time as any to start drinking wine.

I move to the kitchen, grab three glasses and pull a bottle of rosé out of the fridge. I pop it open as Liz and her mom whisper to each other with wide eyes.

For the briefest of moments I wish my mom and I could share moments like this. But that would require her to care about anyone besides herself and that's not going to happen.

I bring the glasses to the table and set them in front of the conspirators.

"FIVE HUNDRED NIPS" Katherine shouts out of the blue and causes me to spit the wine I had started to sip back in my own face.

I blink and reach my hand out for a towel and she hands one to me "Sorry Nora," she turns back to Liz. "Gina ordered 500 airplane booze bottles?"

"According to Sal, yes."

"What could she be doing with that, pool noodles, balloons, and spray foam?" Katherine wonders out loud. "Any spray paint orders?"

"I'll text Angie and ask."

"What do you think she's up to?" I ask.

"Well my guess is that's she's going to do some sort of fish tank thing but that seems like a lot of work. Oh no, what if she's doing a James Bond theme?"

"Why would you think that?"

"Like a villain with a huge fish tank in his lair." Katherine's face is etched with worry.

I'm finding it difficult not to laugh.

The three of us spend the next two hours finishing the bead curtains, starting the dress pattern for Michelle, and tidying up as much as we can before Kyle gets home.

18

Ain't Handin' Out Your Number

JIMMY

"Hey Angie, do you have Nora's number?"

"No. You want me to text Liz for it?" She answers from the front of the store.

"Nah, that's okay."

Suddenly Angie is at the door of my office, she's breathing heavily like she ran. "Why do you want her number?"

I lean back in my chair and cross my arms. Angie and I have come to a truce over the last 8 hours but I'm still not sure I'm ready to gab away with her about a girl.

"None of your business." I say.

Angie rolls her eyes but instead of leaving she comes in and sits in the chair in front of my desk. "You two looked pretty cozy this morning."

"I'm sure we did." And I'm still not sure what to make of it. I'm not complaining but why did she come by this morning? Why did she initiate a kiss?

"And she mentioned on her way out that she was meeting you for dinner tomorrow." Angie leads.

"She did?"

"Ohmigod this is so middle school! I will not pass notes back and forth between you two or schedule a locker meet up. You are both into each other just admit it."

"I have admitted it!" I say louder than I mean to. Angie's eyes grow wide.

"Oooooh," she crows. "You like her, like her. What is she playing hard to get or something?"

I rake my hands through my hair. I need to get closer with my guy friends so I don't have to have this conversation with my sister.

"Honestly, I'm not sure what game she's playing. I get the feeling she doesn't either." Angie tilts her head to the side in question. "She has said, over and over, that she doesn't date. That she doesn't do relationships. But at the same time she's opened up to me and came here this morning to check on me. That's relationship-y right?"

I inwardly cringe at the desperation in my voice.

"Yeah it is." Angie pauses to think. "Maybe she hasn't been in a relationship before so she doesn't know what to do. Maybe that's the game she's playing?"

"You think? How could she not have had a relationship before?"

"Well, I haven't." Angie says with a shrug. I get the sense that she's sensitive about this. "And you really haven't since Bethany."

I think about it, she has a point. I haven't had a relationship since Bethany and we started dating in high school. Getting together back then was a matter of making out in public so people knew you were together.

"That's a good point. So it's the deaf leading the blind?"

"Maybe." Angie says with a smile.

"What?"

"Well, I don't think either of you are blind."

Facts. Even a blind man would know that Nora was hot.

"Speaking of…" I start and Angie kind of sinks lower in her chair. "I talked with Dax today."

"You did?"

"Yeah, and we came up with a plan."

"You did."

"Mhmm, we agreed that my appeal is part of the show's appeal but that we could kind of make fun of it. Like be the guy who can't keep his shirt on."

"You are the guy who can't keep his shirt on. That's how all this started." She says with snark.

"Watch it. You're still on thin ice with me." I point at her.

"Got it. So you're going to make it a joke." She says as she leans forward a little.

"Yeah, I'll always either look at the camera right before or right after I take my shirt off. Let the audience know I'm in on the joke. That way it feels like I'm con-sen-ting," I draw out each syllable, "to being on TV with my shirt off."

Angie gulps. "Jimmy, listen, again, I'm so sorry."

"It's fine."

"It is?"

"Yeah, I'm annoyed, a little embarrassed but if the show does well we get to keep doing this. That's what I want."

Angie smiles and stands up. I stand and round the desk and wrap her in a big hug.

"Okay," she says as she steps backwards out of my office. "I'm going to go and look at Gina's plywood order and make sure we have everything in stock."

"Has she shared her plan for Float Fest?"

"No, but Sal said something about nips to Liz so they're trying to figure it out. Katherine is gunning for it this year."

"Like she is every year."

"Facts but this year Katherine took it up a notch and started buying out supplies from Party Towne two months ago."

"Smart." I concede. It's been years since I've decorated a boat for the fest. Well, the last one was the summer before Mom passed away.

Then something strikes me.

"Ange?"

"Yeah?" She says as she turns around in the aisle.

"Does Dad know about the videos?"

"I don't think so, well," she pauses, "not before today at least."

...

The house is dark when I pull up front. That means one of two things. Dad's already passed out or he's out back.

Hoping it's the latter I park the truck in the drive, hop out, and start walking around the side of the house. As I turn the corner I see him, sitting on a plastic chair, looking out over the back yard to the lake. The grill is smoking and he's drinking a glass of iced tea.

"Hey Dad." I say and I lift my hand in a wave.

"Jimmy?"

"That smells good." I say as I get closer. "Burgers?"

"Skirt steak." He says and then takes a sip.

"How was your day?" I ask as I take a seat in a plastic chair next to him.

"Slow," he says as he looks me over.

This is like pulling teeth. I run my hands along my thighs, letting some of the sweat in my palms rub into my jeans.

I open my mouth to speak but he beats me to it.

"Heard you're a celebrity."

"Ha, yeah, something like that."

"I knew those videos were trouble."

I turn to him. "What do you mean?"

"Oh, I saw your sister posting them a few months ago and had a feeling she was up to something. But she never got a chance to do dumb stuff as a teen so I guess she's doing it now."

"Why didn't you say anything?"

"I assumed you knew," he shrugs. "You two are thick as thieves. Always have been." He pauses and looks out at the yard. "You had to be." He mutters.

"Dad," I start.

"Wait Jimmy." He takes a deep breath. "I understand why you skipped dinner the other night. I'm sorry that I drove you away back then." He turns his head towards me. "Everyday for the last fifteen years I've woken up with an ache in my chest."

"I miss her too Dad." I say.

"I know you do." He stands up and goes to the grill to flip the steak over. He closes the lid and turns around.

He's standing up straighter than I remember. He looks stronger. The bags under his eyes are less prominent and he's sporting a little summer tan.

"Pops sat me down after Angie left the other night. I had

been giving him hell about passing me over.

"He looked me straight in the eye and said that he wouldn't leave the store to a ghost and that you had proven yourself man enough to not let your feelings destroy you."

I look down at my hands that are clasped between my legs. When I lift my gaze to him there are tears in his eyes.

"Jimmy, your mother was my reason for breathing. She was my light. My joy. My comfort. She made it possible for me to do everything and without her, well, it felt like I couldn't do anything.

"Pops pointed out that I had been doing things for the last fifteen years. Because even wasting my life away was doing something."

I try not to chuckle because that's a very Pops thing to say.

"I'm not asking to come back to the store, I'm not ready for that. But I am asking that you and I give talking to each other a shot."

"I'd like that Dad." I say, and I mean it.

"Me too." He clears his throat. "Now go inside and get plates and the bag of potato chips. You'll stay and eat with me."

"You sure we can handle that?"

"Won't know unless we try."

...

Dinner with Dad went well. Well enough. It wasn't easy at times but it had it's moments. I told him about the show. About the store. He told me about some landscaping he and Sal have been working on together.

He asked about girls and I didn't know what to say about Nora so I said there was no one special.

The aftertaste of the lie lingered.

What Angie said earlier was true, I don't know what I'm doing in a relationship either. And knowing how Lakeville gossip works I'm sure Nora knows I haven't dated anyone since Bethany.

I'm kicking myself for scheduling the date for tomorrow. It is giving me time to plan, and worry, but if she hadn't come by the store this morning I wouldn't have seen her all day. The idea of not seeing her turns my stomach into knots.

I think that's why I find myself parked outside of Liz and Kyle's house at 10 o'clock at night. It's not creepy. I'm simply drawn to her.

That's romantic right?

"What am I doing?" I ask myself as I drag my hands down my face. I've been parked out here for the last ten minutes. I don't have any reason to go and knock on the door and I doubt that I would come up with one between here and there.

Defeated, I reach to turn the truck on when suddenly someone screams and I am blasted in the face with water.

"Oh shit! His window was open! Run!" I hear Nora holler and then I see her running into the shadows of the side yard. I get out and dry my face off with the hem of my shirt.

Slowly I stalk in the direction she ran. As I get to the screened in porch I see Liz sitting on the sofa with her legs crossed, chest heaving like she just ran a sprint.

Kyle is sitting with one ankle propped up on the opposite knee and has his hand covering his mouth. I'm guessing he's trying to hold in a laugh.

"Where is she." I growl.

"Oh! Hi Jimmy! How ARE you?" Liz says a little too loudly.

"I'm wet." I say.

"THAT'S WHAT SHE SAID!" Nora screams from behind me and as I turn, I am blasted with water again.

I take off running after her and she keeps hold of the hose so every few steps it sprays across my path. She's fast, but I'm faster. I grab her by the waist with both my hands and pull her against my chest.

She swings the hose around so it is spraying down my back and that's when I reach up and grab her hand in mine, hard.

Her body stills and her fingers release the trigger.

"Jimmy," she cautions, "I'm wearing a designer dress that is dry clean only."

"You should have thought of that before you started this."

"You're absolutely right." She placates.

She's breathing heavily and I can feel in the way her balance waivers because her feet are barely touching the ground. I ease my hold on her waist and she lowers down to flat feet. She turns her head up towards me and I gaze into her eyes.

Slowly I start to smile. I see her starting to smile too. That's when I shoot the jet of water at the top of her head.

She gasps but is too startled to get any words out.

"Whoops, my hand slipped." I say with a shrug.

She spins out of my arms and pushes me backwards and I get a front row seat for the moment she realizes she left me holding the hose.

"Don't you dare." She warns me. I swing the spray nozzle

around like it's a lasso. Her eyes turn wild. "Listen, Jimmy," she flicks a strand of wet hair over her shoulder. "I'm sure we can both be adults here."

"I'm sure we can."

"Good. So with that being the case, why don't we just set the hose down and walk back to the porch. Let's get a beer and talk." She starts to take a step towards me with her hands out stretched, mischief twinkling in her sapphire eyes.

"Or," I cock an eyebrow. She looks at me while she takes another step in my direction. "I could keep the hose and walk back to the porch."

"But that gives you an advantage." She says while keeping eye contact. She's now only a few steps away from me.

"With you, I feel like I need all the help I can get."

Her eyes turn softer for a split second. I almost missed it. She steps in closer and is now right in front of me. Our eyes are still locked together.

I look down at her and her lips open slightly. I lean in and press a kiss to her warm lips. As her lips caress mine, her hand reaches up and squeezes the trigger and water blasts us both in the chest.

In my surprise I try to pull back but she jumps onto me like a spider monkey and screams like a banshee. With the arm that isn't trying to wrestle back control of the hose I hold her up under her ass.

We're both drenched and laughing when Sal next door comes out onto his porch and turns on the flood lights.

"Knock it off it's late!" He yells.

"Sorry Sal." I say, breathless, as Nora buries her head in my neck and giggles. "Truce?" I whisper in her ear.

"Truce." She whispers back.

Slowly I lower her to the ground and I drop the hose as well. We both put our hands above our head to indicate that we aren't going to make any sudden movements.

We walk towards the back porch and Kyle tosses me a towel. Liz grabs Nora by the arm they start giggling as she drags her into the house. I shake Kyle's hand and follow him up the steps.

"Beer?" He asks.

"Sure." And I towel off my hair and arms. Nora comes back outside with a glass of wine, settles into the sofa, and tucks her bare feet up under her.

"Not that I'm not glad to see you, but why'd you come over and park outside?" She asks over the rim of her wineglass.

I smirk. "I didn't have your number."

"Why do you need my number Jameson?" She asks with a wise ass smile spread across her face.

"I wanted to text you." I say matter of factly.

Liz and Kyle come back out to the porch. Kyle hands me a beer and we clink the necks together.

"So Jimmy, use any of my lines today?" He asks with a twinkle in his eye. Was it really just this morning that I discovered I was a social media sex symbol?

"Fuck off Kyle." I mutter with a smile as I take a sip. "It's been an interesting day."

"You know, you should have asked me to take your boudoir photos Jimmy, I'm very talented." Liz teases.

"I'll keep that in mind." I reply. Nora is watching this exchange with interest. I turn to her. "What about you? Anything to add?"

"Me?" She says as she raises her eyebrows. "Nope. Well, actually, I would have liked to know right away who I was getting myself involved with. Your fans are not going to like the fact that we've hooked up, twice."

"Eh, my count is at three."

"Three?" Nora questions, as Liz scoots forward to the edge of her seat.

"Yeah, my truck, my place, my office." I say as I lift a finger to tick off each one. "Oh, and just now in the yard." I add another finger to my count.

"Your office and the yard don't count, those were just kisses." Nora says.

"Hold on. When did you kiss him in his office?" Liz asks.

Nora pauses before answering, "This morning." She says quickly then she takes a sip and ducks her chin into her chest.

"Holy freaking mother Gary." Liz says.

"I don't think you have that quite right." I mutter. Liz shoos my comment off like a fly.

"Nora Lucinda Heely," Liz starts, Nora shakes her head in humor. "You have kissed our Jimmy Lewis here on," she looks down at her palm like she's checking her notes, "four different occasions?!"

"Maybe." Nora answers.

Liz slaps her knee. "Well I'll be Hoover Dam-ed."

"What?" I ask looking between the girls who seem to be exchanging some sort of secret code with their eyes.

Liz squares her shoulders to me before turning her head in my direction. She sets her wine glass down on the table and steeples her fingers while balancing her elbows on her knees. Nora rolls her eyes and mutters "here we go" under her breath before taking a sip of wine.

"Never, in my many many, many years of friendship with Nora Alexandria Heely has she ever kissed the same man on four separate occasions."

I smile and look over at Nora.

"Really?" I ask, interested.

Liz answers for her, "Really."

"Interesting. And this whole time she's been telling me not to fall in love with her." I tap my chin with my finger. "Seems like maybe she's falling in love with me."

"Okay, no, wait a minute." Nora says, leaning forward to put her wine glass down. "I'll concede that what Liz has said is true, you," she looks at me, "are the first guy to get me to kiss him four separate times. But, it's only because I'm stuck in this tiny town and Sal's lips look too dry."

Kyle laughs, Liz smirks, and I just stare at this beautiful girl.

"Sal huh?" I ask.

"His overalls are cute." She says with a shrug and picks up her wine glass again.

Now she and I are locked in eye contact and I can feel Liz looking back and forth between us. Kyle clears his throat.

"So, Jimmy, how are things at the Fallons' house?" He asks.

"Great actually, Angie came up with this idea to put the word 'fresh' into the penny tile on the floor when you walk in to the kids' bathroom so that's what I worked on today."

"Oh that's such a cute idea." Liz says. "We'll have to remember that when we redo our bathroom."

"Just let me know when and I'll be here to help."

"How's the show coming?" Nora asks.

"So far so good." I shrug. "I had a chat with the camera man today and we came up with a plan to kind of play into my special talents."

"What's the plan" Nora asks.

"Why do you want to know?" I tease.

"Exactly." Liz adds.

Nora shoots a dagger at Liz. "No reason, just wondering how he's going to handle it."

I stand up, "Actually this shirt is feeling a little uncomfortable now, seeing as it's all wet." I reach for the hem and start to pull it up.

Liz whoops, Kyle starts doing some weird beatbox sound, and Nora covers her eyes with her hand.

"Nah, I won't waste the goods on you guys." I say and then I take the last sip of my beer. "Thanks for the beer Kyle."

"Sure thing man." He says.

Liz stands up and pulls on Kyle's shirt sleeve. "C'mon lets let these two kids say goodbye."

"You're so weird," Nora says as she stands up.

"I know you are but what am I?" Liz retorts before sticking her tongue out as she steps inside.

Nora chuckles and rolls her eyes. "See what I deal with?"

"I do," I throw my thumb over my shoulder, "walk me out?"

"Sure."

I hold open the screen door for her and she steps in front of me. Her bare feet hit the grass and the primal feelings I had a few nights ago flood my system again. I want to tell myself that she's getting comfortable here. Comfortable enough to not put on those sexy, but impractical, strappy sandals. That she's comfortable enough to walk barefoot in the grass.

It's only been a few days but the girl in the pencil skirt seems to have softened and it makes me desire her even more.

"So, how about that number?" I ask as we walk towards my truck.

"Why do you need it again?"

"So I can——"

"Text me." She finishes for me in a baritone voice.

"Yeah, exactly." I say with humor.

"I don't think so Jimmy. I already agreed to dinner tomorrow." She says like it's her final decision.

"That's all the more reason to give me your number." I say as I step up closer to her, she's between me and the truck now.

Her hand reaches up and lands softly on my chest sending radiating heat throughout my body.

"I told you, I don't want you getting attached." She says.

I lean in and whisper, "I don't believe you."

"What do you mean?" She whispers back.

"I think you're the one who doesn't want to get attached. And you're scared because you already are."

I pull back and see her eyes dart from side too side.

"Give me your number or don't Nora, but either way we're having dinner together tomorrow." I say as I step back and walk backwards towards the front of my truck. "Wear something nice."

I toss her a wink and turn. When I climb in, my seat is still wet from where the water was sprayed and I catch her standing by the open passenger window staring at me.

She leans in and crosses her arms on the window. "Be

careful, Jimerson." She says.

"Careful with what?"

"About giving me fashion advice." And with that she turns and walks back towards the house. I smile and start my engine and drive home.

19

The One Where Nora Goes On Her First Date

Nora

Wear something nice.

Dumbhead.

Of course I'm going to wear something nice. My closet has multiple sexy options for weeknight dates.

Problem 1: That closet is in my apartment in the city.

Problem 2: I've never gone on a premeditated dinner date.

Sure, I've eaten with guys before. But usually it goes like this; we meet for the first time while sitting at the bar. We exchange some flirty banter, maybe light touching. He asks if I'm hungry, I say yes. We ask the host for a table, eat, and then enjoy each other for dessert.

In fact, I can afford to add the sexy weeknight clothes to my closet because of the number of free Michelin star meals I have enjoyed over the years.

Which brings me to my next problem.

Problem 3: We're meeting at The Whale.

When I was in there on Monday my shoes stuck to the floor, some of the vinyl of the stool rubbed off onto my shorts, and if Angie hadn't shown up dressed to the nines, like I taught her to, I would have been the dressiest person there. And I was in one of the most casual outfits I own.

I'm standing in front of the guest room closet looking at the few outfit options I have. I lift a white dress out, examine it, and put it back. He's already seen me in my bodysuit and that's not a date night outfit anyways. Guys can't figure those things out and unbuttoning your own onesie in front of him is not sexy. Another option would have been my corset but that garment is a goner.

I turn towards the bed and tuck the towel around me in a little tighter. I look at the leather miniskirt and ribbed high neck tank top I set out earlier. This will have to do.

With my feet snug in the purple fluffy slippers, I sit on the edge of the bed, and look at myself in the mirror. The purple slippers draw my attention and I smile down at them. I'll order Angie a new pair, because at this point these are mine.

My phone buzzes on the bed next to me and I reach over pick it up. It's a TikTok message notification.

I open up the app and go to my messages. I tap on the username and am greeted with a video of Jimmy flexing his back. A smile immediately spreads across my face.

Under the video there's a message.

CountryCraftsman31:
Get *back* to me soon.

I laugh because it's just so corny. With a girlish grin across my face I start typing my reply.

StylishSleuthNH:
That's a back-handed way to
get my number.

CountryCraftsman31:
But it got you talking back to
me.

StylishSleuthNH:
Back up, how did you get my
handle?

CountryCraftsman31:
Back channels.

Little laughs of air leave my nose with each rapid fire response. The part of me that hates how much I am enjoying flirting with Jimmy is shrinking away to the back corner of my mind.

StylishSleuthNH:
Well this back-and-forth has
been fun but I need to get ready.
I've got a date tonight.
I hope he can handle it.

CountryCraftsman31:
Right back at-cha.

...

I park on the street in front of The Whale. I considered walking to town but these heels aren't the most comfortable ones to walk long distances in.

I did not do it because I hoped to spend the night at Jimmy's and then drive myself home in the morning instead of walking through town in the light of day.

Nope.

Not even a little bit.

Liar.

I straighten out my miniskirt and drop my keys into my purse. I push the door open to The Whale and the stale beer smell hits me like I've walked into a locker room. I exhale through my nose and question why I agreed to this.

At the bar I take a seat and order a gin and tonic. The bartender delivers it and asks if I want to start a tab when I feel a hand on my lower back.

I turn and watch as Jimmy says "put it on mine" to the bartender before he turns towards me and flashes a smile.

"Hi Nora." He says and my insides melt a little.

"Hi." I reply. I take a second to look him over. He's in a light blue button up shirt and the top two buttons are open which delivers a hint of his chest hair, the sleeves are rolled up to expose his muscular forearms. The hand in his pocket pulls the shirt to the side and offers a view of blue jeans that fit him perfectly. Not too tight but not baggy. He has a pair of white sneakers on.

No baseball cap tonight. Instead his thick hair is swept back, still curling slightly behind his ears and at his neck. He trimmed his beard so it is tidy but still full.

"I thought you only had one dress shirt?" I tease and take a sip of my drink through the straw.

"I went and got something new for our date." He steps back and does a little twirl. "Do you like it?"

"You went shopping without me?" I ask, offended.

He laughs. "I won't let it happen again."

"See that you don't."

The bartender sets down a beer for Jimmy and he picks it up. There is a bead of condensation on the outside that runs down the bottle and drops onto my bouncing knee. The droplet is freezing against my heated skin.

Jimmy leans in to whisper something in my ear. I lean forward a little bit and inhale his fresh scent.

"I'm nervous Nora." He whispers.

I pull back and look him in the eye. There's no hint of teasing in his features. Instead his eyes bore into mine and there is almost a fear in them.

"Wow," I say and I fan my face with my hand. "You are leading off by dropping truth bombs like that? It's a first date!" I say as I toss my hair over my shoulder. He looks at me and smiles. My heart opens to him and so I lean in and whisper, "me too."

"I know." He says as he lets his hand drag down my arm to rest on my knee leaving a path of firework ash in its wake. He clears his throat. "So, you have a decision to make. The Whale has the best nachos I have ever tasted but I want only the best for my girl on our first date. So I have reservations at three different restaurants."

"Oh boy, you came prepared."

"Like I said, I'm nervous. I've had to channel this energy

into something and there was no more work to do at the site today so I looked up restaurants for two hours."

"Two hours?"

"Yeah," he concentrates on twirling his beer bottle on the bar.

"That's thorough." I tell him with a smile. "What are the options?"

"Well, two towns over there is a tapas restaurant that got a lot of good Facebook reviews. Then south of us about twenty minutes is a microbrewery that is supposed to have the best burgers in the area. Finally, there's Sandy's picnic."

"Sandy? Tome Raider Leader, Scoops & Sips Café, Sandy."

"Yes, she packed a picnic for us."

"She did?"

"Yes. Liz told her mom about our date and Mrs. Collins told the Tome Raiders, and Sandy showed up at the store this afternoon with a basket packed full of food."

"This town moves fast."

"Only when it comes to good gossip," He says as he takes a sip of his beer.

"Hmmm." I draw out the decision. "Let's do Sandy's picnic basket."

"Yeah?"

"Yeah." And I drain the rest of my drink and set it back on the bar.

Jimmy pulls out some cash and leaves it on the bar. He gives a wave over his shoulder at the bartender before placing his hand on my lower back and ushering me to the door.

"Where are we going to have this picnic?" I ask as we step outside.

"Well," he sticks his hands in his pockets. "I've got a spot if you don't mind a short drive."

I look down and rotate one foot on the stiletto heel, "As long as I won't be walking much I'm game."

"Honey, I'll make sure of it." He says as he reaches for my hand. Glitter travels through my veins slowly like molten lava at his easy use of this affectionate term. No guy has used a pet name for me before.

Jimmy threads his fingers through mine and spins his grip to keep our connection as we reach his truck. He opens the door for me and lets me use his arm to steady myself as I climb in. Everything about this night is new, including the collection of emotions I'm experiencing.

Nervous and excited.

Comfortable but on edge.

Terrified and, happy?

Is that what I am?

I've felt accomplished. I've felt proud. I've felt in control.

This is the most chaotic my life has been since I was a child, and I should be working tirelessly to get it back under control, but instead I'm going out with Jimmy for a picnic dinner packed by the town gossip.

Who am I? And what happened to the old Nora Heely?

Jimmy drives us north out of town, a direction I haven't traveled yet. We continue around the lake for a few minutes. We pass the Inn and the entrance to the summer camp Kyle manages.

He has the windows open and I let my hand roll through the air as he drives. The radio is on but it's low. I can't tell what the music is.

Jimmy turns left onto an unmarked gravel road and I bounce a little in my seat. The rocky ground drowns out the radio completely. There's only room for one vehicle on the narrow road and the trees are so close I can almost touch them.

Suddenly the tree cover opens up and a large empty lot appears with a view of the lake. There's a dock in the water and a shed near the tree line but no other building.

Jimmy does a three point turn so the back of the truck faces the lake and then he turns off the engine and climbs out. He comes and opens my door and helps me down.

"Where are we?" I ask.

"It's a parcel of land. Someone will build a home here one day but for now it's mostly used for camping."

"I'm regretting my miniskirt." I say as I take a few steps towards the lake.

"I'm not." Jimmy says from behind me.

I turn and glare at him but he only smirks and motions for me to come back towards the truck. He steps to the tailgate and unlatches it. He climbs up and pulls a blanket away which reveals another blanket laid out on the bottom of the bed and several pillows scattered around. The picnic basket is in the middle.

I look at up at Jimmy with a question in my glare as he jumps back down to me. Before I can get my question out he holds up his hand.

"Let me stop you right there, Angie helped me set this up because she owes me for a lifetime for the videos, and if you had picked the tapas restaurant or the microbrewery I would have rushed through those meals only to bring you here afterwards."

"A man with a plan."

"Sometimes." He shrugs and puts his hands on my waist.

He lifts me up to the tailgate and my butt lands with a thud. I curl my legs to the side and make my way onto the blanket. He sits down across from me and pulls the basket towards him.

"Alright, let's see what we've got." He says.

We both peer inside and find bowls of mixed nuts, a tray of cut up fruit, a plate of cheese and crackers, a large fudge brownie in a pastry bag, and three bottles of wine.

"So Sandy's plan is to get us drunk." I remark as I pull out one of the bottles.

"Seems so." Jimmy says with a laugh as he starts to unpack the food. "Although, we don't need any help from booze to get together."

I look down at the bottle in my hand and slowly realize that he's right. All of the times we'd been together I hadn't been drinking at all. Well, one beer at the bonfire but that hardly counts as anything.

Usually I need two or three glasses of wine at the bar or at dinner before taking a guy home. They usually have bourbon, whiskey, or scotch, sometimes red wine. It's never been sloppy but it's never been entirely sober either.

"Nora," Jimmy says and he looks at me. "I'm dying here." He rubs his hands on his jeans. "I'm so nervous because a date has all these expectations tied to it." He takes a deep breath. "I'm just gonna level with you."

"Okay." I say with a little laugh.

"I haven't dated anyone in a long time. I started dating my last girlfriend in high school. I have no idea what I'm doing but I do know that I like you, a lot. I enjoy talking with you. I look forward to seeing you." He pauses, "and I find you sexy as hell."

I blush and look down at the cracker I had picked up off the tray, suddenly finding the grains of salt on top fascinating.

"I'm sure I'm not as smooth as the guys you normally date in the city, but tell me what to do and I'll do it. I want to make sure you have a good time."

"Sexually?" I tease before looking back up at him.

I did not expect his gaze to darken.

"Tell," he pauses, "beg. Same difference."

I flash my eyes down to his crotch and feel my heart rate speed up. He leans over and whispers "Now tell me something honest Nora."

I swallow hard. Honest? Where do I begin?

That he is the sexiest man I have ever met?

That I have broken all my rules for him?

That I want to jump on top of him as soon as possible and then later tonight just talk to him?

"Honest? Well, Jamestown, I already know we're good together physically but," I pause and look off towards the shoreline, "I am terrified that we might be good together in other ways. Emotional ways."

"Why does that scare you?"

"Because I do everything alone."

He sits up and instead of pouncing on my vulnerability, or making some sort of innuendo joke about doing things alone, he reaches for a piece of cheese and brings it to my lips.

I take a bite and he pops the other half into his mouth. He looks out over the lake as he chews. After he swallows he turns to me and says, "then let's figure out how to do this together."

20

I'm Not Finished With You Yet

Nora

I don't think I have ever just watched the sun set.

I'm sitting between Jimmy's legs with my back to his chest and together we watched as the reflection of the sun on the lake changed from orange, to purple, to midnight blue. The moon's reflection now casts a glow across the water.

We haven't spoken in several minutes, but instead of my mind racing with questions and doubt, I've simply observed. Sat quietly noticing the colors, the slight ripples in the water, the leaves rustling in the trees.

"Part of me doubted if I'd have enough to say tonight." Jimmy says.

"Really? You've been carrying the conversation so far." I say, and he has. He has lead us on discussions of cooking, baseball, and has asked me questions about fashion and shopping. He touched on my job a little bit but I deflected. I got him talking about building a custom home for himself and he really lit up.

"Well you ask good questions." He says.

"That's something I learned on the job. Asking questions gets a prospect to open up and they slowly drop cookie crumbs about their interests and desires. Then we can tailor our ask to suit them."

"Makes sense. What's the biggest deal you've closed?"

"I did a 12 million dollar bequest last fall."

"Woah!" He leans forward to look at my face. "That's a lot."

"It was, and it was with a prospect our client had been trying to secure for a few years so it felt good to be the one to bring it home."

"What do you do to prepare for a meeting?"

"Look at you with the good questions!" I say as I turn and look at him over my shoulder. "We actually have databases on the donors. We can see their giving history to the school, and we cross reference with our other organizations to see if they give anywhere else. Like the symphony or something. Then there are pages of notes from every meeting someone in our firm has ever had with the person. I'm talking details on their kids, spouses, affairs, cars, vacation homes, everything."

"Whoa."

"Yeah it's kinda creepy but I never let them know I have all that information the first time we meet."

"How does that work?" He asks.

"Questions." I smile. "I get them to open up and share some of the information I already have and then we keep the conversation going."

"Interesting. I never knew this kind of thing was a job."

"I didn't either until I got to college." I pause but Jimmy doesn't say anything so I continue. "I was a junior and needed to apply for more scholarships. My advisor sent me to the development office to ask if there were any obscure funds I might qualify for."

"What does that mean?"

"So sometimes people designate their gifts for like, I dunno, Redheads from New Jersey with 3.95 GPAs and Cat Stickers on Their Planners."

"You have cat stickers on your planner?"

"Had, Jimmy, I *had* cat stickers on my planner."

He laughs.

"Turns out I qualified for a few smaller scholarships so I secured them and was able to buy my books for two semesters with the funds. The development office lady, Claudia, would chat with me when I came in and I just found her job interesting.

"She believed so strongly that the work she did would help others and I was the one sitting there receiving the help. My senior year I started helping her in the office. Then I heard about Fosters and set my sights there."

I stop talking for a minute while I remember the way that Claudia had taken my picture at graduation when Mom didn't show up on time. How she helped me work on my résumé. How she still checks in on me a few times a year.

Jimmy is trailing his knuckles up and down my arms which are resting on his thighs. Heat radiates off of him and warms my entire body. I'm comfortable, cozy, and Jimmy's hands on my arms is soothing.

These sensations of comfort and trust must be why I've let myself open up. I barely know him and I've told him stuff I haven't even told Liz. These are the parts of me that I keep protected. Things that don't get to see the light.

That's the only way to prevent shadows from falling upon them. If the cruel world got it's hands on Claudia's importance to me I'd be devastated. Updating her on my life, my goals, is a brief moment where I can soak in the appreciation of someone else.

Of someone who is more of a mother to me than mine will ever be.

"You're incredible." Jimmy whispers.

"Yeah, well, someone has to be." I quip and then I lift my body and hug my knees to keep me from leaning against him. Jimmy doesn't laugh at my line. Probably because I've scared him off. I was too honest. Too vulnerable.

"Let's head back." Jimmy says as he stands up. He goes to take a step and he limps, hisses, and violently shakes his foot.

"Oh fuck! My foot's asleep." He continues limping around the truck bed. It's like something a cartoon character would do. Girly giggles are bubbling up my chest and I find myself laughing at his discomfort.

"It's not funny!" He cries. "It's painful!" He slows himself down and tries to walk normally.

"I'm sure it is. Will you be able to get down?" I ask, realizing that could be a problem.

"Just leave me." He says dramatically, draping an arm over his eyes. "Save yourself Nora!" He performs an interpretative version of the dying swan as he collapses back down on the blanket.

I watch the whole thing from where I'm standing in the middle of the blanket. He's laying below me now. He lifts himself up on one elbow and reaches his hand out to run his fingers up the front of my foot to my ankle. He looks up at me and I stare down at him. Something flashes in his eyes and he moves himself to kneeling.

I'm frozen to the spot. His eyes have darkened with lust and I find my inner walls contracting around nothing. The intensity of this instant reaction is something I've only experienced with Jimmy. My knees quiver as he comes closer and runs both his hands up the back of my legs. Their heat radiates through my entire body and I feel my knees quiver. He reaches the hem of my skirt and toys with it. So close to touching me where I need him most.

I bite my lip to keep myself from panting.

"Jimmy." It's a plead.

"Nora." It's a promise.

I look down to see his eyes reflecting the need in mine. He rises off his heels and his head is lined up to my center. Keeping his eyes locked with mine he stands up, dragging his hands up my hips to my waist. He leans down and kisses me while pulling my body towards his. My hands anchor me on his biceps.

Jimmy pulls his head back and looks at me. My eyes are searching his for a clue as to what's next. He brings his head forward and his mouth lines up with my ear.

"It's time for dessert. Can you keep quiet while I eat you out right here?"

The words to answer him are stuck in my throat. I nod and his grip on my hips tighten. I can already feel my arousal pooling between my legs.

Jimmy tugs down on my hips and helps guide me back down to the blanket. He slides a pillow under my head before positioning himself between my legs.

I close my eyes and concentrate on feeling his every move.

The way his rough fingers slide up my outer thigh, dragging my skirt with it.

The way his beard scrapes against my soft skin.

The warmth of his breath as he lowers himself down to me.

With one hand he hooks my underwear off to the side. Opening me to him like a curtain. I start to roll my hips to chase any friction I can but his other palm grips my thigh and stills me.

Slowly he glides his thumb through my seam, spreading my wetness. I glance down when I feel his fingers leave me, my thong snaps back into place. Then I watch as he swipes his knuckles along his lips. My head rolls back to the pillow.

"Jimmy." I whimper.

That's all it takes, his mouth lands on me, his tongue working quickly, while he holds my panties off to the side. He pulls on the fabric which delivers a delicious pressure around my waist while he sucks my mound into his mouth.

My teeth bare down on my bottom lip to trap my moans. My insides begin to flutter.

"Oh…my…god…yes." I grit out.

Jimmy responds by burying his head between my legs and drawing me into his mouth. My head is rolling side to side and my hands are white knuckling the blanket.

Suddenly Jimmy's hands leave me and I curl up onto my elbows to see what pack of wild horses is dragging him away. His eyes are closed and his mouth is still on me over my panties but his hands are working his fly open.

He uses one hand to pull himself from his boxer briefs and

he grips his cock at the base. His other hand returns to move my thong to the side as his mouth connects again with my bare skin. I lay back down and relish how hard he got while getting me off.

He continues his rhythm and even with the image of his delicious manhood in my mind, I've fallen into a trance. Sensations continue to bloom from my center but the tension is no longer building.

I've plateaued. It was so good to start, and it doesn't feel bad now, just steady. Almost relaxing. I try to tune in to what he's doing, the feel of him, but there's no increased pressure.

I've lost my orgasm. I'll slip into a performance of an orgasm just to give him the satisfaction. It started off so good. He's so hot. He knows exactly where to touch me. But I lost it.

I try one last time to feel him and get myself back on course. The tickle of his beard. The warmth of his breath, the pressure of his tongue. C'mon Nora, find it.

"Nora?" Jimmy says.

I look down at him and he's crouched on all fours looking up at me. Our eyes connect and he leans forward, closer to my stomach. I can see the way his pulse is fluttering at the base of his neck and my heart pounds against my breast bone.

"I'm not finished with you yet." He says before he places both hands on my hips and rolls me to my stomach.

Then he pulls my hips up so my back is arched and my head rests on my folded arms. He uses both hands to slide my thong down to my knees. I feel a rush of arousal travel to my center from the change in position.

Jimmy leans over me pressing his chest to my back. He pulls a piece of hair over my shoulder and whispers, "Spread your legs Nora."

I pull my knees apart, straining the fabric of my thong. The elastic digging into my thighs. Jimmy runs his hand down my backside and then pushes three fingers inside me. I gasp at the fullness, the pressure.

He increases the speed of his fingers as they curl out and return to me again and suddenly I'm clenching around him. The pressure is building. My clit is throbbing.

I feel him lower himself and he grazes his teeth against my butt cheek. He pulls his fingers out slowly and I feel empty. My insides clenching around nothing.

Then his mouth is on me again. His tongue is exploring inside my entrance while his hand grips my ass hard. I tuck my head under to try and watch him eat me out from behind but all I can see is the way he strokes himself.

He grips his base, slides his hand up, curls his palm over the top and flips his hand to run back down his length. He pumps a few times and runs his hand back to the tip.

The pattern will be a salacious core memory.

His tongue brings me back to my own pleasure as he taps it against my clit. He draws me into his mouth and sucks while continuing to flick the swollen nub.

Once.

Twice.

I feel liquid flood between my legs. My limbs are shaking. Not just my legs but my arms are trembling which has never happened to me before. Behind me Jimmy grunts and he slips his thumb inside me.

It's just enough friction to finish me. I barely remember to keep quiet while I experience the shockwaves of bliss shooting through my veins.

Jimmy carries me through my orgasm, massaging my insides and slowly running his tongue up and down my slit.

He rests his forehead on my ass and I feel the increase in speed as he handles himself. I curl to look between my legs and feel his heaving breath along the back of my thigh. Suddenly his hand stops and squeezes at his base. I watch as the first ribbon of him explodes onto the blanket. He slowly runs his hand higher up his shaft and another follows.

Right now he is everything I could ever desire.

And I feel desired by him.

He rolls his forehead and places a kiss on my hip as he tucks himself back into his pants. He gently pulls my thong back up my legs. When he tries to pull my skirt down into place it doesn't budge.

I push up onto my knees and bring my legs closer together before pulling the skirt down into place. Jimmy stands behind me and I pivot around so I'm kneeling in front of him.

He brushes his fingers against my face and stops at my chin. He tugs and I rise up, steading myself on his legs, then abdomen, then chest as I stand.

He leans down and kisses me gently. Our breaths regulating together. Then Jimmy rests his forehead against mine and I close my eyes.

"Stay with me." He whispers.

It isn't a question.

I tilt my chin to press a kiss to his lips. "Okay."

21

No More Games

JIMMY

I will die a happy man. At this very moment. Everything could fade to black and I would have no regrets.

And if I ever find myself needing to pick one, Nora's pussy is what I want for my death row meal. Fuck. She was sweet, sour, warm, soft, wet.

I hold her hips as she slides off the edge of the tailgate. When her feet hit the ground I press myself up against her and she pushes herself back into me.

A give and take.

That's what it has been with us. One of us giving, the other taking and then giving it right back.

I open her door and hold her hand as she climbs in.

"So, Jimothy, are we just going to tear each other apart tonight or do you have something else besides sex planned?"

I pretend to think about it. "Nope, just sex."

She grins. "Good."

"But maybe we make it interesting." I venture. I closer her door and wink at her through the windshield as I walk to my side. We shared so much earlier, but my craving for Nora Heely knows no end. I want to know what makes her laugh, cry, angry, hungry.

"How so?" She asks as soon as I open my door.

"A game."

Her eyebrows raise. Good, she's curious.

"What kind of game?" She asks as I drive us back out to the main road.

"20 questions."

"Like the guessing game?" She asks, a little disappointed.

"More like, 20 questions to get to know each other. The basics."

"That's not a game." She says as she crosses her legs and starts bouncing her black stiletto clad foot. Nora is tall but in the front seat of my truck there's enough room for her and she's not afraid to use it. "That's a stall tactic while you get the feeling back in your dick."

I laugh. "True. You haven't gotten your hands on him yet tonight and he's already asking for electrolytes." She smiles. "But I'm thinking quick touches or kisses as a reward for each question."

"Interesting. That could be fun."

"You first." I say quickly.

"What's your favorite position?" She asks as she places her hand on my thigh.

"Going for the big guns I see."

"It's important information. So, what is it Jimmy?"

"From behind. Second is when your ankles are resting on my shoulders and I get to hold your legs against me while I pound into you."

I see her pulse flutter at the base of her neck. Her breathing increases. She knows I just delivered an answer to her question and a promise for later.

"My turn." I reach across the console and grip her thigh. "How do you take your coffee?"

"That's your question?"

"I want to get to know you." I counter.

She shakes her head in a laugh as she crosses her arms over her chest. "I like my coffee black, like my underwear." She pauses. "Sometimes with a splash of almond milk."

"Almond milk in your underwear?" I ask.

"Coffee."

"Ah, got it." She smiles at my showman ship. "Your turn Nora."

She brings her hand up to the back of my head and plays with the hair along my neck. "Do you like dogs or cats?"

"I've never had a pet but I like your pussy."

"Smooth." And she rolls her eyes at me. I grin back at her and squeeze her thigh hard.

She laughs and I love that I've broken through her tough outer skin to see the more playful side of her. "Morning person or night owl?" I ask.

"Night owl."

I make a gameshow buzzer sound and her eyes grow wide. "Sorry, wrong answer."

"There can't be a wrong answer. That's not how it works."

"Well, I'm a morning person and I just don't see this working out now that we're so different so, sorry Nora I'm taking you home."

"First of all, I drove here myself." She crosses her arms.

"And second, that doesn't matter because I don't mind being woken up for morning sex and then falling back asleep."

It's my pulse that flutters this time at the though of lazy, warm, morning sex with Nora before starting my day.

"We'll table this issue for now." I say then I turn onto Willow Beach Road towards my apartment.

"My turn." Nora says as she pulls her shirt off over her head. Her black lacy bra barely contains her silky breasts and I am seriously regretting my own game right now. Thankfully there aren't other cars on the road because I'm distracted. "What makes you cry?"

I flash my eyes up to her face and see that she's serious. The fact that she took her shirt off before asking me that question ignites a fire in my soul. Fuck yeah, she wants to get to know me. What makes me tick. But she's hiding it behind a veil of sexuality. I'm definitely not complaining and I'll let her do what she feels she has to in order to protect her heart.

I look back out to the road and answer her question.

"Certain movies, and visiting my mom's grave."

"Ah shit, Jimmy I'm sorry, I didn't mean to bring that up." Nora rushes through her words and pulls her shirt in front of her beautiful chest and holds it to her. "I was trying to razzle you."

"It's fine. I'll ask you a silly question next to lighten the mood."

"You sure?"

"Nora, honey, you took your shirt off and then covered yourself back up, I'll do anything." She breathes out a laugh. "What's your favorite flavor of ice cream?"

"Mint chocolate chip. Yours?"

"Same."

"Does that negate our morning person versus night owl incompatibility?"

"When you mentioned morning sex I decided you were flawless."

She stares at me and I can see how her mind goes to the same images as mine. I pull into my parking spot, turn off the truck, and get out. When I open her door I swivel her in the seat. I place one hand on her thigh, the other at the back of her head, and bring her mouth to mine.

She immediately deepens the kiss by opening her mouth and pushing her tongue against mine. I bring her to me and lift so she slides off the seat. Her toes hit the runner board and she breaks the kiss.

"Jimmy, what question were we on?"

"That one right there was number twenty." I tell her firmly. I lower my voice. "Get upstairs and strip."

Fire dances across her eyes and she hops down and rushes upstairs. She reaches for the zipper on the side of her skirt as I unlock the door. She slides it down her legs and the fabric falls to the floor. She reaches forward and unbuttons my jeans while toeing off her shoes. I whip my buttoned shirt off.

I bend down to pick her up but she takes a step back.

"You okay?" I ask, breathless.

"I want to watch you walk into the bedroom." She says with a sly smile.

"Yeah?" I ask with an eyebrow raised.

"Yeah." And her voice is husky and shallow. Like she can't get a full breath.

I hook my fingers into hers and start to walk away. She

follows behind me and I feel her fingers press into the divots above my ass.

We step into the bedroom and at the foot of the bed I pull her under my arm so she's standing in front of me. Her red hair catches the light from the other room. I reach up and comb my fingers through it and she rolls her head along with the movement.

I connect us with a kiss and feel her as she reaches for my boxer briefs and tugs them down my legs. Her finger tips run back up my thighs and my cock jumps to attention. Her hands continue up my sides burning my skin with her touch. They round up over my shoulders. I lower my head and kiss her while her hands trail down along my back.

I reach around and unclasp her bra and pull it down her arms. She pushes her bare breasts up against my pecs and I savor the tantalizing sensations of her hardened nipples grating along my chest hair.

She hooks one leg back onto the bed and then the other and she's kneeling as I stand in front of her. I loop an arm around her waist and place a knee on the bed. Together we move until her head rests on the pillows.

I position myself next to her and prop myself up on one elbow. She trails her hands down my stomach and around my throbbing cock.

"Such a tease." I scold.

"You have no idea."

I close my eyes to feel the way her hand runs up and down my thigh. Closing in on my balls but not touching them. My cock is growing stiffer by the second and I'm surprised she hasn't accidentally bumped it.

My free hand finds her breast and begins to roll her nipple between my fingers. Her back arches into my touch so I increase the pressure. I release it and cup her entire breast in my hand pushing it up and feeling the weight before squeezing it, hard.

She hums and I feel the vibration in her chest. I repeat the gesture with the other breast and watch as a satisfied smile dances on her kiss swollen lips.

Nora tilts her head towards me and kisses me as her hand connects with my cock. She circles the base with her hand and rolls her fingers up increasing the pressure. Then she pulls her hand up the underside and tops it over the head. Her palm is wet when she pushes her hand down the topside to the base.

When she reaches the base again she tightens her hold and pumps twice.

It's my rhythm.

"You learn quick." I say against her mouth.

"I want him to feel comfortable." She jokes.

"Honey, he's so sick of my hand he's comfortable with anything you'll give him."

She smiles against my lips as we kiss again and I slide my hand between her legs, finding her already wet.

"Let's do the ankle thing." She says as she lays down on her back. I reach for a condom from my night stand. I slip it on while she plays with her tits lying on her back in front of me.

This seductive woman has no idea how gone I am for her. I will do anything she asks. Our physical connection is unreal. It's overwhelming. My need for her is nothing short of urgent.

Telling myself to go slowly, I move between her legs. I grip my base and line up with her entrance. Her back arches as I slip in my first inch. My hand catches her under her waist and supports her back as I push in further.

Her feet are resting on the bed on either side of my hips and I pick them up by the ankle and hook them around my back. Her heels dig in and I slide into her another inch. Her body responding with enticing ripples and feminine whimpers.

I grip her hips and pull her up my thighs, pushing in further. Her inner walls bear down on me.

"Nora, stop that."

"Stop what?" She has the nerve to ask as she bears down again.

"That." I say quickly as I hold her thighs and push the rest of the way in.

She gasps as her pussy spasms around me and I lift my face to the ceiling and suck in a deep breath. She asked for this. I need to make it last. But my arousal is overpowering.

I plant myself inside of her and run my hands to her knees. I swivel them so they are pressed into my chest and I lean into them.

Nora pushes back and curls her hips just enough to create a new angle even though we've hardly moved. My dick is stone hard and my balls are getting heavier.

I want to take this slow as quickly as I can. I peel her ankles out from where they were tucked against my abs and bring them up to my shoulders.

I sit up off my heels and her ass lifts into the air. I'm still buried deep inside her but I pull out just enough to push in again, hard.

"Fuck," she whispers through her seductive lips.

"Yes Nora, so fucking good." I reply and I pull myself all

the way out before I slam myself back in. Her tits bounce with the movement and I reach up to hold her ankles while I pound into her again.

And again.

Her legs start to shake.

I tighten my grip and pull out and thrust in again.

"You don't have to be quiet Nora. We're not outside anymore." I tease as I pull out and shove in.

"Jim-my." She says through pants of breath.

"Yes Nora?" I ask as I slowly pull out. I can tell we're both on the precipice and I refuse to come before she does. I let my heavy dick hang between us as I run my hands up and down her legs.

I slide my thumb along her entrance and press into her clit.

"Fuck!" She shouts. "Get back inside me!"

Yes ma'am. Without a word I press on her clit with my thumb and push myself back in to her warm, wet pussy. Neither of us is going to last long now.

I hold her ankles together with one hand and keep her legs pulled up against my chest. My other hand presses down on her pubic bone and I push my chest forward so she begins to tilt at the hips.

I can't hold myself up so I drop my fist to the mattress just outside her shoulder and increase my pace in tune with her gasps, whimpers, and pleads.

"Ah, Jimmy…oh…my…god…fuck me!"

Grunts escape my mouth and I growl her name. Her hands fly to my biceps and she holds on tight as her insides convulse around me. Her inside grip on me clamps down like a vice and I piston myself hard against her, the sound of slapping skin filling the room. She bears down one last time and I explode. I pump my hips into her as everything in me travels through my body into hers.

Pleasure hardly describes the feeling in my bones. Everything feels so fucking good. I've never experienced anything as intense as this and each time with Nora the sensations are stronger, better than the last time.

I look down at her while our bodies settle together. Her breaths are as ragged as mine. I drag my gaze down her body to the point where we are still connected. Her warm channel cradles me as the final waves of her orgasm flutter against me. In this moment I know that nothing will ever be better than being with Nora.

Does she feel the same way?

Is she going to stay?

We talked through so many things tonight but we barely skimmed the surface of her future, let alone our future. I fully believe in living in the moment and being present but is she going to be in the moment with me?

Slowly her grip on my biceps relaxes. I roll myself back and guide her legs down to the mattress. I'm lying next to her and her eyes are closed and her face is serene. Satisfied.

I kiss her shoulder and move off the bed to toss the condom and wash up. When I come back from the bathroom she's curled up under my blankets, her red hair fanned out across the pillow behind her.

Fucking gorgeous.

Nora smiles at me and I climb in. She places her hand gently on my chest and gives me a quick kiss before sliding out and walking to the bathroom.

My heart hammers in my chest. I glance at her side of the bed, the sheets are crumpled. I run my hand over the spot and it's still warm, ready to welcome Nora back to my bed.

The thought that I could be happy with any other girl after Nora is laughable. Nora is it for me. I can feel it. It has happened quickly, but what started as an intense physical attraction has deepened to more.

The mission to make her crave me seems to have worked. Not sure what I did to accomplish it but it's clear she wants me. Nora told me earlier that an emotional connection scares her. My new goal is to make Nora want me emotionally. She's here, she's staying, can I press my luck and get her to open up more to me tonight?

She comes out of the bathroom and smiles. I take in her full naked figure and every square inch is perfection. In this moment I decide that if she doesn't want to talk any more, I'll happily not talk with her for the rest of the night.

"I'm going to get some water." She says before walking out of the room towards the kitchen.

22

Curiosity Killed What Again?

Nora

Jimmy takes my water glass from me as I slip back into bed. He takes a sip and sets it on his bedside table. He lifts his arm and I curl into his side.

"Back to our game?" He asks.

"Twenty questions?"

"Yeah."

"Okay, whose turn was it?" I ask as he clasps my fingers in his and my other hand floats up to caress the back of his hand. He shrugs quickly and I laugh because I forgot too. "I'll just start, ladies first and all."

"Go ahead." He says with a kiss to my temple.

"Okay, if you could travel anywhere where would you go?"

"Denmark."

I lift my chin and look up at him.

"Really? Why?"

"Because their furniture design history is so incredible. It's simple, sophisticated, and timeless."

"Hmm." I agree and I lean down to rest my head back on his broad chest. My fingers find his chest hair and the course texture tickles my fingertips.

"My turn," he says, "if your job falls through what do you think you'll do?"

I playfully shove at his chest as I sit up. "Seriously with that question?"

"Yeah," he insists. "You were so passionate about why you got into fundraising in the first place when we talked about it earlier. I've been wondering ever since."

I rest my head against his chest again and think. I haven't really thought about there being an alternative to getting my job at Fosters back.

"I'd need to find a job with big gifts or grants involved. I find smaller giving and organizations too stressful."

"Why?"

"Because I don't want the anxiety of not making enough to support a program or an employee."

He just nods.

"I'm not sure a university would hire me if I get fired from Fosters, at least not on the east coast." I shrug. "I haven't really thought much about it, I'm confident that I'll get Fosters back."

I pause and drag my fingers across his chest. "Okay, my turn to ask a question."

"Fire away."

"What's your favorite way to spend a day off?"

"What's a day off?" He jokes. I smile up at him and enjoy the way my heart pitter patters in my chest when I see his smile. These small moments are sneaking up on me with increasing frequency. His question about my future plans sent a pulse of anxiety through my system. I've been distracted the last few days. But, never has getting distracted felt so right.

"Well, I haven't had a whole day off in a while. Between the store and projects I usually work a little every day. But when I do have a few hours to myself I'll drive to the west side of the lake and go on a hike."

"Errrrrrrrnt." I buzz.

"Wrong answer?" He winces.

"Wrong answer. We were looking for," I hold out my palm like I'm checking my notes, "shopping."

His laugh inflates his whole chest and my head bounces with it. He squeezes my side and I squeal in laughter.

When our laughing slows down he reaches for my chin and pulls me up to kiss him. He ends the kiss too soon and whispers, "Nora, I'd go shopping with you any day."

"I'll hold you to that." I say with a pointed expression.

"I expect you to."

...

"Nora?"

"Mhmm?"

"Nora."

I curl my shoulders into myself and pull the blanket up higher under my chin. Relishing the cozy environment surrounding me.

"Honey, move." My eyes fly open as a hand lifts my waist in the air and then plops me back down. I roll onto my back and see Jimmy shaking out his hand.

"What's going on?" I ask while poking the sleep out of the corners of my eyes.

"My hand is asleep." He says. "Damnit." He mutters.

I roll the rest of the way to face him. "Is it okay?" I'm kind of worried by the look of pain on his face.

"Yeah. Sorry. I was going to wake you up slowly for morning sex. Slide in behind you and fuck lazily from the side," I inhale sharply and rub my thighs together because, yes. "But my arm was asleep. It was shooting daggers and I couldn't concentrate on your body."

He lets his hand fall down to his side and lets out a frustrated sigh. I can't contain my giggle. He turns towards me with an eyebrow raised.

"This funny to you?"

"No." But the word is laced with laughter.

"You sure?"

"Mmhmm." I nod but the frown I'm forcing is fighting me.

"I see." Jimmy says. He pulls me up onto his chest and runs a hand down my back.

"The lazy morning sex sounded great. I'm sad we can't do it now." I say with a pout.

"Oh we're doing it. It just won't be lazy."

My breath hitches as he drags my thigh across his body. His obvious desire pushing against my stomach. He rolls us up to a seated position and cradles my ass while his mouth sucks in one nipple and then the other. Each time his mouth closes around me a stampede of dragonflies travels through my veins.

"If I was behind you I couldn't do this." He says as he moves back to the first breast.

My hands rake through his hair as his hands grip my backside. I roll slightly and am reminded of our first time together when I straddled him in his truck.

This time there's nothing between us.

Jimmy leaves my chest and reaches to grab a condom. He rips the foil with his teeth as one hand begins to finger me.

"Shit Nora, did you wake up this wet?" He growls as he feels the evidence of my need.

My body does my speaking for me. My hands take the condom from him and roll it down his length. I tug up to make sure it's in place and he lifts my hips just enough to line up to my entrance.

Sitting on his lap I brace my hands on his shoulders and he pulls me down onto him. In one swift movement he has filled me. My body stretches and molds to him like a lock and a key that were designed for each other.

I wrap my arms around his neck as he buries his face in my chest and together we increase our speed. Our skin dampens. Our breathing increases. Our shared grunts and whimpers providing the soundtrack to the morning.

Sooner than I'm prepared for, my inner walls start to tremble. He feels it and whispers a "yes, Nora" against my neck as he showers my body with kisses.

He tilts his hips and pushes up into me harder. My thighs open slightly wider for him. Jimmy's arms tighten around me and his body stills as he rolls his head to look up at the ceiling.

"You okay?" I ask when he pauses.

"Yes," he chuckles. "I'm trying not to come yet."

Involuntary flutters race through my body and he groans. "Honey, you can't do that."

"You do that to me." I say as I kiss him and lift myself off him for a split second before lowering back down slowly.

"Ooh fuuck." He breaths.

"Yes Jimmy." I say. Saying his name sets him off because his speed increases and he's guiding my hips up and down on his length. My insides clench. My back arches. The world fades to black until fireworks explode behind my eyes.

He pounds up into me without leaving as I ride out the last wave of my orgasm. His grip on my thighs tightens and then I feel him swell inside me.

Jimmy's head falls forward to my shoulders and I cradle his head in my hands.

"Nora, you're gonna kill me." He says before he lifts me off him and sets me down on the bed.

He stands and goes to the bathroom to clean up. I hear the shower start and I curl up under the covers. My breathing slows and I relax into the pillows that smell like Jimmy. My eyes drift shut and I fall asleep.

...

I hear faint sounds from the kitchen, music playing softly. I keep my eyes closed as I bring the blanket further up on my shoulder. I nuzzle into the pillow when I hear footsteps approaching.

I peek one eye open and am face to crotch with Jimmy's denim clad bulge. Both eyes open and I roll to my back to look up at him. He smiles and leans down to kiss my forehead.

"I've gotta head to the site but there's some food on the counter for you and coffee in a traveler mug to keep it warm."

"Thank you." I stretch my arms up over my head and curl up to lean against the headboard. The sheet is draped across my breasts.

"Mmmm," Jimmy hums appreciatively as he leans in again for a kiss. "And your toothbrush is by the sink."

I playfully slap his chest and he chuckles. His handsome face makes up for the fact that he just called my breath stinky.

"See you around." He says as he backs out of the bedroom. I hear him swipe his keys off the counter followed by the door clicking shut behind him.

"Toothbrush my ass," I mutter as I breathe into my hand to check my breath. Oh, yeah, that's bad.

I hop up to the bathroom and start brushing my teeth right away. I pee, tidy up my makeup from last night, and promise myself I'll do a face mask tonight to make up for sleeping in my makeup again.

Back in his bedroom I see my bra on top of his dresser, no thong though. I clasp the bra around my waist, spin it around and pull the straps up my arms. I open up his dresser drawer and find a t-shirt to slip on and then I snag a pair of his boxers.

With my bits covered in crazy comfortable cotton I pad out to the kitchen. Next to the travel coffee mug is a bowl of cereal and a note that says 'I know this is gross cereal but it's all I've got. Milk is in the fridge.' I laugh to myself and clutch the note to my chest as I take my coffee with me to explore his apartment.

Under his TV, along the far wall, is an entertainment unit. I open the cabinets to find some dusty DVDs, a worn baseball glove with a ball in the mitt. There's a box of pencils and a small graphing paper notebook.

I close it and move to the next cabinet where I find a blanket on the top shelf and a dusty box on the lower shelf. I lift the lid, knowing full well that I am snooping and not caring. Inside are stacks of photographs.

I pull the box off the shelf and carry it to the coffee table. I settle in on his sofa and grab the first few photos on top. A pretty woman who looks a lot like Angie is smiling into the camera. I stare at her for a few beats before moving on to the next photograph. This one is of Jimmy's whole family. His dad is carrying Angie on his shoulders, she's maybe four or five. His mom is standing on the other side of the photo with Jimmy between them. They're swinging their arms up high. His face is blurry but I can feel the unbridled joy this family shares.

The next photo is of Jimmy with chocolate cake all over his face. His front tooth is missing. Then a few photos of him in his little league uniform. And the last one in the stack is of his family around a bonfire.

I set these to the side and reach for the next stack. As I pull it towards me a piece of paper slides out and falls to the ground. I feel for it under the sofa but I can't reach it.

With a huff I set the photos down and get on my knees to look under the sofa. I see the piece of paper and I reach for it. Once I have it in my hand I realize it's more like plastic than paper. I pull it out and see that it's a hospital bracelet.

LEWIS, EMILY ELIZABETH

Hospice.

I freeze as I hold this relic of Jimmy's painful past. I glance away but my eyes settle on the top photograph of Emily. She was beautiful.

My vision blurs as tears well up in my eyes for a person I've never met. I sniffle then I feel the first tear fall.

I sputter out a soggy laugh and wipe away the tears with my fingers. I dry them on the hem of the t-shirt I'm wearing and I stand up. Hovering over the coffee table, I pack the bracelet and photos away, close the box, and put it back.

I stand tall, tilt up my head to the ceiling and suck in a breath. After a shake of my arms I pick up my coffee and carry it with me to the island. When my eyes settle on the full bowl of cereal the tears burst from my eyes and I sniffle out sobs I didn't know I was holding in.

I've lost my damn mind.

I slump onto the stool. I shovel a spoonful of dry cereal into my mouth and try to chew it. But it's terrible. As I mutter "ugh, gross" to myself I stand up and pull the milk out of the fridge.

Still sniffling up tears I eat the cereal and entertain the type of thoughts I have expertly suppressed over the years.

Why am I crying over a woman I never met?

Why am I crying over a bowl of dry cereal?

Why am I snooping around trying to learn more about a guy I'm sleeping with?

Why does saying 'a guy I'm sleeping with' make me feel icky?

I know the answer to that one.

Even my brain knows Jimmy means more to me than that. The more I've gotten to know him the more I've wanted to keep getting to know him. Not just sleep with him. That's new for me.

Why the cereal? Because it has been a long time, decades, since I've let anyone take care of me and I hate how much I like the feeling of it.

Why am I crying over a picture of Jimmy's mom?

Well, because, *just admit it to yourself Nora*, the idea of a loving and joyful mother makes me sad, and it's even sadder that he lost her while my mother is still around.

The tears start again and I let them fall. This time I use the sleeve of Jimmy's shirt to dry them up and blink towards the ceiling to try and stop anymore from falling.

My skirt and top from last night are folded on the table behind me. I slip them on, hiking Jimmy's boxers a little further up my leg but keeping them on. Then I toss the t-shirt into his laundry basket.

I hear voices on the street outside his apartment. I peek out the window to find Liz wrangling three dogs into her studio. Maybe she needs some help.

23

We. Do. Not. Have. Time. For. All. This. Chatter.

Nora

"Please sit?" Liz begs to a giant Saint Bernard who is standing in front of a green screen in her studio.

"What's happening here?" I ask as I walk in.

"Ugh, Fluffy is not listening. I'm trying to capture him sitting next to this fake box of dog food but he just stands there like a dope!"

"Well there's no need for name calling," I joke.

"Help me?" She asks with a pleading grin on her face, one that shows most of her teeth.

"I will, but don't make that face around the dogs. They'll think you're aggressive."

She laughs and hands me a baggie of dog treats. I walk up to Fluffy and pat his? her? head. With a little scratch behind the ears I make eye contact and say "you're a good doggie, here's a treat."

The dog laps the treat out of my hand and then I turn so I'm off the back drop and hold the bag of treats above my head.

Fluffy immediately sits and lifts her head in the direction of the treats.

I hear Liz's camera shutter as she captures the pup. She lowers her camera to check the shot and I toss a treat at Fluffy. The other two dogs that are tied up to the desk behind me start to yap.

"Alright, alright, everyone gets one." And I give a treat to them both.

"So how was your date last night?" Liz asks, while pulling out another fake food prop. "I saw your car on the street here this morning." She teases.

"And I'm staying at your house so you should know that I didn't come home last night."

"Oh yeah. That too." She admits. "But the Tome Raiders saw your car and reported it."

"Ugh, freaking small towns are the worst."

"They are not. Lakeville is amazing."

I look out the front window of her studio and watch as Sandy scurries down the sidewalk towards the café. Across the street, I can see Angie sitting at the front counter of Lewis Hardware. Sal walks past with his coffee and cuts through the alley to get to his store. I pause as the understanding of how invested in the town I've gotten over the last week settles in. In the city I occasionally saw familiar faces at the coffee shop and dry cleaner but I definitely don't know anyone's name. I barely made friends with my coworkers and I saw them every weekday.

The little neon sticky note map Liz made for me earlier this week is still in my purse but I haven't had to use it for a few days now. And I have a feeling if I ever did find myself lost I could ask the first person I saw and get reliable directions.

"Level with me oh she-who-doesn't-date," Liz taunts as she pulls me from my thoughts. "How did it go?"

"It was amazing." I admit and I watch as Liz does a double take snapping her attention back to me after her question.

"Reeeeal-ly?!" She stands up tall and squares her shoulders in my direction. Her brown eyes searching me for clues as she cocks one hip out to the side.

"Shut up." I roll my eyes. "But, yes it was."

"Tell me about it."

I sit down in her desk chair and the two dogs sitting there start nuzzling my legs for attention. I reach down and scratch them behind the ears. "We met at The Whale."

"As one does when dating in in Lakeville."

"I suppose." I shrug. "Then he gave me three options for dinner."

"That's cute, nice work Jimmy. What where the options?"

"Tapas, burgers, or a picnic."

"Interesting. What did you pick?"

"The picnic."

Liz pauses her efforts to get Fluffy to lie down and looks over her shoulder at me. "Go on."

"He walked me to his truck and drove me out to a plot of land near the camp. When we got there he parked and unveiled a picnic set up in the back of his truck. There were blankets and pillows and he had the picnic basket ready to go. Well technically Sandy had packed it but he had it waiting."

"Smooth."

"Definitely. And we unpacked the picnic and talked until the sun set."

"What did you talk about?"

"Stuff. Geesh you're nosy!"

"Sor-ry but there isn't a lot of first date discussion around here anymore." Liz admits as she comes over and unhooks the Westie's leash.

The dog bounds towards the bag of treats I had set on a stool. In one swift move, like she secretly has a black belt in karate, the pup knocks the bag of treats over and starts snacking away. Fluffy hustles over to join in on the piñata smash and I reach down to unclasp the last dog's leash.

Liz shrugs and starts to take pictures of them eating the treats.

"At least I'll have some photos to send the brand." She says as the pups sniff around for any remnants. "Remind me not to do pet campaigns again."

I turn around to find Fluffy squatting and leaving a little, well giant, present on the floor. I start backing away, grab my purse off her desk, and when I reach the door I quickly say, "Good luck, and that," I point to the floor, "is your reminder not to do pet campaigns again."

I swivel out the door and push it closed behind me.

Gross.

Across the street the door to the hardware store opens and Angie waves wildly in my direction so I cross the street.

"Hi Nora!" She greets me as I step up on the sidewalk. "How are you this morning?"

"Hi Angie. I'm good. How are you?"

"Good, good." She mutters. Then she looks up and down the sidewalk before grabbing me by the arm and dragging me into the store. "Ohmigod! Guess what?"

I literally have no idea what she could be talking about and it must show on my face because she keeps talking.

"Holden just texted me and asked what my plans were for Float Fest." She finishes her sentence with a little *eep* noise of excitement.

"That's awesome." I offer.

"So I was going to ask you if you had plans. After he basically ignored me at trivia night I don't want to seem too available. Or maybe he's asking like as a friend if I know of any parties."

She rounds the checkout counter and sits on the stool. She picks up her phone and reads me the text.

"Okay, so this is what he said." She clears her throat and annunciates each word. "Hi Angie - what are your plans for Float Fest?"

She looks up at me expectantly.

"Sounds like he wants to know your plans." I wince. "So, what are your plans?"

"Well, I was going to ride along with Maeve and her family and then go with them to the carnival. But if he has a boat and wants me to ride on it with him I totally would. Maeve would understand."

She drills her fingernails along the desk. "Or maybe he doesn't have plans and wants me to invite him along on mine." She looks off in the distance for a minute.

"What are your plans?" She asks as she turns back towards me.

"Ah, I think I'm riding on the Collins's boat and tagging along with them the rest of the day."

"Jimmy didn't make plans with you?"

"No, should he have?"

"No." She says quickly. "I mean, I just figured since you're like dating now you'd be doing everything together."

"Who said we were dating? Did he say that?" Good golly, I sound like a smitten teenager.

"I heard Sandy at the coffee shop this morning telling Sal that you spent the night at his place after your date. She was the one who said she expects to hear wedding bells by spring."

I have to temper my eye roll so I don't pull a muscle.

"She couldn't be more wrong." I pause. "Well, about the wedding bells thing. I did stay the night after our date last night. But we're not officially dating."

"How can you date but not be officially dating?" Angie asks.

"I don't know but I can tell you we're not." I look down at my feet. "I've never officially dated a guy before so I'm not the one to ask."

"Wait, never?"

"It's against my policy." I look up at Angie.

"Like insurance policy?" She asks, genuinely confused.

"No, more like my personal philosophy. I see guys once. Only once. Sometimes we'd share a meal before going home together but other times we'd meet at a bar and a few hours later get down to brass tacks."

Angie's eyes double in size. I shrug.

"I never got their numbers, they never got mine. It was a transaction. We both got what we wanted and moved on."

"Don't you ever get lonely?"

"I don't let myself think like that." I pause and see that she doesn't quite understand so I clarify. "I make my plans, I work my plans, and I stay focused. I can only count on myself. So with me for company, I never get lonely."

"Huh, that's an interesting way to look at it."

"I'm pretty great company." I laugh. She laughs too and then looks back down at her phone.

"I'm going to tell him I have plans and that maybe I'll see him around."

"I like the sound of that."

Across the street Liz comes out of her studio wrangling the three dogs again. I tell Angie I gotta go. I reach Liz and take one of the leashes out of her hand. Together we walk the dogs to their respective homes and then circle back to town, get my car, and drive back to her house.

Mrs. Collins's car is parked in the driveway when we get there and Liz and I both take bracing breaths before we head inside.

"Girls! Thank goodness!" She yelps as we step inside. This is the worst mess yet. The rug glitters under my feet.

Liz rolls her eyes, "Mom, Kyle is going to have a coronary seeing this place so messy."

"Then we'll have to work fast so we have time to clean up." Katherine replies matter of factly.

She tosses a bottle of something to Liz who bats down it out of the air. "Mom! What the hell! At least say heads up?"

"We. Do. Not. Have. Time. For. All. This. Chat-ter." Katherine says with a clap on each syllable.

Liz and I exchange a glance. Katherine is on the next level and we have to catch up quickly. Here's where I shine.

"Liz, you grab a notebook and pen." I say as I point at her. "Katherine, I know you're anxious to get this finished, but I need you to chill out long enough to tell us everything that needs to get done."

"I can do that." Katherine says while jumping from side to side like a tennis player waiting to receive a 100mph serve.

Liz bounds back into the room with a notebook and pen. "Ready."

I point to Katherine, "Go."

"Okay, we need to attach the beads ropes to the velcro strips," she's counting on her fingers as she continues to bounce. "And then attach the second side of the velcro strips to the boat. We need to finish Michelle's dress and the loot bag for our murderer." She spins around like she's on super market sweep.

"Oh! We need to glue each one of these mirror pieces to that foam half sphere to create a disco ball. We need to cut the green felt for the top of the tables and coolers so they look like card tables."

Liz is furiously writing this down as I scan the room for anything we missed.

"Charles is going to handle getting the booze and filling the coolers. Kyle volunteered to do the playlist. Bond is already in a suit so he doesn't need anything. So, I think, that's it." Katherine says.

I walk over and take the notebook from Liz. I read through the list and an action plan formulates in my head.

"Liz, you're on bead strings and velcro duty. Pop on some jams and get it done. Katherine, you finish Michelle's dress since you have the end design in mind. I'll go to the hardware store for glue and come back and start on the disco ball."

Liz and Katherine exchange a look.

"What?" I ask crossing my arms.

"Oh nothing." Liz says like it's definitely something.

"You're just awful eager to go to the hardware store is all." Katherine adds.

"You two are ridiculous. He's not even working at the store today, he's at the Fallon's house."

"Sure." Liz nods.

"Of course." Katherine chimes in.

I cross my arms and huff off to the guest room to change clothes. I'm not more than one step down the hall when I hear Liz say to her mom, "She's got it bad."

"I know." I mutter to myself.

24

Thirst Traps and DM Slides

JIMMY

Countertops are one of the more difficult parts of a remodel. They have to be cut exactly to the space, they're breakable, and they weigh a ton.

I recruited some buddies to help me get the kitchen counters in today. In Angie's design, we went from a small galley kitchen to an open concept with three walls of countertops and a gigantic waterfall marble island.

There's a lot of marble to sling today.

I step out of the house into the front yard and wipe my brow. I'm sweating and exhausted already. Part of it could be that I was up later than usual last night. But I don't think any red blooded man would have slept any more than I did with Nora in their bed.

My stomach curls at the idea of Nora in another man's bed. It's been a week. We've gone on one date. And when I asked her to stay with me at the end of our date I definitely meant the night. Nothing more.

Sure keep telling yourself that, asshat.

Hey! No need for name calling.

But you're right. I meant stay longer.

Forever.

She has infiltrated my every waking thought. I think I see her everywhere I turn. I catch a flash of red hair in my rearview mirror. I see her around the corner of the aisle at the market. Even now she appears before me like a mirage.

I'm a man on the verge of heat exhaustion. Dehydration must be closing in because Nora The Mirage is getting closer.

Ah, I can feel my muscles relaxing as she smiles at me. Her mouth painted a beautiful shade of reddish orange. The hue is just darker than her hair.

My head swirls with the possibilities of that mouth. Too bad I'm dying out here in the heat before I can experience its pure bliss again.

"Jimmy?" Her voice is melodic.

She's getting even closer, and she's getting clearer. She's waving her hand in front of my face.

I feel my face light up in a smile.

"Jimmy!" She's snapping her fingers in my face now.

"Huh?" I blink and feel my head rush. "Ah," I stumble backwards. "I need to sit down."

"Oh shit, okay. Here." Nora helps guide me to the porch step. "Hold on, let me get you some water."

She stands but I reach out and grab her wrist. I pull her down to me.

If I'm going to die I'm to do it kissing her. The voice in my head says.

"You're not going to die dummy, you're just dehydrated." She reassures, then she pecks my lips, and walks to my truck.

She comes back a minute later with my water bottle and an apple. "Here, drink this." I take a few sips. The water feels good as it travels down my throat.

"Now, eat this." She hands me the apple. I pick it up and take a bite. The sweet and tart flavors combine on my tongue and remind me of how she tasted last night.

"Stop growling." She scolds. I must not have a filter right now. Nora places her hands on my shoulders and folds at the hips so her head is tucked in next to mine. "You won't get to taste me again if you don't hydrate."

I freeze as she pushes herself off my shoulders and comes back to standing. I feel feverish but I don't think it's the heat, I think it's her.

I finish the apple and toss the core into a bucket of scraps on the porch. After another sip of water I'm feeling better but with Nora standing in front of me I don't want to move. I want to sit here and watch the muscles in her legs flex as she shifts from side to side in her heels.

"Whatcha thinking Jimmy?" She asks.

"About your legs, and those shoes."

"Ah, I see." She looks off to the side. "And ugh, how are you feeling?" She asks looking anywhere but at me.

"Better." I say as I reach out and take her hand in mine. Her fingers are so soft, delicate. I lace them together with mine and pull. Again she bends at the waist and she meets me for a kiss.

The only parts of our bodies touching are our lips and our hands. I picture the way her ass must be popped up behind her and groan hungrily while I deepen the kiss. My fingers clasp just a little tighter on hers.

"Ew get a room!" Angie scolds and Nora stands up immediately. I turn to where Angie is standing in the driveway with Dax who has the camera pointed at us.

Nora wipes at her lipstick and turns to Angie but not before flashing big eyes at me. I chuckle.

"Angie, just the girl I was looking for," Nora says as she strides over to the driveway. I don't hate watching her go. "I need some spray adhesive or hot glue or something that will attach mirror pieces to foam."

"Float Fest?" Angie asks.

"Float Fest." Nora confirms.

"I'm sure we can find something for you. Let me just drop off these tiles to kissy pants over there and we'll walk over together."

Dax is still recording and he follows Angie as she walks up to me holding a small box of tiles.

"Here are the penny tiles for the wording in the bathroom upstairs. Dad picked them up last night."

"Dad did?"

"Yeah, I was telling him yesterday that I wasn't sure how I was going to cover the store and get up to the supplier to get these. He offered to do it."

"Wow, that's…" surprising, suspicious, thoughtful, selfless? I settle on, "great."

"Yeah, he's really making an effort these days." She says and I see her eyes flick to the camera and I understand that she wants to talk more about it but not with a national audience.

"That's great." I repeat because I'm not really sure what else to say. "Ah, let's take them up and see how it looks."

"Yes!" Angie says and then she steps past me into the house. I stand and put a hand on Dax's shoulder. He pauses his recording and looks at me.

"Did you, ah, film…"

"Your sexy as hell kiss with the redhead?"

"Ugh, yeah, that."

"I did."

Shit. "Are you gonna use that?"

"Not sure, it would depend on a lot of different factors."

"Like what?"

"Well I'm not the editor or director but I would guess they'd include it if she makes appearances in other episodes, if she's part of your story."

"And if she's not?"

"Then probably not. I think they have a plan to promote you as this hot shot contractor and sharing your girlfriend doesn't really fit that ya know?"

"Sure, yeah. Okay."

"Yeah?"

"Yeah." I say. He gestures for me to lead the way up the stairs.

When we get to the landing I turn towards the bathroom and look out the front window, Nora is standing in the driveway talking with Marla. The hairs on the back of my neck prick up but there's nothing I can do about their conversation now.

In the bathroom Angie is trying to pick one of the tiles off the sheet with her fingers. I flip open my pocket knife and pry it off for her.

"Thank you!" She chirps and then bends down to place it into the spaces I left open. I pry out the next one and keep handing them to her and she starts to fill in the word.

"This looks so cool." She says as we're about halfway through.

"It really does." I tell her. "This is something unique just to this house and I think they're going to love it."

"I agree." She says as she stands up. "Okay, you finish putting these in and text me a picture before you cement them down."

"You don't really cement tiles in…"

"You know what I meant smartass." And she rolls her eyes at the camera as she walks past me down the hall.

I give the camera a shrug and a smirk and after a beat Dax lowers it and chuckles.

"That was gold." He says as he starts walking back downstairs.

My buddies all got a little break while I rehydrated and messed with the tile but we've got four more slabs to go. I meet them in the kitchen and Dax lifts the camera.

"Alright men." I start like it's a halftime speech. In a way it is. "We've put in a lot of hard work already. And I'm proud of you. But we need to deliver a marble waterfall kitchen island today and that ain't gonna be easy. It's gonna be heavy. It's gonna take precision. It's gonna take ah,"

"While?" Holden chimes in.

"Yes!" I say as I point to him. "It's going to take a while! So drink some water, dry your hands, stretch your lower back."

"I did my sciatica stretches already." Cole hollers from the back.

"Good on you Cole." I continue, "I know we can get this done and later the first round at The Whale is on me."

My group of dedicated workers let out a whoop and a cheer and we get to work.

...

Beers taste better when shared with friends. Even better when they've been earned by a hard day's work. And I should have realized that my buddies were going to invite more guys out tonight to try and get in on the free round.

Never miss a chance at a free beer.

I should get that on a poster or something.

"So Jimmy, you and that new girl seem pretty serious." Holden says as he leans on the bar next to me.

"Seems that way." I answer non-plussed before taking a sip even though my insides are churning at the casual way he referred to Nora.

"She's just in town for the week?"

"That's what she said."

"And then she's going back to the city." It isn't a question.

"Probably, why?"

"Well if you're not going to keep seeing her I might introduce myself tomorrow. I head into the city often enough for meetings and we could make a," he takes a sip of his beer, "a regular hook up thing work."

My blood is boiling. It started increasing in temperature slowly as Holden continued talking and his admission right there has me over the edge.

But as much as I want to grab him by the collar and tell him to back off I don't know if I can. She probably is going back to the city. If she doesn't want a relationship with me she might want a regular hook up.

I don't know.

"Easy bud," Holden says as he sets his hand on my shoulder. "Your shoulders are practically kissing your ears."

I try to laugh it off. "Not sure if she'd be into that kind of arrangement." I say and hope that I haven't just stuck my foot in my mouth.

If she doesn't want a relationship then I'd gladly take a regular hook up arrangement. Anything to be near her, next to her, inside her. She quickly has become a pillar in my life, something that I can never live without.

If I was her boyfriend I'd shoot her a text right now. Something fun and laced with innuendo. But I don't have her number so I can't.

Wait, I can.

I set my beer down on the bar and leave cash next to it.

"Whoa you're leaving?" Holden says.

"Yeah, I just remembered there's something I gotta do."

I leave The Whale and cross the street and head around the back of the hardware store to my apartment. Once I get inside I instantly spot the half eaten bowl of cereal and the coffee mug Nora used this morning.

I smile at the idea of us sharing a space. Of me getting to tidy up after her everyday. As I move the dishes to the sink, I think about my next move.

I slide into one of the chairs at my dining table and pull out my phone. I prop both elbows in front of me and open the app.

I have her TikTok handle. I already sent her one video. This next one needs to be perfect. What do other people send? Is this even a thing?

With the app open video after video come at me at an alarming rate. Slow motions of people kneading bread. Dance numbers with groups of girls doing the exact same moves. The same few songs playing over and over as each clip passes.

This isn't going to help. I close the app and search the internet instead. Yeah, that's the answer.

I type "romantic TikTok videos" into the search bar and instantly thousands, maybe millions of results come up. I click on the first one and am taken to a 7 second video that starts with a picture of a man gripping a woman's leg, with the words "when he possesses your body and soul" written in bubble letters over it, then suddenly a series of pictures flash behind the words. All different images of a couple together.

It's kinda hot. But not really romantic. I could be barking up the wrong tree here.

I go back to the browser and scroll down to the next video. It starts the same way, a picture of a couple holding hands in the front seat of a car. The words "He calls you a good girl when you're being bad" written across it. Then again, a flurry of images pass. These are all in black and white which I appreciate. It's an artful choice.

Still not any closer to an idea of what to send Nora, I go back to the search page and type in "TikTok flirting" because apparently I'm desperate.

The first article that comes up is titled "Thirst Traps and DM Slides; How Dating Has Changed In The Age of Social Media." This has promise.

The article explains what different acronyms mean. What a thirst trap video is, and I realize that is what Angie has been posting of me. Once again, gross. And then the article covers how to start a conversation with someone through their Direct Messages, DMs.

Huh, I don't have to send a video to direct message her. Who knew? I open the app again and go to my messages. Hers is the only one there.

> CountryCraftsman31:
> Did you get what you needed
> this morning?

That's good right? It could go either way, sexual or about whatever she needed at the store.

But now what? I just wait? Am I expected to just sit here patiently without worrying and over analyzing and—

Ooo, she's typing.

> StylishSleuthNH:
> I did, but I might have to come
> back for more.

She's good.

Very good.

So now, what do I say back. C'mon Jimmy *think*.

> CountryCraftsman31:
> Tell me what you need and I'll
> make it happen.

Again, good. It could go either way but if I know Nora it's probably leading the sexual way.

She's typing.

> StylishSleuthNH:
> I forget exactly what your favorite is. Can you remind me?

My favorite what? Position?

Because that's the first thing that comes to mind. But if she's talking about cereal I could make a total ass out of myself here.

I messaged her to try and push her a little bit. To entice her to come over or at least consider coming over. I am not ready for whatever we have to be over.

> CountryCraftsman31:
> My favorite is you.

25

Up Before The Tequila Sunrises
Nora

My favorite is you.

I bite my bottom lip to contain my smile. I'm sitting on Mr. and Mrs. Collin's dock while they scurry around putting the finishing touches on things for tomorrow.

Charles has volunteered to sleep on board tonight so no one can lay siege to their decorations. Katherine is busy trying to set booby traps throughout the yard by tying yarn between trees. Liz and Kyle are cooking dinner.

And I'm exchanging flirty DMs with Jimmy.

StylishSleuthNH:
You sure know how to make a girl blush.

CountryCraftsman31:
You know how to make a man want to make a girl blush.

I cringe. Not his best work.

CountryCraftsman31:
Okay, that sucked. I'm out of
innuendo.
What are you up to?

StylishSleuthNH:
Sitting on the dock watching
Charles make himself a bed on
the boat while Katherine runs
around setting traps for
potential saboteurs.
You?

CountryCraftsman31:
Sitting in my apartment
wishing you were here.

StylishSleuthNH:
Smooth Lewis.
What are your plans
tomorrow?

CountryCraftsman31:
I'm going to ride out with
Holden and then hang out at
the carnival.

StylishSleuthNH:
You aren't like festival
chairperson or committee
head.

CountryCraftsman31:
It's a task force. But no, I
haven't helped out since high
school.

Liz calls to us that dinner is ready. Suddenly texting with a boy and getting called to dinner feels like I'm in high school. Except when did my mom ever cook me dinner?

StylishSleuthNH:
Dinner is ready. I'll see you
tomorrow.

CountryCraftsman31:
Goodnight Nora

...

Ding Dong. Ding Dong.
Knock. Knock.
Pound. Pound. Pound.
Ding, dong.
"Up and at em!" Katherine bellows through the door.
I roll over and check the time on my phone. 5:45am. I hear Liz shuffling down the hallway and opening the door.
"Mother." She says flatly.
"Why aren't you dressed?" Katherine asks surprised.
"Why *are* you dressed? It's not even 6 in the morning." Liz gripes. I open the door to my bedroom and lean against the doorframe while I listen in on early morning mother-daughter antics.

"Liz, you know as well as anyone that getting a good position in the parade is an important factor. The judges see your boat early on before they've seen any others and that gives you an advantage."

Kyle walks out of the bedroom with a pair of shorts on. He barely opens his eyes but he nods in my direction and mumbles "morning" as he passes by.

"Now, get yourself dressed so we can meet your father." Katherine sticks her head down the hallway. "You too, Nora! Chop chop!"

I smile and head back into my room. I pull out my swimsuit and a cover up, lay them on the bed and head to the bathroom. After I wash up and brush my teeth I head back into my room.

"Oh shit!" I yelp because Katherine is sitting on my bed.

"Didn't mean to scare you pumpkin. But I wanted to see what outfit you had planned." She points to my suit on the bed. "Is this it?"

"Yes?" Liz told me that this event is essentially a day drinking event so I figured a swim suit and cover up would do the trick.

"Where did you get the perfect outfit at the last minute?"

"I didn't. This is what I packed." I say with confusion.

"Well aren't you just made for French Riviera Meets Lakeville?" Katherine crosses over and plants her hands on my cheeks. "It's like you're meant to be here!"

She kisses me on the forehead and marches out of my room and right into Liz and Kyle's.

"MOM! Get out!" Liz cries and I hear a thud that sounds a lot like a broad shouldered man falling over.

"Whoopsie daisy." Katherine sing-songs as she backs out of

the room and closes the door. She turns and winks at me while crouching into her shoulders. "Seems like my daughter is trying to get knocked up before her wedding."

I shake my head and close my door to get dressed. I slip on the berry pink bikini and the tan mesh cover up. I twist my hair up behind me in a clip and put in gold hoops. I grab my sunglasses, tinted SPF, lip gloss, and phone and toss them in a woven tote. I slide into my wedge espadrilles and sit down on the edge of the bed while I tie up the ribbons at my ankles.

When I open my door I hear Liz giggling on the other side of hers and roll my eyes.

I walk down the hallway and find Katherine in the kitchen standing at the counter. She's tapping the front of the coffee maker like it's an elevator call button and muttering something to herself.

"Did Charles make it through the night?"

"He did." She says proudly.

"And did anyone fall victim to the booby traps."

Katherine sighs and her shoulders sink. "Sadly, no. I did see a bird perched on one of the lines this morning though."

"I guess that's something."

The coffee maker beeps and Katherine starts filling up travel mugs. She hands me one and clears her throat.

"You okay?" I ask.

"Oh yes, yes. Nervous. Are you okay?"

I'm surprised by her question because it seems like she's asking about more than just in this moment. And it feels like a complicated answer.

She sets the coffee carafe down on the counter. She looks up at me and says, "I just worry about you sometimes."

"Me? Why?"

"Well, we don't see you much. You work so hard, Liz said this was the first vacation you've taken since you started." I wince because that's true, and this was a forced vacation. "I know things with your mother are complicated."

I look off to the side and nod.

"And you seem to see a lot of different men."

I turn back and raise an eyebrow at her.

"Oh Liz tells me a few things here and there. Sometimes she's jealous of your adventurous life."

"Adventurous?" I scoff. "Hardly."

"No? I think so. You live in the big city all by yourself. You work on these deals that help so many people. You dress just as well as Cynthia Harris. That real estate agent even comes to yoga in the park dressed up." She mutters. She looks back up at me. "You've got it all figured out. Always have."

I look down at the counter. That might have been the case before but certainly doesn't feel true now.

"That was part of what made Liz's first few months at home so tough. She had big plans," Katherine continues. I chuckle because she really did. "But Liz's plans didn't work out for her. Now, don't get me wrong I think she's better off for it, but it wasn't easy for her to watch you from afar as you executed your plans. Leaving her here to figure things out on her own."

"I know, that's why I pushed her to set up the Monday FaceTimes. She wasn't talking to Kyle but she was talking to me. I've never told her but I would give him updates on how she was doing. Especially with her photography. "

"And thank goodness she had you to do that for her."

Katherine looks down the hall to where her daughter and future son-in-law are leaving their room.

She reaches over and pats the top of my hand. "Just remember that it's okay not to have it all figured out once in a while."

And with that she scoops up the coffee mugs, distributes them to Liz and Kyle and then shoos us out the front door.

...

The sun has barely risen over the trees but I am drinking a tequila sunrise, sitting on a pontoon boat with my best friend, her fiancé, her parents, and a collection of cardboard cutouts. If you had asked me two weeks ago I wouldn't have come close to predicting I'd be here. But it feels right.

I haven't been able to shake Katherine's advice from this morning out of my mind.

It's okay not to have it all figured out once in a while.

I've been walking through this week without any sort of plan and that has scared me.

Scared by how much I've enjoyed it.

I enjoyed the surprises.

I enjoyed slowing down.

I enjoyed breaking my one-and-done rule.

I enjoyed that a lot.

We raise our glasses in a toast to Katherine and her vision and I watch as other boats come into view.

Everyone lines up at the public dock and then at 9am the parade starts. The procession takes us around the perimeter of the lake, past the Inn where the judges are stationed, and then once each boat has passed it becomes an all out party.

Charles and Katherine have been sharing stories of years past. How the kids would get into trouble and they'd pretend not to know.

Liz tells us about when she tried to intercept a pass between the high school quarterback and his cousin and ended up belly flopping into the lake. Luckily it started a party where everyone was jumping in.

I'm standing next to James Bond drinking my third, fourth?, uh-oh, drink when an airhorn sounds.

"Oh gosh, oh my, this is it." Katherine says as she sets down her drink and begins to fuss around the boat.

"Alrighty, here we go!" Charles calls out as he puts the boat into gear. The pontoon starts to inch slowly forward and I realize that this is probably the top speed. It is going to take forever to get to the Inn.

We're at the front of the line so when we turn to head back down the other side of the lake we get the chance to see some of the other boats. There are a few that look like tropical huts. A few that look like a children's birthday party with streamers and balloons. Then at the back of the line is a boat with rotating colored lights and a big board hanging off the side.

Katherine is standing at the front of our boat and staring that one down.

"Is that Gina's?" I ask.

"Yes, and I can't figure out what that board is." Katherine says through clenched teeth.

"Can't do anything about it now." Kyle says as he claps Katherine on the shoulder. "C'mon, let's get out the snacks."

We cruise past the Inn and there is a folding table set up on the end of the dock. Three judges are sitting there with clip boards, taking notes. They snap a few pictures while we pretend to be gambling with celebrities.

It's the most ridiculous three minutes of my life but I will fully admit that I love it.

Charles turns the boat back towards the center of the lake. Katherine kicks her shoes off and grabs a bottle of champagne. It's like a light switch flipped and she's no longer stressed or worried at all.

"C'mon let's party!" She hollers as she takes a sip straight from the bottle.

"Yeah, Play Hard Nora, let's party!" Kyle says as he knocks me in the shoulder. I laugh at the old nickname and shimmy my shoulders.

"Anyone have coconut rum?" I ask with a smile.

26

Allow Me To Introduce Play Hard Nora

JIMMY

Lakeville always comes out strong for the Christmas Carnival. The Valentine's Day Sadie Hawkins Dance maxes out the capacity of the high school gym.

But nothing gets the town out like Float Fest.

Maybe it's the decorating competition. Or maybe because it happens in the summer. It is only 10am and I can tell already people are getting into the party spirit.

I borrowed Holden's jet ski with the sole mission of getting Nora to take a ride with me. I told him it was because I wanted to visit several boats and make sure the decorations were safe.

Not sure if he bought it but I don't care. The Collins's boat is just ahead of me so I slow down and pull up next to it.

"Well ahoy there sailor!" Nora says with a sloppy salute. A smile cracks across my face as I take in her rosy cheeks and the way she's swaying with the waves.

"JIMMMAAAYYY" Liz hollers as she comes up and slings an arm around Nora's shoulders. "Have you met my dearest friend in all the world, Play Hard Nora?"

"I don't believe I have."

"Oh, well, here she is." Liz wobbles backwards as she holds her arms up to display Nora. Nora obliges with a curtsey.

Kyle is sitting on a seat behind them and rolls his eyes.

"I was hoping I could take Play Hard Nora for a spin around the lake."

Liz and Nora exchange a look over the top of their sunglasses. I take the moment to really appreciate the beauty in front of me. A deep pink string bikini is tied around her neck and back and between are just two little triangles over her breasts. Little ties rest on her hips, her shapely legs curve down into shoes held on by ribbons. Every tidy little bow is begging to be untied and I'm feeling about as patient as a kid on Christmas morning.

"Permission granted." Liz announces.

"Yeah?" I ask.

"Play Hard Nora is coming for a spin around the lake." Nora says as she sits down and starts to untie her shoe. I stare intently as her fingers pull on the knot. Slowly I drag my eyes up her shin to her knees and get lost in the dark shadow between her legs.

"Heads up." Charles barks as he tosses a rope my way. I'm a second too late to grab it so I fish it out of the water and pull myself closer to the side of the boat.

Nora walks over to the side of the boat. I stand to help her step across to the jet ski. As soon as her hand lands in mind a zing of electricity shoots through my veins.

She straddles the seat and I sit back down. Her thighs squeeze into mine and I wrap her arms around my torso. The feel of her tits against my bare back is incredible. I'm going to ask her to be the big spoon tonight.

"You know how to swim?" I ask her.

"Yes dad, I know how to swim." She grumbles.

"Hey I don't know what you city folk do for fun." I reply laying on the dumb townie accent a little thick.

She responds by twisting my nipple.

"Ow!" I yell and everyone on the boat looks at us.

Nora leans a little closer and whispers "I do a lot of things for fun." And her palm slowly caresses my chest.

"Hold on." I say as I toss the rope back on the boat and slowly drive us away. Once we have some space between us and the boats I rev up the speed and revel in the sensation of her arms tightening around me.

Her laughter floats to my ears as the wind rushes past us

"Faster!" She hollers and I kick it up another notch.

I turn us towards the south side of the lake, past the Inn. Most of the boats are circling on the north half near downtown and the park where the carnival is held tonight.

I slow the jet ski and we move leisurely through the water. The back of the homes on the lake appear every few hundred feet in clearings of trees. Dad's house is at the very south end of the lake. I drive us that direction.

"These homes are so pretty." Nora says in my ear.

"They are." I point straight ahead of us. "That one is my dad's."

She pushes herself up so she is standing on the back of the jet ski and can see over my shoulder. "Is that where you grew up?"

"Yeah, my parents bought it right after they got married and then Dad worked to rebuild it, project by project, for the next decade."

I smile at the memory of there always being a construction zone in the house. How my mom always complained about the mess but would have the next project in mind before the current one was finished.

"Your dad still lives there?"

"Yeah." I whisper.

Nora settles back down behind me and hugs me. "I'm sorry your mom died." She says.

"It's okay, it was a long time ago."

"I know, but still. It's not fair that a mother who loved her kids had to die while another who doesn't even care that her kid exists is still around."

"You mean your mom?"

"Yeah. I shouldn't be so harsh. She did not have an easy time of it when I was a kid. Whoever my father is wasn't around at all, my mom did her best to keep us going but her best wasn't much." Nora pauses and I reach a hand down to hold her calf wishing I could be holding her against my chest.

"We still talk so I guess she does know I exist, but the only time she really cares is if she needs something."

"I'm sorry." I offer, knowing it isn't enough.

"It's okay. I've come to terms with it. I've gotten better at ignoring her and not worrying too much about her. But she gets herself in shady situations and I know one day I'll get a call from jail or a hospital."

"Nora, that sucks."

I feel her shrug her shoulders and she leans her head against me. I run my hand up and down her leg and then squeeze her arms against me before turning the jet ski back towards the party.

"Tell me more about Party Hard Nora." I say as we make our way back towards the parading boats.

"Well, she loves coconut rum, art galleries, and can turn pretty much any game into a naked version."

I laugh. "Oh yeah? Like 20 questions."

"Exactly! And horseshoes, and croquet, and Catch Phrase."

"Naked Catch Phrase?"

She thinks about it. "Well, Liz loves Catch Phrase and she's freakishly good when she's drunk. And I just take my clothes off every time I miss one so yeah, naked Catch Phrase."

"Can't wait." I say and then I speed up and feel the wind bite across my face. We're about halfway back up the lake when Nora taps me on the shoulder. I slow down and turn towards her.

"Move, I wanna drive." She says.

"Nora, have you ever driven one before?"

"No, but how hard could it be?" She says confidently as she stands up and starts to climb around me.

Holden specifically told me to, and I quote, "not fuck up my jet ski," when I borrowed it this morning. I think flipping it over would fall under the category of fucking it up.

I scoot back on the seat and lean a little away from Nora to help offset her weight. She lifts her foot to step across so I lean back towards the middle and just that little movement sends her toppling into the water.

She shrieks and I reach for her but she's already half under water by the time our fingers brush. I stand, pull the coil on my wrist to kill the engine, and dive in after her. When my head pops up I get a splash in the face before I even open my eyes.

"I can't believe you pushed me in!" Nora calls.

I wipe the water from my brow and flip my hair back. When I open my eyes I see Nora climbing back onto the jet ski. I swim over to her and grab her ankle.

"Where do you think you're going? You can't almost capsize a watercraft and then think you get to drive it back?"

"That's exactly what I think." She replies as she searches around for how to turn it on. I hold up the lanyard on my wrist.

"Looking for this?"

She glares at me over the edge of her sunglasses and I laugh. Nora would hijack a freight train if the mood struck. I climb back onto the jet ski and she makes a show of keeping it steady while I do.

I reach around her and put the clip back in place and then restart the engine. I can easily reach around her to hold the handlebar and before she is really settled in I squeeze the throttle and we take off. Nora slides back into my body and I place a kiss to the side of her neck.

She points to the empty lot where I took her for our date and then turns to look at me. I release the throttle and she stands up. I hold her thighs to keep her steady but she turns around and curls her finger for me to stand with her.

The jet ski has enough momentum to keep us moving towards the lot. It feels like we are walking on the water. I lace my fingers through hers and pull her back against my chest. My chin rests on her shoulder as we take in the view of our first date from the water.

Does she know she's the first girl I've taken there?

Does she I bought the land a few years ago?

Does she know that I haven't thought about building a home on it until she asked me to describe my dream home?

And that I was picturing the home on that very spot?

With her?

Nora settles back down into the seat and we cross back over the lake at a leisurely pace. We pull up next to the Collins's boat and I hold on to the side while Nora climbs aboard. I offer a quick wave to everyone and then I look at Nora.

"Can I come back and hang out?"

"On the boat?" She asks confused.

"Yeah on the boat."

"Umm, sure I guess so. How will you get here without the jet ski?"

"I'll swim." I say with a shrug and then push off and steer the jet ski back towards the public dock.

...

Carnival setup is well underway as I walk through Sunfish Park on my way to the public beach. I pass the game stalls and decide to win a stuffed animal for Nora tonight. The smell of fried dough from the funnel cake stand wafts through the air. There is a fried Oreo stand, a fried pickle stand, and a fried peanut butter and jelly stand too.

I turn down one of the walkways towards the beach. I plan on diving in and swimming to their boat when it comes closer to the park. Everyone slowly circles around throughout the day so it's just a matter of time.

Someone steps out from between two stalls and I run into their back.

"Shit, sorry."

"Watch your mouth son." Dad says as he straightens up.

"Dad?"

"Jimmy." He says as he brushes his hands on his pants.

"What are you doing here?" I ask. It sounds accusatory and I don't mean for it to but he hasn't come to Float Fest since Mom died.

"I'm helping them get set up." He says like the answer is obvious.

I look around wondering if this is some sort of joke. Pops sticks his head out from the other side of the aisle.

"Jim what's taking you so long? Oh, hi Jimmy."

"Pops."

"Did you come here to help us old men? We could use your youth!" Pops says with a laugh. I look between them.

Dad looks to Pops and says "Give us a second Pops." And then he guides me over to a picnic table and takes a seat.

"Sit down Jimmy."

"Okay." I agree with trepidation. For the last fifteen years Dad has been a ghost of his former self. As I take a seat I see the color in his face more closely resembles the olive in mine. His brown eyes aren't clouded. His movements, although slow, are steady.

"Jimmy," he starts, he takes a deep breath. "I can see the shock in your face and it's tearing me up inside."

"What do you mean?"

"Well," he looks off towards the lake and inhales, "we talked the other night but when your mother died my world ended. I thought that everything revolved around her and with her gone I had no reason to keep going." He turns back to me.

"I know Dad," I start but he reaches across the table and puts his hand on my arm to quiet me.

"It took me too long to realize that I was ignoring what was left of your mother in you and your sister.

"When Angie came back from school she looked so much like your mother it physically hurt. I could hardly look at her. I tried to escape the pain and find comfort in the bottom of a bottle but that did no one any good.

"When you missed dinner," he continues, "Pops had had enough. He came over the next morning and yelled at me like I was seventeen and had been caught with my hand up the skirt of the ministers daughter."

"Did you?" I joke.

There is a sparkle in my dad's eyes I haven't seen since I was a kid. "I wasn't a saint before I met your mother."

"I can't wait to hear that whole story." I say as I sit up straighter and scratch at my beard.

"Maybe tonight at a bonfire."

"Yeah?" That's how we used to celebrate Float Fest each year. We'd close down the carnival and everyone would parade down Cherry Blossom Drive to our house for a bonfire.

My parents would set up tents and neighbors would party and then crash in the wee hours of the morning if they didn't live close by. As a kid I always tried to stay up as late as the grownups but would inevitably end up falling asleep in a chair and getting carried into the house by Dad.

The memory warms me from the inside out. It would be painful to do it without Mom there. But maybe that pain is something we need to work through, together.

"If you and your sister want to come by tonight after the carnival I'll have a fire going. Think about it." He pushes up and stands from the table. "Gotta get back to work."

"Okay, Dad." I say and I stand too. He holds out a hand for me to shake and I grasp his in mine.

This feels like a turning point. Like he's ready to move forward. To participate in town life again. In our lives again. What will it feel like to have him around? Have him helping at the store? Or on jobs?

There is a lot to figure out but, like I've done with nearly everything since Mom died, I'll take it one day at a time.

27

Step Right Up Play Hard Nora

Nora

"Gina, you sonovabitch!" Katherine grumbles as she swims over to retrieve a dart that just bounced off the plywood. "This is so much fun!"

Katherine lines herself up and whips the dart towards a blue balloon. It pops and Katherine squeals with delight as she dives forward to retrieve her nip and the dart.

Gina created a carnival game on the side of her boat. She stuffed balloons with airplane bottles of booze, blew the balloons up and then superglued them to plywood that she painted to look like a carnival game stall.

It is super fun.

We've all gotten turns and are swimming with our prizes back to the boat. Jimmy never came back after he dropped me off but that hasn't stopped me from giving Play Hard Nora the time of her life.

We climb back up and Charles hands us each a towel. I dry myself off and toss it to the side. The sun feels amazing on my skin. Warm and cuddly.

Maybe that's the booze.

I unscrew the whiskey I won and dump it into a cup. Kyle hands me a ginger beer and I dump half in my cup and hand it back to him. He empties the rest into his cup and then tosses it in the recycling bag.

"Who's ready for *Snackooterie*?" Kyle announces the question like a game show host.

I gasp in delight. "Really! I haven't had one in years!"

"Step right up Play Hard Nora. The Float Fest *Snackooterie* is a time honored tradition." Kyle says with a level of self importance I haven't seen from him before. "We have been stock-piling snacks for weeks."

"And we bought a new tray!" Liz adds as she stumbles towards the front of the boat. She digs through a bag and then stands up triumphantly holding a white tray over her head. It doesn't look like anything special.

She looks at it above her head and then goes 'oh' before turning it around. There's something written on it but the words are upside down.

"Babe." Kyle prompts.

Liz pulls it down in front of her face which makes the words fall right-side up to her. I giggle because I could see little comedy act this never ending.

Liz stares at the tray confused and then holds it up again but it's upside down to us. Kyle steps over and takes it from her hands gently. He places a kiss on her temple and carries the tray over to us.

"You're a snack." I read out loud.

"Isn't that cute?" Liz asks excitedly.

"Totally."

...

"All ashore that's going ashore!" Charles yells out as we pull up to their dock. I'm not sure what time it is but the heat of the afternoon has worn off a little and while the sun is still high in the sky it's getting close to the tops of the trees.

I collect my things and get off the boat. It's been a long day in the sun and I am looking forward to a minute inside. Kyle helps Charles and Katherine carry things up to their house.

"So, what's next?" I ask Liz who is busy trying to untangle one of the bead curtain strands from her bag.

"Shower and then carnival." She says.

"Dinner?"

"I usually eat there. You could make something at home first if you wanted." She gets the strand free and turns towards me. "Did Jimmy make plans with you?"

"Umm no, not really. He said he'd be back to the boat but then never came."

"Hmm," Liz considers, "We would have heard if he like drown or something."

"Ohmigod don't say that!"

Liz's eyes widen as she looks at me. "Why, because you like him?"

"Because that's a terrible thing to say about your friend." And, yes I like him.

"Sure sure. Well, I'm sure he just got caught up helping someone at the carnival. He'll probably be there."

"That's what I figured. So what do you wear to the carnival?"

"What do *I* wear or what should *you* wear? Those are two very different questions."

I chuckle. "True. I have a short white sundress that would be cute with these shoes," I hold up the espadrilles, "and they're comfortable enough to walk around in all night."

"Cute." Liz says as she links her arm in mine and walks us towards the car.

...

The warm shower water felt hot against my skin. I was careful to apply sunscreen but there's no avoiding a sunburn when you're a redhead and spend the day in the sun.

Before I leave the bathroom, I towel dry my hair, roll it into curlers, and blast it with the blow dryer. With my towel wrapped around me I step into the hallway. There are only three steps to my bedroom but before I make it, I hear Jimmy's voice in the font of the house.

On my tip toes I creep to the end of the hallway to try and hear what he's saying. He and Kyle just stepped out onto the porch so I creep a little further into the kitchen. I crouch down under the window and try to listen in.

"I'm just not sure what to make of it." Jimmy says.

Make of what? Of me?

"What do you think your pops said to him to make him want to change?"

Hmm, maybe they're talking about his dad.

"I don't know but he said he hadn't been yelled at like that since he was seventeen." Jimmy chuckles. "It must have been a compelling argument though. He seems to really want to turn things around." Jimmy pauses, maybe to take a sip of beer. "He asked me to come over for a bonfire tonight."

"Really?" Kyle asks.

"What the hell are you doing?" I turn and see Liz standing at the end of the hallway with her arms crossed.

"Shhhhhh, get down here before they see you." I hiss and wave.

"Who sees me? Kyle?" She whispers.

"And Jimmy."

"Ooooh."

"Shut up, I'm trying to listen."

Liz settles in next to me and holds her breath. I roll my eyes a little bit but only because I love her so much.

"I don't think he's invited anyone else, not even sure if Angie knows he's planning it, but I feel like I should meet him there. Just feel it out."

"I don't think it could hurt. Will you tell Angie?"

"Yeah, I want her to come with me. She must remember these parties even if she was younger when they ended."

"I'm sure she does. I haven't attended one in person but I've heard stories. They sounded unforgettable."

I turn and look at Liz and she nods. She jerks her head to the side and starts to walk in her crouched position back towards the bedrooms. She waves for me to fall in behind her.

Once we reach the hallway she leads me to my room.

"What is Jimmy talking about?" I ask as I pull my dress off the hanger.

"So growing up his parents always hosted a late night bonfire party after Float Fest."

"Hosted, as in past tense?" I say as I slip my underwear on under my towel.

"Yeah, they stopped when Jimmy's mom got sick." Liz

looks off in the distance. "There was talk of having another one for her funeral, or memorial service I guess, but Jimmy's dad was in bad shape so it never happened."

"Ugh, that's so sad." I say as I fish my strapless bra out from the drawer.

"How's your mom?" Liz ventures after a pause.

"Same old, same old with her. She called and said she had a new job this week. Mind you, it's not like she's starting a job at a store or a business, no, it's probably some sort of illegal substance distribution scheme."

Liz winces. "Still?"

"As far as I know, I don't really ask for details."

"Yeah." Liz glances at the clock on the nightstand. "Ah, we better get going and see if Mom beat Gina this year!"

She hops off the bed and marches down the hall, yelling, "Kyle McShoulders Sutherland finish that beer, we need to leave!"

I chuckle and slip my dress over my head. I pull out the rollers, fluff my hair, and pick out a pair of earrings. As I slip them in I hear a light knock on the door.

Jimmy is standing there with his arms braced on either side of the frame.

"Hey." He says.

"Hi."

"Sorry about earlier." He says earnestly.

"It's fine. We had a super fun day!"

"Yeah?" He looks off to the side. "I did too, now that I think about it."

"What kind of fun did you have?"

"I helped my dad and Pops finish setting up the carnival. It was the first time the three of us worked together on a project in a really long time."

I sit down on the edge of my bed and slip my shoes on. "That's great. I can't wait to see the work you put in."

He pauses and watches me as I tie the ribbons around my ankles. "What?" I ask.

"I ah, this is probably going to sound whiny or needy but, you're not mad at me are you?"

"Mad at you? Why would I be mad at you?"

"Because I didn't show up after I said I would," he sticks his hands in his pockets and rocks back on his heels.

"Jimmy," I stand, walk over to him, and place my hands on his chest. "I'm not mad, even if we were in an actual relationship I wouldn't be mad. I can take care of myself and I don't rely on other people."

"You sure?"

"I'm sure. My only expectation is orgasms, lots of them. So if you keep that, ah, coming, I will never be mad."

"Never say never but I think I can agree to those terms." He leans down and kisses my temple.

I've seen Kyle kiss Liz on the temple a thousand times. It seems so innocent but as his breath caresses my hairline and his beard brushes against my eyebrow my knees wobble. I feel my eyes flutter closed.

"Stop making out and let's go!" Liz yells. "Mom is gonna lose her dang mind if we're late."

Jimmy steps backwards and I lead the way down the hall.

...

"And the winner of Lakeville's Eighth Annual Float Fest

Decoration Contest is..."

"Holy shit, holy shit, holy shit." Katherine chants next to me. Her fingers are crossed and I imagine if she was sitting down she'd be crossing her legs, elbows, and toes too.

"Katherine Collins!"

Katherine squeezes my arm so tight I think I'm going to bruise. She's screaming and jumping up and down next to me. She holds onto my arm as she wraps Liz, and then Kyle, and then Charles in a hug which means she drags me around in a circle with her.

"Oh sorry!" She says as she releases my arm and then runs her hands down her dress to smooth it. Everyone is clapping and smiling and Jimmy slides up next to me.

Katherine climbs on stage and accepts her certificate.

"Wait, there's no cash prize?"

"Nope. A certificate that gets printed at T.H.E. Library and bragging rights." Jimmy tells me. "Although I think Katherine will be dining out on this story for years. No one has bested Gina since the contest started."

"Wow, I'm even more proud to be a part of this win."

"I bet, for the right price, you could get a second certificate printed to commemorate this achievement." He teases.

"I would expect so." I dish back.

Jimmy reaches down and slides my hand through his arm before leaning down to my ear. "What are you hungry for Nora?" He whispers.

My tongue nearly rolls out of my mouth because, you, obviously I'm hungry for you. But also whatever fried pastry thing I'm smelling because, yum.

"Are there funnel cakes?"

"Yes there are, and fried Oreos. I like to get a basket of those, a basket of fries, and a beer to start off my night."

"Start? I mean, yes, that sounds delicious but where can a person even go from there?"

"To bed. And not in a sexy way. I think that's partially why my parents's bonfires were such a hit. People stopped eating carnival junk but then stayed up and walked around."

"Worked it off a bit, but not in a sexy way?" I ask.

"Exactly."

28

Care To Make It Interesting?

JIMMY

"I'm not sure you're holding that correctly." I venture with my hands held up like I'm approaching a hostage situation.

In my defense, Nora is standing with the air rifle held up against her belly and is trying to aim it at the target to win, and I quote, "her own damn prize."

"Let me do it!" She hisses as she pivots towards me causing the game attendant, myself, and the group of people behind me to duck. I cup my balls for good measure.

She turns back to the game and settles in. Suddenly all her muscles seem to tense and she pulls the trigger.

She opens her eyes, which means she closed them in the first place, and looks at the target in front of her.

Nothing.

"What the hell?" She asks and she tips the barrel up towards her face. I step in quickly and grab the gun. I set it down on the counter and the attendant snatches it.

"Easy there Annie O." I say with a smirk. "Here, let me show you how it's done."

She scoffs. "I'd like to see you try!"

I hand the attendant $5 which gets me three shots. Same three shots Nora got. She's standing next to me so with my fingertips to her stomach I gently push her backwards a step. She crosses her arms and cocks a hip. I wink at her before turning towards the game. I pull the rifle up to my shoulder, check the view finder, exhale, and fire.

The target flips over and falls backwards.

"Lucky try." Nora comments.

I line up again, exhale, and fire.

The target falls backwards.

"You're cheating."

"No I'm not, but I am willing to make a wager with you."

"Oh yeah whatcha thinking?"

"If I make this next one and win that," I point to the giant pink teddy bear hanging off the top of the stall, "you have to carry it around with you all night."

"And if you don't make it."

"You have to come home with me."

She laughs, "Nice try big shot. If you don't make it, I get to decide what kind of face painting you get."

As if this scene was scripted, a little girl runs behind us with her face painted like a butterfly complete with glitter.

"Deal." I reach out and we shake hands. She takes a step back while also pressing her tits together in her dress which makes them pop just a little bit more.

"Trying to play dirty Heely?"

"Never." She smirks.

Ignoring my pulse that has risen slightly in the last few moments I pivot towards the target again. I line up, exhale, and shoot leaving the rifle in place until I know the target fell.

Ting.

I set the rifle down and point to the giant pink teddy bear. Nora is standing there dumb struck.

"Here you go, honey." I say with some extra sweetness drizzled on top as I hand her the teddy bear.

If looks could kill.

Wow.

With her ice blue eyes laser faced on me, Nora reaches out and snatches the bear from my hands. She loops her arm around it's middle and hugs it to her waist.

She turns and stomps off towards the next game.

I jog a few steps to catch up with her.

"C'mon, you said earlier you'd never get mad at me."

"I'm not mad at you." She clips.

"You sure?"

"I'm mad that you paid off the attendant to rig the game or something and that I didn't think of it."

Laughter bubbles up. I can't tell if she's serious. And if I've learned anything from teenage Angie it's to always assume things are serious and then walk it back to a joke later.

I step in front of her and walk backwards.

"I didn't rig the game or bribe the attendant." I tell her earnestly and see her eyes narrow. "But I didn't tell you that I had done JROTC in high school."

"That's information counsel would have appreciated before she made an ass out of herself."

"Who, you?" I tease. "No way. It was adorable. And I'm sure if we went back and tried again you'd be nailing the targets easy peasy."

She looks back over her shoulder and for a split second I

think she's considering it. But then she smiles at me and points behind me. I turn around and see the ping pong ball toss.

"I challenge you to a do-over." She says as she strides up to the tent. She sets the bear down on the ground and pats its head like a dog.

"Alright, how many chances do we each get."

"It's six shots for five bucks." The attendant says.

"Three v three?" I ask.

"Deal."

"Flip to see who goes first?" I ask.

"No, ladies first." She says with a little dip of her shoulder.

I hand over the cash and the attendant hands us each three balls.

"Alright, if you get one in down here," he waves his hand over a collection of vases right below us, "you earn one point. Up here," he points to the middle level, "three points. And up here," he points to the top level, "seven points. Anything over eight points total wins a prize."

"Easy peasy." Nora turns to me "most points gets to pick the prize?"

"That seems fair. Alright, as soon as your ready."

"Shut it, I'm considering my options." She growls. I smirk and stand back to give her room.

She lines up her first shot and tosses it. She does a little hop move like it's a free throw. Either way the ball bounces off the top level and lands in the middle level giving her three points.

"Yes!" She hisses as she pumps her fist. "Your turn."

I step up and with a flick of my wrist the ball lands in the top row. I turn to her with a smile and she returns with a scowl.

"Seven," I say pointing at my chest. "To three." I say

pointing at her. She knocks my hand down and starts to curl the two ping pong balls she has left in her hand. I have turned into a horny teen because my balls tighten a little imagining her with her hand on them instead.

"Yeah, yeah. Okay." She lines up and does her little hop toss thing and it lands in a top row cup. "YES! Suck on *that* Lewis!"

"Nice job." I concede because I have no clue what the physics are behind how that went in, but it did. I step up, flick my wrist and sink a ball in the top row.

"Fuck." She mutters besides me.

"Careful, there are kids around." I tease. "Okay, last throw, score is me, 14, you, 10."

"We can all do the math, Jimbob." She mutters as she comes up for her final shot. She lines up and raises her arm, and then lowers it. She looks over at me. "I don't like losing."

"I figured as much."

She squares up again and I step forward so I'm standing right behind her. A mere inch separates our bodies.

"It's only losing if you let it stop you from getting what you want." I whisper.

She nods and rolls her shoulders back. She lines up, hops, and throws. It bounces off the top row, down to the second row, and then dribbles down to the bottom where it lands between two cups and hits the plywood.

"Damn." She says as she steps back.

I walk up, hold the ball in my hand and lift it to shoulder height before dropping it. I don't aim at all, just wanted to get the last toss out of the way.

It lands with a plop in a vase.

"Ugh! Even when you don't try you win." She turns, grabs her pink bear, hoists it up to her waist, and marches off.

The attendant holds up two stuffed animals for me to pick from, a neon blue monkey and a fluorescent orange tiger.

I grab the tiger, toss him a "thank you" over my shoulder, and chase after Nora who is already closing in on the food carts.

"Hey! Nora, wait up."

"No, I'm hungry."

"Alright, what do you want?"

She looks around at the different options and then points to the popcorn booth. I get in line for a bag of kettle corn.

Nora waits for me, thankfully, and when I have the popcorn in hand I make it look like the tiger is carrying it when I hand it to her. She smirks, I can tell she fought it, and I sling my arm around her shoulder.

Together we walk towards a bench and take a seat. She sits up the pink bear next to her and it feels like there are three of us on this bench.

I rest my arm on the back of the bench behind Nora. She holds out the popcorn bag to me and I take a handful. I start dropping pieces from the palm of my hand into my mouth as she pinches one piece at a time.

"Having fun tonight?" I ask with a mouthful.

She smiles "I am, more than I expected to." She looks around at the carnival. The sun has set and the flashing lights from the rides create a kaleidoscope of colors across her white dress. Music from the different rides compete with the live band playing on the other side of the park. Conversations flow and squeals of kids' laughter float through the air.

She sighs.

"What's that for?"

"I don't have a plan. I'm sitting here right now, enjoying myself, trying not to jump your bones," she adds quickly, "but I don't know what I'm doing tomorrow."

I place my hand on the crook of her neck where it meets her shoulder and wait for her to continue.

"I always have a plan. I always know what I'm doing tomorrow and the next day, month, year."

We sit and contemplate her words in silence. She turns her face towards me and the concern in her features matches the sharp pain in my chest.

"My Gran used to say something that I didn't really understand until recently. She'd say 'if you control everything you control the magic too'. I always thought she was saying it as encouragement to plan and control things. And I leaned on that after my mom died. But now I'm starting to think that she meant controlling everything doesn't leave any room for magic to work its, well, magic."

Nora turns her head back towards the carnival. She's quiet for a long time before she speaks.

"I think I controlled everything to the point where there was no magic at all."

Past tense.

"And now?" I test.

"And now, there's some magic." She whispers. "Everything fell apart at my feet and I had no choice but to let go of the reins. And this week has felt scary but also exciting, fun. And I've never experienced this type of connection with," she pauses, "people."

People or me?

"What are you thinking now? What non-plans do you have in mind?"

She smiles. "I'm trying out this one moment at a time thing. Let the magic do the work for a while."

29

Pulling The Rip Cord

JIMMY

Nora and I finish the popcorn while we watch high schoolers sneak off into the darker area of the park.

"Should we head in there and show them a thing or two?" Nora jokes.

"Nah, it's best they figure it out for themselves. That's the kind of thing that requires on-the-job experience. It can't be taught."

She laughs. We stand and start to walk back towards the carnival. We turn a corner and see Liz and Kyle enjoying some ice cream together. Liz waves at us and we walk over.

"Hey you two!" She says.

"Hey." Nora answers.

"So are you going to your dad's tonight?" Kyle asks. Liz and Nora exchange a glance before Nora turns towards me.

"What's going on at your dad's?" She asks.

"He invited me over for a bonfire. I figured I'd see how the night went with you before I decided what I was going to do." I say to Nora with a small shrug.

"And, how's your night going with Nora?" Liz asks.

"So far so good." I say and I catch Nora's smile. "Let's go find Angie and see if she's going. Then we can decide."

We wave to Liz and Kyle and start walking away. Nora leans in closer to me and whispers. "I'm willing to go, or meet up with you later, or be the excuse for why you couldn't go. Whatever you need."

"Thanks." I say, trying to fight the worry in my stomach. Why am I worried though? Dad will be nice to Nora, he'll regale her with stories of my youth. Angie already loves her and will ask her for advice on fashion or guys or whatever else she needs input on.

Dad's eyes were clear earlier and he told me he hasn't had a drink since the dinner I missed on Tuesday. Yeah, that's only a few days but it's a start. He and I chatted and joked around with Pops as we assembled the stage.

I asked if he was going to come to the carnival and he said no, that the lights and sounds and crowds would be too much for him right now. And I respect that. He seems to understand his limits.

Nora and I make our way through the crowd, I say hello to a lot of people as we pass them. We spot Angie standing in line for the restroom. Nora hands me the giant teddy bear before joining her in line. I watch as they inch their way forward, chatting and laughing the whole time. Nora stands out as the most beautiful girl here but she fits into Lakeville perfectly.

When they're finished they walk towards me and Nora takes the giant bear back and hooks it under her arm.

"So you want to go to Dad's after this, huh?" Angie starts.

I look at Nora and she shrugs. That's not exactly how I put it but it's where I was leaning.

"I think so, yeah. What about you?" I reply.

"I'll go if you go and we set a safe word slash develop an exit strategy."

"You live there." I remind her.

"True but I don't hang out with Dad very often. We share meals, he goes to watch TV, and I go to my room."

"Let's go to his place, and if either of you needs to end it ask me how my cat is doing and I'll storm off in a hissy fit." Nora states like this settles the matter.

Angie looks at Nora with questions written all over her face.

I lean forward and inform Angie, "Her cat died last week."

"Oh-kay." Angie manages. "That could work. Dad could never handle any hysterics so if you storm off, Jimmy has to follow you, and I'll just say I'm tired at that point. I like this, this could work."

"We're not plotting a bank heist. We're going to hang out with our dad." I say.

"Po-tay-to, po-tah-to." Angie replies.

...

"What can I get ya to drink?" Dad asks as we walk through the house towards the back yard.

"Water is fine for me," Nora says.

"Same." I answer.

Angie heads to the fridge and gets herself a sparkling water as Dad pours waters for us.

I slide open the screen door and stand back so Nora can walk through first. Dad already started the fire so it's burning bright. The moon's reflection is glistening off the lake behind the fire. The joy of my childhood rushes back as the smell of the fire meets the chorus of crickets, frogs, and squirrels in the trees.

"So Nora, how long are you in Lakeville?" Dad asks, going straight for the jugular.

She smiles, turns to me, "I'm not sure." She says.

Shooting stars race through my body.

Is she planning to stay?

She turns back towards my dad and continues.

"My job is on hiatus at the moment and I haven't had a break in a really long time. I'm trying to just sit back and enjoy the moment for awhile before plotting my next move."

I don't even try to contain my grin. Dad continues walking with Nora down towards the fire and Angie slides up next to me.

"So are you two like a thing now? Do I need to start developing a celebrity couple name?"

"That's the first I heard her say something like that. I'm not sure what it means."

"Interesting." Angie says as she takes a sip of her water.

"Yeah."

We settle into the Adirondack chairs that surround the fire pit. Dad is finishing up a story about how he would secretly microwave the hotdogs that we used to cook over the fire because my mom was afraid of undercooked food.

I chuckle at the memory. Angie threw a total fit when she saw Dad sliding cooked hotdogs back into the packaging before coming outside. She went on this whole tirade about how they were liars and she can't believe they would trick their kids like this.

It was around the time she had found out about Santa from kids at school so her entire belief system was being tested.

"Remember playing kick the can with Mom?" She asks.

"Of course I do. She was so good. She always won." I say with a laugh.

"She was patient." Dad says. We all go still because no one knows how talking about Mom will affect him. "She'd lean against the shed, she didn't even try hiding, but you two were trying so hard to be sneaky. Your whispers always gave you away."

He looks towards the shed and takes a sip of his water.

"I'd watch her from here, our eyes would connect, and I'd marvel at how this incredible, extraordinary, beautiful woman had created this life with me."

Angie and I exchange glances. I turn and catch Nora's eyes meeting mine.

"She sounds wonderful." Nora says as she lays a hand on my dad's arm breaking his trance with his memories.

"She was one hell of a woman that's for sure. Angie, you're her spittin' image. She was a hopeless romantic too. And you Jimmy, you hold the world together like she did." He exhales a laugh. "But all your handyman skills you learned from me."

The three of us laugh because Mom was not handy in anyway. She did more harm than good if she tried to help. Nora smiles softly, taking in our family trip down memory lane. I watch as a shadow crosses through her eyes and they cloud over.

"I ah, um, my cat died." Nora says curtly. She stands up abruptly and walks back to the house.

I stand up and start to follow her but Dad holds up his hand to stop me.

"Jimmy, I don't know what you've got going with that girl but don't let her get away."

"I won't Dad."

"Good," he nods. "Now go."

I jog up the grass and catch Nora just as she's reaching the deck.

"Hey, Nora, what's going on?" I ask, concern dripping from every syllable.

"I just," she wipes at her face, shit she's crying. "I just got overwhelmed seeing the love you all share."

My arms act before my brain does and I pull her tight against my chest. Her head rests against me and she wraps her arms around my waist. We stand there, my heart reaching out to hers through this embrace.

Telling her I am here for her. Telling her I will wait for her. That I will help her figure things out. That I want to face uncertainty with her. That I have love to share with her too.

She sniffles and straightens up. I keep my arms around her but loosen my hold just enough to allow her to look up at me.

"Seriously, I'm like allergic to Lakeville." She laughs at herself. "I never cry."

"Then you had a lot to let out. You've broken the seal."

"Like when you pee for the first time while you're drunk?" Her humor attempting to slide up and protect her from being vulnerable.

"Exactly like that." Her smile tells me that she is glad I didn't push further. I'm learning to read her, to understand when she's willing to open up, when to sit back and let her think things through on her own, and when she needs to shut everything down and reset.

"So you pulled the old 'my cat died' line, does that mean you wanna get out of here?"

"Yeah. Can I come home with you?"

"I wouldn't have it any other way."

...

Because a deal is a deal I'm standing three steps below Nora as she climbs the stairs to my apartment giving the giant pink teddy bear a piggy back ride.

I squeeze past them both and unlock the door. Nora walks in and tosses the bear on the sofa. Then she takes the time to make sure it's sitting up straight so it can see the TV. She leans against the back of the couch and pulls one ankle up to her knee and starts untying her shoe.

I step up to her and gently move her ankle back to the floor. I kneel down in front of her and finish untying the first ribbon before guiding her foot out of the shoe. I move to the second.

When her shoes are off and she's standing barefoot in front of me, in the apartment I built, I can feel roots starting to grow.

A possessiveness washes over me and Dad's words ring in my ears.

Don't let her get away.

My hands travel up the back of her legs, pulling up the skirt of her dress with them as I reach her thighs. At the junction of her legs and ass I grip and lift her up against me.

She gasps in surprise but her legs instantly wrap around my waist. Her arms curl around my neck. Unable to resist a moment longer, I crash into her mouth as I carry her to my bedroom.

I set her down at the foot of the bed and she places her hands on my chest and pushes me backwards. After a few steps my calves meet the overstuffed leather chair in the corner of my room.

She reaches for the hem of my t-shirt and I help her pull it off. Her hands run up my torso and my muscles ripple under her touch. She presses down on my shoulders easing me back into the chair before she climbs onto my lap.

"Jimmy, my mind is saying we need to talk," her hands are on each side of my neck.

"But?"

She smiles.

"But, my body is begging me to give in to my need for you." She says as her eyes zero in on my pulse.

I inch forward and kiss her, my hands on the tops of her thighs. This is so similar to the night I met her. The memory of her rain soaked body, the way she rolled her hips on top of me, how she gripped my shoulders for leverage, plays in my mind while I grow harder underneath her.

She pulls back and puts her fingers on my lips.

"Let's play a game."

"Strip Parcheesi?" I ask with a wink.

"No."

"Seven Minutes in Heaven?"

She laughs and playfully slaps my chest.

"No, Two Truths and A Lie."

"Naked?"

"Winner gets to undress the other." She says. "You go

first."

I lean back in the chair and she settles down onto my thighs. Our fingers are interlaced and her thumb is drawing circles on my palm.

Nora is giving me a chance to open up. To be vulnerable. I think she wants to use this game to admit her feelings to me. Maybe not all her feelings, that's fine. I'll take what I can get.

The question is, do I admit my feelings? Or only part of my feelings? Will going for broke scare her?

What's my goal here? Short term, getting Nora naked in my bed and doing everything I can to hear my name on her lips in pleasure. Long term, creating a life with her.

That's too much to admit now. She'd go running for the hills.

"Okay. I got it. I can't stop thinking about you. You saying my name is my favorite sound in the world. I'd be willing to make some major life changes if it meant we could stay together."

Where's the lie?

Her face softens and I see the wheels turning.

"The lie is that you'd make major life changes."

"Nope." I smile.

"So you *can* stop thinking about me?" She adorably crosses her arms in front of her chest and raises an eyebrow in mock anger.

"Nope. You saying my name is my second favorite sound in the world. Your laughter is my first."

Her arms stay crossed but her body relaxes. She leans forward.

"You cheated." And she hops off my lap and starts walking

to the door.

I jump up, grab her around the waist, and twirl her back into my arms. I gently lean her up against the wall and press my body against hers.

"No. I'd never cheat. Not in a silly game, not when it comes to cutting corners to save money or time on a job, and never, I repeat, never would I cheat on you."

"Jimmy, that's not what I meant."

"But I need you to hear it." I keep my body close to hers. Her hands are on my ribs, bracing herself. "Your turn."

Nora's sapphire eyes grow wide as she inhales.

"You make me question everything I ever thought was certain. I've never felt so scared in my life. And, I think your bedspread is ugly."

She grins.

"Easy, the bedspread."

She doesn't respond. I raise an eyebrow at her. She just stares into my eyes.

"I win." I whisper, "so now I get to do this," I play with the strap on her shoulder. "But we're going slow."

"Slow can be good." She breathes.

"Why are you scared?" I whisper the question into her ear before gently kissing down the column of her neck. She rolls her head to the side giving me more room. The hint of her perfume is intoxicating but I need to hear her answer so I still myself.

"Close your eyes." I pull back and watch as she flutters her eyes closed. I return to placing kisses along her neck and down to her shoulder.

"Nora, why are you scared?" I ask between kisses.

"Because I don't know what's going to happen." She gasps in a breath as I gently bite her shoulder. "Because what if we try and fail? I don't take risks if I can't calculate them."

She tucks her chin into her chest.

"But, honey, what if we try and don't fail?" I press my hand along her side and pull my head back to look at her. Nora's eyes are still closed and she's biting at her bottom lip.

"Nora, look at me." Her eyes open and desperately search mine for answers. "I don't have any answers, I don't know what's going to happen, but I do know I'm scared too."

"You are?" Her words are barely audible.

"I am. I'm scared of letting you slip out of my grasp. Of living a life without you, knowing you're out in the world without me. I've seen my father and grandfather lose the women they love," her hand rises from my side to rest on my wildly beating heart. "And while the loss wrecked my Dad I know he would live it all over again if he could have one more day with her. One more moment."

I rest my forehead against hers. Both of us breathing heavily because of the emotions we're feeling and sharing.

"Nora, I have no idea where you came from or how you ended up here with me but I want to always be there for you. To help you make plans. To help you not make plans. To pick you up when you stumble and to try and watch you win carnival games."

She laughs and sniffles. I open my eyes to see a tear running down her cheek. I catch it with my thumb and then turn her head up to mine.

"I think I love you." I admit to her, and myself.

The world around me is silent. The sound of no sound

bangs against my ears. Nora's eyes are clouded with tears that won't fall. She blinks and one slides down her cheek.

"I think I love you too."

30

Putting Pen To Paper

Nora

Jimmy's grip on my waist tightens. Good. Because I am waiting for the earth to crack open and swallow me up whole.

I think I love you too.

I meant it when I said he scares me. Not Jimmy the person, but everything about a relationship with him. Since I was a child I have only had myself to rely on.

My mother would poke fun at me in high school for how organized I was. She'd laugh at the chore chart I made to make sure I kept up with the laundry and remembered trash day. In some of her crueler moments she said no man would want to get with such a tight ass woman.

I decided I'd rather be a tight ass than give anyone else the reins.

It's why hook ups worked for me. It's why I've risen so quickly at my job. It's why my closet is organized, my meals are planned. My manicures scheduled regularly.

Control.

And as soon as my life began to spiral Jimmy found me.

Before I knew him, he was there to pick me up in the storm.

He was there when I cried on the bench.

He was there when I was overwhelmed at his dad's house.

And he's here now.

Embracing me as I admit to the feelings I have for him. I don't know what love towards a man is supposed to feel like but this tug and pull between the way he energizes and calms me is something I've never experienced before.

"Nora," he whispers.

"Yeah?"

"I need to make love to you."

My knees quiver as his words hit my ears. He picks me up in a hug and carries me towards the bed. Unlike before he doesn't seem rushed. He sits me on the bed and drags his fingers up my arm, holds my wrist, and places a kiss to my open palm before resting my hand on his shoulder. My limbs are putty in his hands.

He slides the zipper of my dress down to my hip. He pulls me up to standing and the dress slides down to the floor.

I reach around behind me to unclasp my bra but he shakes his head. "Rules were that the winner got to strip the other."

"Oh right." I smile.

I'm standing in front of him at the foot of his bed. Each second that passes increases my need for him. I want to be physically connected to him, with him. I want to feel his body on top of mine.

He brings his lips down to mine and his kiss sends lightning through me. Immediately I open my mouth to bring him closer. His kiss swallowing the moan that escapes my throat.

He grunts and unclasps my strapless bra and it falls to the floor between us. I'm standing naked in front of him. Emotionally, I'm completely bare. Physically only my panties remain. His hand finds the elastic of the waistband as he kisses me and he hooks his fingers under the thin band.

He steps forward so his leg is between mine and with an arm around my waist he lowers me to the bed. I slide myself backwards so my head is on his pillow. Thinking he's going to follow me, I lay back and close my eyes. Waiting to feel him on top of me.

When he doesn't, I curl up and lean on my elbows. He's standing at the end of the bed looking at me as he rubs the side of his face with one hand, the other sitting on his hip.

"What's wrong?" I ask, trying to temper the panic that rushes through me.

"Nothing, I just, ah, got to thinking."

Oh no, oh shit, he's changing his mind. He wants to stop this. Stop us. I sit up all the way and curl my legs off the side of his bed. Before I can stand he's rounded the bed and is standing in front of me.

"Where the hell are you going?"

"Jimmy, I'm not just going to lay here on your bed and watch you change your mind about me."

"That's not what I was thinking." He says as a headiness settles over his eyes.

"No?"

"No."

"Then what were you thinking?"

I swallow to try and dispel the moment before the roller coaster drops feeling in my stomach.

"Well, I was thinking about what to do with you first. And then the idea of binding your wrists to my headboard got in my head and, honestly, it broke my brain for a minute."

Oh.

It's breaking my brain too.

I look up at him and reach for his belt buckle. He lets me work it open and unbutton his fly. He helps me push his jeans down off his hips and the belt buckle crashes against the floor.

I wet my lips and see his cock twitch in his briefs in front of me. The things I could do with him race through my mind.

More than a night's worth, more than a week's worth.

A lifetime's worth?

I smile and pull his briefs down, then slide back and lay on his pillows again. He kneels onto the bed and moves closer to me. He hooks his thumbs into my thong and pulls it down my legs.

"We have plenty of time to try all sorts of things, Jimmy," I say as I pull him down on top of me. "Tonight, I want to be with you."

Our kisses turn urgent and our bodies respond to one another's. He tests my readiness with his thumb and finds me fully aroused.

"Nora, I want, no I need to be inside you." He mutters sounding frustrated.

"Then do it."

He lunges for his bedside table and I let out a giggle. He roughly pushes the condom down his length and comes back to me. Bracing himself with his elbows on either side of my head he pushes all of himself into me quickly.

His chest pushes up against mine and my arms hold on to

his neck like I'm hanging on a tightrope. I'm surrounded by him. He's surrounded by me. And from the containment of him alone, I feel my orgasm building.

He thrusts in and out of me, my name a chant on his lips. My chest tightens as I cry out his name. A blissful type of pain concentrates there, pushing against my chest as every other nerve in my body zeroes in on my center.

Together we fall over the edge. My inner walls holding him and his need meeting my own.

While he's still inside me he lifts up and brushes my hair back from my face.

"Nora," he breathes, "I love you."

I stare back into his eyes and warmth washes over me.

"I love you Jimmy."

He smiles, pulls out of me, and goes to the bathroom to wash up. I'm lying alone in bed, fighting the urge to kick my feet and squeal with delight. By the clock that was a quickie but I have never been so satisfied.

"What are you smiling about?" Jimmy says as he slides onto the bed and lays his hand on my stomach.

"I might be having a psychotic break." His eyebrows rise and I feel his body tense. "No, not for real, I'm completely sane. I think." I shake my head. "I'm laying here, enjoying the come down from the first orgasm I've ever experienced from containment alone and feeling thrilled that I don't know what is going to happen next."

"Thrilled?"

"Yes, nervous, obviously, but more excited than I think I'm willing to admit."

"So does this mean you're staying in Lakeville? Will you

stay with me?"

"I don't know." I say slowly, wondering who this version of Nora Heely is. For the first time I don't have a plan. I don't know what's going to happen next.

But I do know I'm willing to leave some room for magic. This past week, this man, has changed my heart forever. I sit up and Jimmy curls up on his elbow too. He searches my face as I look down at him.

"Actually, I take that back." I sit up next to him, "Do you have a notebook and pen?"

"Sure, let me grab it."

Jimmy stands and walks over to his dresser where he slips on a pair of gym shorts. I use the bathroom and then settle back in his bed under the covers as he carries in two glasses of water and has the notebook and pen tucked under his chin.

I laugh as I grab the notebook and he kisses me on the forehead after he releases it. He takes a sip of water and offers me the other glass before climbing in next to me.

He wraps his arm around my back and rests his chin on my shoulder.

"Whatcha doing?" He asks.

"I'm doing what I do best. I'm making a plan."

"Do I get to help?"

"I was hoping you would."

At the top of the page I write 'Nora's Next Steps' and jot the date down in the corner. I'm not sure if it's late Saturday or early Sunday. I don't feel the need check, I write Saturday's date with a little star next to it.

This is the moment my life changes.

"Okay, I need to give a 30 day heads up to my building if

I'm going to break my lease. I'll email them in the morning." And I write 'email landlord' on my list.

"Next, I need a job."

"What are you thinking?"

I rest the notebook on my knees and look at Jimmy.

"I'm thinking that I can call my boss on Monday and pitch her my solution clearly. I will tell them that I need an answer from them by Friday."

"What if they give you your job back? Wouldn't you have to stay in the city?"

"Not necessarily, I might have to travel to the city for meetings but the drive isn't that bad. And then longer trips traveling to see the clients would be the same as if I still lived there."

"Okay. This seems reasonable." He pauses and his fingers play with the spirals of the notebook. "What if you don't get the job back?"

"Then I look for another one. But I can't solve that problem until I know it's something that needs solving."

"Wow." Jimmy says reverently.

"What?" I look straight at him.

"You're amazing. Can you really not worry about something like that?"

"I've never been much of a worrier." I always thought that was a good thing but Jimmy has helped me realize the control I had on my life didn't allow things to veer off the plan.

"Okay then, Zen Master, you've got a plan. Now let's put that away and spend time on each other." He says as he reaches for the notebook. I pull it up against my chest.

"Actually, I have one more list I need to make."

"You do? What is it?" Jimmy asks.

I turn the notebook page and write 'All The Things We Want To Do To Each Other' on the top.

Jimmy's eyebrows skyrocket and he sits up straight. He snatches the notebook out of my hand and plants a kiss on my lips. He pulls away quickly.

"Give me that pen, I'm going first."

31

That Wasn't On The List

JIMMY

"I might need a diagram for that one." I say as I read the five word description of the, ah experience, Nora just wrote in the notebook.

"That's fine, I'll coach you through it." She starts tapping the pen on her chin. "Oh! I know." And she writes down number 48 on the list.

That's right, we've officially hit four dozen different ways we want to explore each other. The first dozen went quick since we've only spent a few nights together. Then she brought up the ties on her wrists idea I had mentioned and the next dozen stemmed from there. We went down the list of different locations next. And I have a feeling that section will grow the more we think about it.

We also turned the page and wrote out a new list of the different supplies we would need. Nora said she had a few of them at her apartment and I had to stop myself from dragging her out the door right now to drive to the city and get them.

"What do you say we get to fifty and then try some of them?" Nora asks me nonchalantly.

"Write this down; 49. 100m Dash - where we try to get each other there as quickly as possible. And 50. 100min Marathon - where we can't get off for 100 minutes."

"Oh, I like that," Nora says as she writes it down. She clicks the pen shut when she's done writing. "So, where are we gonna start?"

"At the top." I say, as I slide the notebook off her lap and onto the floor. I take the pen from her hand and drop it off to the side.

"Honestly, I can't believe we haven't done that yet."

"I've been saving it, it's one of my favorites."

"I know," she smiles and kisses me deeply. I'm already hard from picturing everything we've put on the list. I'll need to pace myself because once I'm inside her I won't last long and I want her to enjoy my favorite position too so we can return to this one again and again.

...

"Hand me the pen." I say and Nora reaches over to her nightstand. She hands me the pen and I place a checkmark next to number 12.

We went a little out of order after number 1 so we have checks next to 1, 4, 23 and 24, one rolled into the other there, and now 12.

"I don't want to admit this but I need some sleep." I say and like my body heard me a yawn escapes my lips.

"That's okay babe."

Babe, she called me babe.

"You're not tired?" I ask, because number 24 involved

some concentration on her part.

"I'm a little tired." And a yawn escapes her lips too.

I roll down on the bed a little and lift my arm to invite her to snuggle with me. Her body presses up against my side and her hand rests on my stomach.

I stroke my hand up and down her back. She sighs against me and her exhale tickles my skin.

"How about number three in the morning?" She asks.

Number 3: Shower Sex.

"How early can I wake you up?" I ask seriously and she playfully rolls her eyes.

"After number three what do you want to do tomorrow?" She asks me, a hint of vulnerability in her voice.

I pull strands of her beautiful red hair through my fingers.

"Well, I think after number three we enjoy breakfast together, decide which numbers to tackle next," I pinch her side and she laughs, "and then we get your stuff from Liz's and bring it here."

"Okay. I like that plan."

"Yeah?"

"Yeah." And she gently pats my chest. "I'm going to get some water, do you want some?"

I glance at my empty glass on my night stand. "Yeah, thank you."

She leaves her side of the bed, I fucking love that she has a side of the bed, and takes our water glasses with her to the kitchen.

Once she opened up to me, things have fallen together quickly. If she's feeling any doubts, she's not showing them to me. And I'm fine if she's nervous. I'll be confident enough about this relationship for the both of us.

I close my eyes and let my imagination run with the life I can create with Nora. I envision dropping on one knee and asking her to marry me, I envision the home I build for her, our wedding day, she's going to look so damn good walking down the aisle to me.

I see a family, I see us hosting friends around a bonfire. I see us both working and coming together at the end of the day to reconnect.

Based on Pops and Dad I know I'll go gray. Will she?

Will our children have red hair like her? I fucking hope so because it is the most beautiful shade of amber under the sun.

Nora already gets along with Angie, and her best friend lives in town. She's shown she can hang at Float Fest and her kind words to Dad around the fire demonstrates her depth of character. How much she cares about those she loves.

Maybe I'm putting the cart before the horse but when she said *I think I love you too* my heart cracked open and made room for hers. I felt it shape shifting to accommodate a life with Nora.

"Oh shit!" She hisses from the kitchen.

"What?!" I fly out of bed, snag my shorts off the floor and step into them as I stumble towards her.

"I gotta go." She says as she sets her phone down on the counter.

"Why? No. What's going on?"

She storms past me and picks up her bra, clasps it, spins it, and slides it up into place. She's tearing around in the sheets for her thong. "Where is it?" She mutters with frustration.

"You know what, fuck it." And she stands up straight and gathers up her dress and starts stuffing her limbs into it.

"Nora, what's happening?"

"Nothing, just, ugh, my mom."

"Your mom? Is she okay?"

"Probably, but I just gotta go."

"Is there anything I can do to help?"

"Nope. Ugh, actually." She looks up at me and pauses with her hand on her purse. "Can you drive me to my car?"

"Of course. But I don't want you driving while you're upset. Where are you going?" I slip into a t-shirt and slide on sandals.

"My mom is in my apartment right now and nothing about that is good." Nora says darkly as she opens my door and starts walking down the stairs barefoot.

"I'll go with you, let me take you." I say as I lock up behind her. She freezes on the step and turns to look up at me.

"No. Absolutely not. Just take me to my car."

"Nora." I plead.

"Jimmy, you know what, never mind. I'll call Liz to come and get me. Or bring my car here and then walk home or something, I don't need your help."

"But I want to help!" I almost yell as she pushes open the door to the alley.

"No, you don't. Not with this." She says as she starts walking towards the sidewalk.

"Nora, stop. I'll drive you to your car. I'll stay behind. But it's going to kill me."

She turns and marches back to the truck. She opens the door, climbs in, and I start the engine. We're sitting next to each other. My hand itches to reach out and touch her for the entire drive. We're sharing the same air but she's a million miles away.

I pull up in front of the house and without a word she slides out of the cab and walks barefoot to her car. It's by the light of the moon that I watch her get into her car.

When she closes the door I hear her engine start and she pulls out of the driveway. Her eyes find mine as she passes. Then I stare in my rearview mirror and watch Nora drive out of town.

32

A Bad Comedy Act

Nora

My palm hurts from pounding it on the steering wheel.

Why did I check my phone?

I could be cuddled up in bed with a man, my man, who makes me feel fucking feelings but noooo. I'm driving back to the city because of a text.

> Mom:
> Where's your vodka and why is there a cat in your freezer?

"She's IN MY FUCKING APARTMENT!" I scream at my dashboard. She never comes to the city. Thank Heavens. The people and the noise and, let's be honest, the sirens give her anxiety.

The only thing that brings her to the city is if she has to pick something up for a job or if she's hiding from a job.

My guess is that today, she's hiding.

Hence needing the vodka.

How'd she get in to my place?

Is she alone or did she bring a guy?

Is she trying to stash something at my place until her scent cools off?

I never ask my mother for details on her jobs because I figure the less I know the better. Plausible deniability and all that. She has hinted at moving drugs for guys in the past. Hopefully just weed, but who knows.

When I was little she'd disappear for two days and then come back with a handful of cash. We'd dine like queens and then there'd be famine for a week or two. I was old enough to know she didn't make her money like other parents at my school but I wasn't old enough to try and figure out what she did to earn it.

One month, when I was twelve, she dated the grocery store manager. That was a whole month of eating like queens because he gave us a discount. I tried to stock up on canned goods, knowing they'd eventually break up and the going would get tough again. Mom would put them back on the shelf saying "Girlie we don't want him thinking we're using him. Even though we are." And then she'd cackle cough us towards the deli counter.

I exit the highway and start driving through the grid of Manhattan towards my apartment. Even at 3am there is activity in the streets.

Cabs zig and zag down the avenues.

Bakery lights are on behind the grille door fences.

And my mother is most likely sitting on my sofa drinking whatever booze I had in my apartment.

I park my car and head to the front door of my building. I see Manny, the night time security guard there. He greets me with wide eyes.

"Hi Manny."

"Ms. Heely. How are you this morning?"

"Oh I'm fine. I'm just trying to figure out why there is a woman in my apartment."

"She said she was your mother and that she had a surprise for you and that I would spoil it if I called you for permission."

I massage my temples. That's not even a good lie. "Okay. Was she carrying anything?"

"Yes ma'am. She had a big, colorful tote bag on her shoulder and a black duffle bag in her hands."

"Okay, thank you Manny. In the future, always call me, surprise or not."

"Yes ma'am."

I head to the elevator and press the call button. My body is trying to decide if it is tired or wired from the adrenaline coursing through my veins.

As the doors close behind me I'm met with my reflection. How many times have I used this last-chance mirror to make sure I was put together. Checking my hair, lipstick, or if my skirt was straight.

As I look at the girl in the slightly distorted stainless steel now, I don't feel any urge to adjust. She's sporting bags under her eyes. Her date makeup is faded and smudged. The curls in her hair have fallen.

She is sporting an outfit Old Nora would approve of. Ivory fitted dress and heels. I hitch the chain of my purse up on my shoulder as the doors open and march purposefully down the hallway.

I reach my door and stop to listen before opening it. I hear the TV on but nothing else.

That might be a good sign. Maybe she is alone.

As quickly as I can I unlock the door and push myself in. My mom's head pops up from the sofa and I pray to anything listening that she's alone. That I didn't just interrupt something.

"Nora! You're back!" She scans my outfit. "Have fun tonight?"

"It was a good night until I got your text."

She stands and turns towards me. I'm close enough to confirm that no one else is on the sofa.

"Well it took you long enough to get here." She huffs. She crosses her arms and cocks a hip. "I'm assuming you continued the fun after you got my text."

"No, I was upstate, so I immediately got in the car and drove here."

"What were you doing upstate?"

"Visiting my friend."

"Friend? Or *friend*?" She teases.

"None of your business." I say as I cross over to my bedroom and begin to change into leggings and a long sleeve t-shirt.

She marches after me. "Don't be like that! C'mon, we can share dick stories!"

"No!" I pull the t-shirt over my head before continuing. "You're my *mother*! I am not interested in sharing dick stories with you. Now, be honest, why are you here?"

"To visit."

"Try again."

She levels me with a stare. Our roles are reversed. The parent should be the one scolding the child asking for the truth in the middle of the night, but here I am treating my mother like she's a teenager who broke curfew.

"I'm waiting." I inform her.

She shifts her weight and crosses her arms.

"Fine, don't tell me but I'll just call the cops and have them come and remove this intruder from my home."

"Wait! Wait. Fine." I look at her expectantly. "Eddy got nabbed this afternoon because he had a taillight out and left half the fucking stash sitting open on his back seat."

I roll my eyes.

"So before he could start blabbing I packed up and came to visit you, pumpkin!" She tries for sweetness but all I taste is sour.

"What's in the bag?" I demand as I jut my chin towards the duffle that's sitting on the floor next to the sofa.

She looks at me like she might not tell me. Or she's trying to figure out if she can lie.

"I'll just open it myself then." I say and I take a step towards it.

"Wait! Wait." She steps into my path. "Okay. Fine. It's pills."

"Pills." I repeat.

"Yeah, Eddy knows a dirty doc who writes prescriptions. We get them filled and then help distribute them to his clients."

"Fucking hell," I mutter to myself.

"It's a good paying gig!" She protests as if that'll change my mind.

"I'm sure it is. Listen. It's 3 in the morning so you can stay the night but tomorrow you are leaving, taking *that* with you, and you're never coming back here again."

"Fine."

"Fine." Both of us sound like teenagers now. I get a glass of water and walk to my bedroom. I close the door, sink into my bed, and as my head crashes into my pillow the first tear falls down my cheek.

...

"NORA! Door!" I roll over and return to consciousness. I register a knocking sound in the background. I slide myself out of bed and walk into the main living area.

"Who the fuck is at your door this early?" Mom complains from the sofa.

"I don't know Mom." I say, exasperated. The clock on the oven confirms that I only got four hours of sleep.

I open the door while rubbing my eyes and I see Jimmy standing on the other side. I slam the door in his face and turn around with my back against it.

"Cops?!" Mom is awake and at attention now. She stands, grabs the duffel, and starts to back towards the bathroom.

"No, it's not the cops." I hiss. And he knocks again.

"Nora? Hey, let me in." He says through the door.

His voice sends shivers down my spine. How did he find me? How did he get upstairs?

I run my fingers through my hair and poke at my eyes to try and get the sleep out of the corners. I roll my shoulders back and open the door again.

"Hey Nora." He says as his eyes soften.

"Jimmy." I say tersely.

A question forms in his eyes and he looks past me and into the apartment.

"Uhh, can I come in?"

I step back and open the door wider. He steps inside and it feels wrong. His presence in this place where I brought all those other men taints him.

"What are you doing here?" I ask as my eyes dart to the bathroom door.

"I came to check on you. I was worried." He turns to me after surveying the apartment. "And someone was too stubborn to give me her number so I had no other choice but to badger her friend in the middle of the night for her address."

A small laugh escapes and I hate him for making things feel lighter. For teasing me. For bringing his charm here. I need to get him out before my mom sees him and ruins it all.

"Well, as you can see I'm fine and so now you can leave." I say with as much pep in my voice as I can.

I can tell I overdid it because he steps further into the apartment.

Shit.

"I like your place." He says.

"Thank you. It's a really nice building."

"It is. It is." He says as he steps around my sofa, his gaze is sweeping my apartment. It's only a moment before he stops on my mom's bag sitting against the wall.

He continues to glance around and then stops again at the little cat scratch tower and donut cave I got for Sir Harold for his birthday last year. He looks back at me.

"I bet he loved this." Jimmy says and it breaks the dam on the tears I didn't know were forming in my eyes.

A dramatic sob escapes my lips and I pull my hands into my sleeves to press the fabric into my tears. Jimmy crosses over to me in two steps and wraps me up in his arms.

I hear the bathroom door swing open and slam against the wall.

"Unhand her you fucking dick!" My mother yells. Jimmy spins with me still in his arms and I'm stumbling to catch myself.

I pull my hands away from my eyes to see my mother racing towards us with my curling iron hoisted over her head like a billy club.

"Mom stop!" I yell as Jimmy releases me and takes a step back.

Thankfully my mom stops her forward charge but she keeps the iron in place.

"Who is he?" She demands.

"None of your business." I say as Jimmy says "James Arthur Lewis The Third."

"Why is he here?" Mom continues.

"None of your business." I grit out as Jimmy says "Just checking on Nora, ma'am."

It's like a bad comedy act.

"Mom, chill. He's my…friend." I turn towards him and see the disappointment at the label after everything we shared last night. "Mom, Jimmy, Jimmy, my mother."

My mom drops the curling iron and holds out her hand like a debutante.

"Pleasure to meet you James Arthur Lewis The Third. What do you do for work?"

I roll my eyes as Jimmy takes her hand in a shake and then puts his hands in his pockets. "I own a hardware store ma'am."

Mom looks at me, "went for the old blue collar this time huh Nora? What did you make your way through all the men in the financial district? Or did you just get a hankering for lower class D?"

Shame flushes my face as Jimmy turns to look at me. I can't meet his gaze so I just stare at the spot where my toe disappears in my plush carpet.

Jimmy grabs my elbow and without a word he brings me to my bedroom and closes the door. I hear my mother's cackle cough from the other room. I slink down to the floor next to my bed and bury my head.

"Nora." He says softly but I can't look at him. I can hardly bear him looking at me. "Nora, c'mon honey, look at me."

I lift my head and take in the concern and tenderness in his features. Tears well up in my eyes.

"Lets go, I'll take you back." He say as he stands and holds his hand down to me.

I shake my head. "I can't."

"What do you mean?"

"I mean, I am back. This is my apartment, my life." I say as I throw my arms out to the side. "*That's*," pointing towards the door to where my mom is likely listening on the other side, "my life."

Jimmy doesn't say anything. He just steps next to me and sits on the bed. He leans forward and rests his elbows on his thighs. His head bows and he holds his hands clasped in front of him.

"Listen," I say, resolved to my fate. "We had a good time. I, for one, enjoyed myself. And I think maybe I got swept up in everything this past week, swept up in you. I'm sorry for getting your hopes up last night but I think I need to stay here."

"Even without a job and a dead cat in your freezer." He whispers.

I look up at him and smile, knowing the gesture doesn't reach my eyes. "Even so."

I take a deep breath and push myself up so I'm sitting next to him on the bed. "This never would have lasted." But the words sound like a lie even to me.

"I disagree." Jimmy says. "We never even got a shot."

"No, we didn't." I admit.

"Nora," he pleads as he turns towards me.

"Don't Jimmy, it's for the best." I stand and face him. "Head back upstate, do the show, get super famous, and marry a celebrity. I'll cheer for you from afar and tell people you're the one that got away." I try to sound light but I don't think it's working.

"That's not what I want." He says.

"Well, that's fine, but you don't want me."

He stands and starts to pace my tiny bedroom. "I don't know what to do here, Nora." He admits.

"About what?" I sit on the bed.

"You!" He yells. I'm startled and jolt back from the surprise.

"Sorry, I'm sorry, you." He says more gently as he comes to kneel in front of me. "I don't know what to do about you."

"There's nothing to do about me Jimmy, except let me go." I rest my hands on his shoulders. "I told you not to fall in love with me."

I meant it to be a joke. I tried to bring a smile to my face. To bring us back to a few days ago when the connection between us didn't feel so strong. Before we told each other about the love in our hearts last night. Before the planning together. But instead of finding humor, Jimmy's eyes intensify and his jaw sets.

"What?" I ask, tempting fate.

"I've never been good at following directions." He says before he pushes forward and kisses me. His hands hold onto my thighs as I spread them to make room for his body.

He leans forward and tilts his head to deepen our kiss. His arms wrap around my body and I am surrounded by him.

Both of us are pouring every emotion into this kiss. I feel my racing heart slow down as I savor the comfort being in his arms provides.

Maybe I can bottle this feeling so even after I let him go I can keep him with me forever.

33

Oh, the Internet Searches I Do For Love

JIMMY

Our kiss tastes the same but it lacks intensity. I can feel her pushing me away. Pulling herself back inside her protected bubble. She's putting the walls up around her heart.

I move my lips to her neck and bring my hand to the back of her head where I tuck her into me. She's holding me tight as if she doesn't want to let me go.

That sensation is what I hold on to. What I desperately cling to.

My heart is bleeding for her. I meant what I told her last night. I'm ready to share the burdens of life with her. But not just the burdens, the joyful moments too.

And after just one short interaction with her mother I want to hide Nora away from her forever. There was a cruelty to her tone I'd never heard in a parent's voice before.

Liz told me this morning when I went to her house to get Nora's address that if her mom was involved it was bad news. That Nora would shut down. That she always did when her mom popped up.

Liz said Nora has compartmentalized her mom into a once-a-week FaceTime and outside of that she operates as if she didn't have the scum of the earth as a parent. That growing up she only had herself to rely on so now she's fiercely independent. To a fault. I laughed to myself thinking of her trying to win her own prize at the carnival.

Her best friend then continued to tell me that she saw Nora lowering her guard this week as the two of us spent more time together. That us together is a good thing, a really good thing, and that I need to fight for her.

And Liz doesn't know the things we said to each other last night. What we planned. What we shared.

Nora's breathing slows as she melts against me and I place a kiss on her temple. I pull back and see how tired she looks.

She's still the most beautiful woman on the planet.

"Let's tuck you in for a nap." I say as I help guide her to her pillows. She's too tired to protest. I pull back the blankets and she slides in. She yawns.

"Jimmy?"

"Yes honey?"

Nora pauses and when her eyes flutter open and she turns to look up at me I see defeat in them. It breaks me.

Her eyes search mine. I try to convey that I would go to the ends of the earth for her if she asked. She opens her mouth, another pause.

"Never mind."

And with that she rolls into herself and closes her eyes.

I can only bear to watch her for a few seconds before tears well in my eyes. This woman is not the one who shared my bed last night. Who comforted my father, encouraged my sister, who helped her friend's mother win a silly boat decorating contest. The selfless, vibrant, kind, and sassy woman I fell in love with this week is gone.

Before I finish cataloging the changes in the Nora drifting off to sleep in front of me, I turn and leave her bedroom. Closing the door quietly behind me.

Her mother is sitting on the sofa watching TV, none the wiser to the broken daughter behind her. It isn't my place to put her in hers. Yet. That's a privilege I hope to earn as Nora and I build our relationship.

Instead, I cross to the kitchen to clean out the refrigerator. Knowing Nora hasn't been here in a week I hope her mother ate something rotten in her fridge because I doubt she went to the market herself.

There isn't much in her fridge. There's a collection of dressings that all seem fresh enough, butter, some cheese, and sparkling water.

I open a cabinet next to the refrigerator and find less than half a loaf of bread and some almond flour crackers. Peanut butter, almond butter, and a box of dried pasta. I can do something with the pasta but that's about it ingredient wise.

As soon as I place my hand on the freezer handle I remember Sir Harold. Mentally I try and prepare myself for what a frozen dead cat might look like. I slide open the drawer and I see a tuff of grey fur exposed from beneath a tea towel.

Emotion stings my nostrils as I imagine Nora wrapping her beloved companion in a dish towel and placing him ceremoniously into the freezer.

I pull out my phone and search "what to do with a dead cat" and pray that no images come up in the results. Instinctively I squeeze my eyes shut and then peel one open after I hit the search button.

Oh, not so bad. You can take it to the vet and they'll cremate it for you or dispose of the, gulp, carcass on your behalf.

Trusting Nora to be organized and have her vet's information on hand, I open up a drawer to look for a business card or promotional flyer or something. After two strikes, but respecting the level of organization in each drawer, I reach the final drawer on the peninsula.

Jackpot. It's her junk drawer. It still has little divided compartments to corral loose change, paper clips, and, yes, business cards. Smiling at how even her junk drawer is under control, I grab the stack of business cards and start filing through them.

Bagel shop and coffee punch cards, one for her dentist, a personal shopper's business card, a gift card to some store called Credo, a nail place punch card, something called Sugar Pop hair removal, and finally a Dr. Wilde, Veterinarian.

I see that they're closed on Sundays, but I program the number into my phone so I can call tomorrow and make arrangements.

"She's got nothin' worth takin'," Nora's mom says over her shoulder. "I already checked."

"No? Not even this bagel card that only needs one more punch before a free one?" I ask laying the sarcasm on thick.

"Nah, it's only good to me if it was the free one."

I roll my eyes and pocket the punch card in case her mom changes her mind and decides to spring for one bagel in order to get a second one free.

"So, you must be sitting on a pretty little nest egg if my Nora is chasing your tail. Do you invest in bitcoin or something stupid that kids do these days?"

"No, just the hardware store that's been in my family for three generations." I think about the TV show but don't mention it.

"Interesting. That's not like my Nora."

Grating at the term 'my Nora', I pull out a little pad of paper and a pen from the junk drawer. On the first one I write a note to Nora. I peel it off and set it to the side. On the second one I write out a grocery list.

I'm going to make Nora dinner, probably can't avoid her mother eating some of it but I'll know deep down that it wasn't meant for her. Then I'm going to snuggle with Nora in her bed for as long as she'll let me before heading back to Lakeville at the last possible moment.

We're taping tomorrow morning, it's furniture delivery day. The plan is to film from 9:30-10:30 and then Angie can head back to open the store at 11.

With my notes in hand, I slip into Nora's room. Her face is soft and relaxed. I kiss the tops of my fingers and brush them as gently across her temple as I can. She barely stirs.

I place the note on the pillow next to her. After I stand up straight I look around hoping to find her purse or keys.

Turning towards her dresser I spot the purse she had yesterday, black with a gold chain strap. Inside is her lipstick, a makeup compact, her ID and cards, and the photos we took together in the festival's photo booth.

I make a mental note to find a frame.

No keys. Which makes sense, you don't put your keys back in your pocket or bag when you get inside your house. No, you hang them up on a hook or set them in a bowl on a table.

Nora seems like the decorative bowl on the table type so I make my way out of her room and close the door gently. Next to the door is a tall square table, maybe a foot wide. There's a bowl on top and I see sunglasses perched next to it.

Once I'm standing at the door I see her keys and smile at the cat keychain she added. I pick up the keys and leave for the store.

34

I Thought You Left

Nora

The sound reaches me like it's coming from a thousand miles away, or maybe I'm underwater. My almost conscious mind registers an apartment door closing.

It could be a neighbor's.

It's probably Jimmy leaving.

Or it could be my mother finally clearing out.

Wouldn't that be nice.

Hoping against hope, I climb out of bed. Stiff from my nap but also feeling just a little bit more refreshed. I open my bedroom door and am greeted by the back of my mother's head.

Shit.

She's still here.

So if it was my door closing that means Jimmy left. Disappointment floods my system as I search for any sign of him while I cross over to the bathroom.

"That man of yours didn't stay long." Mom says from the sofa as she changes the channel. "And he rummaged through all your stuff."

Ignoring her I close my bathroom door and lock it. That flimsy lock providing me with a false sense of security. The same I have relied on during interactions with my mother since high school.

I step up to the mirror and take in my appearance. My hair is still slightly curled from yesterday. My skin looks a little more flushed than tan but hopefully it'll turn golden in a day or two. I lean closer to the mirror to examine the bags under my eyes.

They're bad. I open one of the drawers and pull out the under-eye masks that Imogen Skye recommended on TikTok and set the package on the counter to use after my shower.

I turn on the water and strip down. My mind is on an endless loop of Jimmy and the last 24 hours. The feel of him as he held me against the wall and said I love you. The laughter in his eyes as we made our sex list.

His embrace before he tucked me in for a nap.

That is the one I'll need to erase from my memory. That connection held promise. Hope.

And hope isn't going to get me anywhere.

Once I'm in the shower I wash my hair and use my favorite lemongrass body scrub hoping the sugar crystals will dissolve away the hurt I feel crawling over my skin.

Hot, angry tears well in my eyes as I step out of the shower. Whoever said 'it's better to have loved and lost than to have never loved at all' deserves a kick in the crotch.

How is this feeling of despair, of emptiness, of anger better than the baseline numbness I lived with before?

The only feelings I shared with another being was total adoration of Sir Harold, and somedays he'd reciprocate by allowing me to pet him. Other times he'd flick his little tail and show me his butthole while walking away.

But Sir Harold was a cat who had his own litter box, an automatic food and water dispenser, and a mountain of toys to entertain himself with. We shared the same apartment but we didn't rely on each other.

Well, I maybe relied on him a little but not nearly as much as I have relied on Jimmy this last week.

I grind my teeth and sniffle deeply to stop the tears threatening to spill over. It stings but I will not cry over him. I step up to the mirror and put the eye patches on.

Once they're in place I stare at the warrior woman in the mirror.

"You don't need him. You don't need anyone. You are Nora Fucking Heely and you take care of yourself." I growl to my reflection.

She matches my energy and I feel ready to move forward. Enough of this sappiness. Emotions are for losers.

Sure, let's go with that.

Determined to summon the Nora from 10 days ago I begin to style my hair. **Volumizing** mousse, nourishing oil, and then a heat protecting spray followed by a blow dry.

I peel the under eye patches off and toss them. I pat the residual serum in with my ring fingers before running through my entire skincare routine.

I toss my hair over my shoulder and wrap my robe around me tighter. My mother will likely still be on the sofa and I have to walk past her to get back to my room to get dressed.

"Took you long enough." Mom mutters as I open the door.

"I like to take my time."

"Had to wash that handyman off ya huh? Didn't want any evidence of you slumming it."

Rage boils up from my toes and rings in my ears. I step in front of her, blocking her view of the TV.

"Hey, move!" She says as she starts leaning to the side. "I'm watching that."

I grab the remote and turn it off. And Mom lets out a string of curse words as she stands up.

"First of all, don't talk about him like that, you don't know him." I see my mom's eyes twinkle with interest because I'm defending a man, something neither of us have done in a long time, maybe ever.

"Second, don't act like this is your apartment. Third, when are you leaving?"

"First of all," she says in a sassy, mocking tone, "I'll say whatever I want to, freedom of speech baby! Second of all, what kind of daughter doesn't welcome her mother into her home with open arms. Mi casa, su casa, right?"

I feel the muscles in my jaw tensing, I'm afraid they'll pop if I squeeze any tighter but I am determined not to let her see any emotion from me. "And I'll leave when I damn please. I housed you for 18 years so you can give me a few nights on your fancy sofa."

I'm not expecting anything more from her. She smirks, grabs the remote out of my hand and flops back down.

"Go on now, step aside." She says and I walk away to my bedroom.

I close the door behind me and take a deep breath. I walk over and stand in front of my organized closet. Color coordinated, sorted by fabric weight, or garment length, or both in the case of my dresses. Most of the items are my business clothes.

Pencil skirts, suit jackets, suit dresses, wide leg pants. My collection of pumps lined up on the bottom shelf.

I can still stick to part of the plan we came up with last night. I can still call Trisha tomorrow and pitch my idea. Mom doesn't know I don't have a job at the moment so I'll have to make the call from somewhere else.

Unless she decides to leave in the next 12 hours.

But based on how comfortable she looked, I doubt that will happen.

I'll have to text Liz and see if Kyle is coming to the city soon. He could bring my bag back. Most of it was my casual and weekend clothing. I can live without it but the empty hangers in my closet serve as a reminder of the week I spent in Lakeville.

It's a Sunday afternoon and usually I'd wear a pair of jeans and a top to run errands and do my meal prep. I don't feel like I have the energy for meal prep today. Good news is that I could do it tomorrow since I've got no where else to be.

I reach for my jeans and a boxy cut, black and white striped top that feels like loungewear but looks more put together. Once I'm dressed I walk back to the bathroom and as I hang my robe up behind the door I hear my front door open.

Terrified that Mom somehow got a spare key and gave it to Eddy or that the people looking for her and Eddy know where I live I open the bathroom door just a crack and peer out.

Mom doesn't react. I try and regulate my breath, waiting for whoever is entering my apartment to make it around the corner. I know some self defense but at the moment I'm hoping I can just barricade myself in the bathroom and stay safe.

I start to think about what I can use to block the door when a tall, broad body walks around the corner carrying bags from the market.

Jimmy.

I whip the door open and basically run to him. He barely has time to set the bags down before I jump into his arms.

"I thought you left." I say as I squeeze my arms around his neck.

He laughs, "Not a chance. Didn't you see my note?"

"What note?"

Jimmy sets me down, grabs my hand, and walks me to my bedroom. He leans over onto the bed and plucks a piece of paper off my pillow. He turns and hands it to me.

"Oh." I smile sheepishly and read the note. 'Nora, I'll be back soon. Love, J'

I look back up at him and he grins.

"I see you showered without me." He says as his fingers toy with the ends of my hair.

"Whoops." I say with a shrug and he laughs.

"You'll find a way to make it up to me I'm sure. Now, I have a feeling you'll want to be the one to unpack the groceries. Make sure everything ends up in the right place." Jimmy says and I blush because, yeah, he's not wrong.

"Why don't you do that and then sit down and enjoy the iced coffee and fancy fashion magazine I got you while I take a little nap." He leans down and I feel his breath pass over my ear. "I didn't get much sleep last night."

And with that he kisses the side of my neck which sends shivers down my spine. He steps back and toes his shoes off followed by his pants. He folds them in half and sets them on the foot of the bed and then he slides in.

"Mhmm," he hums as he snuggles into my pillow. "It smells like you."

I laugh and step over to give him a kiss. He loops his arm around the back of my legs and holds me up against the side of the bed.

"I don't want to let you out of my arms, and if you're out of my arms I don't want you out of my sight. But I almost fell asleep standing in your elevator so I'm going to nap for 20 minutes. Wake me up with that beautiful mouth of yours."

Thank heavens he's holding my legs up because that was a bone melting declaration. I don't want to be anywhere besides his arms, or in his line of sight.

But I won't be able to appreciate being in his arms with my mother in the other room.

I lean down and kiss him, briefly he lifts his head and deepens it before resting back down on the pillow. He lays a quick slap to my ass before he tucks his hands under his head and settles in for his nap.

That little tap sent sparks flying inside me. My mind flies to our list. I can't wait until we do number 10 together.

35

A Man With A Plan

JIMMY

Naps in the city aren't quite as rejuvenating as naps at home. Not that I nap often.

My brain is stirring back to life because it is trying to make sense of two women yelling. It must be on the sidewalk just outside because it's loud. I can make out everything they're saying.

"You're an ungrateful little bitch who doesn't understand everything I sacrificed for her. I hope you get knocked up and have to raise a little brat with a stick up her ass."

"I'm not a brat."

Nora.

I whip the covers back, grab my jeans, and jam my legs in as I hear her mother continue.

"Yes you are. You're a spoiled brat who always thought she was better than everyone else. You still think so with your fancy clothes and apartment and job. Well, you're not much different than me. I fell for a blue collar piece of tail too and had to live with that regret the rest of my life."

"I do not think I'm bett—" Nora starts but stops as she sees me pull the door open. "Jimmy, sorry, let me just show you out."

"No." Nora's eyes widen. I turn to her mother. "Get out." I growl.

"Who the fuck do you think you are? You can't tell me what to do."

"I absolutely can. No one comes into Nora's home and insults her. No one insults her period when I'm around."

"Jimmy, it's fine." Nora says to me as her eyes graze the floor. I cross over to her and grab her by both arms.

"It's not fine. You are not the person she just described, got it?"

Nora's eyes widen as she stares at my face. I hope she can see how serious I am. How strongly I feel.

Her mom is still standing in front of the sofa looking at us. I pull Nora into my chest and turn towards her mom.

"It's time to leave. I'll give you two minutes to gather your things and leave on your own before I do it for you." I tell her and my tone darkens. I guide Nora by the arm back to her room and have her sit on the bed. I kiss her forehead and close the door behind me.

"Fine." Her mom huffs from behind me. "I'll go but only because I can't wait to watch her kick you to the curb for speakin' for her. That little hussy knows to never let a man have the power. It's why she fucks around so much, she gets her needs met but she doesn't have to deal with a man telling her what to do. You stupid men think you're getting what you want but she comes out on top. Conniving bitch is what she is."

She takes her bag and steps over to the door. She opens it, stops, and looks back at me.

"Stupid, stupid man." She says as she walks out and closes it behind her.

I rush back into Nora's bedroom and find her frozen on the edge of the bed. Her arms are straight and her hands are gripping the blanket. Her head is bowed forward.

"Nora?" I say, gently.

She looks up at me and where I expected to find tears there is admiration. It's almost a smile. She stands and takes two steps in my direction before pausing and clasping her hands together in front of her.

"Thank you." She whispers.

"For what?"

"For making her leave. For not letting her poison get to you."

"Never Nora, honey, never." I look at this beautiful woman in front of me and all the words I want to say get stuck in my chest. I step closer and my hands tingle with anticipation of touching her again "I cannot believe that you, a person who is selfless and thoughtful and funny could have grown up with such a horrible mother."

"I figured a lot of things out on my own." Nora says. "And I guess I've always been just that, on my own."

I'm prepared for her to push me away. To make comments about herself and her need to be alone. And, arguing against a girl's reasoning is not what most people would advise a man to do in this situation.

But any arguments she might have for us not being together are, simply put, bullshit. We are meant to be together and I feel that in my bones.

Standing in front of me is a woman wearing a pair of blue jeans and a fancy t-shirt on a Sunday when she's going to stay home. She is most comfortable, most confident, when she feels put together.

I can see how she is cracked open by the emotions of the last few minutes. Her pointer fingers press into the backs of her hands to help ground herself and keep things under control. I can see how she's not open to hearing compliments. She'll feel them as platitudes, not genuine truths.

How she needs to freeze in this moment of pain. Maybe not quite pain but neutrality. I want to hold her while she sits with the emotions swirling through her. I want to lift her up when she's ready to let it go.

"I've dealt with loss and had to do things on my own too. But I had a community to support me. And none of that cruelty." I say. "You don't have to do this alone."

"That might be true, but she isn't anyone else's responsibility." She counters.

"That woman is not your responsibility." I sneer because the anger in me is rising. How dare her mother bring Nora down like this. "That woman is only responsible for herself and she's barely capable of that."

"Jimmy, don't. It's not her fault. She didn't want to get pregnant and when she did I was too much for my dad to handle so he left. She had to raise me all on her own. She didn't finish high school. She had nothing and so she figured out how to survive and had to keep me alive as well."

"Don't defend her." I reach out and grab Nora's arms. The need to connect with her is overwhelming. I'm praying my touch brings her back to her senses. Helps her snap out of this trance she is in.

"I'm not defending her, I'm just explaining."

"I don't need an explanation. I need for you to realize how incredible you are and how nothing, *nothing* that woman said is true."

Nora shakes her head no and steps back out of my reach.

Fuck, this is worse than I thought. Does a part of her actually believe what her mom said? I flex my fist because anger is rising in my chest. Anger won't help Nora so I breath in through my nose, out through my mouth, and re-center my focus on the woman in front of me.

Best case scenario, she's spiraling. That I could try and stop and reverse.

Worst case is that she's defeated. That requires finding a way to scrape her off the pavement and puff her back up.

I reach for her hand and she makes me tug before she loosens her clasped grip. I stare at her hand in mine. Her nude but with a slight sparkle nail polish, the freckles that dot her skin. I turn her hand over in mine and see the lines and the flesh of the palm that just yesterday was plastered against me as I drove her around the lake.

I lift her hand and bring it to my lips. I press a kiss to her palm before curling her fingers with mine.

"Nora," I smile as her eyes connect with mine. "Wanna hear the plan?"

Her face lights up. It is a beautiful sight.

"You made a plan?" She whispers.

"Honey, I'm a man with a plan." And I punctuate my bravado with a wink and I pull her out to the living room. She sits on the sofa and I grab the notepad from her junk drawer before joining her.

"Number one, I'm going to spend the day with you. Doing whatever you want to do with me. You're in charge."

"Okay." She says, still a little too timid for my taste.

"Number two, I'm going to cook you dinner. This, you are not in charge of. You will be forced to sit and watch or take a bath while I cook."

"I think I can manage that." She says and some of the sparkle returns to her eyes. I keep going.

"Number three, is that you'll do the dishes." Her eyebrows raise so I lean over and stage-whisper, "Because I have a feeling you're particular about loading the dishwasher."

She laughs and internally I give myself a high five.

"Number four," I start.

"Wow this really is a thorough plan." She interjects.

"I'm trying to impress a girl." I tell her. "Number four, is that we go out for dessert. You pick the spot."

"Ooh I've got a good idea already."

"I figured you would. Then after dessert we're going to stop at a market to get a styrofoam cooler."

She looks at me confused. "Why?"

"Because after dessert we're coming back to your place and I do not expect to leave, or put on clothes, until the early morning."

She laughs, "Okay, fine, but why do we need the cooler?"

"Because the rest of the plan happens tomorrow morning."

"I still don't understand why we nee—" I cut off her question with a kiss.

"I'm only sharing the first five steps of my plan with you now." I look at the notepad, "Alright, the first thing on the list was spend the day together," I glance at my watch. "It's noon, what do you wanna do before I start dinner?"

Nora's smile is wicked as she leans over to my ear. She places a kiss to my ear lobe which send shivers down my spine before whispering a series of numbers in my ear.

"Six, six*teen*, forty, and then eleven."

She stands, reaches for my hand, and then pulls me towards the bedroom. My mind starts racing trying to remember what each of those were. I feel like sixteen involved her favorite vibrator.

"I can't remember what each of those were." I admit. "You're scrambling my brain, Nora."

I stand behind her and while she's facing away from me I reach for the hem of her top. I pull it over her head and watch her shoulder blades shift back into place. The dip of her back showing the path of her spine is beckoning me.

My fingers trail up the valley to where her hair dances across her back. I reach up and try to unclasp the bra but end up fumbling with it and snapping her back.

"Ow!" She yelps playfully.

"My bad. I don't think I've ever taken a bra off from back here before. It's like trying to button pants when the button is on the wrong side."

"That usually means they're ladies pants." She says over her shoulder as she reaches up and unclasps her bra.

"Well, either way, it's tricky." My hands curl around her ribcage and rise to knead both of her breasts at the same time.

Nora's head rolls back and rests against my chest. Her back arches and that pushes her tits further into my hands. She reaches behind her and starts to unfasten my jeans while I start to plant kisses along her neck and down to her shoulder.

She steps forward and crawls onto the bed. I finish taking off my pants and follow her. She looks back at me over her shoulder and draws her bottom lip into her mouth.

I've never seen anything hotter. I fish a condom out of my wallet and roll it on while she brings her fingers to her center and slowly moves them in a tight circle.

"Impatient today Nora?"

"Yes. Fuck me already Jimmy." She demands. The words clash in my ears. I pull my knee off the bed and stand back.

Nora rises up and looks at me. "What's the matter?"

"I don't want to fuck you."

"What?" She scowls as she sits up and reaches for her pillow to cover herself.

"No, no, honey, that's not what I meant. I meant I'd rather make love with you." I reach up and brush her hair away from her face.

"Semantics Jimmy."

"No Nora, listen to me. When I enter you in a minute you need to know that I'm giving myself to you. And I feel the way your pussy clamps down on my cock. You're giving yourself to me too. We're physically demonstrating our love. Not just our physical chemistry."

Nora looks up at me and doesn't say anything. In her eyes I see fear, anticipation, and, best of all, love.

"Can you do that with me Nora?"

"Yes." She whispers.

I bring her up to me for a kiss, our mouths demanding the depths from each other. I continue to kiss her as I start to rotate her body back down onto the mattress. She breaks the kiss and let's her hands fall in front of her.

Gripping her hips I drive into her in one push. Her body opens up for me and as our hips melt together and I physically feel my heart opening up to her again. I prop up my leg to get at the essence of number six and somehow I find more of myself to give to her.

With each thrust, each whimper from her kiss swollen lips, my heart opens to make room for more of her.

Again.

More.

Deeper.

My control is slipping as my climax approaches.

"Jimmy, oh, fuck, I'm almost there."

"Wait for me honey."

She whimpers in protest but I hear her force a deep breath to help cool herself down.

I slowly press my thumb at the point just above where our bodies are joined. Nora's body clenches inside and out. That response does me in.

"Nora, aah, fuck." I say on an exhale as I still on top of her. My orgasm ripping up my legs.

"Yes." Nora hisses as her hands grip into the blanket. I feel the way she pulls out every ounce of me as she rides the waves of her orgasm.

I slide out of her and she stands. She stands on her tip toes to kiss me and I hold on to her ribs to steady her, and myself.

"I'll be right back." She says and then she slips out of the bedroom.

I tie off the condom and use a few tissues to wipe up. I toss both into a garbage pail by her door and then return to her bed.

I make myself comfortable and run my hands through my hair. The last twelve hours have been a turbulent roller coaster. The ups and downs of my dad, of admitting feelings to Nora, of going back to my apartment without her.

After an hour of pacing around trying to talk myself into and out-of different actions, I texted Kyle. He replied and said Liz would make me a coffee and I could come over and talk about it. When I got there she sat me down on the sofa.

"Nora has been making the plans and following them for most of her life. So the thing you must understand is that she sort of freezes when there's a change she can't figure out. She's not impulsive unless she's out for the night but even that is pretty innocent fun. Oh, here's a good example, when she buys something new for her closet she knows exactly where it will hang before she brings it home."

The thought has me looking towards Nora's reach-in closet. The items, mostly tans, browns, olives, and ivories are organized by color. The closet is full but it isn't over stuffed.

Her shoes are all lined up on the bottom row and I marvel at why she'd wear these heels on a regular basis.

Behind me the door opens and Nora has something held behind her back.

"Six was fun, but I'm looking forward to sixteen now."

And I grin as I hear a faint buzzing sound.

36

The Styrofoam Cooler Question, Answered

Nora

"This is obnoxious." Jimmy says as he stares at the dessert I insisted on ordering for him.

"You don't have to eat it all if you can't handle it." I tease.

Honestly, I'd be impressed if he ate it all. I got him what Liz and I usually share but don't finish.

Jimmy is the proud owner of a donut sundae. Three old fashioned donuts in a paper sundae boat topped with three scoops of ice cream (vanilla bean Oreo, chocolate caramel swirl, and strawberry cheesecake). On top of the ice cream is a sprinkling of toasted hazelnuts, a drizzle of chocolate syrup, a drizzle of caramel, colorful sprinkles, and a cherry on top.

I'm holding a single scoop of mint chip ice cream with half a chocolate sprinkle donut as the accoutrement.

"I'm not sure two people could finish this." He says as he scoops up a spoonful of the vanilla Oreo ice cream.

I laugh before admitting, "Liz and I can't finish one. Either Kyle helps or we end up putting it in the freezer and having it for breakfast."

"Breakfast of champions."

"Absolutely."

I reach over and take a scoop of the strawberry cheesecake ice cream. Jimmy tugs the sundae away and whines "no mine" before lunging at the spoon I quickly bring to my lips.

I can't wait any longer. I have held onto this question all day. Except for during our bedroom times when my mind, body, and soul were at Jimmy's beck and call. We'll be revisiting sixteen again soon.

"Why do we need a styrofoam cooler?" I ask. Because why beat around the bush.

"Ah, I suppose I should share the rest of the plan with you before I fall into a sugar coma." Jimmy takes a bite of donut. "We need a styrofoam cooler," he says while chewing. He swallows and then finishes, "To bring Sir Harold up to Lakeville tomorrow."

"What?"

"The rest of my plan consists of helping you pack up as much as you want to bring with you now. Texting a list of the closet organizer items you need for my place so Angie can place an order for them, maybe trying sixteen again," he wiggles his eyebrows and I nod excitedly. "And then in the morning bringing you, your clothes, Sir Harold, and your vibrator with me to Lakeville."

"Okay!" I laugh as my smile cracks wide and reaches my eyes. I can't think of a better plan than this one.

"Yeah? Okay!" His smile meets his eyes too and he takes a big bite of ice cream. Suddenly pain washes over his features and he sucks in a deep breath.

"Ah! *Brain freeze*!" he hisses.

"Stick your tongue to the roof of your mouth." I coach. He looks at me questioning. "Do it, it works. Liz and I looked it up after Kyle told us to do it."

I see him try it and after a few seconds he turns to me.

"Holy shit that does work."

"I know. It's a secret solution that should be all over the internet but isn't."

"Let's be the ones to put it on the internet then." Jimmy says and he reaches for his phone in his pocket. He opens up TikTok and navigates to record a new video.

He turns to me and says "Okay, I'll introduce myself, share where we got the sundae, and then I'll introduce you."

"Okay."

"Then you feed me a bite of ice cream and I'll complain about brain freeze and you'll share the trick and I'll do it and then when the brain freeze goes away I'll kiss you."

"Ha no need to kiss me at the end."

"Hey, I'm the one with acting experience," He says with a fake baritone voice.

"Sure, sure you are." I say as I pat his chest. He lifts his phone and begins to count down.

"Five, four, three," then he mouths two and one before tapping record. "Hello Internet, I'm Jimmy Lewis and I'm here in NYC enjoying a Donut Sundae in Hell's Kitchen with my girl Nora, say Hi Nora."

He flicks the camera over to me and I wave and say "hi."

"Nora got me this monstrosity of a sundae band it is incredible. She got herself a mini sundae and I'm about to try a bite of her mint chocolate chip ice cream."

I was able to get most of my cup of ice cream on the spoon and I lift it so it's in the screen next to his face. He opens up and gives me wide eyes knowing I just guaranteed brain freeze.

"Mmm, oooo ow ow ow ow," Jimmy says with his mouth full of ice cream. "Brain freeze!"

"Oo," I start like I just thought of it, "press your tongue up to the roof of your mouth! That'll help."

"I harf roo sworow ris firs."

I giggle and plant a kiss on his cheek. "Okay babe, you do that." Then I turn to the camera and say "Follow for more tips!" Before I reach over and stop the recording.

Jimmy is still trying to swallow the ice cream but is struggling to contain his laughter.

He coughs a bit and I jump up from the curb expecting him to spit ice cream everywhere. Instead he looks up at me, inhales through his nose, and then swallows the rest.

"That was perfect Nora." He says with a smile. "Now get back down here." He nods his head to the side and I take a seat next to him.

I rest my head on his shoulder and he leans his head down to rest on mine. Together we sit side-by-side and eat our desserts.

...

I'm standing in front of my closet and Jimmy is perched on my bed behind me. His thumbs are poised to send Angie the details of what to order for my closet.

"I honestly need to see your closet to know exactly what supplies I need." I say as I put my hands on my hips and turn towards him.

"What's a supply you'd use no matter what? Because I have wire hangers and…judging by the look on your face right now that's…bad."

I try to wipe the horror off my face. "You have wire hangers? Not even plastic ones? Where did you even get wire hangers?"

"I dunno," he shrugs. "Pops gave them to me I think."

"Is there rust on them?" I ask afraid of the answer.

"It's possible. I haven't looked closely."

"Okay, that's okay." I say out loud to myself. "Ah, tell Angie we need 40 cedar hangers with a pant bar. And 20 cedar hangers with pant clips."

Jimmy types away and then mutters "pant clips" before I hear the text send.

"What else?" He looks at me.

"Again, I'm not sure what space is there but a shoe rack probably."

"Any preference on which one?"

"The Yamazaki Home Tower Shoe Rack in White."

"You had that ready to go. Spell Yamazaki for me."

"Y-A-M-A-Z-A-K-I."

"Got it," and I hear the text send. He looks up at me, "Okay, what else?"

"Let's start with that, once I can measure your closet and your clothes I'll know what other organizers to get."

"Measure my clothes?"

"Yeah, to see how much space they'll use up. Like how grocery stores plan their shelves down to the quarter inch."

"Interesting, I never really thought of it like that."

"I put way too much thought into closet and drawer organization." I say as I come and sit next to him on the bed.

"That's a damn pretty closet though, I'd say your planning paid off."

"Yeah?" He has no idea how much that means to me. It might be crazy to care so much about someone appreciating an organized closet. But it's something that brings me so much joy when it works out perfectly. When you swap a shelf in the modular system one notch lower and it fixes all the issues.

It's magical.

"So what are you going to pack up tonight to take with us tomorrow?"

The plan is to drive with Jimmy back to Lakeville tomorrow. Then next weekend he, and maybe Liz and Kyle, will come down with me and we'll pack everything that's left.

I emailed my landlord earlier while Jimmy cooked dinner and he said he'd end my lease early since it's easier to get tenants in September than October. I already saw my apartment listed on his website.

Together Jimmy and I called Holden while we were eating dinner to ask questions about the next steps for Sir Harold. I could allow them to perform an autopsy, but based on his age and that he went in his sleep, Holden thinks it was just old age.

I started to cry when he offered to handle the cremation details for me and ensured me that Sir Harold would be in the best hands for his final care. Jimmy thanked him, ended the call, and pulled me into a hug. After consoling me for a few minutes he whispered something dirty in my ear.

"Wanna show me how to load the dishwasher?"

Oh heavens, I felt my whole lady region clench in excitement.

"Now," Jimmy says as he sets his phone to the side and I come back to the present. "I have a question."

"What's your question?"

"Can I get your number?" His smile spreads slowly.

I bring my hands to cover my face. "Ohmigod how have we not exchanged numbers yet! I mean, I said I *love* you before I even gave you my number?"

"You're under my spell." He jokes as he picks up his phone, unlocks it, and hands it to me.

"Should I just write Nora Heely or do you want some like sexy code name for me?"

"Hmm, that's something to think about." He taps his chin. "It can't be something like Perfect Ass or Redhead With Great Tits," I laugh, "because I can't be getting boners every time you text me."

"Yes, we wouldn't want that."

"You call me babe so obviously I'm going to be 'babe' in your phone."

"Obviously." I deadpan. "You call me honey," I say with a shrug.

"That I do. Okay you can put your name in as 'Honey Tits'."

I bark out a laugh. "Shut up." And then I put my number in his phone under 'Honey T'.

He leans over to see what I've entered. "Cute." And he kisses me on the nose. Then he grabs his phone and types out a text.

My phone is in my purse on my dresser and I hear it buzz with a notification. I look at Jimmy and he smiles before I stand up and get my phone.

I swipe open the notification and read the text out loud.

"Hey Honey T, it's," I look up to him with 'get real' eyes, he smiles and points to the phone for me to continue. "It's Big Dick Babe, put me in your phone as BDB."

I roll my eyes and smile. He stands and comes to look over my shoulder at what I've typed in.

"Aww c'mon that's not what I said."

I send him a gif of a celebrity making a heart with her hands and the contact appears in my list as Jimmy followed by a heart eye emoji.

"I know, but I can't be getting aroused every time you send me a text thinking about your BD."

"Why not? I love the idea of warming you up via text before meeting you at home."

"Trust me, BD, I'm not going to need a lot of warming up. I've got it for you bad."

"You do, don't you?" He teases as he wraps his arms around me. He gives me a hug and then releases me.

"I heard your dishwasher stop so come show me how to unload it." He whispers in my ear as he grips my shoulders and starts to massage them.

"I just told you I have it for you bad, stop trying to get in my pants with your sexy talk." I tease as I push my ass into his crotch before walking to the kitchen.

"Stop bashing that tight ass against me if you want my help with chores."

"That sounds like a threat." I tease as I hand him a plate and point to a cabinet.

"It is, but not really. I'll always help with the chores."

"Somehow I believe you." I admit.

"Why wouldn't you believe me?" He asks.

"Because men aren't the ones who do the chores. Women do the cooking and the cleaning."

"Since when?" He asks. "I mean, maybe in 1950 but honey, I've been cooking, and cleaning, and working, and playing all on my own for a long time now. I had to take care of Angie, and Bethany and I shared chores when we lived together. And since then I've had to take care of myself."

"I guess that's true."

"It is. And while I am willing to let you take the lead and show me how you want things done, I'll always do my fair share of the chores."

My hands still before I grab the next dish. Visions of Jimmy and I doing the dishes together in his apartment flash in my mind's eye. He's standing at the sink and I'm next to him. We're talking with each other as we work.

I blink and reach for a serving bowl when I place it in the cabinet the vision changes.

Now we're standing in our own home, not his apartment, a home. We're in the living room with a creamy wrap around sofa, large windows overlook the lake which is glistening in the sun. He's vacuuming while I fold laundry.

"Babe?" I get his attention after he puts the salad servers away. "I like the idea of doing chores together."

He steps up and runs his hand from my shoulder down to my hand before grasping my fingers in his.

"I do too, honey."

37

The Life From My Country Songs

JIMMY

"I think that's it for now." Nora says with a shrug as she slides Sir Harold's cooler off the counter and carries it to the door.

She slips her purse over her shoulder and grabs her keys. I wheel the last suitcase out behind her. I've already taken two suitcases down to the truck.

I watch her determined profile as we move down the hallway together. She's been quiet since I woke her up, moving robotically through the motions of getting ready. Her lack of energy is making me anxious.

Are we moving too fast?

Is she having reservations?

Did I push her too far by assuming she'd not only come back to Lakeville but move in with me?

How quickly do frozen dead cats, umm, thaw?

Nora presses the elevator button with her elbow and I shake my head behind her. I have a free hand. She's so used to taking care of herself that she hit the button with her elbow instead of relying on me.

Time will change that.

We get in the elevator and I look down at her as she stares forward at the closing doors. Her reflection stares back from the elevator's stainless steel interior.

"Are you alright Nora?" I ask.

"Yes, I am. Sorry, I'm just not used to being up this early."

"Ah," I scratch at my beard. "That's right, you're not an early bird."

"No, but if you're fine with it, I'll sleep on the ride up."

"I am fine with that. As long as you're okay with whatever I put on the radio."

"Ha that's fine. I don't really care about music. Except that country music kind of makes me cringe."

I turn to her with a shocked look on my face. I'm tempted to joke that this will never work out but we're still in her elevator and she could easily agree with me and go back upstairs.

That can't happen.

"I happen to love country music." I say. "But I'll keep the volume real low while you're sleeping."

She laughs. "That's fine. Maybe I'll subliminally start to like it. But if that happens, I'll never admit that to you."

"We'll see. Some Hayes Farrow, Zach Bryan, and Luke Aldeen drifting in your ears while you relax could have you singing a different tune."

"Literally." She says with a smirk.

The elevator door opens and Manny, her doorman, gives me a wave. We've come to an understanding after the first time I stormed in and demanded to be let inside.

My truck is parked right outside of her building with the hazard lights on. I hold open the door for Nora, she walks through, and then I swing around her to open the back passenger side door.

Her face erupts in a smile when she sees the giant pink teddy bear sitting in the seat, buckled in.

"Ohmigod Jimmy! Why did you bring that?" She says with laughter.

"Because she's yours." I state matter-of-factly. "And if you weren't going to come back with me ,I was going to leave her with you. She's yours forever."

"Forever?" Nora asks as she slides the cooler into the middle seat next to the bear.

"Yeah honey, forever."

When she turns around she studies my face. I hope she is seeing the sincerity and devotion I am feeling in my heart. I take her hand and lead her towards her door, gently pressing a kiss her temple as she steps past me.

She climbs up into the cab and I close her door, Pinky's door, and walk around back to slide her suitcase into the bed of the truck. I lift the tailgate closed and get in the drivers seat. When the engine starts, little clock on the dash says 6:24.

"Uggh it's so early." Nora complains.

I reach back and unbuckle Pinky before dragging her up to the front seat.

"Here, snuggle up with this."

Nora shifts in her seat and positions the bear against the window. She leans down onto it and then quickly pops back up and turns to me.

"Did you spray the bear with your cologne?"

"Maybe."

I see her roll her eyes as she settles in and gets comfortable. I shift the truck into drive and pull onto the street. I stick my phone in the console and let the navigation guide us home.

I wait until Nora has drifted off before turning on the satellite country station. I adjust the speakers in the truck so most of the music is playing on my side of the cab. And then I drum as quietly as I can on the steering wheel as the lyrics fill my head.

Angie texted last night that she placed the closet supply order. She also said she put a few flower vases in my cabinet so Nora wouldn't have to use a mason jar like a peasant.

I thanked her, let the dig slide, and then texted Dawn to order a bouquet from Water's Edge Nursery & Florals.

I'm sure all the Tome Raiders have been informed of my inquiry.

Fine. I don't plan to hide Nora. It'd be impossible. I'm going to do everything I can to help her settle into Lakeville and make it feel like home for her.

When I was younger, I thought my life waited for me outside of town. That college, jobs, and adventure were my future. It wasn't just Mom passing away, or Pops needing help, or Angie needing a parent, that changed my viewpoint. It was feeling the connections and the support of the community. Of being able to support them in return. I didn't want anything outside of Lakeville. I wanted the small, slow life from my country songs.

Hayes Farrow's hit Electric Sunshine begins to play. I read that he wrote this song when he was falling in love. I remember reading that and wishing a girl would inspire that kind of poetry in me. Glancing over at Nora, I understand his lyrics. She is the sun shining in my life. The light.

Especially while she is sleeping cuddled up with a giant pink carnival bear sprayed with my cologne.

And, I want to be her light. Her shining sun. Her guiding star. I want to be her roots, her foundation. The person she turns to when life knocks her down.

My chest squeezes in pain imagining her pain. She looked so defeated after the things her mother said to her and I never want to see her looking that way ever again.

I feel tears well up in my eyes. I try to blink them away but that only forces them out and one rolls down my cheek.

"You crying over a country song Jimateo?"

I sniffle and turn to Nora who has her wide eyes turned to me with her head still laying on the bear.

"What? No." I lie through my teeth.

She smiles and pushes herself up. She reaches over and places her hand on my thigh and I drop my hand on top and grip hers in mine. The next few miles pass quietly like this, the only sound is the soft music playing in the background. I hear Nora exhale a laugh and I glance in her direction.

"What?" I ask.

"I was just thinking how crazy this is and how crazy I must be to just, I don't know, go with it."

"Can I admit something?" I glance over and she's looking at me nodding her head. "I think this is crazy too. But in a way, it feels like we'd be crazy not to."

"Right? That's exactly it." She smiles. "Jimmy? Can I admit something?" She pauses, I nod. "I have never felt this happy in my life."

I squeeze her hand before bringing it to my lips to kiss her palm. Her fingers brush tenderly across my cheek and I have to fight every cell in my body that is begging me to pull over.

"You want coffee honey?" I ask.

"Yes please."

"Okay, there's a spot at the next exit, we'll pull over and grab a quick bite and some coffee. Then it should only be 30 minutes until home."

Nora turns and settles in with the teddy bear again. She looks out the window and whispers "home" to herself.

...

We arrive at the apartment with only fifteen minutes to spare before I'm supposed to be at the Fallons' house for furniture placement and filming. Nora grabs the teddy bear and her purse, I carry up the cooler with Sir Harold inside. I unlock the door, push it open, and then stand in front of Nora so she can't go in.

"What are you doing? You're running late."

"I want to carry you over the threshold, so wait here."

"Jimmy that's ridiculous, we didn't get married." But my girl stays just outside the door with one hip cocked, resting a giant teddy bear on it waiting for me.

"No, you're right, we haven't gotten married…yet." And I scoop her up and carry her inside. I want to take her to bed and never leave but I'll be back with her tonight.

I press a kiss to her nose. She lifts her chin and presses a kiss to my lips. The give and take with Nora is unlike anything I could have imagined. It feels like we are equals in this.

I toss Nora on the sofa and then go back to carry the teddy bear in the same way.

"It's a good thing you've got your own television show." Nora laughs.

"Why's that?"

"Because you're a showman."

I lean over the back of the sofa and kiss her. "I am, but really all I want to do is make you laugh."

She smiles. "That's sweet."

"It's true."

"You're so mushy." Nora says as she runs her hands up my arms and comes to kneel on the sofa facing me.

"Honey, I'm anything but mushy, you know that. Hard as steel." I flex my biceps under her hands and fire dances through her eyes.

"Now, I've got to go and lift heavy things so a family can move back into their house this week. What are you going to do today?"

"Start unpacking and then coming to watch you lift heavy things."

"I like that plan." I peck her lips with a kiss and stand.

"I'll carry up your suitcases now. I also texted Holden about Sir Harold and he said we can bring him over whenever. Maybe around lunch today? I'll come pick you up."

"Okay, that works." She pauses and sinks back on her heels. "And Jimmy?"

"Yeah?"

"Thank you."

"There's no need to thank me" I pause, "but you're going to pay me back in there." And I point to the bedroom.

She laughs.

"I was already planning on it." She calls after me and I almost trip on the first step down to the truck.

...

"Well aren't you just the luckiest bastard there is!" Dax says as he pulls me into a hug and claps my shoulder. "I'm so happy for you."

"Thanks. But, uhh, sorry. What are you talking about?"

"Nora! You two making it official and all." He says like it's obvious.

"How do you know about that?" I ask as I see Angie pull up to the house. The delivery truck is already here so once she gets her mic on we'll start filming.

"Saw your video. You both have heart eyes for each other, it's so evident in the way you interact." He lifts the camera and starts to get it ready. "Honestly," he lowers his voice to a stage whisper, "Marla was pissed because she planned to market you as single and ready to mingle but I think this is a better story."

I feel like I missed a day at school, "Wait, what's a better story?"

"The hot, small town contractor," Dax points to me, "you, and the even hotter city slicker, Nora, falling for each other. It's like opposites attract and will give every single girl in a city who watches our show hope that she's just one blown tire from being rescued by her hunk."

"It was an empty tank of gas." I mutter.

"Okay, I'm ready!" Angie yells from her car before closing the door again. Dax lifts the camera and hits record. He gives a thumbs up to signal to Angie that he's ready and she pops out of the car like she just pulled up.

"Yay! The truck is here!" She squeals and she claps her hands together like a seal. That has never been her reaction to furniture day before but I try to match her energy.

"Yes it is. I haven't unpacked anything yet." I say as I give her a high five. "I've learned my lesson."

"That's right, wait for the brains of the operation." Angie says as I lift the door on the truck and it rolls open.

"Now this is all the new furniture right?" I ask even though I know the answer, it feels like explaining on camera could be helpful.

"Yes, when we moved everything out I talked with the Fallons about what pieces they loved and wanted to keep and which ones they were willing to part with. Their dining set will arrive tomorrow, it's been passed down for three generations now."

"Wow, that's cool."

"It is, so that we obviously kept. There is also a set of Jenny Lind bunk beds we kept and a dresser for the parents' bedroom but other than that they were willing to go new."

"That explains the full truck." I say as I survey the work ahead of me with my hands on my hips.

"It does, and the truck tomorrow has the vintage furniture we bought, this is only the brand new stuff." She grins. "But I got you some help."

She steps back and I see Dad walking up the driveway. He extends his hand to shake and I take it in mine.

His eyes are clear. His face has more color to it.

He looks good.

"Jim Arthur Lewis Jr reporting for duty." He says as we break the handshake.

"Glad you're here. We need all the help we can get."

38

Showbiz Buzz Strikes Again

Nora

"Liz? Liz? Anyone in there?"

I'm waving my hand in front of my best friend's face as she stands in front of me in shock. Not literally, I know she's just messing with me, but even I will admit that the news I broke is shocking.

"So, wait, back up." Liz blinks. "You are moving in with Jimmy? Like, Lakeville's James Arthur Lewis The Third."

"Yes, that very same one."

"What? When? How? Huh?"

I laugh and guide Liz down to the sofa in her studio. I bring the iced coffee straw to her lips and force her to sip like she's a hospital patient recovering from surgery.

"Well you're the one who gave him my address so really it's all your fault."

"False. Nope. I gave him your address because I assumed he would come down, try to be a hero, and then you'd kick his ass to the curb."

"Almost but nope, he came down, told my mother to shove it, and then took care of everything."

"Everything?" She cocks an eyebrow.

"Yes everything…he got up in it, but I also mean like making plans and organizing the to do list."

"You let him do that?"

"Liz, the man runs a business and builds homes for a living, he can keep things organized." I clarify as I take a sip of my iced coffee. Mitchell tossed a little bit of cinnamon syrup into them this morning and it's divine.

"True, but when have you ever let someone else do any planning for you?"

"That would be never."

"Right? So you see why I'm thrown off here?"

"I do, and I told him this morning that I feel crazy. He said that he feels it too but that he also feels like he'd be crazy not to and that hit me here." I fist bump my chest to try and make a joke out of it even though it was one of the most profound moments I've ever shared with another human being.

"Wow." Liz drags the word out as she looks me over.

"What?"

"Nora Leann Heely, you're in love."

That's the first time she's used my real middle name in the history of this game.

And while my best friend has hit it right on the nose, I can't cave that easily.

"Nuh uh." I challenge.

"Uh huh!"

"Fine. Maybe I am."

Liz's eyes double in size.

"Wait, seriously? I was teasing!"

"I know but I think I am. I mean you fell in love with Kyle quickly, why can't I fall in love with Jimmy quickly?"

Liz doesn't say anything, just stares at me.

"Right?" I demand as panic starts it's rampage through my veins. I stand abruptly and start pacing around Liz's studio. "Holy shit. Can I fall in love that quickly?"

I hear the panic in my own voice which only spurs me on.

"This is a *major* life decision that I just made on the fly. I followed my gut. And yes, I trust my gut and I've followed her for years but I've also planned and plotted, and pro and conned, and SMART goaled my way through things after my gut made the suggestion.

"I've never just climbed into some guy's truck who I've known for a week with three of my suitcases and my dead cat."

"Hey hey! Chill Nora. You *can* fall in love that quickly." Liz stands and stops my worried march with two hands on my shoulders. "You can totally make a major life change quickly. It's fine. Stop pacing in those heels, I'm afraid you're going to sprain your ankle."

I look down at the pumps I slid on. Today is Monday and every Monday in the last four years, barring holiday Mondays, I've worn these heels.

I had to replace them two years ago and was going to shop the Labor Day sales next week to replace them again.

"Okay, that's better, now c'mon and sit down and tell me more about how he took care of everything." She wiggles her eyebrows.

I barely hear what Liz says as my gaze stays locked in on my shoes.

My job is still up in the air.

My apartment is about to be rented by someone else.

My shoes are about to become obsolete in my new small town life.

"Oh god, what have I done?" I whisper.

"What are you talking about?" Liz asks as she takes a bite of her pastry.

"Liz, I think I just realized that everything is going to change."

"You're just realizing that now?" Liz confirms slowly as she finishes chewing.

"Yes, I was thinking earlier that it would be like last week, where I could run around Lakeville helping your mom with some project or following you as you take photos or just chilling out wishing I had a hobby besides true crime podcasts but I can't do that. Can I?"

"I mean, I'd make finding a hobby a priority because Lakeville isn't that exciting, but why can't you do that?"

Why? Why is it a bad idea to give everything up and change my life completely?

Will Liz even understand? She had someone give it all up for her. And that's not even what happened but Kyle was the one that moved to Lakeville to be with her.

"Nora?" Liz interrupts my internal debate. "Why can't you be in Lakeville while you plan your next steps?"

"Because," I exhale, "what if I can't do this? What if I can't be in a relationship?"

"Oh Nora." And Liz pulls me into a hug and hot tears fall down my cheek. She gently rocks me back and forth for a minute before pulling back and looking me in the eye.

"One, you can be in a relationship. You'll be great in a relationship. In fact, you've been in one with me for years and I have no complaints." A phlegmy laugh escapes my throat and Liz smiles before she continues. "And B, if for some crazy reason it doesn't work out then you move in with me and Kyle and we make a plan from there. Okay?"

"Okay." I sniffle.

"Now, I've got a pregnant lady coming in for photos in five minutes and I will not have you crying in front of her. Trust me, once the pregnant clients start crying the shoot is as good as over. They just don't stop."

I laugh and give Liz a big hug. With my iced coffee in hand I walk back over to Jimmy's apartment.

I set my iced coffee down on the island next to Sir Harold's cooler and look down at the set of keys Jimmy gave me. I brush my thumb along the grooves of the key as I look around the room. The dining table with flowers in the center. The sofa with the teddy bear sitting on it. I toss the keys up into my hand and then set them on the counter too.

With determination in my step I cross over to his dining table and pull out my phone. Before I can chicken out, I dial Trisha's number and, like I expected, it goes to voicemail.

"Hi Trisha, it's Nora. I know we aren't supposed to be communicating right now but I have an idea for how to salvage the Cornell gift. If we make a case for the Veterinary school she might reconsider. Something to think about. And, I need to start figuring out my next steps if Fosters isn't going to be offering me my job back. Do you think I can expect an answer by the end of this week?"

I pause to gather my thoughts.

"I loved working at Fosters and learning from you and the other talented members of our team over the last four years. I hope we can continue to work together going forward. Talk soon, bye Trisha."

I end the call and set the phone down in front of me. I tuck my hands in my lap and resist the urge to just sit and stare at the black screen hoping a call will come through.

With a deep breath I push myself back from the table and stand up. I can see one of my suitcases in Jimmy's bedroom.

Correction, our bedroom.

I roll my suitcase over to the closet and flip on the light. I haven't been in here except to steal his one button down shirt and I am pleasantly surprised.

Rusty wire hangers aside.

He's got a few shelves and plenty of hanging space. The only hanging items are his new button down from our date, a suit coat, and dress pants. There are a handful of flannels that any lumberjack would be proud to own.

Don't be a snob Nora…he practically is a lumberjack.

I open one of the drawers and find a stack of folded jeans. The dresser in his bedroom has his boxers, socks, and t-shirts so I'm curious about what else is in these closet drawers.

I open the second drawer, empty.

The third, empty.

The fourth and final drawer is…

Empty.

I smile. There are three empty hanging rod bays and three empty drawers at my disposal.

There are a few boxes on the shelf at the top of the closet. I drag a step ladder from the laundry room into his closet and step up to peek inside.

The first box is heavy and I almost drop it when I pull it down. I carry it over to the bed and pop the lid off.

Sweaters.

With the lid back in place I try to lift the box back over my head to place it on the shelf and struggle more than I'll ever admit to Jimmy.

The second box slides off the shelf much more easily. It almost feels empty. Still standing on the ladder I lift the lid and find a Hawaiian shirt. I rest the lid on the ladder and dig deeper to find a swim suit and a pair of flip flops.

The final box isn't as heavy as the first but heavier than the second. A real Goldilocks scenario. I carry it off the ladder and bring it to the bed.

Inside are baseball hats. Lakeville H.S. is on the top one, under it is a Lewis Hardware hat that has worn out sections on the brim. I brush my thumb across the logo and place it gently back into the box.

After I return the box to the shelf I step back and look at the closet again. It feels like he was holding this space for me.

I'm startled out of my admiration for his closet space when my phone pings with a text notification.

> LIZ:
> Mom just sent me this from the
> Tome Raider chat...

LIZ:
🔗 The Morning Show Showbiz Buzz

I swallow, swipe open the message, and tap the link. The same two women from last week appear on the screen and their dresses are equally saturated.

"Welcome back! It is time for Showbiz Buzz and we have a fun little update from upstate New York."

"That's right Rashmi, remember the handsome contractor we shared with you last week? Well, I'm sorry to say it ladies, but he's taken! Take a look."

The women disappear and then the video of Jimmy and I eating the donut sundaes appears. They show the whole thing and then cut back to the hosts.

"I mean, adorable right?"

"So adorable. And they were right here in the city! We did a little sleuthing and figured out that the lucky lady in the video is Nora Heely. She lives here in the city and works for the prominent fundraising firm Fosters, Henderson & Associates."

"Well, Janet, she *worked* for them. When we called them looking for her they said she no longer works there."

"Really? Well maybe that means she's moved upstate to live with her man!"

"That's really the only conclusion to make." The host volleys back and then they move on to airing details of someone else's life.

Before I realize what I'm doing I am racing down the stairs and out onto the sidewalk. I run past Liz's studio, the coffee shop, the boutique. My heels are pounding into the pavement, leaving click, clack echos in my wake.

I turn the corner to the Fallons' house and can see Jimmy carrying one end of a sofa into the house. My pace picks up. My feet knowing how much I need to be in his arms.

He sees me barreling up the sidewalk. He mutters something to the person holding the other end of the sofa before he sets it down and turns to me.

Jimmy braces himself as I crash into him. His arms wrap around my waist and the tears fall.

"Nora, honey, what's the matter?" His voice strained with terror. "Are you okay?"

"No. I'm not." I wail.

"Hey, hey, it's okay." He brings one arm up and starts to stroke the back of my head. And when I feel him start to set me down I cling on tighter. "Okay, not ready yet, got it."

Then he just stands there. Holding me. Waiting for me. He doesn't seem to be in any rush, doesn't seem to care that he was in the middle of something else moments earlier.

It's like I'm the most important thing in the world.

As my crying stops and my breathing regulates he sets me down. This time I let him.

"Now, tell me what's going on." He urges.

"The news showed our brain freeze video."

"What?"

"The video of us eating the sundaes yesterday with the brain freeze tip. Well, the producers must be following you now or something because they just showed it on showbiz buzz."

"Why? I don't understand why they would do that? Why do they care?"

"Because you're supposed to be this hot, *single* guy. The show needs to promote you that way and now you're not. Single. I mean we haven't had the talk I guess, but I'm moving in with you. We've said I love you to each other so it feels official. It didn't even cross my mind that this would be an issue."

I'm rambling. It's like I've pulled the loose thread just enough and now the rest is coming apart.

"The worst part is that they called Fosters looking for me and Fosters said I didn't have a job with them anymore. And I had already called Trisha this morning like we planned."

"What did Trisha say?"

"She didn't answer, I left her a voicemail and then saw the segment."

"How'd you see the segment?"

"Liz sent it to me. She got it from Katherine who got it from the Tome Raiders chat."

He pulls his hand down over his face. "Okay, not ideal. I've got to think about the job thing a little bit more but Dax said this morning Marla likes the idea of us being together."

"What? You talked to them about it?"

"I didn't mean to, Dax brought it up and we chatted for a minute before Angie and Dad showed up for furniture day."

Remembering that I ambushed him at work, where there are cameras, I quickly wipe at my eyes and step back from him. Over his shoulder I see Angie with a concerned look on her face, their Dad who oddly looks happy, and Dax with the lens pointed at us.

Jimmy reaches up and brushes at the tear stains on my cheek.

"Let me help Dad get this sofa inside and then I'll take you home for lunch. We'll call Holden and take Sir Harold over to his office."

"Okay." I say and he reaches for my hand and walks me over to the porch. Angie gives me a hug, his Dad offers me a smile. Dax gives me a thumbs up as I sit down on the stoop.

I pull out my phone and see a missed call from Liz, several "you okay?" texts from her, and a text from my mom.

MOM:
Thought I recognized that guy you brought home this weekend! Nice work getting a celebrity while he's up and coming. He'll be less likely to ditch you for some younger, hotter thing in a few years.

39

Never Rush A Grand Gesture

JIMMY

"What the hell is that?"

Nora looks up at me. I just stepped out onto the porch and read her mom's text over her shoulder. The urge to pick up her phone and chuck it across the street is strong.

"Just a note from my mom." Nora says as she pockets her phone.

"Nora, that's not okay. What she said. And it's not true."

"I know," is all she says.

Needing to get Nora out of here before Dax can record any of this I grab her hand and drag her out towards my truck. Her heels sink into the grass as she tries to keep up.

"Jimmy! Hold on."

I stop, reach down, swing my arm under her knees to pick her up, and carry her the rest of the way. I open the door and hoist her inside. I stand next to it with the door open behind me and look into her eyes.

"We're buying you new shoes. Add that to the to do list."

"Why do I need new shoes?" She says as she crosses her arms. Universal code for 'watch out dude, she's fired up.'

"Because you don't need to be running around town in heels."

"Maybe I like my heels." She counters.

"Honey, I like them too, but when you're running around trying to get to me, I want you in sneakers so you can run to me as fast as you can."

"Fine, but I get to pick the sneakers."

"Fine."

I close the door and smile. She seems alright. Her mood is light enough that I imagine she'll recover quickly.

Knowing I'm the one she ran to, being the one that she can count on, fills my chest with pride. I want to be the man she comes to. I want her to be the woman I go to.

And the one I come home to.

The drive back to the apartment is quiet. Nora is looking off out her window. Things have changed, very quickly for her, and I'm going to have to remember that as we discuss things together. Does she feel like Bethany felt? Like she sacrificed everything for me? I can't have her feeling that way. I don't want her thinking she's the only one making changes.

I knew the show would bring around some fame and notoriety for me but I never expected my love life to be the center of attention. I don't like the idea of everyone knowing who Nora is. Or of her being known as my girlfriend.

She is my girlfriend, and everyone needs to know that, but she's also her own woman. She's created a life for herself and up until this past week she didn't plan to share it with anyone.

What can I do to show her that I want to change my life too?

As we pass the market an idea pops into my head. I pull over and Nora turns to me with questions written all over her face.

"Wait here." I tell her.

And then I hop out of the truck and head inside.

...

"Jimmy, the bag isn't hiding anything. I can see that you bought a box of cereal and condoms. Did we really need to stop for that right now?"

"Yes we did. And this isn't just any cereal."

She looks down at the box and then back up at me, still not getting it.

Maybe this wasn't the grandest of gestures, or the most obvious, but there is sentiment behind the box of cereal Nora is pulling out of the bag and examining.

"Did you like put a ring in the box or something? Because, cute, I guess, but I am not ready to get engaged."

"No, there isn't a ring in the box. And I know you're not ready, but I've got plans for when you are." She looks at me with wide eyes. "No, the cereal itself is the gesture."

"I don't get it."

"I picked up on that," I turn towards her in my seat. "The first night you stayed over, when Angie was drunk on the couch. You criticized my generic brand cereal. Something along the lines of 'Knock off cereal is for homeless shelters.' if I recall correctly."

"What I said was, I don't know anyone who buys generic cereal and eats it themselves, instead of donating it."

"That was it," I snap my fingers and point at her. "And in my ill-planned grand gesture here I went into the store and paid 70% more for the name brand cereal for you."

"Jimmy, I don't know what to say." She says as she brings her hands to her heart in mock appreciation.

"Alright, enough with the sarcasm." She grins. "With more planning I can do a grand gesture like the best of 'em."

I turn back to the wheel and drive us the rest of the way to the apartment. When we get inside she slides the box of cereal into the cabinet. She turns around and pulls me into a hug.

"Thank you, it's actually a lovely grand gesture."

"It feels like you're being sincere." I say with skepticism.

"Because I am. Listen," she pulls back and places her hands on my chest while mine rest at her waist. "Was I freaking out this morning about all the changes I've decided to make in the last 24 hours? Yes. Yes I was."

Shit.

"But the second I was in your arms again I knew everything was going to be okay. That we were going to figure it out together."

Phew.

"That's all I want Nora, is to figure things out with you."

She smiles and then takes a deep breath. "Okay, it's time to deal with Sir Harold. I'm afraid to open that cooler."

"I'll call Holden."

I grab my phone and dial the clinic's number. His receptionist answers and she transfers me to his office.

"Hey man! Calling about your cat again?" He says when he hops on the line.

"Yeah and it's Nora's. He died a week ago."

"Gross. Where has he been since then?"

"Gross? Are you serious? Where's your bedside manner man?"

"It's not your cat so I didn't think I needed it." He clears his throat and drops his voice. "I'm so sorry to hear about the loss of your new girlfriend's beloved animal."

"You're a turd."

He laughs.

"So can we bring him in? He's been in her freezer until this morning and we have him on ice in a styrofoam cooler on my kitchen island."

"Good thinking. Ah, yeah, my calendar is pretty open this afternoon so why don't you drive him over and we'll take it from there."

"Thanks man."

"See you soon."

Nora is sitting on a stool at the island with her hand resting on top of the cooler.

"He said we can bring him over now. Are you ready?"

"As ready as I'll ever be." She says and she stands and lifts the box.

I take it from her and then follow her out the door and down to the truck.

"Am I a bad cat mom if I don't want to hold the cooler on my lap. I'm seriously so freaked out."

"Not at all. Everything about this is weird."

She laughs and opens the back door for me to slide Sir Harold onto the seat. She closes the door and takes a deep breath.

"Okay, let's do this."

...

"So that's it?" I ask as Holden takes the cooler from us.

"Yeah, that's it. We'll cremate him here and call you when his ashes are ready."

Next to me Nora cringes a little bit.

"What happens if we don't want the ashes?" I ask, just in case.

"Then we dispose of them for you." He turns to Nora. "Any other questions?"

"No, I think I'm good." She says.

"Alright, well I'll give you a call tomorrow when it's all done. So, will we see you at Trivia tonight?"

I look at Nora who offers up a little shrug.

"Maybe. We'll see."

Holden shakes my hand and then extends his to Nora. He opens his office door for us and we walk out into the hallway.

"Dr. Monaghan?" Nora starts.

"C'mon, it's Holden. No one calls me Dr. Monaghan."

She chuckles. "Okay, Holden, where would you take a date to lunch if you really wanted to impress her?"

"Well, let's see. If I was taking a girl to lunch it would have to be good so I can get a second date and take her to dinner."

"A man with a plan." I say with an eye roll as I follow behind them.

Ignoring me, Holden stops and turns to Nora and says, "I'd take a lunch date to Pastoral Provence outside of Avon. It's fancy but also inviting and their quiche is delicious."

"Thank you for your help!" Nora says and then she turns back to me. "Did you hear that? Pastoral Provence in Avon."

"I heard. Thank you Holden, see you later."

"Enjoy lunch!" He calls after us as we exit the waiting room. I turn and see him sporting a grin from ear to ear and I flip him off as I walk away.

He knows as well as I do that Pastoral Provence is the most expensive restaurant in a 20 mile radius. There is an engagement almost every night because it's the only fancy restaurant around here.

Not that I don't want to go with Nora but right now, she at least looks the part. She's wearing black peep-toe heels, long tan wide leg pants, and a cream sweater tank top.

I, on the other hand, am in a sweaty t-shirt, jeans, and work boots.

We're going to get some looks at lunch.

40

We Fancy Like

Nora

Pastoral Provence is…unique. It's like they visited every three star French restaurant in the city and tried to replicate it. But they're also on a tight budget or maybe they think mismatched place settings are charming. I'm trying not to be a snob but the food better be incredible if it's where Holden would take a girl to impress her.

I am, however, thoroughly enjoying the fact that they made Jimmy slip on a suit coat.

Sitting across from me is a man trying to relax his shoulders in a coat that is easily two inches too narrow for his broad frame. His t-shirt has a dirt mark along the collar. His tan boots take up a lot of space under our little bistro table.

He's out of place here and I only hate how much I love it a little bit.

A waiter approaches our table.

"Bonjour Madame and Monsour."

Mon-sour?

Don't be a snob.

Don't be a snob.

"Vhat can I geet you started vhit today?"

I see Jimmy trying to contain his laughter too. This guy clearly has never spoken French a day in his life. I wonder if the restaurant asked him to do it this way or if it was a choice all his own.

"I'll start with a glass of the Chardonnay and the escargot, please." I look across the table to Jimmy.

"Water's fine."

"Alright! Coming right up!" And with that our waiter skips off behind a red curtain.

"So, what do you think?" Jimmy asks with his voice full of humor.

"I think Holden doesn't try too hard to impress his dates."

He laughs. "Nah, that usually isn't Holden's MO. He likes them as superficial as they come."

"What do you mean?" Should I be telling Angie this?

"In college, mind you I was still here in Lakeville, but in college he figured out that you had better odds of taking a girl home if you approached a group of them. He'd start talking to one, if the vibe wasn't there he'd pivot to another."

"It's not the worst strategy."

"No, it worked out pretty well for him. Now that he's settled back home I'm not sure how much he goes out like that since there aren't really gaggles of women hanging out in Lakeville."

"Well, there might have been if I hadn't snagged the hot celebrity contractor."

He barks out a laugh. "True. Thank you. You not only saved me but you saved Holden the embarrassment of constant rejection."

"I dunno, he seems to fill out that doctor coat pretty well." I tease.

"Like I'm filling out this coat?" Jimmy tries to lift his arms but gets stuck. I burst into a fit of giggles.

Our waiter comes back with my glass of wine and scowls at our laughter. I bring my hand to my mouth and try to literally wipe the smile off my face.

It's not happening.

I manage to say thank you as the waiter mumbles "I'll give you a minute."

Jimmy reaches forward for his water and has to shimmy in his seat to get close enough. I watch him struggle and the giggles come sputtering out of my mouth.

Along with a little bit of my wine.

"Hey, this is a classy joint. No spitting your wine." Jimmy scolds me.

"Sorry." I mutter with as much seriousness as I can muster but the smile breaks through.

"What are you going to order?" Jimmy asks while making a show of trying to pick up his menu.

"Definitely something that requires cutting because I can use my arms freely."

"Oh fuck, I didn't think about that."

I laugh, "I'm honestly trying to picture you eating and all I see is that coat ripping down the back or a sleeve ripping off."

"Drink that wine, eat whatever you already ordered, and then I'm taking you someplace else."

"But don't you want to impress me?" I say with humor.

"I can think of other ways to impress you."

Different numbers from our list start floating through my mind. I feel myself flush. It's almost like I can hear the buzzing of my vibrator in this restaurant.

Wait, that's my phone.

I move quickly to answer the call from a number I don't know.

"Hello?"

"Nora? It's Angie." Jimmy looks at me with questioning eyes. I mouth 'Angie' and he nods and tries to sit back in his chair but his shoulders are still curled forward, stuck in the coat, and it is a sight to see.

"Hi Angie, what's going on?"

"Well two things, one I got confirmation that your hangers and shoe rack are going to come in tomorrow. Usually our deliveries are pretty early so I'll bring them up to you when they arrive."

"Oh fabulous. Yeah I was looking at his closet and I think once I get everything hung up I'll place another order for the remaining organizers."

"Great. I'll order whatever you need."

"That's awesome, thank you."

"Now my second thing," Angie starts and I hear her take a breath, "Jimmy was telling us this morning that the closet in your apartment was organized to perfection. Your kitchen and bathroom was too. Even your junk drawer had sections!" I make eye contact with Jimmy and his expression is questioning but I smile with pride. "Anyway, I've got to get the mud room figured out at the Fallons' house and I was hoping you could take a look at it with me and tell me what you think?"

"Oh sure, I'd love to."

"Really? Okay! Just umm, think you could come by tomorrow afternoon? Jimmy and I switch shifts at the store at noon so I can walk with you over to the house then?"

"Sounds good."

"Okay! Yay! Okay, I'm gonna go before you can change your mind. Kay, bye!"

I laugh, "Bye Angie."

"What was that all about?" Jimmy asks and he leans forward and tries to rest his forearms on the table. The seam at his shoulder is splitting. This jacket isn't going to last long.

"Angie asked if I would help her organize the mud room at the Fallons' house."

"Yeah?"

"Yeah. Apparently someone was saying how organized my apartment was."

"I might have mentioned something while we were unloading furniture today."

"Your escargot," our waiter says as he sets the garlic sauced snails down in front of us. Jimmy leans back a little and I lean forward to waft the smell into my nose.

"Mmm, smells wonderful, thank you."

"Merci," the waiter mumbles.

"Think he meant *de rien*?" I ask as I pull an escargot onto my plate.

Jimmy struggles as he pivots to look back over his shoulder.

"Judging by the way he's shaking his head in shame, yeah, I think he did."

I chuckle as I bring the snail up to my lips. Jimmy is watching me.

"What?" I ask.

"Nothing."

"It's not nothing. What is it?"

"I've never had this before so I'm watching you for guidance." He admits.

I offer him a smile and pop the delicacy into my mouth. The garlic and the butter and the herbs combine with the briny meat and my taste buds melt into bliss.

"So good." I say as I finish swallowing.

Jimmy leans forward.

"That was kinda hot."

I reach for my glass of wine and wink at him. "It was kinda hot, wasn't it? Try one for yourself."

He reaches forward but can barely bring his hands together to pull out the meat from the shell. I chuckle and help him.

I slip the snail onto his fork and feed it to him. He keeps his eyes on me the whole time. I watch has his brown eyes widen as he registers the surprise of how delicious it is.

"Wondering how you've ever lived without this?" I tease as I take my second bite.

"Yeah, exactly." He says as his eyes intensify.

I don't think we're talking about snails anymore.

I grab my wine glass and gulp down the rest. It's not that I want to be drunk. It's that I want to get the hell out of here.

"Would madam like another chardonnay?" Our waiter asks.

"Ah, no, I'm okay."

"We'll just take the check." Jimmy says quickly.

"You're not going to order meals?"

"Nope. We're just going to pay you and then head out."

"I see, and were there any issues with your appetizer sir?" Jimmy looks pained as he tries to keep his voice even.

"Nope, nope. Everything was great. We just have somewhere we need to be."

"I see, okay…" and without another word he walks away from our table.

Jimmy and I look at each other and both start snickering again. He reaches for his glass of water but freezes. His eyes meet mine.

"Shit." He whispers.

"What?"

"I heard a pop."

"Like when you ripped my bodice off?"

His eyes darken and I see the memory flash in his mind. I try not to laugh again as he slowly brings his arm back to rest at his side.

"Honey, I'm gonna bust the seam in my fly if you keep talking like that."

I bark out a laugh but stop when I see the pain in his face.

"Oh no, you're serious?"

"Nora," he tries to lean forward and can't so I start to giggle again. Before Jimmy can continue our waiter arrives at the table with the check.

Jimmy tries to reach down to pull his wallet out of his front pocket, but the suit coat gets in the way. Instead he stands up and walks over to stand next to me.

I'm eye to fly and can see the bulge looks a little fuller than it had when we first arrived. He twists a little bit.

"Nora, can you get my wallet out of my pocket please?"

I hear the waiter gasp a little.

Slowly, I drag my hand up his thigh and reach into his front pocket all while keeping eye contact with him. I pull the wallet out and hand it to Jimmy.

Without breaking eye contact with me he slides a card out between two fingers and holds it out for the waiter who takes it and scurries away.

"You're not playing fair." Jimmy says as we wait for the waiter to come back so he can sign.

"I'm well aware." I admit as I uncross my legs and scootch my chair back. I watch as Jimmy watches the movement.

"Here you go. I hope you come back for a full meal sometime." The waiter clips at us, his fake accent almost completely gone.

Jimmy signs and I stand up. We walk towards the host stand and then he tries to slip out of the jacket but can't. I stand behind him tugging the sleeve down on one side just a few inches before going to tug down on the other.

With his arms behind him like he's an olympic ski jumper I'm able to pull on both sleeves at once and the jacket finally slides off his arms.

"Come here." Jimmy growls as I toss the jacket at the host. He wraps me up in a hug and then smacks my ass.

"That's for the move you pulled taking out my wallet."

"Seems like a reasonable repercussion." I say as he wraps his arm around my shoulder and we walk out to his truck.

...

We got burgers and fries at a drive-in diner on our way back to Lakeville. Then Jimmy dropped me off at Liz's to pack up my stuff. He went to the Fallons' house to finish up for the day. Later I'm going to meet him at his place, I mean our place, before we go to The Whale for trivia night.

He agreed to be on The Know Jobs with Liz, Angie, and me as long as we didn't mime giving a blow job when we got a question right.

I kinda forgot we had done that.

After I changed my outfit, I walked out to the living room to find Liz and Kyle sitting around their coffee table reading Trivial Pursuit cards. Apparently when we kept The Nine Inch Males in check last week we unlocked a beast mode of trivia competition in this town.

I still think male lobsters should be called Peens.

Just saying.

"So you really think just reading these random facts is going to help you tonight? Isn't there like a theme?" I ask.

"Yes there's a theme. And we don't know what it is. So I'm trying to capture as much knowledge in my brain as I can." Liz mutters as she flashes two more cards in front of her face.

I highly doubt she's retaining any of this. I continue to watch them "study" as I drink my water.

"Nora, let me tell you a few things about Lakeville." Kyle says as he flips over another card.

"Be nice." Liz warns.

"Absolutely. I love it here. But Nora is a fellow outsider and I have some tips."

"Fire away Kyle, I'm all ears." I say.

"First, never park your car on the street in front of someone's house. They'll think it's suspicious. If there is room in the driveway use it and deal with everyone having to move their car to let yours out when you need to leave."

"Ha, random, but okay."

"Second, never complain about power outages, I let it slide last week because I didn't know you were gonna stay but when the power goes out we band together and find a way through."

"Noted. And thank you for your forgiveness."

He nods his head.

"Finally, be ready for everybody to know everything. Not just the Tome Raiders although they are usually where information starts. But the men are just as chatty as the women. Everyone here feels like one big family.

"As an only child I had to kind of get used to that. I know you like to run things on your own too so just be aware."

"Thanks Kyle. I have been used to doing everything on my own, for a long time. It's honestly, kind of nice not to have to."

Liz slaps the cards she was reviewing down onto the table. She looks at me like I'm an alien sitting on her sofa.

"What?" I ask her.

"You keep saying stuff like that and it makes me do a double take. I've never heard you say you want someone else's help before. Let alone admitting to liking it."

"I know, it's weird for me too, but I'm trying to tap into my feelings and listen to what they're trying to tell me."

"It's shit like that!" Liz yells. Kyle lifts his head to look at her, "sorry, shit like that, Nora Heely doesn't have feelings."

She looks to Kyle, "I mean, of course she does, but am I wrong here? She's not acting like herself?"

"Babe, I think she's acting totally like herself. It's just not the self she lets people see."

Liz pauses and stares at her fiancé.

I'm staring at him too.

"Wow," Liz says. "That's deep."

"That's what she said." Kyle replies and after a beat we all start laughing together.

"Alright ladies, the Nine Inch Males need me. Let's go." Kyle says as he stands up. He lends a hand to Liz and pulls her up too.

She raises her hand in the air like Joan of Arc and calls out, "to The Whale!"

41

You Make Me Feel. Period.

JIMMY

I am in my element. The theme of trivia tonight is music and The Know Jobs are cleaning up.

Liz has musical theatre covered.

Angie knows both pop and R&B.

I've got country in the bag.

And Nora keeps saying that if we wanted to know the details of the several outfits Rihanna wore at the 2016 VMAs, or the order of songs from her Super Bowl Performance she could help. And something about a Lady Gaga Meat Dress which I vaguely remember. Then there's been a lot of muttering about Taylor not getting the respect from the industry she deserves and that fans came through and shut them up.

Her knowledge seems to be limited to Rihanna, Lady Gaga, and Taylor Swift.

We're entering a round where they'll play one second of a song and everyone gets a chance to name the artist. If no one gets it, they'll play two seconds. The amount of points you can win diminishes with each extra second they play.

"Anyone need another?" I ask the ladies.

"Yes please."

"Sure."

Angie slurps up the bottom of her drink. "Yep."

I head to the bar and lean against the edge. I laugh to myself remembering how I struggled with basic movements while I was stuffed in that jacket from Pastoral Provence. Nora is going to have a tough time getting me in a suit coat ever again, even if it fits.

Subconsciously I roll out my shoulders and I hear Nora giggle behind me. I shoot her a look and she immediately looks away and tries to hold in her laughter.

Her shoulders give her away.

Holden slides up next to me.

"Hey man. How was lunch?"

"Humorous." I reply and he scrunches his eyebrows in curiosity but I just shake my head.

"I ah, actually, have to tell you something," he says.

Immediately Sir Harold's kitchen towel wrapped, frozen carcass comes to mind.

"My assistant just sent me this." And he holds out his phone to me. I see a text from his assistant that says "Weren't they in the office today?!" above a link to an article.

The summary headline reads "Homecraft Network Darling Hires High End Hooker"

I flash my eyes up to Holden and he grimaces.

"So you haven't seen this yet? Shit, I hate being the bearer of bad news."

"No I haven't seen this yet, but send it to me. Who else has seen it?"

"Not sure, Sofia spends most of her free time on trashy gossip sites so there's a chance no one else in Lakeville knows. Plus we aren't supposed to have phones out during trivia. You know how Rick gets about cheating."

"Right, okay. Well, thanks."

I return to the table without drinks and Liz and Angie complain but Nora takes one look at my face and asks, "What is it?"

"We gotta go." I tell her as I hand her my phone.

"What? Why?" Angie asks. "If you leave we won't have enough people for trivia!"

"I'm not worried about trivia right now Ange, I'm worried about Nora."

"Everything okay?" Liz asks.

"No, but it will be." I help Nora step off the stool as she reads the article.

She looks up from it and I see the disbelief, anger, and grief in her eyes. She turns to Liz, "I'll call you later."

And together we walk out the door to my place.

●●●

"I can't believe that she would do this! Why would she do this?!" Nora paces in front of the sofa. I'm sitting with my hands between my knees trying to regulate my blood pressure.

All signs point to Nora's mom as the source of the article. She had weird details about how Nora likes to celebrate her birthday with a new pair of shoes, and that she doesn't dye her hair, just conditions it well.

The article is otherwise completely false. Nora admits that she told her mom about a few of the free fancy dinners she had gotten from guys when she was younger but maybe only two before she stopped sharing any details at all.

Knowing I don't really want to know the answer but asking the question anyways I say, "Did you keep a list or a record of the guys you brought home?"

"Why?" Nora says and she's practically spitting venom.

"I'm asking because maybe your mom found it when she was in your apartment and that's why she thinks this. I don't know, Nora. I'm trying to figure this out too."

"Oh," she softens a little and sits down next to me. "Yes and no. I used to keep their names written in a notebook just in case I, you know, caught anything. I'm totally clean by the way."

"Me too."

She nods. "But I sort of stopped, I dunno, a while ago."

"Why'd you stop?" The way she muttered 'I dunno' has me on high alert. Did one of those men hurt her? Try to stalk her? I will find the asshole who hurt her and kill him mysel—

"I stopped when I got Sir Harold because I stopped bringing guys home."

Oh. Wait. "That was three years ago."

"Yeah."

"So you haven't brought a guy home in three years?"

"No, that's not exactly true, but instead of like one a week it went down to one every several months."

"I see." I say, and my satisfied smirk breaks through.

"What are you smiling about?"

"Just that this girl who all last week was saying *I only do one night stands, no numbers, just sex* wasn't actually as promiscuous as she made herself seem."

"Well, she was a whore for her cat's dismissive love."

I laugh and then I glance at my watch, it's almost midnight.

"Did you call Liz yet?" I ask.

"No, but I sent her a text that I'd call her in the morning. She said that she was going to ask her sister if there's anything we can do."

"Maggie?"

"Yeah, she's like a political advisor now so Liz said she deals with bad press all the time."

"Huh, who knew. Alright Heely, let's get ready for bed. I've gotta be at the Fallons' house early and you have a closet to organize."

"Yes, this is true. Oh, and Jimmy?"

"Yeah honey?" I turn and see her perched on the edge of the sofa.

"I'm sorry about all this. How my mom got this article published, how our video affected the show. I'm so ashamed of the chaos I've created."

I cross back over to her and step up in her space. One of my legs fits between hers and I slide my knee in until it's touching the sofa and pushing her skirt taught. I place my hands on her jaw.

"You did not cause any chaos. Do you hear me?" She nods. "All of those things happened around you, but not because of you. Other people made the choice to publish lies and try to find details about small town businessmen."

She chuckles.

"You are anything but chaotic. You're an anchor. My anchor."

"Okay." She whispers.

"Do you believe that? Do you believe that you're my gravity? That I was just floating through life not attaching myself to anything until you came along?"

"Yes, I believe you."

"And will you let me be your anchor? Let me ground you and support you? Care for you? Because," I pause as tears clog my throat. "Nora, I've watched my father and my grandfather lose the women they love and if I'm going to suffer their fate I need to know I gave you everything."

She reaches up and kisses me and I wrap my arms around her and pull her into a hug. She sniffles, I sniffle. She pulls back and wipes away the tears on her face and when she looks up and sees the tears in mine she lets out a laugh.

"You've turned me into a sap!" She jokes.

"I love you." I tell her, she smiles. "Can I say something without you thinking it's really weird?"

"Maybe?" She says with a questioning tone.

"Okay, so, don't make this into a big deal. I'm just sharing what's in my mind right now."

"Go on," she says tentatively.

"You remind me of my mom."

"You're right that's really weird." She starts to walk away.

"No wait, wait, wait, wait." I grab her wrist and spin her to me. She slides her hand in mine and I reach for her other hand to clasp them together. "I meant, just being in your presence is comforting. Like, I know there's a shit storm blowing outside, but you're the eye of the storm."

"I'm teasing, that's really sweet." She looks to the side and sighs. "That's just so the opposite of how my mother makes me feel so I don't really understand it."

"I get that." I tug her hands and pull them around my back so she is forced to step in closer to me. She rests her chin on my chest and looks up at me. "How do I make you feel Nora?"

She smiles. It's like the sun's first light in the sky.

"You make me feel. Period. I'm not even sure how to name all the feelings I have for you. I never expected to fall in love and now that it's happening, I can hardly believe it."

"Believe it." I say and I press a kiss to her forehead. She tucks her head so her cheek is resting against my chest.

Can she hear how wildly my heart beats for her? Can she feel the way it is ready to burst out of my chest and go to her. How it is ready to open up and consume her?

I wiggle my fingers out of her hand and bring my arm around to rest at her waist. Slowly I sway us back and forth and she nuzzles her nose into my chest.

"Are you dancing with me?" She asks.

"If you want me to then yes, if not, I'm just shifting my weight from side to side."

"I want you to dance with me."

And those are the last words we say out loud. Our hearts connecting. Passing silent love notes back and forth to each other as we sway around the living room to no sound.

Nora is the music in my head, the song in my heart. With her in my arms I don't need anything else in the world.

42

The Early Bird Gets Three Job Offers

Nora

"I've always wanted to do this." Jimmy says from the side of the bed.

I peel one eye open and look up at him. Beautiful. Shirtless, neatly trimmed beard lining his jaw, low riding gym shorts, and he's holding a baking sheet.

Hold on, what?

I rub my eyes and start to sit up a little bit against the headboard. I open my eyes again and, yes, that's a baking sheet. With a bowl of cereal, bowl of fruit, and a cup of coffee balanced on it.

"I'm going to have Angie pick out a tray for this but I made do with what I have."

"Very resourceful of you." I say as he sets the tray on my lap and sits down on the bed in front of me.

He watches me expectantly as I take a spoonful of the cereal and bring it to my mouth.

"What?"

"Nothing, I am just so freaking excited to give a girl breakfast in bed. And not just any girl, my girl."

I smile. "Okay, I'm glad you're excited, and I am excited to be the recipient of breakfast in bed, but I'm realizing that it's super awkward to eat cereal from my lap, especially when my devilishly sexy boyfriend is staring at me."

His eyes go wide and I shove the spoonful of cereal in my mouth quickly before any more stupid, unplanned words pop out.

"You said boyfriend." He says while wagging a finger at me slowly. I bat it out of the air and slosh some coffee onto the tray. He lifts it off my lap and moves it to the bedside table.

Jimmy comes back but this time he crawls onto the bed so he's straddling me. I busy myself with chewing and looking anywhere but at him.

"You said boyfriend," he repeats.

"Nuh uh." I say while I finish chewing.

"Oh yeah honey, I heard it." He waits while I swallow and then grabs my ribs and drags me down the bed so I'm lying on my back.

My smile cannot be contained and I bring my hands up to cover my face.

"Oh no you don't, no hiding." Jimmy says as he reaches up and pins my hands over my head. He moves down so he's laying on my pelvis but holding himself up on an elbow so I can still breathe.

"How did you sleep Nora?" He asks.

"Really well, once my boyfriend stopped getting boners."

"Hey now, I didn't stop, I decided it was time to let you sleep. And I don't think girlfriends are allowed to complain about too many boners."

"You called me your girlfriend." I taunt.

"Eh? Did I?" He pretends to think about it. "No, I think I referred to girlfriends in general, not specifically to you Nora, my girlfriend."

He grins.

His smile makes every muscle in his face move. His face brightens, his eyes shine, and the little crinkles at the corners add depth to his expression. I want to hug him to me but he still has my wrists pinned so I wrap my legs around him instead.

"Hey now girlfriend, what are you trying to do?"

"Hug you."

"With your legs?"

"Well, my arms are pinned." And I offer up the best shrug I can with my arms over my head.

"If I recall, girlfriend, this is number 14 on the list."

"I believe you are correct boyfriend." And he nuzzles in against my neck and begins trailing kisses up and down my body. I feel him harden as he rests between my legs and I start to rock my hips and press my heels into his ass.

He starts to rock his hips too and I pull one of my hands out and slip it down the front of his shorts.

He hisses at the contact but pushes himself into my hand. I pull him out and line him up with my entrance.

Jimmy's eyes connect with mine.

"Nora," he breathes, "are you sure?"

"Yes Jimmy, I want nothing between us ever again."

He brings his hand down to my hip and in one thrust, all of him fills me. I gasp for air as I feel my entire lower half tense.

"Relax Nora," Jimmy breathes. He starts to pull out and I feel my walls cling to him to prevent him leaving.

"Oh fuck, you're clawing for me Nora." And he pushes back inside me while gripping my hip. His head falls forward and rests on my shoulder.

My body reacts to him quickly and every nerve ending from my head to my toes is focused on his movements. After an agonizingly slow push into me, he pulls his hand off my wrist, and brings it to my hip. Holding me in place he pushes forward, barely leaving, just pushing up and up into me.

He has no where else he can go but he continues like he's searching for new depths within me. I hold his head in one hand and cling to his back with the other.

Our physical closeness matches the intimacy of our hearts. Together we hold each other as the room fades to black around us. We cling to each other as we both return to earth.

"Wow girlfriend." He whispers in my ear as he rolls himself to cuddle behind me.

I giggle. "I know boyfriend."

"You're fucking incredible." He sucks in a breath. "And you're mine."

I tuck my face into his arm and sigh as I let these feelings wash over me. The emotions of being claimed by him. Of claiming him for myself.

We lay there together for a moment. My heart racing faster than my mind which slowly begins to come to life.

"When do you have to be at the job site?" I ask.

Not because I want to rush him out of here but because there is a plan for the day and I will not let sex derail it.

"The truck is going to meet us there at 7." He murmurs into my hair.

"It's not even 7 am!" I say and sit up straight looking for the clock. Jimmy laughs behind me.

"I took a chance and woke you up early, hoping I could get some morning sex before leaving."

"You woke me up to try and feed me."

"True, I was going to feed you and then try to get in your pants."

I slap at his chest.

"This is the last time you wake me up in the," I spot the time and growl, "fives, unless the house is on fire do you understand me?"

"Yes ma'am." He says. "Noted, now, since you're up, let's give number three a try."

I roll my eyes but let him hold my hand and lead me to the bathroom where we not only try number three but we mix in a little number eight and twenty-two as well.

...

"Knock knock!" Angie calls from the door. I left it open when she texted to say the hangers and shoe rack had arrived.

"I'm in the closet!" I call back.

She walks into the room and comes to a halt. Every single piece of clothing I have, plus every single piece of clothing Jimmy has, is either laid out on the bed ready to be hung or folded neatly in rows along the floor. Our shoes are lined up next to the windows and my purses are standing side-by-side in the chair.

"Not wasting anytime I see." Angie says as she steps over things to get to the closet.

I finish wiping down the shelf I just moved and stand back to look at the space. Jimmy had a few extra shelves for the modular system tucked away in the laundry room and he said he couldn't care less where I put things.

Since I got such an early start to the morning, I'm on track to finish the whole closet before lunch.

"Wow, this closet is huge!" Angie admires it as she steps inside. "I'm jealous!"

"It's awesome isn't it. My closet in the city was a reach-in so I had to be creative and use vertical space as much as possible." I spread my arms out wide in the middle of the walk-in closet. "I feel like there's room to get dressed in here!"

"Totally. You could hang a mirror here," Angie points to one of the empty bays next to the door.

"I like that idea. I was going to hang bags there so it was like a grab on your way out thing, but bags could go here instead." I point to my left. "Maybe add a little table for jewelry."

"Yes! I love that. You'd have to get better lighting but it's a step in the right direction."

We give each other a high five and I follow her out of the closet to the main room.

"I wish I could stay and help you but I gotta get back downstairs. Meet me just before noon and we'll head over to the Fallons' together. I'm so excited to see what you can do in the mudroom."

"Me too. Thanks for thinking of me."

"Of course! I'm only interested in organization for the pretty bins to put the stuff in. I don't always think about what the best location for stuff is."

"That's where my mind goes every time I step into a room."

"Really? Okay, good to know." Angie crosses over to the door and gives me a wave over her shoulder as she leaves.

…

"Aaaaand done." I say to myself as I put the final hanger on the rod. I step back and survey my, I mean, our, closet.

Each section is organized by color, by weight of fabric, and length of garment. Going shortest to longest from left to right. My shoes are stacked on the shoe rack along the back wall and my purses are sorted on a shelf.

All of Jimmy's clothes are back in the closet, fluffed and organized too.

I glance at my phone and see that I've got about 25 minutes until I meet Angie so I grab an outfit out of my closet, hang it on the door, and begin to change clothes. I slip into a pair of wide leg pants and tuck my ribbed tank into them.

Normally I'd toss a blazer over my shoulders but I don't think I need to be in business formal attire today. I select a necklace and a bag and then turn towards the shoe tower.

I glance down at my feet and see that I need a heel of some sort or these pants will be dragging along the ground. In the city I'd wear my black pumps if I was going to work. I'd wear my black peep-toe pumps for a flirtier vibe.

I grab the peep-toe pumps, slip them on, snag my quilted black bag with the gold chain, and leave the closet. Decisions have been made, no need to second guess them now.

After I pack my purse I head out of the apartment. Moving in my clothes helped it to feel like my space. I wonder if there are other things I should do to make the space more mine? Actually, I'll talk with Angie about it because she'll have plenty of ideas.

I bet she's been dying to get her hands on that place for a while.

It's not bad, or ugly, it's just a lot of browns, iron, leather, and stainless steel. He could use some linen or something to soften it up.

When I hit the sidewalk I hear "Hi Nora," and look to see Gina from the boutique walking towards her store. "You look exquisite this morning!" She says.

"Thank you Gina! Good morning."

She reaches me and loops her arm through mine, dragging me with her past the door of the hardware store. I glance up to see Angie shrugging at me so I shrug back.

"Nora, I was hoping that you would come and work at the boutique. I need someone with your fashion sense to help me appeal to a younger crowd. You could help me with purchasing, styling, merchandising, whatever you want."

"Oh wow, Gina, thank you, that's a kind offer."

"But you're going to refuse it."

"I've never worked retail before. I have no experience."

"Oh that doesn't matter one bit." She bats her arm down shooing away my comment. "You've got instincts, you're smart, you could run this boutique with your eyes closed."

I laugh. "Okay, well, then, yeah, maybe."

"Don't sound so committed next time you interview for a job." Gina deadpans.

Again I laugh. "I'm surprised. That's all. You caught me off guard."

"Well, I wasn't going to talk to you until the next time you came in the store, but when I saw you out on the town looking like this," she gestures to my outfit. "I had to stop you and ask now."

"I'm flattered Gina, I'll think about it and let you know."

"That's probably all I can ask of you." She says as we reach the boutique. "Well, this is me! Enjoy the rest of your day darling!"

"Thank you Gina, you too. I'll see you later."

She smiles and unlocks the door. She steps inside and flips the sign to open and starts turning on the lights.

I turn around and start walking back to the hardware store.

From across the street I hear "Nora! Youhooo!" I look up and see Sandy waving me over to the coffee shop.

"Hi Sandy!" I say with a wave as I cross the street.

"Nora! Hi. I saw you talking to Gina but before you make any decisions I want to tell you about an exciting opportunity here at the coffee shop."

"Ha, okay?"

"Well, I wanted to offer you a job at the shop. I think you'd be a perfect fit. Especially if you drink even half as much coffee as your friend Lizzy does, she practically keeps us afloat. It can be whatever you want really, serving coffee, invoicing, or supply ordering. Basically, tell us what you want to do and you can do it."

"Wow, Sandy, thank you for the offer…"

"But?"

I smile. "But nothing. I'll think about it and let you know."

Sandy grins and pulls me in for a hug. When she pulls back she squeezes my shoulders and says bye.

I stand there a little stunned by the two job offers I received out of the blue, and also the affection I've received from these women I've only known for a week. I turn and see Liz standing in the door of her studio.

"Well hello." She says.

"Hey Liz."

"A little shaken up by the attention and affection?" She asks.

"Yeah kind of." I admit.

We both let out a little laugh and she walks with me across the street to the hardware store.

"So Maggie did confirm it was your mom behind the article." Liz shares. I wince. "I was angry and texted my mom about it. She then texted the Tome Raiders. And they decided that they were going to take you under their wing and basically adopt you."

"What?" Why would they do that? Why would these women try to help me?

"I don't ask questions of the Tome Raiders' way but my mom called me like five minutes ago and asked me if I thought you'd be interested in helping her start a party planning business."

"Oh no."

"Oh yes. Apparently the Float Fest win has gone to her head. And she's started to talk about my wedding. She's going to need help and I honestly think you're the one for it."

"Ha, tell her what I told Gina and Sandy…I'll think about it."

"Fair enough." Liz says as we cross the street from her studio towards the hardware store. "What are you up to today?"

"Actually, Angie asked me to help her organize the mudroom at the Fallons' house so I'm headed over there with her now."

"That's cool. Good thinking Angie. She might have gotten a leg up on the Tome Raiders." Liz says impressed.

"She'll have to write down the details of how she accomplished this and submit it for the official town record or something." I say, meaning it as a joke.

Liz looks at me straight faced and says "That's brilliant," before she pushes through the hardware store yelling "Angie!"

I pivot towards the door to follow her, but stop when I hear my name.

This time it's not Gina, or Sandy, or Katherine.

It's Jimmy.

I watch as he steps around the front of his truck. In just a few long strides he reaches me and pulls me to him for a kiss.

"Hello beautiful." He whispers against my ear.

"Hello boyfriend." I say with a smile.

"How has your morning been?" He asks as he takes my hand and pulls me down to sit on a bench in front of the store.

"Really good! I got the closet organized." He raises his eyebrows, impressed. "And I got three job offers."

"What? That's amazing! Where from?"

"Gina, Sandy, and Katherine." I share. His expression falls a bit.

"So, not real jobs."

"Oh no, they're very real jobs. And actually I could see myself being very good at each of them."

"Yeah?" He asks hopefully.

"Yeah. I told them I'd think about it. I'm still not totally used to the idea of not working at Fosters. Once that settles in I'm sure I'll have a clearer picture of what to work towards next."

He leans over and plants a kiss to the side of my head. "That sounds great. So are you excited to organize the mudroom?"

"I am. Did you do your job and unpack everything?"

"Of course I did. You'll be very impressed by my taking shoes, boots, coats, and sports equipment out of boxes skills."

I laugh, "I'm sure I will be."

With that the store door opens and Liz walks out followed by Angie. Jimmy and I stand up.

"Ready sis?" Angie says and then her face freezes in horror.

I laugh as I feel Jimmy tense up behind me.

"Ohmigod, ohmigod, ohmigod, I'm so sorry! I didn't mean it like sister-in-law, like you guys were going to get married, I mean, please do, but like don't do it because I said so, do it because you actually love each other and want to spend the rest of your life together, and I'm going to try and stop talking now."

Jimmy looks down at me as he places his hand at the nape of my neck.

"Angie, chill. I have every plan of marrying Nora someday."

Then it's our turn. All three of us girls freeze and tense up. Slowly I look up at him and he's smiling one of his whole face, eye crinkle, smiles.

"Really?"

"Honey, I'd marry you today if you'd let me, I'm all in."

"Oh, okay, good to know." I mutter and then Liz shoos Angie in my direction so she can escort my stunned body away from here. Jimmy kisses my head again and whispers "I'll see you later. Love you, girlfriend."

And I wave at him in a daze as Angie guides me down the sidewalk.

43

Are You Proposing To Me?

JIMMY

It's been a busy afternoon at the store. First Mitchell, then
Sal, and then Cole. They were all looking for random things
that they didn't end up buying. I got the sense they came into
the store looking for an excuse to talk to me.

And to ask about Nora.

Dad is the latest one to come by and he offered to help me
with inventory. Things have been better between us since we
worked to set up the festival together. He naturally stepped up
to help unload the furniture at the Fallons' house yesterday and
finished up with Angie while I took Nora home.

"So Angie said that Nora moved in with you?"

"She has, I don't really know how to explain it Dad, but it
feels like I've known her longer than a week. It feels right."

"I completely understand how you feel. The right woman, a
good woman, will do that to a man."

"Did you feel that way with Mom?"

"Of course. And your Pops did with Gran."

I nod as I hand him a box of drywall anchors that need
labels.

"Dad?"

"Yeah?"

"Something has been bothering me when it comes to Nora." He sets down what he's doing and he looks at me with clear eyes.

"What is it?"

I pull my cap off and run my hand through my hair before fitting it back on my head. "It's that she gave up everything for me. That she moved here. My life isn't changing at all but hers is now completely different." I pause as I fiddle with the drywall anchor pack. "Is she going to resent me?"

My hand is still playing with the corner of the box when Dad lays his hand on top of mine, stilling my fidgeting.

"Son, that's a very real thing to be afraid of, especially with how Bethany left you. But from what I understand Nora's job left her which forced her hand, the apartment, I dunno, but the only thing you can do is talk to her about it.

"Make sure you ask her how she's doing, really doing. Don't let her stop at 'fine' no one is ever just fine. I always found your mom was most receptive to deep talks before bed."

"You and mom talked like that?"

"Of course we did. We shared everything. And once you kids came along there was plenty to discuss and fret over. It's part of what drove me so low after she died," he swallows hard, "I missed my best friend."

I reach over and pull my dad into a hug. He wraps his arms around me and returns the embrace and together we sit with the memories of Mom.

He pulls back after a minute and coughs to clear his throat. I reach down under the counter and hold out the box of tissues for him to take one. We both blow our noses and let out a sigh.

"Tell me how the show is going." Dad says as he resumes his work of labeling packs.

"I think it's going well. Dax says so at least. He has been sending the footage to the editor every night and they're putting the show together."

"That seems fast." He says.

"Yeah, I think it's just for the first one, the pilot. They want to air it during the first week of October when they preview a few different new shows."

"I see, and is your sister enjoying it?"

I laugh, thinking about Angie's acting "skills".

"Yeah, I think she is. She's a little nervous about it but she'll get better."

"She was talking kind of funny when the camera was on her yesterday." He chuckles.

"I'm hoping Marla or Dax say something to her so I don't have to." I admit and we both laugh.

"Did you enjoy helping out at the house yesterday?" I ask.

"I did, it felt good to move my muscles again and it felt really good to be with you and your sister."

"It was fun." That's the honest truth. "If you make the pilot you might have to join the crew." I tease.

"That or man the store, someone has to be here while you two are off being movie stars."

"Cable television stars you mean."

"Right, right, that's an even bigger responsibility." He teases.

The door chimes and we both look up as Sandy walks in.

"Hello Sandy," I greet her, "What can we do for you?"

"Well I just had to see for myself that the Lewis men are working together."

I look over at Dad, "We are. So, how can we help?"

"Oh I don't need anything. Just wanted to check this out. But now that I'm here," she turns to face me and plants her hands on the counter. "Has Nora said if she's going to work for me, or Gina, or Katherine." She mutters the other two names quickly as if to brush them under the rug.

"She has not yet no, but thank you so much for making the offers."

"Of course! We were not about to let some horrible woman's lies result in our Nora not having a job!"

Our Nora.

"What do you mean?" Dad asks.

"Well, Liz sent the article to Maggie last night and she told Liz this morning that it was indeed Nora's mother who got paid for that article. Liz told Katherine and of course Katherine put it in the Tome Raiders' chat. It was shocking to hear that it was Nora's *mother* who wrote it. Well, we all about had heart attacks together.

"I mean, what kind of mother would, oh well, never mind, the point is we all agreed that we'd take care of your girl."

I blink rapidly at Sandy.

"Sandy, that gossip factory you run finally did some good." Dad chuckles.

"I wouldn't say finally Jim, but yes, I'm proud of us today."

"Thank you Sandy," I say quietly. "You have no idea what this means to me."

She reaches over and pats my hand. "Jimmy this town has been taking care of you all your life. When your sweet mother passed away we made sure you, Angie, and Jim were taken care of. Sure we did it from a distance sometimes, but we knew you three had to learn to live without her.

"And now, seeing you fall in love this week, here, surrounded by the town that loves you, well we're all just over the moon. We're a wise group of women, who have seen almost everything, and we're going to make sure your Nora sticks around."

"I appreciate that Sandy, thank you."

"Of course. Oh look there's Mitch, I snuck out as he was doing the deep clean on the pastry case, whoops!" And she swings open the door and struts out onto the street.

My Dad and I watch as Mitchell greets her with a kiss and then loops her arm in his as they walk towards home.

...

"Honey! I'm home!" Nora calls as she opens the door. I rush out of the bedroom and race to pull her into a hug.

"Not that I don't love being smashed against your body, but why such a tight hug?" She asks.

"Can't a boyfriend just hug up on his girlfriend?"

"He can, and he should, but I need to pee."

"Oh!" I say as I release her and step back. She hurries past me to the bathroom. I stick my hands in my pockets and lean against the back of the sofa.

"When will we have been dating long enough for me to talk to you while you're in the bathroom?" I call out.

"Never, we'll never be dating long enough for that." She responds before I hear the toilet flushing.

She reappears, she has slipped off her shoes so her long pants are pooling over her feet. "Hi." She says.

"Hi." I reply.

"So you know my mom did the article."

"Yeah, Sandy actually was the one who told me." I wince, Nora's been around long enough to know that if Sandy knows, everyone knows.

"Yeah, Liz said Katherine told the Tome Raiders. But it's all good. That's why I got three of four job offers today."

"Three of four?"

"Gina offered me a job at the boutique, Sandy at the coffee shop, Katherine wants me to start a party planning business with her."

"Oh boy."

"I know. And then I got a call with a very interesting offer while I was walking home."

"Oh yeah?"

Nora holds her phone up and hits play on a voice mail.

"Nora Heely? This is Darlene Smithe, we had breakfast a few weeks ago with that suit from Cornell. Anyway, I got a call from someone at your office, Trisha or something, who asked if I'd like to have a meeting about making a gift to the veterinary school. I asked her where you were and she said you had been let go. I hung up on her then and there and made my assistant find your number. Anyways, I like you Nora, and I need someone to help me plan my estate. Call me to talk it through but you're the woman I want for the job. Toodle-oo!"

I look up from the phone to Nora's face and she's beaming. The biggest smile I've ever seen on her face. Joy rushes through me and I pick her up and spin her around the room.

"Nora! This is incredible! Congratulations!"

"I know, I'm so excited."

Suddenly the thought that she'd have to go back to the city hits me. I set her down and step back from her.

I will not stand in her way. I will not be the reason she settles for a life that isn't everything she dreams of or has worked for. Letting her leave will crush me, I'll never be the same, but I couldn't live knowing I'd forced her hand.

I'd resent myself.

"Jimmy? Why did your face just go all sad on me?" She asks as she steps up next to me and caresses my cheek before settling her hands on either side of my neck.

"Because Nora," I reach up and hold her hands in mine. "I'm sad that you're leaving, going back to the city."

"Who said that?"

"Well this is your dream job. I won't stand in your way." I close my eyes because I can't bear to see the emotions that might be in hers.

"Jimmy, open your eyes, look at me." I do, slowly, her expression is soft and her smile is gentle.

"I already called her and told her that I would love the job but that I needed to do it from Lakeville."

"What?"

"And she said that was splendid because she has a property up here she loves to use and we can meet here and if I need to accompany her to meetings in the city we'd be able to arrange that."

"What?"

"I said that I'd have to talk it through with my," she pauses and looks down at the floor and takes a deep breath before continuing, "fiancé, and—"

"What!?"

"Listen, I know, but you said it first on the sidewalk today and I felt like the word boyfriend didn't do justice to our relationship."

"Are you proposing to me Nora Heely?"

"No."

"I think you are."

"No Jimathon, I'm not."

"And," I continue, "I would have appreciated more of a grand gesture but I'm going to say yes because I love you."

"I love you too…don't go digging around in your generic brand cereal box for a ring. It isn't in there."

I bark out a laugh and pull her to me. She rests against my chest and her arms loop around my waist.

Nora steps back and presses a kiss on my lips.

"What do you want to have for dinner boyfriend?"

"Fiancé." I correct and she gives me a look that could freeze the lake in July. "Fine, fine, **Pre-Fiancé**."

Nora rolls her eyes. "What do you want to have for dinner **Pre-Fiancé**?" She asks with sass.

"I have some chicken defrosting, a fresh zucchini from Mitchell's garden that he dropped off at the store today, and for dessert I'm planning to have you."

"You start with the vegetables, I'll just slip into something more comfortable and then come join you."

She walks backwards into the bedroom and when she turns I watch her disappear around the corner. I stand and walk to the kitchen and start gathering ingredients.

I put my country station on the speaker and I set my phone back down on the counter. Lyrics about buyin' dirt, about life moving fast, about the love of a good woman, fill the air. I smile. I've found love like a country song.

Nora slips behind me and wraps her arms around my torso, her hands pushing up to my chest.

"Hey honey," I say and then I spin around to find her in a creamy satin slip with lace trim along the top. "Wow."

She smiles. "Did you think my something more comfortable was going to be sweatpants?"

"Do you even own sweatpants?" I ask.

"No." And she drags her fingers under the hem of my shirt and starts playing with the band of my briefs.

"Should I get more comfortable too?" I ask as I reach for the collar of my shirt and tug it over my head.

Tossing it to the side I gather her in my arms and bring her lips to mine. Our kiss deepens immediately and her whimper sends shockwaves straight through me.

I walk her backwards around the island and then when one of the stools is right behind her I end the kiss and lift her up onto it.

"What number was kitchen sex again?" She asks as she slowly spreads her legs open.

"We can look it up later." I grumble as I step forward and kiss her again.

"Will dinner get cold?" She asks.

"It hasn't even been cooked yet." I reply as I toy with the hem of her slip.

"Oh well, best laid plans and all." She says with a smile.

EPILOGUE

The Results Are In

Nora

"You comfortable?" Jimmy asks as he fluffs up a pillow behind my back.

"Yes very. Stop fussing."

"I'm nervous." He whispers into my ear.

"I can tell, it'll be fine." I reassure him and I try to settle him with a hand to his thigh.

He looks down at it.

"Maybe, if we…"

"No."

"Real quick?"

"No."

"C'mon I can be quick."

"That's not something you should brag about to your pre-fiancée."

"True, true. You're right," he develops a false bravado, "I never shoot off quickly because I'm with the sexiest woman on the planet."

I laugh to myself and kiss his shoulder. He settles in and puts his arm around me as he looks back behind us at the crowd gathering.

Lakeville decided to host a viewing party for the pilot. They put up a movie screen and projector in Sunfish Park. Katherine helped to decorate.

She strung lights through the trees, found a red carpet for everyone to walk down. She even got a popcorn cart and a hot dog vendor to set up at the back.

Angie helped her gather up blankets and quilts and cushions and pillows from the Tome Raiders. Then they set up little areas for everyone to watch the show from.

The one for Jimmy and me is right up front. Next to us is Angie's, her dad, and her friend Maeve too. Pops is just past them in a wicker chair with a foot rest. And on the other side the Fallons have a blanket set up and their kids are chasing each other around it in circles.

"I can't believe they did all this for me, for us." Jimmy says as he turns back around.

"Lakeville takes care of their own." I say and love how in just the span of six weeks this place has become my own too.

"Okay everybody!" Katherine shouts through a bullhorn. "The show is about to start!"

Cheers and clapping erupt from the whole crowd and I am almost overcome with emotions.

Almost.

"Jimmy? Angie? Want to say anything before we get going?" Katherine asks as she shakes the bullhorn in our direction.

"Sure." Jimmy stands up and then offers a hand to his sister. I pull out my phone to record a video.

He holds up the bullhorn and it squeals with feedback.

"Shit sorry guys," he says as he adjusts it and the noise stops.

"Language!" Someone yells from the back.

"You're right, this is a family show, and I'm sure they had to do plenty of creative editing to make it so."

Angie pulls the bullhorn towards her and adds "but don't worry, Jimmy's muscles are still on display…that's in the contract."

The crowd laughs and Jimmy rolls his eyes.

"We just want to thank you all for supporting us as we not only built this business but started something new. For all the years of your loyalty at Lewis Hardware and," he pauses and grabs Angie's hand, "for your support as we learned to live without Mom."

I see Angie squeeze his hand and Jimmy clears his throat. I know he's close to tears, hell even I am close to tears again.

"We don't know if the show will continue after this but I do know that we won't stop helping you build the homes of your dreams."

Angie is nodding her head.

"Anything to add Ange?"

She shakes her head no.

"Okay then, thank you, and, umm, enjoy the show!"

Jimmy hands the bullhorn back to Katherine and then wraps Angie in a hug. They cross back over to our blankets and settle in. The crowd's clapping stops as the screen flickers to life and the familiar Homecraft Network logo appears.

The voice over goes "And now, the premier of Homecraft Network Original, Design and Shine."

The park erupts with noise and I kiss Jimmy on the cheek before turning my attention back to the screen.

An upbeat music plays, there's a little bit of a country twang to it, and short clips of Jimmy and Angie move across the screen. The final one is a slowmo of Jimmy wiping his brow with his shirt and I feel my insides clench.

Yummy.

The show opens with Jimmy and Angie talking in the hardware store. They're doing the "we've got to go over to the Fallon house today" speech where they get the audience up to speed.

You can tell Jimmy is relaxed, almost like he doesn't care how this goes. Angie is tense and speaking really quickly.

The show then moves on to Jimmy giving Angie a tour of the bathroom and she shares her idea for the penny tile. This time her cadence is normal and she sounds much more relaxed.

Scenes of Jimmy working, shirtless, and of Angie shopping for furniture fill the next several minutes.

At the commercial break people stand and move around. Jimmy and Angie talk to each other. I smile at Jim and he gives me a thumbs up.

Maybe I am more nervous than I think I am. His small gesture does reassure me a little bit that this is going well.

The show comes back on and Angie is examining the finished tile. Then it shows Jimmy installing the countertops. The shot is of him walking outside and bracing his hands on his hips with exhaustion.

I expect the clip to cut but instead it follows Jimmy outside and then it captures me walking up to him.

It's a weird thing to see yourself on a TV show. Dax and his camera have captured my genuine emotions.

In my face I see affection, sincerity. It's almost like I'm relaxed.

We watch as I give him some water, an apple, and then lean down for a kiss. Just our hands are touching and I remember how stable I felt with his hands holding mine. And how his soap, cologne, and sweat smell was clouding my brain.

I remember that the whole town is seeing this too when Angie yelps out "I thought I told you to get a room!"

The whole crowd reacts. There is laughter, several "awww" coos, and a smattering of whistles.

And one "Yeah Jimmy!" from someone who sounds a lot like Holden.

Then a talking head of Angie appears and there's a subtitled question under it.

"Jimmy brought his girlfriend over to the site today to show her the progress, will you be bringing your boyfriend?"

Her face flushes on screen.

"Oh, ha ha ha, no, not today." She says before continuing. "But it is really fun to have Nora around, she's got a great mind for organization."

I lean forward and look at Angie who shoots me a side eye grin.

The segments ends with a truck pulling up the drive and Jimmy lifting it to reveal furniture. Their dad is there and he claps Jimmy on the shoulder as they survey the contents.

Another commercial break and this time I lean over to talk to Angie.

"When did you do that talking head?"

"That same day."

"Wait, like before Jimmy told you about my closet or whatever."

"Yeah, anyone could see that you're organized, almost to a fault. I had plans to channel your skills long before Jimmy confirmed my suspicion with a picture of your closet."

"He sent you a—! You know what? Never mind."

She offers me a fist bump and I settle back in to the cushions next to Jimmy. There's only one segment left.

I might be biased but I like it. The show does an excellent job of demonstrating the love and care that Jimmy and Angie put into their projects.

Marla said she would call after the show to give them the initial feedback and ratings. Test audiences have already seen it and it did pretty well. Some things to tweak, but Marla assured Jimmy and Angie it was nothing big.

The show starts again with Jim and Jimmy carrying in furniture. It shows Angie adding accessories and making Jimmy move some furniture around.

Which he grumbles about.

Then the boxes of the Fallons' stuff arrives and Angie starts to put it away and I walk through the front door and ask if she needs help.

It was what we discussed with Dax when we arrived that day. He asked if I was comfortable with filming and I shrugged and said sure why not. He got me a mic and then said that I was the best dressed extra he'd ever seen.

The camera follows us around as we organize the mudroom, then the playroom, and then the kitchen. I really hit my stride in there and you could tell.

I'm excited and confident and making Angie laugh with kitchen mishap stories.

Our little organizing segment ends and Jimmy kisses me on the side of the head. The words "reveal day" flash across the screen and we are treated to a talking head shot of the family right before they see their remodeled home.

They're talking about how great Jimmy and Angie have been and how excited they are to see inside.

We then get to watch as they open the door and see their home. Mrs. Fallon immediately starts crying and Mr. Fallon ducks to the side to pinch his eyes.

The kids take off through the house, charging up stairs to see their rooms. The Fallons walk through the space and Jimmy and Angie appear from the kitchen.

"What do you think?" Angie asks nervously.

"It's perfect." Mrs. Fallon replies as they all exchange hugs.

"Let's give you the full tour then!" Jimmy says and he leads them through the house, explains the features they added, shows off the organized cabinets. He takes them upstairs and they gush over the "fresh" tile in the bathroom.

It cuts to another talking head of the family telling us how perfect everything was.

Then the final scene is Jimmy and Angie doing a talking head and recapping the project. They're each complimenting the other.

"Couldn't have done it without you bro." Angie jokes as she punches him in the arm.

"Right back 'atcha sis," Jimmy jokes and pulls her in for a noogie.

"Alright you two cut it out." Comes Jim's voice and they both freeze. He slides up between them and says "I'm so proud of you two, good work."

And the credits roll.

There is a beat before anyone reacts and then the crowd erupts. People are on their feet clapping and cheering and rushing forward to give Jim, Jimmy, and Angie hugs.

A few pull me into a hug too and tell me that I did a good job.

Angie's phone rings and the crowd goes quiet.

"Hello?"

We all stare at her.

"Yes, hi Marla."

Jimmy takes a step closer. I've never heard a crowd this large so hushed before.

"That's great."

"What'd she say?" Someone whispers before a chorus of "Shhhhhs" follow.

"Oh, okay, I'll have to ask."

Jimmy's eyebrows raise as if to ask "what?" Angie just shakes her head quickly.

"Sounds good Marla, okay, yes, thank you, talk soon."

And we all watch as Angie ends the call. I don't think anyone in Sunfish Park is breathing.

Angie takes a deep breath and lifts her chin.

"Early results are in…"

"AND!?" someone demands before more "Shhhhhhhhs."

"And, they're good. Like really good."

Cheers erupt and Angie grins at Jimmy.

"They want to film a whole season starting in February."

"Ohmigod!" Someone squeals from the crowd.

"I know, I know, and Marla had one other ask."

"What?" Jimmy demands.

"That Nora organizes each project for us. She actually offered Nora her own organizing only show that could start taping this fall because it's not weather dependent like home construction is."

Jimmy turns to look at me and I feel my shock hit me like I just walked into a wall. What? My own organizing TV show?

"What do you think Nora?" Jimmy asks.

"I'll have to think about it." I reply with a smile.

"Do it!" Someone yells.

And the crowd laughs.

Jimmy takes my hand and I hear a few "Shhhhhhhhs" behind us. He squares himself in front of me. "Nora Leann Heely," Jimmy starts before he takes a deep breath and reaches into his pocket. I freeze as I watch his hand. "Will you watch this video for me?"

He slowly hands me his phone.

I bring it up to my face, look at him confused. He just smiles and nods towards the phone.

I hit play.

Jimmy's face appears on the screen before he backs up. He is standing next to his truck, on the empty plot of land where we had our first date, and he's shirtless.

"Hey Nora," the video starts, "I have been working on something and I want to show you the plans."

In the video he holds up a piece of paper. Then he props the camera up on something and continues.

"Angie said I should do a green screen but I don't know how so here's what I've got. This," he points to a box he's drawn on graphing paper and walks to a spot on the grass, "would be the closet, it is off the side of our bedroom that overlooks the lake, then this is the bathroom with two sinks, two shower heads, and a full length cabinet for towels and whatever other girly stuff you have."

"Awww" Someone starts before "Shhhhhhhhs" erupt.

"Here," he moves his finger off to another square and walks to the other side of the lot, "Is the dining room and then the kitchen, you get to design the cabinet layout. Back here, is the powder room and a butler's pantry. Then this is the main living area and off over here are two more bedrooms and a bathroom. Oh, and the laundry room is here."

In the video he sets the paper down and looks directly at the camera.

"Nora Leann Heely, will you build this home with me? Organize a life with me?"

The video ends and I look up from the screen to find Jimmy down on one knee, holding a ring box in his hands.

"And, will you marry me?"

Happy tears cloud my eyes as I figure out how to say the word "yes."

I must get it out because Jimmy stands and kisses me and wraps me into a hug. Everyone around us is cheering and clapping.

He stands back to slip the ring on my finger.

"It was my mom's," he whispers.

Tears fall down my cheeks. I hold his head with both my hands and kiss him.

He wraps his arm around me and turns me to face the group of people surrounding us. They're all cheering and laughing and I see Sandy and Gina wipe at their eyes.

Liz steps forward and wraps me in a hug and again my tears flow. Kyle shakes Jimmy's hand and behind us I hear a champagne bottle pop open.

Katherine starts to hand out glasses of champagne and when everyone has one Jim holds his high and says, "To Nora and Jimmy."

"To Nora and Jimmy!" The crowd echoes.

As I take a sip of my champagne I look at Jimmy's profile and smile. I never could have imagined that when I first stole a glimpse at that profile in the front seat of his truck, at the end of one of the toughest days of my life, that it was the beginning of my next chapter.

But maybe it's the things you don't plan, what you don't expect, that end up being the most magical.

ACKNOWLEDGEMENTS

PHEW!

I've learned that there are two types of authors - ones who plot, The Plotters, and ones who fly by the seat of their pants, The Pantsers. I fall squarely into the latter group. And Upstate Expectations is a prime example.

In my first draft of Here For It Nora actually got married to Jeff who Liz hooks up with early on but as I rewrote I started to envision Nora better and her story became crystal clear.

And her story was fighting to get out. Thank you to everyone who cheered me on as I did 80,000 words in a week to finish the draft! Thank you to Dan who kept the house running while I did that. Thank you to my kids who opened their own snacks, just a few minutes before dinner, that week.

And an extra thanks to Dan who is the one to keep the house running most of the time.

Thank you to my early readers, Lisa, Liza, and Kelsey. Your feedback made the book so much better.

Thank you to author Sarah Adams who shared her resource for writing captivating novels and to Jessica Brody for writing Save The Cat! Writes A Novel.

To my girl crush author Meghan Quinn for sharing your daily word counts often so I feel a little competitive to keep up. (And for letting me use Hayes Farrow's name in this book…go read The Way I Hate Him now.)

Thank you to Amanda of The Last Chapter Book Shop for your feedback on Here For It and for leading me to platforms and resources for independent publishers.

Thank you to Allyson Voller, Tyler Darby, and producer Jade Pietri for bringing this novel to life in the audiobook. And holding my hand through the process. I now understand the timelines much better!

Thank you to Chelsea Kemp for the cover design. It was such a fun experience to envision Nora and Jimmy and how they should be judged on the cover.

Thank you to the other indie romance authors on social media who answer my questions when I slide into their DMs and for their informative and supportive content!

Thank you to Angela for my logo and website design! I'll babysit in exchange for design hours anytime. And man, how crazy will it be when Baby A goes to preschool!

Thank you to my parents for their support and encouragement. To my neighbors for their questions! And to Meghan B for being my first ever author signing. It is so appropriate that it was at swim lessons.

And thank you, dear reader. I do this for you.

Erin Marie Bassett is a geriatric millennial, wife, and mother of two living in Chicago. (A mile west of Wrigley Field but she, like her husband and kids, are St. Louis Cardinal fans). When she's not reading or writing romance, Erin helps small businesses and local organizations use the magic words to connect with their communities. She volunteers hard at her kids' school and she believes in the power of S.L.O.W. Living. Her doctor tells her not to but she drinks a lot of coffee. Like, a lot.

Connect with Erin Online & Sign Up for Her Tuesday Night Newsletter

erinmariebassett.com

@erinmariebassett

Erin's Favorite Read-Them-Over-and-Over Romances

Nora Goes Off Script by Annabel Monaghan

Highland Fling by Meghan Quinn

The Vancouver Agitators Series by Meghan Quinn

Portrait of a Scotsman by Evie Dunmore
(And all her League of Extraordinary Women Books)

Rock Bottom Girl by Lucy Score

Emma of 83rd Street by Audrey Bellezza and Emily Harding

One Day in December by Josie Silver

The Twelve Dates of Christmas by Jenny Bayliss

Set on You by Amy Lea

The Dead Romantics by Ashley Poston

Love on the Brain by Ali Hazelwood

Northanger Abbey by Jane Austen

But wait! There's more!

Read Liz & Kyle's story in *Here For It*, available now
on Amazon, KindleUnlimited, eBook format,
Bookstore.org, and signed paperbacks are available at
erinmariebassett.com

And stay tuned for Angie & Holden's story, *Don't Call
It Puppy Love*, coming May 14, 2024.